Praise for *I Do Not Come to You by Chance*

'Beautifully written . . . More than just a brilliant read, it
¹so turns the whole idea of Nigerian 419 scams neatly on its
head, using wit and warm humour to bring to life the stories
of the email recipients themselves' *Sunday Herald*

'This is a fast, fresh, often hilarious first novel, by one of the
remarkably talented young African writers who are rapidly
making everyone else look stale' *The Times*

'[Nwaubani] not merely explores a side of modern existence
that touches millions every day, but does so with wit, warmth
and insight' *Independent*

'Poignantly funny' *Waterstone's Books Quarterly*

'Sparklingly funny debut novel' *Wired*

'In this touching tale, the Nigerian author traces a '419' plot
back a generation – a generation full of hope and promise'
Pride

'[Nwaubani's] pointed and poignant first novel is a lively,
good-humored and provocative examination of the truth
behind a global inbox of deceit' *Washington Post*

'Nwaubani does a great job of detailing the frantic pulse of
urban Nigeria' *Time Out*

Adaobi Tricia Nwaubani grew up in the eastern part of Nigeria, among the Igbo-speaking people. She now lives in Abuja, Nigeria. *I Do Not Come to You by Chance*, her first novel, won the Commonwealth Writers' Prize for Best First Book, Africa Region and a Betty Trask Award from the Society of Authors.

I Do Not Come to You by Chance

Adaobi Tricia Nwaubani

PHOENIX

A PHOENIX PAPERBACK

First published in Great Britain in 2009
by Weidenfeld & Nicolson
This paperback edition published in 2010
by Phoenix,
an imprint of Orion Books Ltd,
Orion House, 5 Upper St Martin's Lane,
London WC2H 9EA

An Hachette UK company

5 7 9 10 8 6 4

Copyright © Adaobi Tricia Nwaubani 2009

First published in the USA in 2009 by Hyperion

A CIP catalogue record for this book
is available from the British Library.

ISBN 978-0-7538-2697-3

Printed and bound in Great Britain by
Clays Ltd, St Ives plc

The Orion Publishing Group's policy is to use papers
that are natural, renewable and recyclable products and
made from wood grown in sustainable forests. The logging
and manufacturing processes are expected to conform to
the environmental regulations of the country of origin.

To my parents . . .

Chief Chukwuma Hope Nwaubani
(Ahanyiefule 1 of Omaegwu, Oke Orji Abia)

Chief Mrs Patricia Uberife Nwaubani
(Nwanyiejiagamba 1 of Omaegwu)

. . . for giving me the very best of their best.

Prologue

People in the villages seemed to know everything. They knew whose great-grandmother had been a prostitute; they knew which families were once slaves of which; they knew who and who were *osu* outcasts whose ancestors had been consecrated to the pagan shrines of generations ago. It was, therefore, not surprising that they knew exactly what had happened in the hospital on that day.

From what Augustina had been told, as soon as she came into the world and the midwife smacked her buttocks so that she could cry and force air into her lungs, her mother took in a deep breath and died. The dead woman was the most recent of five wives, the youngest, and the most beloved. But because she had died a bad death, a death that was considered as much an abomination as a suicide, she was buried immediately, quietly, without official mourning.

When Augustina's father took her home, everybody complained that the child cried too much, as if it knew that it had killed its mother. So her grandmother came and took her away. At age seven, when it was confirmed that her right hand could reach across her head and touch her left ear, Augustina moved back to her father's house and started attending primary school. Being long and skinny had worked to her advantage.

Six years later, the same village experts said it was foolish for her father to consider sending a female child to secondary school. It was a waste of time; women did not need to know too much 'book'. Reverend Sister Xavier was outraged and came all the way to talk it out with Augustina's father.

'Good afternoon, Mr Mbamalu,' she began.

'Welcome,' he said, and offered her a seat.

The white woman sat and stared right into his eyes.

'I hear you're not allowing Ozoemena to attend secondary school.'

Ugorji, Augustina's elder brother, who had been assigned as interpreter for the day, repeated the woman's words in Igbo. It was not as if their father did not understand English, but when he received word that the headmistress was coming, he had panicked, fearing that his feeble grasp of the foreign language would not withstand the turbulence of the white woman's nasal accent and fast talking.

'I want her to learn how to cook and take care of a home,' Augustina's father replied. 'She has gone to primary school. She can read and write. That is enough.'

The white woman smiled and shook her head.

'I'm sorry to disagree with you, but I don't think it's enough. Ozoemena is such a smart girl. She can go a very long way.'

Ugorji did his thing. The white woman sped on.

'I've been living in Africa since the thirties. In all my over twenty years of missionary work here, I've come across very few young women as smart as your daughter.'

Sister Xavier sat upright, hands clasped as if she was in a constant state of preparedness for prayer.

'All over the world,' she continued, 'women are achieving great things. Some are doctors who treat all types of diseases, others have big positions with the government. You might be surprised to hear this, but in some countries, the person who rules over them is a woman.'

From her position behind the door, Augustina noticed that her brother did not give the correct interpretation for the word 'rules'. It was little things like this that made her the smart one.

'Mr Mbamalu, I would like you to reconsider your stand on this matter,' Sister Xavier concluded.

To date, nobody is sure if it was the sister's words, or the rapid way she fired her sentences, or simply the shock of a woman telling him what to do, but Augustina's father consented. She would attend secondary school with her brothers. Another five years of the white man's wisdom.

Augustina was thrilled.

2

In the end, though, it did not matter that she had made the highest scores in her class during the final-year exams, or that she spoke English almost with the same speed as the reverend sisters themselves. After secondary school, the topic of formal education was officially closed and Augustina was sent as an apprentice to her father's sister who was a successful tailor. Her aunty was married to a highly esteemed teacher. So highly esteemed, in fact, that everybody called him Teacher. That was how she left Isiukwuato and moved to Umuahia.

Augustina had been living with Teacher and Aunty for some months when news reached them that one of Teacher's friends was coming to visit. The friend had studied Engineering in the United Kingdom, was now working with the government in Enugu, and was returning to Umuahia for his annual leave. As soon as his letter arrived, Aunty went about broadcasting the news to all the neighbours. Most of them knew the expected guest from reputation. They said he was good-looking. They said he always wore shoes, even when he was just sitting inside the house reading. They said he behaved like a white man, that he spoke English through his nose and ate with a fork. Some even swore that they had never known him to fart.

When Engineer turned up in his white Peugeot 403, Augustina, Aunty, Teacher, and the five children were dolled up in their Sunday best and waiting on the veranda. As soon as Augustina caught that first glimpse of him, she decided that even if Engineer's steps had not been leading to their courtyard, she would have crawled over broken glass, swum across seven oceans, and climbed seven mountains to see him that day. He was as handsome as paint. His back was straight, his hands stayed deep inside his pockets, and his steps were short and quick as if he had an urgent appointment at the end of the world. Anybody passing him on the way to the stream could have mistaken him for an emissary from the spirit world on special assignment to the land of mere mortals.

After lunch, they all sat in the living room. Engineer crossed his right leg over his left knee and reeled out tales of the white man's land.

'There are times when the sun doesn't shine,' he said. 'The

3

weather is so cold that even the plants are afraid to come out of the ground. That's why their skin is so white. Our own skin is much darker because the sun has smiled too long on us.'

They opened their mouths and opened their eyes, and looked at themselves from one to the other.

'During those times, the clothes they wear are even thicker than the hairs on a sheep. And if they don't dress that way, the cold can even kill.'

They opened their mouths and opened their eyes, and looked at themselves from one to the other.

'The way their streets are, you can be walking about for miles and miles and you won't even see one speck of sand. In fact, you can even wear the same clothes for more than one week and they won't get dirty.'

They opened their eyes and opened their mouths, and looked at themselves from one to the other. If anybody else had narrated these stories, they would have known immediately that he had spent far too much time in the palm wine tapper's company.

'That's why education is so important,' Engineer concluded. 'These people have learnt how to change their world to suit them. They know how to make it cold when the weather is too hot and they know how to make it hot when the weather is too cold.'

He paused and leaned back in his chair. Then he beamed the starlight on someone else.

'So how have the children been doing in school?' he asked.

Teacher shifted in his seat to adjust the extra weight that pride had suddenly attached to him.

'Oh, very, very well,' he replied. 'All of them made very high scores in Arithmetic.'

Engineer smiled.

'Go on . . . bring your exercise books. Show him,' Teacher said.

The children trooped out like a battalion of soldier ants, the eldest leading the way. They returned in the same order, each holding an orange exercise book. Engineer perused each book page by page and smiled like an apostle whose new converts were reciting the creed. Finally, he got to the last child, who was about four years old. As soon as he held out his exercise book, his mother leaned over and landed a stout knock on the little boy's head.

'How many times have I told you to stop giving your elders things with your left hand?' she glared. 'Next time, I'm going to use a knife to cut it off.'

Engineer jumped in.

'Teacher,' he said, 'it's not really the boy's fault if he uses his left hand sometimes.'

'Children are born foolish,' Teacher replied sorrowfully. 'If one doesn't teach them properly from an early age, they grow up and continue that way. He'll soon learn.'

'No, no, no . . . What I'm saying is that the way his brain is arranged, he uses his left hand to do things that other people normally do with their right hands.'

Teacher laughed.

'I'm very serious,' Engineer said. 'It's the white people who found that out.'

'Engineer, it doesn't matter what the white people have found out. The white people may not mind what hand they use to eat and do other things, but in our culture, it's disrespectful for a child to give something to his elders with his left hand. You know that.'

'I know. But what I'm saying is that, no matter what culture says, it's not the fault of any child who does this.'

'Engineer, I think you're taking things too far. You need to be careful that the ways of the white man don't make you mad. The way it is, people are already saying that you're no longer an African man.'

'How can they say I'm not African?' Engineer chuckled. 'My skin is dark, my nostrils are wide, my hair is thick and curly. What other evidence do they need? Or do I have to wear a grass skirt and start dancing around like a chimpanzee?'

Teacher looked wounded.

'Don't forget I've also gone to school,' he said. 'But that doesn't make me believe I have to drop everything about my culture in favour of another man's own.'

Yes, both men had been classmates in secondary school, but only

5

one of them had gone on to university – to university in the white man's land.

'My learned friend,' Engineer replied, 'we are the ones who should know better. Any part of our culture that is backwards should be dumped! When I was in London, there was a time I was having my bath and my landlord's son came to peep at me because he wanted to see if I had a tail. Do you think it's his fault? I don't blame the people who are saying that monkeys are our ancestors. It's customs like this that give rise to that conclusion.'

At that point Augustina lost control of her mouth and broke all protocol by speaking.

'Monkeys? Do they say that men and women are the children of monkeys?'

Both Teacher and Wife turned and looked at her as if she had broken the eleventh commandment. The children looked at her as if she had no right to interrupt their day's entertainment. Engineer looked at her curiously, as if he were peering through his microscope at a specimen in the laboratory. This girl was trespassing – a conversation between men.

'What is your name, again?' Engineer asked.

By that time, Augustina had repented of her sin. She cast her gaze to the floor.

'Young woman, what is your name?' he repeated.

'My name is Ozoemena,' she replied solemnly.

'Go and bring in the clothes,' Aunty said, as if she wished she were near enough to fling Augustina against the wall.

Regretting all the exotic tales she was going to miss, Augustina went outside and gathered the dry clothes from the cherry fruit hedges. Afterwards she felt awkward about rejoining the group and remained inside the bedroom until Aunty called her to carry out the sack of yams and plantains they had prepared as a gift for Engineer. Engineer saw her heading outside, excused himself, and followed. He opened the car boot and helped her place the items inside.

'You have very beautiful hair,' he said.

She knew that was probably all that he could say. As a child, Augustina's family had jokingly called her *Nna ga-alu*, 'father will marry', because she had been so ugly that the experts had said her

6

father would be the one who ended up marrying her. But Nature had compensated her adequately. She had a full head of hair that went all the way to the nape of her neck when plaited into narrow stems with black thread.

'Thank you,' she replied with head bent and a smile on one side of her face.

'Why did they call you Ozoemena?' he asked. 'What happened when you were born?'

She was not surprised at the question. Ozoemena means 'let another one not happen'. The only shocker was that he had actually cared to ask.

'My mother died when she was giving birth to me,' Augustina replied.

'Do you have a Christian name?'

She nodded.

'Augustina.'

She was born on the twenty-seventh of May, on St Augustine's Day. It was the nurse at the missionary hospital who had written the name on her birth certificate.

Engineer bent and peeped into her face. Then, he smiled.

'I think a child should be named for his destiny so that whenever he hears his name, he has an idea of the sort of future that is expected of him. Not according to the circumstances of his birth. The past is constraining but the future has no limits.' He smiled again. 'I shall call you Augustina.'

Augustina meditated on his words as she walked back inside. One of her cousins was named Onwubiko, 'death please', because his mother had lost seven children before he was born. She had another relative called Ahamefule, 'my name should not get lost', because he was the first son after six girls. And then her classmate in secondary school was called Nkemakolam, 'my own should not lack from me', because she was the first child after several years of childlessness. This method of choosing names was quite common but this Engineer man was a wonder. He said things and thought things like no other person she had ever met.

A few days later, Engineer returned for lunch. Afterwards, he asked Teacher if it was OK to sit and chat with Augustina in the garden. Teacher and Wife looked at themselves and back at Engineer. He repeated his request.

Augustina completed her tasks and went to meet him outside. He was sitting on a pile of firewood by the back fence and had pulled a smaller pile close to his side. As she approached, he looked her over from top to toe, like a glutton beholding a spread of fried foods.

'What of your slippers?' he asked softly.

Augustina looked at her feet.

'Why not go and wear your slippers,' he said.

She was used to walking around barefoot. But the way he spoke made her rush back in and fetch the slippers she usually wore to the market on Nkwo Day.

'Augustina, you shouldn't go around with your bare feet,' he said, after she had sat down on the smaller pile of wood.

Augustina kept quiet and stared ahead at a large family of fowls advancing towards them. A bold member of the brood stretched its neck and pecked at some invisible snack by Engineer's feet. A more audacious member marched towards her toe area and attempted to feed. Augustina jerked her leg quickly. The abrupt motion sent the fowls sprinting towards the other side of the compound in a tsunami of fright.

'You know,' he continued, 'when the white man first came, a lot of people thought he didn't have any toes. They thought that his shoes were his actual feet.'

He laughed in a jolly, drowsy way that made her smile a drowsy, jolly smile. She also had heard all sorts of amusing stories about when the white man first turned up. Her grandmother had told her that the very first time she saw a white man, she and her friends had run away, thinking it was an evil spirit.

'You have such beautiful hair,' Engineer continued. 'Have you gone to school?'

'Yes, I've finished secondary school.'

'What of university? Don't you want to read further?'

'I'm learning how to sew.'

'Ah. Learning how to sew and going to university are not the same thing. Look at all these people you see going to the farm every

8

day.' With his right hand, he drew a slow semi-circle in the air. 'Do you know what they could have been if they had gone to school?'

She did not.

'Some of them could have been great inventors, great doctors or engineers. Some of them would have been known in other parts of the world. Have you ever heard of the nature/nurture controversy?'

She had not.

'These people,' he said, turning to face her, 'if they were taken away from this environment and placed somewhere else for a while . . . just a little while . . . they would all be very different.'

He kept quiet to allow her to digest his words. Then she remembered the discussion of the other day.

'Is it true that monkeys are our ancestors?' she asked.

Engineer smiled with gladness.

'Augustina, I like you. You're a smart girl. I like the way you listen and ask questions.'

One of her father's wives had complained that this was her main problem in life, that she asked too many questions for a girl.

'They call it evolution,' he said, and then told her how scientists said that men were once monkeys, that the monkeys had gradually turned into human beings. He said that Christians were angry about this because the Bible says God created man.

'Why was the world originally without form and void? Could God have created it that way?' He shook his head vehemently, as if he were resetting the bones in his skull. 'I don't think so. There must have been another earth that existed before Genesis, which was destroyed. Some parts of the Bible make mention of it. That old earth must have had another man who looked like a monkey. But when creating the new earth, God decided to make the new type of man in His own image.'

Augustina's head swung from side to side like someone in a mini trance. He talked more about dinosaurs and other strange animals that must have existed in that old earth, about how scientists had even been finding their bones. Right there and then, Augustina fell in love with his brain. Throughout that night, his voice led a procession of his words all around her mind. She wondered how

9

all this information could be contained in one head, how all this confidence could be exuding from one breath.

Afterwards, he came more and more often to see her. Eventually, he raised the issue again.

'Augustina, why don't you go to university?'

She smiled on one side of her face and kicked at a passing earthworm. Each time Augustina was tempted to consider the issue, she remembered her father. He would never approve. The sensible thing for a girl to focus on at this time of her life was getting married and building a home.

'I don't want to go back to school,' she said firmly. 'I've decided that I want to sew and that's what I'm going to do. Please stop asking me.'

They sat in silence while she watched the earthworm wriggle away to a better life. This was the first time she had spoken to him sternly. She hoped he was not put off, and she was already composing a suitable apology in her mind when he uncrossed his legs and sat superintendent straight.

'If you go to university,' he said, 'I will marry you.'

Augustina gaped like a trout.

'Augustina, if you agree to go back to school, I'll assist with your fees, and when you finish, I'll marry you.'

That was how he proposed.

On the day that her admission letter to study Clothing and Textile at the University of Nigeria, Nsukka, arrived, Engineer leapt over the moon and back.

'Augustina,' he said feverishly, 'our children are going to be great. They're going to have the best education. They're going to be engineers and doctors and lawyers and scientists. They're going to have English names and they're going to speak English like the queen. And from now on, stop calling me Engineer. Call me Paulinus.'

Then he lost control of himself and did something that he had never done before. He ran his fingers through her hair and told her that he loved her.

Part 1

Ọkụkọ sị na ya anaghị eti ka ẹgbe ji ya haa ya; kama na ya na-eti ka ọha nụrụ olu ya.

The chicken carried away by a hawk says that it is crying not so that the thing carrying it will let it go, but so that the public will hear its voice and be witness.

One

My taste buds had been hearing the smell of my mother's cooking and my stomach had started talking. Finally, she called out from the kitchen and my siblings rushed in to fetch their meals. Being the *opara* of the family, I was entitled to certain privileges. As first son, I sat at the dining table and waited. My mother soon appeared carrying a broad plastic tray with an enamel bowl of water, a flat aluminium plate of *garri*, and a dainty ceramic bowl of *egusi* soup.

I washed my hands and began to eat slowly. The soup should have been a thick concoction of *ukazi* leaves, chunks of dried fish and boiled meat, red palm oil, maggi cubes – all boiled together until they formed a juicy paste. But what I had in front me were a midget-sized piece of meat, bits of vegetable, and random specks of *egusi*, floating around in a thin fluid that looked like a polluted stream.

The piece of meat looked up at me and laughed. I would have laughed back but there was nothing funny about the situation at all. My mother was not a novice in the kitchen. This pitiful presentation was a reflection of the circumstances in our home. Life was hard. Times were bad. Things had not always been like this.

After her Clothing and Textile degree, my mother had travelled to the United Kingdom with my father. They returned armed with Masters degrees. He was posted to the Ministry of Works and Transport in Umuahia; she acquired a sizeable tailoring shop that still stood at the exact same spot where it had been founded all those years ago. My father's earnings alone had been more than enough, but years of rising inflation without any corresponding increase in civil servant wages had gradually rendered the amount insignificant.

Then came my father's diagnosis. For a poorly paid civil servant to dabble in an affliction like diabetes was the very height of ambitious misfortune. The expenditure on his tablets and insulin alone was enough for the upkeep of another grown child. And since his special diet banned him from large quantities of the high-carbohydrate staple foods in our part of the world, he was now constrained to healthier, less affordable alternatives. The little income from the tailoring shop plus my father's pension were what we were now surviving on.

My mother reappeared at the dining table, laden with another tray, which had my father's melancholic lunch on it. The front of her dress was stained with the sticky, black fluid from the unripe plantains that she had used to make her husband's porridge. She arranged the tray at the head of the table and sat in her place next to his.

'Paulinus, come and eat,' she called out.

My father stood up from his favourite armchair. He shuffled to the dining table, bringing with him the combined odour of medication and illness and age. My siblings joined us. Charity sat between me and my mother on my right; Godfrey and Eugene sat to my left. The noise of tongues sucking, teeth chomping, and throats swallowing soon floated about in the air like ghosts. My father's voice joined in.

'Augustina, I need a little bit more salt.'

My mother considered his request for a while. Because he also suffered from high blood pressure, every day she reduced the quantity of salt she added to his food, hoping that he would not notice. Reluctantly, she succumbed.

'Odinkemmelu,' she called out.

There was no reply.

Odinkemmelu!'

Silence was the answer.

'Odinkemmelu! Odinkemmelu!'

'Yes, Ma!' a voice responded from the kitchen.

The air in the room was suddenly invaded by the feral stench of pubescent sweat. Odinkemmelu entered wearing a rusty white T-shirt and a pair of khaki shorts that had jagged holes in several inappropriate places. He and the other girl, Chikaodinaka, had come from the village to live with us. Neither of them was allowed to sit at the dining table.

'How come it took you so long to answer?' my mother asked.

'Mama Kingsley, sorry, Ma. I am put off the fire for the kerosene stove by the time you call and I doesn't heard you.'

My mother ran her eyes up and down Odinkemmelu's body in a way that must have tied knots in his spinal cord. But the boy was not telling a lie; the fumes floated in right on time. We had stopped using the gas cooker because cooking gas was too expensive, and had switched to the kerosene stove that contaminated the air in the house with thick, toxic clouds whenever it was quenched with either a sprinkling of water or the blasts of someone's breath.

'Bring me some salt,' my mother said.

Odinkemmelu took his body odour away to the kitchen and returned with a teaspoon of salt.

'Godfrey, I don't want to hear that you forgot to bring the university entrance forms back from school tomorrow,' my father said to my brother.

Godfrey grunted quietly.

'For almost a week now, I've been reminding you,' my father continued. 'You don't always have to wait till the last minute.'

When it was my turn about seven years ago, I had brought my forms home promptly. My father had sat down with me and we filled them out together. We divided the task equally: he decided that I should study Chemical Engineering, he decided that I should attend the Federal University of Technology, Owerri, and he decided that I must not take the exams more than once. My own part was to fill in his instructions with biro and ink, study for the exams, and make one of the highest Joint Admissions and Matriculation Board exam scores into the university's Chemical Engineering Department. Godfrey did not appear too keen on any such joint venture.

'And I hope you've been studying,' my father added. 'Because any child of mine who decides to be useless and not go to university has his own self to blame for however his life turns out.'

A sudden bout of coughing forced an early conclusion to a speech that could easily have lasted the duration of our meal. To my parents, education was everything. She was the recipe for wealth, the pass to respectability, the ticket to eternal life.

Once, while in primary school, I had ventured to exercise my talents in the football field during break time and returned home with my school shirt badly ripped and stained. When my mother saw me, she stared as if I had huge pus-filled boils all over my body. Then she used a long *koboko* whip to express herself more vividly on my buttocks. Later that evening, my father called me into his bedroom. He sat on the bed, held my shoulders, and adjusted my posture until I was standing directly in front of him. He stared into my eyes forever. Then in a deep, sententious tone, he changed my life.

'Kingsley, do you want to be useful to yourself in this world?' he asked.

I answered in the affirmative.

'Do you want to make me and your mummy proud?'

Again, my answer was the same.

'Do you want people to know you and respect you wherever you go?'

I did.

'Do you want to end up selling pepper and tomatoes in Nkwoegwu market?'

I shuddered. My soul was horrified at the thought of joining the sellers who transported food items from different villages to one of the local markets. Hardly any of them understood what was being said if you did not speak Igbo. Most of them looked wretched.

My father amplified his voice.

'Do you?'

No, I did not.

'Then you must stop wasting your time on silly things. You must read your books . . . focus on your studies and on the future you have ahead of you. A good education is what you need to survive in this world. Do you hear me?'

I heard him too loud and very clear. Still, he continued.

He explained that without education, man is as though in a closed room; with education, he finds himself in a room with all its windows open towards the outside world. He said that education

16

makes a man a right thinker; it tells him how to make decisions. He said that finishing school and finishing well was an asset that opened up a thousand more opportunities for people.

My tender triceps started grumbling. He continued.

He said that education is the only way of putting one's potential to maximum use, that you could safely say that a human being is not in his correct senses until he is educated.

'Even the Bible says it,' he concluded. '"Wisdom is better than gold, understanding better than choice silver." Do you hear me?'

Not only did I hear him, I believed him completely. I was brainwashed. I became an instant disciple. Thereafter, as I watched other little boys squandering their time and energy in football fields, I simply believed that they did not know what I knew. Like the Spiderman, I was privy to some esoteric experience that made me superhuman. And the more my scores skyrocketed in the class-room, the more I kept away from my friend Alozie, who could still not tell the difference between 'there' and 'their', and our neighbour's son Kachi, who was finding it difficult to learn the seven-times table. I continued to outdistance my classmates in academic performance. I had never once looked behind.

My mother reached out and patted her husband's back softly until his coughing ceased. Then she changed the topic.

'Kingsley, when is the next interview?' she asked.

'The letter just said I passed. They'll send another one to let me know. It's going to be a one-on-one meeting with one of the big bosses in their head office. This time, each person's date is different.'

'You're going to Port Harcourt again?' Eugene asked.

'It's probably just a formality,' my father said. 'The first three interviews were the most important.'

'So if you go and work in Shell now,' Charity asked, 'will you move to Port Harcourt?'

There was panic in her voice. I smiled fondly at her.

'It doesn't matter where I live,' I replied. 'I'll come home often and you can also come and be visiting me.'

She did not look comforted. My father must have noticed.

'Charity, bring your plate,' he said.

Charity pushed her enamel bowl of soup across the table, past my mother, and towards him. My father stuck his fork into the piece of meat in his plate and put it into his mouth. He bit some off with his incisors and deposited the remaining half into my sister's bowl. Unlike mine, his was a veritable chunk of cow.

'Thank you, Daddy,' she said, while dragging the bowl back.

I remembered when Charity was born about eight weeks before my mother's expected date of delivery. Though we were all pleased that it was a girl at last, she looked like a withered skeleton, tiny enough to make seasoned doctors squirm. Going to hospital almost every day and watching her suffer must have been when each of us developed a special fondness for her. All of us except Eugene, who was a year younger than Godfrey and a year older than Charity. He was a thorn in her flesh and made her a regular target for his silly jokes.

'Ah!' Eugene exclaimed now. 'Look at your armpit! It looks like a gorilla's thighs!'

Everybody turned towards Charity. She clutched her arms close to her sides and looked about to press the control buttons of a time machine and disappear. My mother's eyes swelled with shock.

'Why can't you shave your armpits regularly?' she asked. 'Don't you know you're now a big girl?'

A cloud fell upon Charity's face. At fifteen and a half, she was still very much a baby. She had wept when Princess Diana died, sobbed when we watched a documentary about people whose body parts were enlarged because of elephantiasis. While other Nigerians poured into the streets and celebrated General Sani Abacha's sudden death, Charity stayed indoors and shed tears.

'Is there any law that says she must shave?' Godfrey intervened. 'Even if there is, who makes all those laws? Whose business is it if she decides to grow a forest under her arms?'

Charity rubbed her eyes.

'It looks dirty,' my mother said. 'People will think she's untidy.'

'Why can't people mind their own business?' Godfrey replied. 'Why should they go about inspecting other people's armpits? After all, those hairs must have been put there for a reason.'

Charity sniffed.

'Actually, you're right,' I added. Not that I agreed that any girl should go about with a timberland under her arms, but for the sole purpose of coming to my darling sister's aid in this her hour of need. 'Scientists say that the hairs there are meant to transmit pheromones.'

'What are pheromones?' Eugene asked.

'They are secretions that men and women have without being aware of it,' my father explained. 'They play a part in the attraction between men and women.'

That was one thing that sickness and poverty had not been able to snatch from him. My father was a walking encyclopedia, and he flipped his pages with the zeal and precision of a magician. He knew every theory of science and every city in the atlas; he knew every word in the dictionary and every scripture in the Holy Bible. It was such a pity that all the things he knew were not able to put money in his pocket.

'No wonder,' Eugene said seriously. 'Like that houseboy on the third floor who's always staring at her whenever she's walking back from school. I guess it's not really her fault the sort of people her own pheromones attract.'

He laughed and choked at his own joke while the rest of us stifled our amusement for the sake of solidarity with Charity. All of us but one. My father transmitted an icy frown that froze the dancing muscles on Eugene's face. We all looked back to our plates. I realised that mine was empty. It was little episodes like this that made it easier for me to forget just how much like sawdust our meals tasted.

Two

Being careful not to disturb Godfrey slumbering beside me, I crawled out of bed and changed into a pair of trousers and T-shirt. Breath stale and hair as dishevelled as a cheap barrister's wig, I made my way out to the kitchen, which served as the route for most of the traffic in and out of our house. The front door was reserved for special visitors. People like my father's sisters and my secondary school principal.

'Bro. Kingsley, good morning,' Odinkemmelu and Chikaodinaka said.

They always woke early to begin their chores.

'Bro. Kingsley, are you go far away or should we kept your breakfast for you by the time you came back?' Odinkemmelu asked.

It was not the boy's fault that his tenses were firing bullets all over the place. Before he came to live with us about two years ago, Odinkemmelu had never set foot outside the village and the only English he knew was 'I want eat.' Over time, his vocabulary had improved. But when it came to tenses, he was never quite sure whether he was standing in the present or dwelling in the past.

Although his position on the family tree could not be described in anything less than seven sentences, Odinkemmelu was introduced to us as our cousin. Chikaodinaka was a more clearly identified relative. She was my father's cousin's niece. Both Odinkemmelu and Chikaodinaka offered their services without pay. Their reward was in kind. Leaving the village and coming to stay with relatives in town was the only opportunity they might ever get to learn English, watch television, live in a house with electricity, use a toilet that had a water system, or learn a trade.

'I'm just going to the post office,' I replied. 'I'll eat when I get back.'

I stepped out into the young morning and walked briskly with my heart playing sweet music. This could be the day that changed my life. For the first few minutes, the only sound that disrupted the early morning calm was the dance steps of dry leaves and debris in the Harmattan breeze. Gradually, a new sound joined in.

'Come and receive divine intervention! For nothing is impossible with God!'

Ring! Ring!

'Come and receive a touch from God! Our God is a God of miracles!'

Ring! Ring!

Soon, I bumped into a group of young men and women dressed in white T-shirts and black bottoms. Their T-shirts were imprinted with some verse of scripture or the other; they were clapping and dancing and chanting Christian choruses. Most of them jangled tambourines. One blared into a loudspeaker.

'Come and receive a touch from God!' he announced. 'Your life will never remain the same again!'

I was familiar with this sort of 'Morning Cry' from my university days. Early in the morning, before others had woken up, some students would take strategic positions along hostel corridors from where they would shout out the gospel of Jesus Christ. Often, groggy students yelled angry abuses at them.

'Get out of that place and allow us sleep!'

'God punish all of you preachers!'

'Ohhhhhhhhhhh! You people should leave us alone! Please! Please! Please!'

Once, one of my roommates had gone as far as opening the door and throwing a cup of water into the face of a self-employed evangelist. The bearer-of-good-news merely turned the other cheek and continued with his 'Morning Cry'. Now an ardent man moved in my direction to hand me a colourful flyer. I sidestepped him deftly and continued on my journey. The last thing I needed was to be harassed by religious fanatics.

The post office compound was as deserted as a school playground on Christmas Day. I walked straight to box 329 and inserted the key. There was a manila envelope with my name printed neatly on the surface. The butterflies in my stomach began a vigorous gyration. I dragged out the thin, white sheet of paper and unfolded it with the panache of one who had performed this same action several times before. Right there and then, my heart stopped beating.

Dear Mr Kingsley O. Ibe,

RE: INTERVIEW FOR THE POSITION OF CHEMICAL ENGINEER (SHP06/06/9904)

We are sorry to inform you that you did not meet the requirements for—

There was no need to read further. I crumpled the offensive letter in my hand and shut my eyes tight. The wind ignored my grief and continued sucking the moisture from my skin as she hurried past on her journey from the Sahara to the Gulf of Guinea. I am not sure how long I stood there. Eventually, I regained consciousness and locked the box. I wanted to weep, to run, to hide away somewhere, never to see anyone again. Anyone except Ola. I wanted to see Ola at once.

Ola was the sugar in my tea. Sitting across from her in the faculty library more than four years ago, it occurred to me that I was in my third year at university and not in any serious relationship. In between attending lectures and burying my head in my books, I had somehow put the issue aside.

That day, I had rushed into the library to snatch some minutes of study before attending my next class. It was not difficult to notice the group of girls in a corner; they were giggling in fifty different sharps and flats. Other library users cast exasperated glances in their direction, yet their banter continued without pause. All evidence pointed to the fact that they were 'Jambites'. Prim appearance, surplus excitement – it was never hard to distinguish a freshman.

Ola caught my attention. Her black hair was swept back in a ponytail and her large brown eyes stood out defiantly in a narrow face. Unlike most girls who had developed a penchant for bleached skin, hers glowed flawless ebony. She also looked innocent. I did not need to be an expert on women matters to know which girls had dabbled in more than their fair share of promiscuity and which were vampires – female Draculas on a mission to drain your bank balance dry. It was as if these girls gave off some peculiar pheromones. Perhaps Nature, knowing that man would someday need it for self-preservation, had implanted this sixth sense so that common folks like me could identify them.

Their noise eventually smoked the library attendant out of his cubicle. He strode to their table with a frown as thick as hail.

'*Oya*, all of you should get up and leave the library,' he ordered, his voice loud enough for everyone to know that someone who had power was in the process of exercising it.

'Must you shout like that?' one of the girls asked.

'Just pack your things and leave!'

'You should even be happy we came,' another girl hissed. 'After all, if we didn't come, you wouldn't have anything to do all day.'

They laughed while gathering their books and dainty handbags. I continued staring at Ola as they sniggered their way out of the library. Her back view was as satisfying as her front.

Ola returned the next day, this time on her own. My heart somersaulted twice when she walked in. She sat about five tables away and spread out her books. My supersonic brain ceased functioning. The words on the pages in front of me started wriggling about like enchanted snakes. I suddenly remembered that I needed a haircut. And that my white shirt was not starched. Ola studied for a full one hour before she got up and left.

She was back again the next day, and the next, and the next. I marvelled at how such a pretty girl could actually make out time to study. Other visitors to the library also seemed to have taken note of this shooting star.

'Hello,' the man whose lenses were as thick as the bottom of a Coke bottle would say.

'Hello,' the man who was about four feet tall would add.

'Hello,' the man who wore the same purple pair of trousers every day would concur.

Ola always smiled and waved at them. Having her in the library was such a delicious change from the usual dreary girls.

23

Even my roommates noticed that something was happening to me. On my way home from school one day, I stopped at the hostel shop and spent considerable time selecting what appeared to be an affordable, musky, macho fragrance. While getting ready for school the next morning, I sprayed the bottle lavishly from head to toe.

'Graveyard, what's wrong with you?' Enyi, one of my roommates, asked.

This nickname had been bestowed on me by another roommate who complained that I hardly ever spoke whenever I was reading, which was almost always. I never responded to it when I was in a bad mood. Today, I was feeling particularly high.

'What do you mean?' I asked.

'Ah, ah. I have never, ever, ever seen you spray perfume before. Never.' He called the attention of the rest, who were also preparing for school. 'Make una come see o, Graveyard don begin dey use perfume.'

The one who had initiated the nickname poked his nose into the air and took in an unnecessarily deep breath.

'You call this one perfume?' he asked. 'This one be like say na insecticide.'

I left them laughing and set off for the faculty with a spring in my steps. All their mockery was not enough to still the drumbeats of ecstasy in my heart.

That day, Ola did not show up at the library.

I did not set eyes on her until about a week later. While walking along the faculty main corridor, I saw her standing and chatting with a group of girls. My feet stopped beside her. The girls quit talking and looked at me. My larynx turned to stone.

'Is everything OK?' Ola asked, her face crumpling with concern. Silence was my answer.

'Would you like me to help you in any way?'

Her voice sounded like a beautiful flower. I could have composed several cantatas and penned unending epics merely by listening to her speak.

'No, everything is OK,' I replied at last. 'I was just wondering . . . I haven't seen you in the library for a while.'

She smiled. To think that she had created that smile especially for me.

'Oh, everything is fine. Just that I was down with a bout of malaria and decided to take things easy. I hope you people haven't taken my space in the library *o*.'

I chortled and assured her that 'her space' was still available. Not knowing what else to say, I remained clutching my folder to my chest and smiling like a portrait. It must be true what somebody once remarked, that shy men and ugly women have the hardest time of all in this world.

Eventually, she spoke.

'Thanks for your concern, eh. See you some other time.'

That was my cue to vamoose. Deflated, I walked away with the sound of hushed giggling bruising my ears. For the first time in my life, I suspected that I was well and truly an idiot.

The next day, I had my face glued to my books when I heard the grating voice of the man with the Coke bottle lenses.

'Hello,' he said.

I looked up. Four Feet and Purple Trousers chanted along. Ola returned their greetings. She smiled as soon as our eyes met.

'How are you?' she asked, when she was close by.

Then she placed her pile of books on my very same table and sat down beside me. The exact same thing happened again the next day. And the next, and the next, and the next. Soon we arrived at affectionate looks and spontaneous giggles, and all the other little actions that precede the grand knotting of two hearts.

Ola was a Laboratory Technology student whose family also lived in Umuahia. She was two years younger than I, enthusiastic about academia and knew exactly where she was headed in life. Her fingernails and toenails were always clean. Her hair never stank, even when she wore braids for over two weeks. She always wore her make-up light and natural and she still had some hair remaining from her eyebrows.

When I was with Ola, my personality changed. Thoughts and feelings that I had never previously paid attention to suddenly found their way from my cerebrum to my lips. She was the only person who told me that I was hilarious. She did not talk much but she always listened attentively when I spoke. Apart from my family and my books, finally something else occupied my mind. At some point, I even started worrying that I might be tipping on the verge of insanity. The flames of our love continued to burn for the remaining years of my stay in school. She was now in her final year at university, while I had been out of school for two years.

Ola was 100 percent wife material. We had already started making plans for our future. She wanted all her four sisters and an additional six cousins on the bridal train; I wanted three sons and two daughters, preferably the boys first.

As much as I wanted to fulfil my responsibilities as *opara* and help my family, I also wanted to get a job because of Ola. Marrying an Igbo girl entailed much more than fairy-tale romance and good intentions. The list of items presented to the groom as a prerequisite for the traditional marriage ceremony was enough to make a grown man shudder. And that was even before you considered the gift items for family members, the clothing for the girl and her mother, and the actual feast itself. Several couples had been known to garner all their financial forces together in the process of organising their marriage ceremony. Afterwards, they could sit back in their new home and gradually transmute to skeletons. At least then they would be married and could die penniless – but happy – in each other's arms.

Still drenched in these thoughts, on the way back home, I did not notice when one of the tambourine-jangling zealots stepped into pace beside me and extended one of his flyers.

'Good morning, my brother,' he said in greeting.

The man sounded as if he had slept on a bed of roses, woken from a scrumptious slumber that morning, and placed his foot right onto the ninth cloud.

'I would like to invite you to fellowship with us on Sunday,' he continued. 'It promises to be a marvellous time. Come and be blessed, for there's nothing impossible with God.'

On any other day, I would have called the man a bumbling buffoon and walked on. But like a well-oiled robot, I automatically stretched out my hand and collected the flyer.

26

Chikaodinaka and Odinkemmelu stopped chattering and resumed servile postures as soon as I entered the kitchen.

'Bro. Kingsley, welcome.'

I grunted and walked past.

I paused at the dining table and exchanged 'good mornings' with my mother and siblings. Breakfast was over but they were sitting and chatting.

'Should I bring your food for you?' my mother asked.

'Not now,' I replied.

Across the room, my father was snoozing in his favourite armchair with his head tilted to one side. A rattling sound rose in his throat like water gurgling in a disused tap that had just been turned on. My mother flipped her head in her husband's direction.

'Reduce your voices,' she said. Despite the fact that we all knew from experience that even the blast of Angel Michael's trumpet was not loud enough to awaken my father from these post-breakfast slumbers.

'Did the letter arrive?' Eugene asked.

I mumbled something. As intended, everybody mistook it for a no. There was no point in ruining everyone's morning.

Pretending that life was still normal proved a bit too difficult, so I went on to the children's bedroom and sat on the bed. Someone knocked on the door. I ignored it. The person knocked again.

'Yes?'

'Kings.'

It was my mother. I did not look up. She sat beside me, put her arm around my shoulders and pushed my head against her neck. We sat in silence for a while. Without asking any embarrassing questions, my mother knew that her first son was still a component of Nigeria's rising unemployment statistics.

'It's OK,' she said.

She stroked my cheeks.

'Kings, it's OK . . . ehn? It's OK.'

I removed my head from her body and sighed.

'Don't worry,' she said. 'Your own will eventually come. Let's

27

believe that there's something better waiting for you. Just don't let all these disappointments get to you.'

'Honestly, Mummy, I'm just tired. What is it I'm doing wrong? I always pass the tests and then they don't want me. I'm really perplexed.'

Perplexed and stupefied and woebegone. As if I was stuck in a maze and each time I found an exit, lightning would strike right across my path. This particular rejection letter was exceedingly painful because I had defied all the odds by getting as far as the last interview. But the way things worked in our society these days, besides paper qualifications and a high intelligence quotient, you usually needed to have 'long-leg'. You needed to know someone, or someone who knew someone, before you could access the most basic things. Still, as I progressed from one stage of the interview to the other, we had all assumed that this time would be different. Someone had identified that I had graduated as best student in my Chemical Engineering class. Surely, they could see that I was an outstanding brain.

'Kings, it's OK. I'm sure things will work out eventually.'

I bent my head.

My parents had been excited when I received my admission letter into university, but the whole experience put an additional strain on the family finances. Tuition fees, books, accommodation away from home – it all needed funding. When my father's illness poured fuel on the flames, my parents were forced to sell our old, grey Peugeot 505 for some extra cash.

At last, Graduation Day arrived. As first son, as soon as I started earning an income, I would automatically inherit the responsibility of training my younger ones and ensuring that my parents spent the rest of their retirement years in financial peace. My family were looking up to me. I was their light, their messiah, their only hope.

My mother held me tighter and rubbed my back.

'Kingsley, I've told you . . . everybody has their own dry season but the rain will always come. You'll see. And you'll remember that I said so.'

She spoke with so much conviction that I almost believed her. In the past, these words would have been tonic enough to brighten my face, push out my chest, and lift my gaze to a more auspicious future. But I had heard this same speech, on this same spot, in this same snug proximity, at least three times in the past year. It was like some sort of déjà vu.

We remained silent for a while.

'Why don't you go and have something to eat?' my mother said. 'There's some powdered milk left in the tin but if it's not enough, I can send Chikaodinaka out to buy some more.'

I stood up.

'I don't want to eat anything. I want to go and see Ola.'

'Why don't you—?'

'No, I'm not eating,' I replied, pulling off my T-shirt.

She left. I started polishing my dedicated pair of black shoes. They were my only pair. Moments later, my mother knocked and came back in.

'Here,' she said. 'Take this and add to your transport money.'

Some naira notes were scrunched up in her palm. I shook my head.

'No, thank you. I have enough for my transport.'

'It doesn't matter. Still take it.'

'Mummy, no thank you.'

'OK, at least use it to buy something for Ola.'

'Mummy, don't worry. I can manage till Daddy gives me my next pocket money.'

'Kings, look. I know it's just for a brief period and that things will work out for you soon. Take the money.'

Disgraceful that a twenty-five-year-old was still depending on his parents, but she smiled and looked tremendously pleased when I took the notes. Right there and then, I decided that the first thing I would do when I got a job was to buy my mother a brand new car.

Three

The 504 station wagon had a handwritten sign on the roof –
UMUAHIA to OWERRI via MBAISE. The vehicle had
originally been designed to carry the driver and one passenger in
the front seat, three people in the middle row, two at the back. But
an ingenious rascal had come up with a more lucrative agenda. Now
two people were sitting beside the driver in front, four in the
middle row, and three at the back. Being last to arrive, I had to
squeeze myself into the back middle seat, the tightest, most
unbearable position in the entire vehicle.

Wedged on my right was an abundantly bottomed lady who
chomped her pungent breakfast of boiled eggs and bread with noisy
gusto. On my left was a man whose eye sockets were empty, with a
boy of about eight years old perched on his lap. From the rugged-
ness of the man's clothes, his random chants and subservient
manner, I could tell that he was a professional beggar. The boy
was acting as his eyes and would not have to pay extra since,
technically, they shared the same space. So we were four in the
back row, sitting in a place prepared for three, which had originally
been meant for two.

The combined stench of the beggar's rags and the woman's egg
almost made my intestines jump past my teeth and onto the floor. I
was eager for take-off, and hoped that as the car increased velocity,
the pressure would force fresh breeze to diffuse the gas chamber at
the back.

'Bring your money!' the driver hollered, stretching a cracked
palm into the car.

I brought out my wallet from my trouser pocket. I shifted the
naira notes aside and gazed at the photograph that I carried
wherever I went. It was one of Ola and me with our arms completely wrapped around each other at Mr Bigg's on Valentine's Day

two years ago. The photograph had been shot by one of those pesky, hawker photographers who hung around restaurants and occasions. At first, I was adamant about not paying, even after the photographer had stood begging for about ten minutes. But when I noticed how much Ola appeared to like the picture, I dipped into what I had reserved for cake and ice cream, and paid for the photographs instead.

Another of Ola's favourites was one that my father had taken when I was three. Ola had asked my mother for the photo during one of her visits.

'I love the way you look in it,' she had said. 'Like a miniature Albert Einstein. Anybody seeing this photograph can tell that you were destined to be a nerd.'

Ola was funny sometimes.

Her third favourite was the one of me holding my rolled up university certificate, wearing my convocation gown and grinning as if I were about to conquer the world. All three photographs were displayed in pretty frames on top of the wooden cupboard beside her bed.

We handed our fares to the driver, who then waited for the little boy to finish unwrapping the diminutive notes and coins which the blind man had extracted from somewhere within the inner regions of his trousers. The boy counted aloud.

'Five naira . . . ten naira . . . ten naira fifty kobo . . . eleven naira . . . sixteen naira . . . twenty naira . . . twenty naira fifty kobo . . .'

More than a minute later, he was still several kilometres away from the expected amount. The chomping woman lost her patience.

'Take this and add to it,' she said, handing the driver some of her own money to complete their fare.

'Thank you,' the boy said.

'God bless you,' the beggar added. 'Your husband and children are blessed.'

'Amen,' the woman replied.

'You people will never lack anything.'

'Amen,' the woman replied.

31

'You will never find yourself in this same condition I find myself.'

'Amen.' This time, it was louder.

'All the enemies who come against you and your children will come in one way and scatter in seven different directions.'

'Amen!' several passengers chanted in an attempt to usurp this most essential blessing for these perilous times.

I wondered why the beggar's magic words had not yet worked for the beggar himself.

Whenever she knew that I was coming, Ola would dress up and wait on one of the concrete benches in front of her hostel. As soon as she sighted me, she would run to give me a bear hug. If I had surprised her by my visit, as I would today, her face would light up in delight. Then she would yelp and leap and almost overthrow my lean frame with her embrace. Then she would place her face against my cheeks and hold onto me for several seconds. At that moment, I could turn back and go home fully satisfied. The whole trip would have been worth it.

An hour and a half later, the vehicle arrived at the motor park in Owerri. I stopped a little girl who was carrying a tray of imported red apples on her head and bought five of the fattest. Then, I boarded a shuttle bus straight to the university gates and joined the long queue waiting for *okada*. These commercial motorbikes were the most convenient way to get around, flying at suicidal speed on roads where buses and cars feared to tread, depositing passengers at their very doorsteps. The *okada* driver that rode me to Ola's hostel had certainly not been engaged in any form of personal hygiene recently. I held my breath and bore the ride stoically.

Inside Ola's hostel, I knocked four times, rapidly, like a rent collector. Three female voices chirped in unison.

'Come in.'

Ola was sitting with some girls in her corner of the room. The girls greeted me, got up, and left. I stood at the door for a while before going to sit beside Ola on the bed. She did not get up. Where were my yelps and my hugs? With bottomless anxiety, I placed the back of my hand on her forehead. Her temperature felt normal.

32

'Sweetheart, are you OK?'

She wriggled away from my touch.

'I'm fine,' she replied stiffly.

Something must be wrong.

'Are you sure you're all right? You look a bit dull.'

'Kingsley, I said I'm fine.'

I hesitated. Her eyes were blank beneath long, pretty lashes that fluttered like butterfly wings. Her rich cleavage was visible from the top of her camisole, and her bare neck was covered with small beads of perspiration. Suddenly, I wanted to lick her skin. I put my lips to her ear and tickled her lobe with my tongue.

'Sweetheart, what is bothering you?' I murmured.

She gave me a light smack in the face and shifted away. With exasperation, she flung her hand in my direction as if swatting a fly.

'Kingsley, you're getting on my nerves with all these questions. Can't you understand simple English? I'm just tired.'

Her words whizzed past my ears like bullets. My eyes were transfixed by her hand. The red-strapped wristwatch was brand new. Dolce & Gabbana. She noticed me staring and dragged her feet under the bed in one swift movement. The action drew my attention to an equally new pair of slippers. Despite my blurred appreciation of the things of this world, I recognised the huge metal design across each foot. Gucci.

Head up, eyes open, I asked, 'Ola, who gave you these things?'

She turned her eyes to the floor.

'They were a gift from one of my friends who travelled abroad,' she replied in a wobbly voice.

I felt strange. Something was different. It was not just her bizarre attitude. Something else was amiss.

'Who's the friend?' I asked.

'I've told you to please stop asking me questions. I'm really not in the mood.'

We remained sitting like that for a while. I wanted to tell her about the letter from Shell Petroleum and about how heartbroken I was. I wanted to tell her how much I was dreading applying for other engineering jobs. But she maintained such a hard look that my voice evaporated. Then I remembered the apples.

'Here,' I said. 'I got this for you.'

From the corners of her eyes, she inspected my outstretched hand.

'Leave it there,' she replied.

'On the floor?'

'Yes.'

I dropped the polythene bag.

'Actually I need to rest,' she said, still without looking at me. 'I've had a very busy week and the week ahead is going to be even busier. You know I'm working on my project.'

I nodded slowly and stood. She accompanied me outside, maintaining a pace or two behind me. When I slowed down for her to catch up, she slowed down. When I stopped and looked back, she stopped and looked askance. Outside the hostel, she halted. I stood with arms akimbo like an angry school headmaster and walked back to where she was standing. The girl needed a severe talking-to.

'Now listen to me,' I began. 'I can tell everything is not all right. If there's something you need to get off your chest, why not just let it out? There's never been anything we couldn't talk about with—'

'Kingsley, I really don't think you should come and see me again.'

My mouth fell wide open. I completely forgot that I had been in the middle of a speech that was designed to bring about world peace.

She hesitated and looked away.

'Right now I just need to focus. I'm really under pressure.'

I sighed. Of course. Her schoolwork was bothering her. Sometimes, project supervisors could drive you up the wall and right into the concrete. Ola was so engrossed in her work, she did not want to be distracted by romance. I looked at her with awe; she had just inspired me with fresh admiration.

'Ola,' I said in the most understanding of tones. 'Take it easy, OK? Just let me know when you've finished your project and I'll come and visit you. OK?'

'Kingsley . . .' she began fiercely.

From her face, I could tell that she was composing a different sentence.

34

'You'd better know that my mother is very unhappy with you,' she said eventually.

'Unhappy with me? Why?'

She averted her eyes.

'Kingsley, I have to go. Have a safe trip.'

With that, she turned and disappeared inside.

Back at the motor park, I located the vehicle going to Umuahia. The station wagon had almost filled up, when a haggard woman approached. Her bony body was outlined under an oversized blouse that was drawn in at the waist. A grey skirt fell to the middle of her legs, her feet were clad in rugged bathroom slippers. She poked her thin face into my window and informed us that her husband was in very poor health.

'My brothers and sisters,' she pleaded, 'I have nine children and hunger is threatening to kill us. My husband has been very sick for over a year and we have no money for the operation.'

She said that we – those of us in that vehicle – were their only hope of survival. If we would only chip in some funds.

'My brothers and sisters,' she begged, 'please nothing is too small.'

Around her neck hung a cloth rope attached to a photograph of her husband. In it, the sick man was lying on a raffia mat on the cement floor. He was stark naked and his ribs were gleaming through his skin. There was a growth the size of two adult heads, shooting out from between his bony legs. The faded photograph dangled on her flat chest as she stretched a metal container into the car and jangled the coins that were inside.

As soon as I saw the photograph, it hit me.

I realised what had been missing from Ola's room, what it was that had been nagging at me all the while I was there. All my photographs – all three of them – had vanished from her room.

Four

The local 7 o'clock news was usually a harmless serving of our state governor's daily activities – where he had gone, what he had said, whom he had said it to. The national 9 o'clock news was different. It always reported something that infuriated my father.

'They're all illiterates!' he ranted. 'That's the problem we have in this country. How can we have people ruling us who didn't see inside the four walls of a university?'

Two days ago, it was the allegation that one of the prominent senators had falsified his educational qualifications. He had lived in Canada for many years, quite all right, but the University of Toronto had no record of his attendance. Yesterday, it was the news that the Nigerian government had begun a global campaign to recover part of the three billion pounds embezzled by the late General Sani Abacha administration. About $700 million discovered in Swiss bank accounts had already been frozen. Today, it was the news that one of the state governor's convoys had been involved in a motor accident. This was the fourth time this same governor's convoy had been involved in a fatal car crash.

'And the most annoying thing,' my mother added, 'is that he's going to go scot-free.'

'Did anyone die?' Charity asked.

'Were you not listening?' Eugene replied.

'One woman died,' Godfrey answered. 'The other one is in hospital.'

The governor's press secretary was careful to add that the injured woman's medical bill was being catered for at the governor's expense.

'It's taxpayer's money!' My father exploded from his chair.

'But why can't they investigate what the problem is?' my mother asked. 'Why can't they ask why this same man has had four accidents in this period?'

'Illiterates . . . all of them . . . that's the problem.'

Had I been less preoccupied with other matters, I would have supplied the answer to that question for free. After the third accident, I had read an interview in which this same governor's press secretary had blamed the governor's enemies, insinuating that they had used a powerful juju to engineer these mishaps in order to embarrass the governor.

Before the news ended, my father had had enough. He stood up and hissed.

'I'm going in,' he said.

My mother followed.

Shortly after, Godfrey dived towards the television and tuned to a channel that was just starting to show a Nollywood movie. I was not a fan of these locally produced Nigerian movies, so I also stood and went into the children's room.

Sleep refused to happen. Three days after my visit to Ola, my mind was still bustling with worry. What was it that her mother was unhappy with me about? Perhaps she and Ola were having a misunderstanding. Perhaps she was angry that I had not been to visit her as regularly as I should have. But then, the woman was always busy. Ola's mother, for the earlier part of her married life, had been a contented housewife. She was forced to start her own business only after her husband defected to some other woman. Now she owned a busy pepper-soup joint somewhere in the middle of town, which she ran with an almost fanatical zeal.

This mystery was going to torment me forever. There was no better way to regain my peace of mind than to pay her a visit tomorrow.

I decided to walk. As I tried my best to avoid the speeding cars and the gaping gutters, I was amazed to see how much this obscure town was developing just a few years after Abia State had been carved out of Imo State, and Umuahia made the capital. There were several more cars on the roads, and neon signs announcing new businesses. There were more and more posters advertising the political intentions of . . . almost everybody. The scallywags hired to post these bills did not spare any available space in the pursuit of their endeavours. Faces of candidates were posted over traffic signs, and faces over the faces of other contestants. There were even faces posted on dustbins. Did these people not realise the subconscious message of seeing a candidate's hopeful face grinning from a container specially prepared for garbage? Perhaps most of them did not go to school.

A red car zoomed past and nearly broomed me off the road.

'*Hei*!' I cried while struggling to keep myself from tumbling into the gutter.

These parts were largely populated by civil servants and traders; the most ostentatious they aspired to was a Mercedes-Benz V-Boot. Anybody riding such an extraterrestrial car must either be a dealer in human body parts or a 419er – a swindler of men and women in distant lands, an offender against section 419 of the Nigerian Criminal Code, which addresses fraudulent schemes.

'Criminal!' I hissed after the flashy vehicle. Was it his dirty money that had constructed the road?

Ola and I had done this journey between her house and mine several times before. It was best enjoyed in the late evening – when there were fewer cars on the road, when the ill-tempered sun was taking its leave, when a fresh breeze was fanning the skin. Walking with Ola was magical. We would take slow steps and talk about everything – our dreams, our fears, what happened to us during the day, how we had spent our time. Usually, I did most of the serious talking. But once in a while, she raised some heavy issues.

'My mother was asking me some things about you today,' she said sometime towards the end of my stay in school.

'Oh, really? What did she want to know?'

'She was asking how I was sure that you would still be interested in marrying me when you finished school and got a good job in an oil company.'

I laughed. Ola's laughter was much smaller.

'She was going on about how she wasted her life trying to please my father, only for him to leave her for someone else.'

I stopped laughing. It had been a painful experience for them.

Following the birth of the first two girls, Ola's father had made it quite clear to their mother that what he now wanted was a boy. Three girls later, he began his coalition with another woman, who agreed to bring forth sons only if he married her. Without informing his existing family, Ola's father paid the woman's bride price, arranged a traditional marriage ceremony, and moved in with her. So far, the newer bride had popped out two bouncing baby girls.

'How can she think I'm so fickle?' I asked indignantly. 'She obviously doesn't know how much you mean to me.'

'That's what I told her,' Ola smiled, and squeezed my hand.

But there was still something else on her mind. It came after a few paces of silence.

'Kings, but how come you haven't given me a ring?' she asked.

'Sweetheart, I don't have to give you a ring for you to know I love you,' I cooed back.

'I know, but other people might not see it like that. They might think we're just fooling around.'

As usual, she had a point.

My next pocket money had been swallowed up by an engagement ring. Ola wore it until late last year when the metal turned green. She did not seem too bothered about a ring these days, but I had promised that when I started working I would buy her one that sparkled so bright she would have to wear Christian Dior shades.

Most times while we walked and talked, I would have my arm around her with my hand inside the back pocket of her jeans. I never held her openly in Umuahia, though; people would think she was promiscuous. Ola never wore trousers in the streets of Umuahia either; girls who wore them were seen as wayward. Men would toss lecherous comments, women would fling snide remarks, children would stop and stare. But in school, we could do whatever we wanted. There were several open fields and bushy gardens. Fortunately, the university budget did not include streetlights.

At Ola's house, I knocked. Ezinne peeped through the transparent glass door, unlocked it hurriedly, and hugged my waist.

'Good afternoon, Brother Kings.'

'My darling little sweetheart, how are you?'

'I'm fine, thank you.'

I pecked her two cheeks.

Ezinne was the youngest of Ola's five sisters. She was a miniature version of her elder sister, both in looks and in personality. And she had taken to me just as naturally, too. We had a special bond.

'Didn't you go to school today?' I asked.

'No, Brother. I ate too much pepper soup yesterday and my tummy was running throughout the night. My mummy said I should stay at home today so that I won't be running to the toilet when I'm in school.'

'So how're you feeling now?'

'I'm feeling better, thank you.'

Ola's mother was sitting on one of the wooden chairs in the meagrely furnished living room. The only chair with a cushion had belonged to the Man of the House. There were some brightly coloured plastic flowers standing in an aluminium vase on the centre table. The table legs were leaning at a 120-degree angle – an extra ten degrees from the last time I was here. I had heard of men who aspired to marry girls from rich homes, but there was something gratifying about having a fiancée whose family house was in a more deplorable state than mine.

All my life, I had heard my mother say things like: 'If not for your daddy, I would never have attended university', 'If not for your daddy, I would still be walking about barefoot in the village'. I dreamt of a wife who would say similarly enchanting things about me, a wife who saw me as Deliverer. 'If not for your daddy, I would never have lived in a house where we didn't have to pay rent', 'If not for your daddy, I would never have lived in a duplex with a high fence and large compound', 'If not for your daddy, I would never have been on a plane, I would never even have left the shores of Nigeria'.

That last one was particularly essential, especially for my children. During my school days, the rest of us had been constantly oppressed by children whose parents could afford to take them away to England and America on holidays. They came back several shades lighter in complexion and never stopped yammering on about their exotic experiences, complete with nasal accents. They

40

flaunted unusual stationery and attracted more than their fair share of friends. Teachers treated them with blatant favouritism. My children would have more than enough to attract the envy of their peers. I would show Ola the world.

'Good morning, Mama,' I greeted.

'Ezinne, lock that door and go inside,' she said without looking in my direction.

Despite the burden of several excess kilograms of fat, Ola's mother was usually as beautiful as her daughters. But today, she was sporting a livid frown. I sat in the chair beside her, feeling the sort of apprehension that you experience when visiting the dentist.

She sighed deeply and placed an arm underneath her chin with the elbow supported by the armrest of her chair. She was wearing two shiny bracelets that were too big to be gold, and a sparkly wristwatch with small white stones that were certainly not diamonds.

'Mama, is everything alright?'

After some long seconds, she turned abruptly in my direction.

'No . . . no! Everything is not alright!' she said without lifting her eyes to my face.

Another spell of quiet followed. At last, unable to take it anymore, I leaned over and patted her hand, hoping to provide some comfort for whatever was troubling her. Instantly, she drew her arm away.

'Don't touch me . . . you hear? Just don't touch me. You'd better make your intentions clear . . . you hear me? Me, I don't know what's happening; I don't know what you're doing with my daughter. This thing has gone on too long. I've said my own.'

So this was what the gloominess was about. Poor woman. I smiled.

'Ah, ah, Mama, but you should know by now that I'm very serious. Ola and I are still very much in love. In fact I saw her in school a few days ago. There's no need for you to be bothering yourself. Ola is my wife.'

'I've been hearing this same thing for how many years now. Me, I'm tired. Every day, "My wife, my wife, my wife . . .", "I love her, I love her, I love her . . ." Is it wife for mouth? Is it love for mouth? After all, love does not keep the pot boiling.'

41

'Mama, but you know the situation. As soon as I get a good job . . . once I'm settled down . . . I won't need anyone to remind me to come and pay the bride price. That matter is already settled.'

She looked at me as if I had just told her that O is for automobile.

'So how long exactly are we supposed to wait for you to settle down? Ola needs to move on, don't you know? She would have been married and settled down long time ago if not for all your rubbish.'

She adjusted her wrappers and laughed. There was no single drop of amusement in the sound.

'Look, let me just make it clear to you. There are other men out there who would gladly marry her, but she's still holding back because of you. Ola is not getting any younger. I've almost finished training her in university. I expected that by now, she and her husband would be the ones taking care of us. Me, I'm getting tired.'

She had a right to be upset. Agreed, Ola's mother had always displayed slight traces of sourness which must have had roots in the many jagged Frisbees life had tossed at her, but every other parent in her situation would feel this way. I was ransacking my verbal storehouse for the appropriate words to soothe her when she hissed. Her eyes were dark and narrowed – focused on me at last. Terror laid firm hold of my heart.

'Other men are finding their way,' she said. 'Other men know what and what to do to move ahead. Your own is just different. Is it certificate that we shall eat? If I say that you're useless, it'll be as if I'm insulting you. But since you people met, I can't see anything at all – not one single thing – that Ola has benefited from you. As far as I'm concerned, you're a complete disappointment.'

My heart rent in two. Different colours of bright little stars danced in front of my eyes. I felt as if she had risen from her chair, balanced one fat foot firmly on the floor, and kicked in my teeth with the other. For the first time, I wondered what my family – what Ola – really thought of me. Did they also feel that, I, Kingsley Onyeaghalanwanneya Ibe, was a disappointment?

Maybe I had not been as smart as other young men who were 'finding their way'. Maybe I had been too carried away by my academic achievements. After all, my father, with all his brilliance, was wallowing in poverty. I shuddered at the thought of ending up like him – full brain, empty pocket.

My thoughts wandered to my mother's half-brother, Uncle Boniface. He had lived with us when I was a child. At the time, he slept on a mattress on the living room floor and ate with a plastic plate on his knees in the kitchen like Odinkemmelu and Chikaodinaka. He had repeated several classes more than once, and eventually left secondary school without a certificate. But Uncle Boniface knew exactly what he wanted from the future. And he never kept quiet about it.

'Kings, sit down and watch me,' he would say. 'Let me show you how rich men behave.'

Then he would puff out his arms and stride around the living room in slow, unhurried steps. Then he would stop and frown and dim his eyes, and look up into the air. Then he would sit in my father's favourite chair, cross his legs, and shout orders at invisible servants.

'Come and take away these plates!' he would bark at one.

'Will you stop wasting my time!' he would howl at another. 'Do you think I pay you so much money for doing nothing?'

Then he would glare at invisible naira notes in his hands and chuck them onto the floor.

'Kings, come and take them and throw them in the bin,' he would say. 'These notes are too dirty to be in my wallet.'

It used to be a fun game that tickled my fancy no end. Not any more. Despite his poor academic record, Uncle Boniface was extremely wealthy. Rumours abounded of his innumerable cars and real estate and frequent trips abroad. And here I was sitting beside Ola's mother, a complete disappointment.

Fear gripped my heart tighter. My mother-in-law-to-be had clearly run out of patience with me. I needed to do something quick. As soon as things turned around, she would become my best friend again. I had seen it happen before. When I was still the only child after five years of for-better-for-worse, my father's family had fallen out of love with my mother. And like Ola's mother, they were very open about their grief.

43

'You need to put on more weight,' one said. 'How can your womb function properly inside such a skinny body?'

'I wonder how you manage the simplest household chores,' yet another one said. 'You look like a dried cornstalk that would break into two at the slightest push.'

'I don't even know what Paulinus found attractive about you in the first place,' yet another one said. 'No breasts, no buttocks . . . yet you call yourself a woman.'

One afternoon, after my father's sisters had visited and left, Oluchi, my mother's niece who was living with us at the time, carried me in her arms and patted my mother's back until her sobbing subsided.

'Mama Kingsley,' she whispered, 'there's something I've been wanting to tell you but I wasn't sure how to say it before.'

My mother sniffed.

'The last time I went home, there's something my mother and Aunty Amaechi were talking about.'

My mother pricked up her ears.

'They said that because of all these problems Papa Kingsley's people have been having since their father died, that maybe somebody from their family has padlocked your womb and thrown away the keys so that you won't be able to have more children.'

My paternal grandfather had died shortly after I was born, leaving behind some few plots of empty land and cassava farms which his living nine-sons-and-fifteen-daughters-from-three-wives had fought vigorously to put inside their pockets. The wrangling had produced such bile that there were suspicions of some family members engaging diabolical means to frustrate others into relinquishing their inheritance. From what Oluchi had said, it appeared that my mother's family regarded her infertility as the outcome of one of such evil machinations.

Oluchi continued.

'Mama Kingsley, I think you should do something about it. There are some native doctors in Ohaozara who I hear are very good when it comes to unlocking people's wombs. Maybe you should speak to Papa Kingsley so that both of you can go there and see one of them.'

My mother insists that her niece's advice went in one ear and out the other. She and my father never consulted any native doctors. They did not swallow any alligator pepper and animal blood concoctions, my mother did not dance naked under the moonlight with a white cock draped around her neck.

'I just kept crying to God,' my mother had told me. 'I knew He would intervene in His own time.'

One look at Godfrey, Eugene, and Charity, and God's intervention became clear. That was what I needed now – divine intervention.

I murmured my appreciation for her concern to Ola's mother and hurried home. Then I ransacked my pile of dirty clothes for the flyer I received from the early morning evangelists of the other day. My very own special miracle from heaven.

Five

As a child, I had gone to church regularly with my parents. So regularly, in fact, that I had perfected the art of sleeping at the precise moment when Rev. Father Benedict permitted us to sit, and waking at the exact point when he chanted for us to stand. On entering university, however, it occurred to me that I did not have to go to church any more. There was nobody to take me, nobody to remind me, no point in going. So I stopped.

This particular Sunday, my parents had left for Mass before I got ready to receive my portion of divine intervention. Agreed, we were not under any particular restriction not to go anywhere apart from 'The One True Church'; still, I knew enough to keep quiet about where I was going. Everybody agreed that the Pentecostals were weird.

But these were dire times. Dire times required drastic measures. Take my Aunty Dimma, my mother's cousin and very close friend. A few years ago, she had boarded a local flight from Lagos to Port Harcourt, and the turbulent voyage had ended with the plane crash-landing on the tarmac. Shortly after that, one of the tyres on her Toyota Carina had burst on the highway. Then a branch had fallen from the tree under which she parked her car and smashed the windscreen, the very same tree under which she had parked for the past five years. All these incidents occurred within the space of six weeks. Aunty Dimma did not need a soothsayer to explain that death was after her life. Somebody invited her to a church where she was assured that all her enemies would flee and all her troubles cease. Believe it or not, my very own Aunty Dimma – the height of elegance and the essence of vanity – had actually succumbed. Today, she was a bona fide Bible-quoting, hallelujah-chanting, tongue-talking Pentecostal Christian.

I lifted the flyer from the dressing table and headed out.

There must have been at least twenty different churches all holding services on the same street, at the same time, on this Sunday morning. Some were in garages, some were in flats, some were under tents erected at the side of buildings. Some even had loudspeakers positioned outside to bellow their live services into the air. I commiserated with every single resident of that street.

My destination turned out to be a three-storey building at the end of the road. A fiery young man was leading the congregation in prayers when I arrived, pacing briskly across the stage with a microphone in his hand and a free flow of mysterious tongues from his lips. Some of the congregation were seated, some were standing, some were pacing about. But every single mouth was moving in varying degrees of celestial conversation. A homely lady, who was smiling a perfect, wide smile approached me.

'Welcome,' she said in greeting.

I returned a smaller smile. She pointed her hand and jerked her head gracefully in the same direction. I took my place beside a pregnant lady who removed a huge, black carrier bag from the bench to make room for me to sit. Almost immediately, a prim young man came and occupied the space at my other side. In a twinkling of an eye, our row was full.

The fiery young man in front clapped his hands slowly and all noise died down.

'Praise the Lord,' he said.

'Hallelujah,' the congregation chanted.

'Praise the Lord.'

'Hallelujah.'

'Next, brethren, we're going to pray for the government of our country, Nigeria.'

He brought out an it-was-white handkerchief from his trouser pocket and wiped the sweat from his brows.

'Brethren,' he continued, striding to the right side of the stage, 'the Bible says that intercessions be made for all men, for kings, and for all that are in authority.' He strode to the left. 'Brethren, let us pray for our government, that God will guide our leaders to make the right decisions.' He strode to the right. 'That every demon of corruption will be uprooted and that we will have people in

47

authority who will favour the cause of righteousness in Nigeria.' He strode to the left. 'Let us pray!'

The celestial conversations resumed with even louder fervour. An elderly woman knelt on the floor and started groaning. Some people who required more space to throttle the demons of corruption moved to the back of the hall and started their vigorous striding about. I closed my eyes and waged my own silent warfare. Then I became curious and opened one eye.

The choir was seated somewhere towards the right of the hall. They looked exceedingly bright in their red satin tops and black bottoms. None of the ladies had her skirt above the ankles; none of the men had his hair barbered to any particular style.

Soon, the man deemed all demons of corruption uprooted. He stopped pacing and clapped his hands. This time, he asked us to pray against the demons of violence – for peace in the land, especially in Kano State, where there had been recent stirrings of yet another Islamic riot. The congregation grabbed the demons of violence by their throats and resumed mortal combat.

By and by, one of the choristers seated towards the edge of the group left her seat, advanced towards the man leading the prayers, and stood calmly by his side with her hands folded behind her and her head bent slightly towards the floor. I assumed this to be some sort of handover cue, because the man immediately stopped striding about and started clapping his hands slowly.

'Father, we thank You,' he began when the hall was quiet.

He spent a few minutes thanking God for answered prayers. Then he handed the microphone over to the lady.

The keyboard and the drum and the guitar went into action. The female minstrel asked us to clap our hands.

'I will sing unto the Lord, for He has triumphed gloriously, the horse and his rider hath He thrown into the sea,' she sang.

The congregation clapped and sang along while she led us from one praise chorus to the other. With each new song, the atmosphere sizzled and several people started wailing and flailing their hands in the air. The young man beside me had tears running down his cheeks. The pregnant woman beside me waddled to her feet. By the time the singing had gone on for over thirty minutes, the atmosphere became as charged as an electric field, and I desperately wanted to sing along as well. But being unfamiliar with most of the sacred lyrics, I was constrained to simply hum and clap instead. Then, a gentleman who had the composure of a seasoned surgeon stood up from the front row. As soon as the lead singer saw him, she ended her song and returned to her place at the edge of the shining squad. I was sad to see her go just when I was beginning to warm up.

The pregnant woman beside me dipped her hand into the black carrier bag and brought out a handkerchief and a plastic fan. She wiped her forehead and fanned herself briskly.

The preacher opened his Bible and stared intently at the congregation. From the concentrated focus of his eyeballs, I got the impression that he was seeing something that we did not and could not ever see. He tapped the microphone twice to make sure it was working. When he opened his mouth, the voice that proceeded was deep, his language was clear, his tone was godly.

'Welcome to service this morning,' he began. 'Please turn round to the person beside you and say to them, "You're here to have a great time this morning."'

We obeyed. The pregnant woman beside me stretched out a chubby paw and clamped my hand cheerfully. The prim lad overdid it with a mini shoulder embrace. All over the hall, men and women, boys and girls, were engrossed in cheerful handshakes and happy hugs and merry verbal exchanges. The bustle soon died down and the hall became quiet again.

The pregnant woman beside me dipped her hand into her carrier bag and extracted a huge meat pie. She opened her Bible with one hand and fed herself eagerly with the other. Her chewing made soft, mushy sounds like footsteps on a soggy carpet.

The preacher boomed out the hallowed text from the book of Luke.

There was a certain rich man, which was clothed in purple and fine linen, and fared sumptuously every day: And there was a certain beggar named Lazarus, which was laid at his gate, full of

sores, And desiring to be fed with the crumbs which fell from the
rich man's table: moreover the dogs came and licked his sores.

He leaned towards us with his hands firmly grasping the wooden lectern. He asked us to take a few moments to imagine. He asked us to imagine how Lazarus had stood at The Rich Man's gate begging for alms. He asked us to imagine how The Rich Man must have felt like a philanthropist because he was feeding a poor man with the crumbs from under his table. I imagined obediently. I was excited at the choice of sermon. Today of all days, they were preaching about poverty and wealth. Just what I needed to hear.

The pregnant woman beside me dug out a boiled egg from her bag. She shelled it skilfully and pushed the whole white mass inside her jaws.

The preacher looked back into his book and continued reading.

And it came to pass, that the beggar died, and was carried by the
angels into Abraham's bosom: the rich man also died, and was
buried; and in hell he lift up his eyes, being in torments, and seeth
Abraham afar off, and Lazarus in his bosom. And he cried and
said . . .

The preacher switched to a shrill voice.

. . . Father Abraham, have mercy on me, and send Lazarus, that
he may dip the tip of his finger in water, and cool my tongue; for I
am tormented in this flame.

He raised his right hand high up in the air, and changed to a deeper voice that ended in an echo.

But Abraham said, Son, remember that thou in thy lifetime
receivedst thy good things, and likewise Lazarus evil things: but
now he is comforted, and thou art tormented.

The preacher stepped away from the pulpit. Using wild gesticulations of the arms and legs, he retold the story of how the two men had ended up in eternity – one in heaven and the other in hell. He asked us to imagine how The Rich Man must have felt, seeing the very same man he had fed crumbs to, relaxing in Abraham's bosom. He asked us to imagine the joy Lazarus must have felt about seeing his personal fortunes change so sharply. He paused for some seconds to allow us time to visualise. I looked round at the congregation. From the mischievous, gleeful expressions on their faces, I suspected that several of them, rather than imagining Lazarus enjoying a better world, were imagining The Rich Man burning in hell.

I wondered why The Rich Man had gone to hell. Was it because he was a bad man or because he was rich? Had the poor man gone to Abraham's bosom because he was poor or because he was good? The preacher did not say. My father was poor. And like Lazarus, he was likely to be the one found in Abraham's bosom.

'It's all stolen money,' he often said with a voice stuffed full of pride, whenever he saw yet another person who had built a house or bought a new car. 'How could he possibly afford that on a civil servant's salary? At least 'I'll always be remembered for my honesty. Nobody can say I stole a farthing.'

I did not think anybody would have been blind enough to accuse my father of stealing public funds. Anybody could see that he did not have any farthings. Uncle Boniface, on the other hand, was foul-smelling rich. Popular gist held that he was a 419er, living large off funds he scammed from unsuspecting foreigners who believed the yarns he spun through emails and faxes. Each time his name was mentioned, my father would go into a tirade.

'I don't know why you people even mention his name,' he would say to my mother. 'You people need to realise that such a person is a disgrace to have in one's family.'

The pregnant woman beside me brought out a small bottle of water from her bag. She sipped in small, hushed gulps.

The preacher returned to Luke and to the deep voice. To further illustrate The Rich Man's sorrow, he knelt down on the cement floor, placed one of his palms upwards in the other, and switched to a high-pitched voice. He mimicked how The Rich Man had begged Papa Abraham to allow Lazarus to fetch him a drop of water and how the patriarch had declined. He described how The Rich Man had requested that Lazarus should go on an errand to warn his family of this place. For one split second, I assumed that he had been there while it all happened.

Suddenly, the preacher's voice evaporated. The electric fans stopped swishing, the lights stopped shining, and the hall became still as death. One of the omnipresent hitches with the National Electric Power Authority supply had struck. In keeping with their more popular acronym – Never Expect Power Always – power had been cut. Some of the men seated in the front row rushed out while the preacher attempted to continue his sermon undeterred. I heard the men pulling the generator starting cord somewhere outside the building. The engine whirred and then died almost immediately. They tried it again, and again, and again. Each time it fired up, each time it was quenched. Had they run out of fuel? Had the engine gone kaput? The men returned to the church hall. One of them approached the preacher and whispered. At that, he stepped away from the pulpit and continued his sermon – without the assistance of any amplifier.

The pregnant woman beside me brought out some white tissue paper from her bag and wiped her lips and her hands, making sure to work the tissue into the cranny between each of her fingers. She resumed fanning herself with the plastic fan.

'My brothers and sisters,' the preacher beseeched us, throwing his arms out in front of him like the antlers of a mighty stag, and shaking his head slowly from side to side, 'verily, I say unto you: In this world, all that really matters is Jesus. Forget about money, forget about fame, forget about all that this world has to offer. All you need is to focus on making heaven. Nothing else is important.'

Despite myself, I laughed. Did this holy man really know what he was talking about? My family was almost destitute, my mother-in-law-to-be had run out of patience with me, my father was wearing an expensive illness. Yet here he was telling me to forget about money and the world. Was this man joking?

The pregnant woman beside me poked a podgy, egg-white-perfumed finger into my shoulder.

'Let me pass,' she said. 'I want to use the toilet.'

I looked at her protruding belly, which was positioned threateningly close to my face, and struggled with the urge to ask her why she did not simply dip into her carrier bag and extract a potty? Grudgingly, I muffled my inner imp and moved my knees aside to allow her past. Her stout thighs got stuck in front of me. Eventually, I had to stand for her to go through.

I did not hear the rest of what the good man said, and not just because the preacher was not using a microphone. Each time there was a pause, I assumed that the sermon was over. Still, he continued. It was when the congregation raised its voice in communal prayer that I realised that, finally, he was finished. He returned to his seat in the front row just as the pregnant woman returned to her seat. The offering basket was going round now, and again, I had to stand to let her through. When the raffia basket arrived in front of us, she dipped into the very same black carrier bag and brought out a green naira note. She mangled it into a tight ball in the palm of her right hand before tossing it into the basket. I watched the container sail past. I had nothing to give.

Towards the end of the service, another man stood up and took the place of the preacher at the front.

'Are there any people worshipping with us for the first time?' he asked. 'Please indicate by raising your hands.'

Some hands in the congregation shot up in the air.

'Please can you take an extra step by standing up for us to recognise you?'

The congregation was asked to make the visitors – those of them who had stood up – welcome. They did so by walking up to them and shaking their hands, as if congratulating them. The young man beside me sabotaged my plan to ignore the ceremony. I had neither raised my hand nor stood up, but he turned to me and shook my hand almost as soon as the call was given. By some mysterious means, he had identified that today was my first time.

'Welcome, brother,' he said.

In total, there were about thirteen of us who had been identified. A lady – the same one who had welcomed me into the church that morning – ushered us all into an adjacent room where a man with an even thicker Bible than the one the preacher had used, came and stood in front of us.

'I'd like to thank you all for honouring our invitation to join us for such a special time this Sunday morning,' he began. 'We're so glad to have you with us at Revival Now or Never Ministries. We are—'

I got sidetracked by the sleeves of his white shirt. They were grimy, almost as black as the corners of his fingernails. His trousers were frayed at the hems, and some threads dangled from two buttons on his shirt.

Somebody handed out some forms for us to fill out our addresses and phone numbers, so that they could keep in touch with us during the week. We did not have a telephone at home. I lied about my house address. This was clearly not the place where my problems would be solved.

'Please don't forget that you're invited to fellowship with us anytime you want,' he concluded. 'You're always welcome. Please consider this place as your home and us as your brothers and sisters.'

On my way back home, I pulled the flyer out of my pocket and crumpled it into a tight ball. I flung it into a nearby bin and shook my head in consternation. The bin was pasted with the bogus smile of a newly declared presidential aspirant.

Six

Going to my mother's shop used to be a lot of fun. She would pick us up from school when she still had her Volkswagen Beetle, and sometimes, we would stop at the roadside where a woman was frying things in a great pan of oil.

'Give me *puffpuff*,' she would say.

With noses flattened against the car windows, we would watch the woman use the hugest spoon in the whole world to remove fried balls from the hot oil and wrap them in old newspapers. My mother would hand the woman some coins and place the wrapped *puffpuff* on the dashboard. The delicious aroma would saturate the car, causing our nostrils to dilate, our mouths to water, and our jaws to contract painfully. But no one was allowed even a bite – not until we got to the shop.

Business had been good then. But over the years, the complicated machines had been to the repairers and back so often that the machines had started shedding tears. Now most of them had packed up. Now the trickling of customers who remained came simply out of loyalty, from having patronised her for so long. Others came only when they needed a tailor to render an expedited service. Now there was hardly any reason for me to stop by, except that at this time of day, the only place where I could have the sort of private conversation I had in mind was in here.

My mother looked up from the buttons she was sewing onto a blue check fabric.

'Ah, Kings!'

Surprise made her dig the needle into her thumb. She locked the tip of the thumb into her mouth and sucked.

'Mummy, good afternoon.'

I sat on her customers' bench.

'How has your day been?'

'Oh, it's been fine,' she replied. 'It's been quite fine.'

She resumed her work with a degree of concentration that showed she was aware that I had something important I wanted to talk about.

'Mummy, there's something I want to ask your opinion about,' I began.

She stopped pretending to concentrate on her work and transferred her full attention to my face.

'I've been thinking,' I continued.

Yes, I had. Since the solutions to my problems were clearly not going to be divine, I had racked my brain until I struck upon a man-made idea.

'I've been thinking of moving away from home. I'll stand a better chance of getting a job if I went away from Umuahia.'

'Ah, ah? But is it not the same newspapers that you'll have to apply through to get a job whether you're in Umuahia or not? All the oil companies put their vacancies in the national newspapers.'

'That's what I've been thinking. Maybe I should start applying elsewhere apart from the oil companies.'

'Elsewhere like where?'

I understood her apprehension. Her first son was a chemical engineer, and that was what she wanted him to remain. But now I was ready to lower my standards. Most of the New Generation banks were willing to hire anybody who could pass their aptitude tests. They did not seem to mind whether your degree was in Carpentry or Fisheries or Hairdressing. All they wanted was someone who could speak English, who could add, subtract, and multiply.

'I'm thinking of maybe a bank.'

'Are there not banks here?'

'There are more opportunities outside here,' I replied.

After all was said and done, Umuahia was still one of the Third World towns in Nigeria. The same bank that would have just one branch in Umuahia, for example, could have thirty in bustling cities like Lagos. Plus, larger cities presented more diverse opportunities for work even if it meant that I would have to trudge the streets and seek employment in any other field.

My mother considered this.

'But where are you planning to stay? You can't afford a place of your own and you can't be sure how long you'll be looking for work.' She paused. 'The only person I can think of is Dimma. Which is good because then you'll be closer to the oil companies when they invite you for interviews.'

I knew that Aunty Dimma would be very pleased to have me at her place in Port Harcourt for however long I chose to stay, but I had other ideas.

'How about Uncle Boniface?' I asked.

My mother laughed and looked at me as if I was trying to convince her that G is for Jesus.

'Mummy, seriously. I think Lagos is the best option. I'm sure I'll get a job quickly. I hear people like Arthur Andersen will give you an interview once they see that you made an exceptional result.'

Uncle Boniface lived not too far away from us, in Aba, but he owned a house in faraway FESTAC Town, Lagos, where his wife and children lived. He probably would not mind my lodging with them, especially since he owed my family a social debt. The youngest of my mother's siblings, Uncle Boniface was the illegitimate son that my late grandfather had fathered by some non-Igbo floozy from Rivers State. Out of anger, my mother's family had refused to acknowledge Uncle Boniface as part of them. And with his failing health, my grandfather had found it difficult to cope. The family made a communal decision. Uncle Boniface moved in with us. Over the years, we had several of these relatives coming and going, but Uncle Boniface's stay was particularly memorable.

A few weeks after he moved in and started attending a nearby secondary school, he drew me aside into the kitchen and whispered into my ears.

'Kings,' he said, 'I've noticed that you have a very good handwriting.'

I accepted the compliment with a smile. He looked over his shoulders and lowered his voice some more.

'Do you know how to write letters?'

'Yes,' I replied, with the confidence of the best English student in his class.

My uncle nodded with satisfaction.

'Kings, I need you to do me a favour. I want you to help me write a letter.'

Such a task was mere bread to me.

Later that night, after the whole family had gone to bed, he summoned me from the children's bedroom. We sneaked into the kitchen, and he turned on the light and started whispering.

'Look,' he said, pulling out a scrunched-up sheet from the pocket of his shorts and unfolding it hurriedly, 'copy this for me in your handwriting.'

I recognised the ugly, bulbous squiggles that were the signature handwriting of the rural classes and the poorly educated. With some slight alterations, this could have been the handwriting of any one of the different people who had come to live with us from the village. I read the first few sentences. None of it made any sense.

'Look at you,' he jeered, planting a biro in my hands. 'Mind you, the person I copied this from is the best student in our class. He wrote it for his own girlfriend.'

My face did not change.

'These are big boy matters. Don't worry, one day you'll understand. Just copy it for me.'

He tore out a fresh sheet from the exercise book he was holding and gave it to me. I placed the paper on one of the kitchen worktops and went to work.

My dearest, sweetest, most magnificent, paragon of beauty a.k.a. Ijeoma,

I hope this letter finds you in a current state of sound body and mind. My principal reason for writing this epistle is to gravitate your mind towards an issue that has been troubling my soul. Even as I put pen to paper, my adrenalin is ascending on the Richter scale, my temperature is rising, the mirror in my eyes have only your divine reflection, the wind vane of my mind is pointing North, South and East at the same time. Indeed, when I sleep, you are the only thought in my medulla oblongata and I dream about you. I was in a trance where I went out to sea and saw you

surrounded by H_2O. In your majesty, you rose from the abdomen of
the deep. The spectacle took my breath away.

I want to rise at dawn and see only your face. I want you to be the
only sugar in my tea, the only fly in my ointment, the butter on my
bread, the grey matter of my brain, the planet of my universe, the
conveyor belt of my soul. I pray that you will realise the gargan-
tuan nature of my predicament. If you decline my noble advances,
my life will be like salt that has lost its flavour.

I am this day knocking at the door of your heart. My prayer is that
thou shall open so that thy servant may enter. The mark at the
bottom of the page is a kiss from me.

I remain your darling, dedicated, devotee,
Boniface a.k.a. It's a Matter of Cash

In the following days, he asked me to recopy the same letter to
Okwudili, to Ugochi, to Stella, to Ngozi, to Rebecca, and to
Ifeoma.

Late one afternoon, we were sitting and watching television
when Uncle Boniface returned from school and handed a sealed
note to my mother. It was from his class mistress. My mother
turned away from the screen and tore the note open.

'How can she say you don't have enough exercise books?' she
asked. 'Is it not just three weeks ago that I bought some new ones
for you?'

She awaited an answer from the scrawny lad standing beside her.

'What happened to all your exercise books?' she demanded.

Uncle Boniface looked at the floor and remained quiet. My
father stood up and walked away to his bedroom. He never made
any input when she was scolding the helps.

'What have you done with all your exercise books?' she asked
again, snatching the bag that was hanging across his shoulder.

Uncle Boniface's face darkened with dread.

My mother opened the bag and brought out his books. Three
loose sheets fell out. She picked them up and started reading. With
each passing moment, her eyes grew wider.

'What is this?'

She looked up at Uncle Boniface and down at the sheets again. Then she turned to me.

'Kings, what is this?'

I was in the last phase of demolishing a meat pie. My teeth froze when I recognised the exhibit in her hand. My mother dropped the schoolbag on the floor and flung the sheets of paper on the centre table. A chunky piece of pastry got stuck in my throat.

'Kings, when did you start writing love letters?! Tell me. When? How? What is this?!'

I could understand her shock. My mother was not the most devoted of Roman Catholics, but she tried her best. She put her hands over my eyes whenever a man and woman were kissing on television; she asked me to go into my room as soon as she perceived that they were on their way to having sex; she once asked me to shut up and stop talking rubbish when I told her about a girl in my class who was so pretty. I could easily imagine the terrible thoughts that were plaguing her mind about where I picked up the lyrics and the inclination to write a full-fledged love letter.

'Who taught you how to write love letters?' she asked. 'Boniface, what are you doing to my son? Tell me, what is this?'

With each question, she swung her head towards the person to whom it was directed. When neither I nor Uncle Boniface agreed to speak, my mother returned a verdict.

'Kingsley, go and kneel down facing the wall and raise your two hands in the air.'

Eager to show repentance, I rushed to start my punishment.

'Make sure that I don't see your two hands touching,' she shouted after me.

I knelt down by the dining table and obeyed her instructions to the letter. Then I heard her hand slam against Uncle Boniface's head.

'Yeeeee!'

'Oh, you want to start teaching my son how to be useless, eh?'

I heard another slam.

'Arggggh!'

'You want him to be useless like you.'

60

Another slam. And another and another. Knowing my mother's usual style when dealing with undisciplined house helps, by now she must have had the front of his shirt firmly in her grip.

'Mama Kingsley, pleeeeese!'

'Don't worry,' she replied calmly, but out of breath. 'By the time I've finished with you, you'll have a scar on your body that will remind you never to try spoiling my son again.'

He must have torn himself away from her grip and fled for dear life. She chased him into the kitchen and back out again. I turned briefly and saw that she had upgraded her weapon to a broom. With the dazzling agility of a decathlete, she chased him round the living room and cornered him between the television and my father's chair. She continued trouncing him until my father came out of the bedroom.

'Augustina, it's all right,' he said. 'Don't wear yourself out because of this nincompoop. Leave him alone.'

She abandoned the howling prey by the wall and went into the bedroom with my father. Shortly after, he came out.

'Kingsley,' he called, 'come here.'

I followed. I knew that my mother had narrated the little she knew, and that he was now about to ask me to pack my bags and leave his house. Inside the bedroom, my mother was sitting on the bed, looking as if someone had died.

'How did you end up writing a love letter for Boniface?' my father asked.

I narrated my very minor part in the fiasco. With each new detail, my father's face became more ferocious and my mother's eyes spread wider and wider.

'Pull down your shorts,' my father said as soon as I finished.

I did. In my mind, I calculated the best place for me to spend the night after my father asked me to pack up. Perhaps I could go to the beautiful grotto in the Saint Finbarr's Church and share the huge shelter with the Blessed Virgin Mary's statue. They had told us in catechism classes that she was the friend of all little children.

My father held my two hands in front of me with his one hand and used my mother's *koboko* to lash me with his other. I wriggled and screamed. After ten strokes that left me unable to sit upright for days, I was banned from communicating with Uncle Boniface whenever my parents were not around.

All these years later, my father still considered Uncle Boniface a pot of poo. So I could understand my mother's reluctance to broach this subject with him. Still, I persisted.

'Just talk to him about it and see what he says.'

'OK,' she replied. 'I can't promise that it'll be today, though. I'll have to wait for the right time. You know how your daddy is.'

'Yes,' I sighed. I did.

Seven

It was not just one of those days when everything seemed to go awry. That day, the devil must have ridden his Cadillac right across our courtyard and parked in front of our house. While brushing my teeth in the morning, I felt some foreign bodies in my mouth and spat out quickly.

'Kings,' my mother called from behind the bathroom door.

'Yes, Mummy?'

'When you finish, your daddy wants to speak with you.'

'OK.'

'Hurry up. He's getting ready to go out.'

I stared into the sink and observed some bristles from my toothbrush drowning in the white foam. I would have to buy a new toothbrush from my next pocket money.

My father was dressed in grey suit and tie, and sitting straight on their bed. My mother was more relaxed on a pillow behind him. Ever since his retirement, apart from going to the clinic for check-ups, he rarely left the house on a weekday morning. But last week, the announcement had been broadcast over and over again on the radio. There was going to be a verification exercise for pensioners.

The government was worried about several ghosts collecting pensions. People who left this world more than twenty years ago were still having monthly funds paid into their accounts, and the government was determined to certify how many people on their books were still breathing. Having the pensioners turn up in person and verified one by one seemed like the best method of confirmation, yet this was the second such exercise the government had conducted in the past fourteen months. Normally, my mother should have been at her shop by now, but whenever my father was going out, she waited so that they could leave the house together.

'Yes, Daddy?' I said.

'Your mummy was telling me that you want to leave Umuahia,' he began.

'Yes, Daddy.'

'What are your reasons?'

I explained in detail. Exactly what I had told my mother, plus some.

'Lagos is out of the question,' he said when I finished. 'Definitely out of the question.'

He went into a bout of coughing. My mother leaned over and rubbed his back.

'Isn't it possible for you to tell them that you're not feeling well?' she asked. 'The way you're breathing, I think maybe you should stay at home.'

'Hmm. Have you forgotten Osakwe?'

The recollection caused a faint breeze of fright to blow through my pores and right into my marrow. Osakwe was my father's former colleague who had been bedridden with some unknown ailment for several years. During the last verification exercise, his children had asked for an exemption, but the people at the pension office insisted that all pensioners – no exception – must appear in person. So the children hired a taxi, lifted their father from his sickbed for the first time in years, and carried him all the way there. They left the door of the taxi open and went inside to call the pension officers who came out and confirmed that Osakwe was still alive and pension-worthy. Shortly after the taxi began the homeward journey, the children discovered that their father had left this world.

'As for looking for other kinds of jobs,' my father continued, 'I understand why you've decided to take this step. But we must never make permanent decisions based on temporary circumstances. Whatever job you might get . . . I don't mind as long as you realise that it's just temporary. You are still a chemical engineer.'

'Yes, Daddy.'

'When do you plan to leave?'

'As soon as possible. I was just waiting to hear what you would say.'

He paused and thought.

'You can go ahead and let Dimma know you're coming.'

'Thank you, Daddy,' I said with a smile.

'Why don't you hurry so that we can all leave the house together?' my mother suggested.

With excitement, I went and had a quick bath. They were waiting in the living room when I finished dressing up. At the junction where our street met the main road, we stopped and waited. I looked at my mother with her man standing erect beside her and saw the pride radiating from her face. Even though his clothes showed too much flesh at the wrist and ankle, anybody would know immediately that he was distinguished. My father always looked like a university professor.

'Ah!' my mother exclaimed suddenly.

'What is it?'

'I forgot! Mr Nwude's wife said she wanted to give me some dresses to mend for her. I promised her that I'd send Chikaodinaka up to their flat to pick up the clothes before I left the house.'

'You should stop taking these sorts of jobs from people,' my father replied. 'If any of them needs someone to mend their clothes, they can stop any one of these tailors who parade the streets with machines on their heads.'

'It's difficult to refuse our neighbours,' my mother said.

'It doesn't matter whether the person is a neighbour or not. You're a fashion designer, not an *obioma*.'

My father appeared quite upset. I recognised that Utopian tone of voice.

'Nigeria is a land flowing with milk and honey,' he had said to one of his colleagues who was relocating to greener pastures in Canada and who had tried to convince him to join ship. 'Just that the milk is in bottles and the honey is in jars. Our country needs people like us to show them how to get it out.'

With that belief, my father had given the very best years of his life to serving his country in the civil service. Today, retired and wasted, he had nothing to show for it. Except our rented, two-bedroom, ground-floor flat in Umuahia town. And the four-bedroom, uncompleted bungalow in the village. It was every Igbo man's dream to own a house in his homeland – a place where

65

he could retire from the hustle and bustle of city life in the twilight of his years; a place where he could host guests for his daughters' traditional wedding ceremonies; a place where his family could entertain the well-wishers who came to attend his funeral. But that dream of owning a home had been relegated to the realms of ancient history when I gained admission to university.

Eventually, I saw a taxi and flagged it down. When the smoky vehicle braked, the people at the back shifted to make space. I held the door open while my father climbed inside.

'Pensions Office,' I said to the driver.

'Bye,' my mother said as I banged the door shut.

He waved. I waved back. My mother kept waving until the car was out of sight.

She continued in the opposite direction while I walked three streets to the closest business centre. I was the ninth person in the queue for the telephone. Things might have moved a bit quicker if not for the young man three places ahead of me who was trying to convince his brother in Germany of the rigours they were going through to clear the Mercedes-Benz V-Boot he had sent to them three months ago via the Apapa Port. The agents were demanding more and more clearing fees. Apparently, his brother thought he was lying.

When it eventually got to my turn, I wrote my number on a slip of paper and handed it to the telephone operator. The attendant got through to Aunty Dimma's line after five dials.

'That's wonderful!' Aunty Dimma sang. 'Having you around will be good for Ogechi. She hasn't been doing well in her maths.'

From there, I went to the newspaper stand round the corner. I had been buying newspapers from this same girl almost every week for about a year. Whenever my budget was tight, she turned away her vigilant eyes and allowed me to carry on as I pleased. Ola had once joked that the old girl had eyes for me. I selected a copy of *This Day* and saw that, in addition to Mobil and Chevron, a few insignificant companies were also hiring. I copied the relevant details before returning the newspaper to the stand.

Yes, Ola had asked me not to visit her in Owerri again, but now that I was aware of the source of her trouble – that her mother was bothered about my insecure economic status – I knew that an update would go a long way in allaying her fears. Ola might worry about my move to Port Harcourt, but in the long run, it would benefit our relationship.

Besides, women are from Venus. Like tying up shoelaces, they are full of twists, turns and roundabouts. They say something when what they really mean is another thing. For all I knew, right now, Ola was hoping that I would pay her a visit and wishing that she had not been so harsh on me the last time.

I confirmed that I had just enough money left over in my wallet and set off on another impromptu trip to Owerri.

Ola was not inside her room. My photographs were still missing. And instead of the wooden locker, there was a brand new refrigerator standing by the wall. Two girls were looking through some clothes piled on Ola's bed. I recognised one of them as an occupant of the room.

'Please, where's Ola?' I asked.

'She's not around,' the roommate replied.

She would either be in the library or in the faculty lecture theatre.

'If she comes in while I'm gone, could you please ask her to wait for me? I'm going to the faculty to look for her.'

The roommate was about to say something. The other girl hijacked her turn.

'Ola isn't in school,' she said. 'She travelled to Umuahia about two days ago.'

'She went home?'

'Yes,' the girl replied.

How could Ola be in Umuahia and not let me know?

'When is she due back?' I asked.

There was an awkward silence. The girl looked at the roommate. The roommate did not return the look.

'She didn't say,' the roommate replied.

'Thank you,' I said, and shut the door behind me.

*

It was late when I returned home. Godfrey and Eugene were huddled in front of the television while Charity was lying on the three-sitter sofa.

'Where are Daddy and Mummy?' I asked.

'They've gone in,' Godfrey replied.

'It's not been long since they went,' Eugene added.

'Daddy said he was having a headache and wanted to go in and rest, so Mummy went in with him,' Charity expatiated.

Their answers came one after the other, as if they were reciting a stanza of poetry and had rehearsed their lines to perform for me when I returned.

I went into the children's bedroom and changed into more casual clothes, returned to the living room and relaxed in a chair.

My mind was moving like an egg whisk. My brain cells were running helter-skelter. How could Ola have come into town without letting me know? What else had her mother been saying behind my back? Poor girl. I would visit her first thing tomorrow morning to allay her fears. Fixing my gaze on the screen, I tried my best to be entertained.

It was difficult. In the movie, a charcoal-skinned father and a charcoal-skinned mother had been cast as parents of an undeniably mixed-race daughter. This was not the only gaffe. Another woman had been cast with a teenage daughter who, based on her appearance, could very easily have passed for the mother's elder sister. Plus, whoever was in charge of that aspect of things had forgotten to replace the large, framed photograph of the family on the wall of the opulent living room with one of the family of actors who had borrowed the house to shoot the scene.

The lead actress had just discovered that the man she was about to marry was her long-lost father, when I heard the first scream. I assumed the noise came from the television. But when Godfrey lowered the television volume, we knew it was there in the house with us. We rushed to our parents' bedroom.

My father was sprawled like a dead chicken by their bathroom door. My mother was crouched over him with her hands on his shoulders and her head close to his chest. She was shaking him, listening for his heartbeat, and screaming.

'*Hewu Chineke m o!*' she cried. 'You people should see me *o*! *Hewu*!'

Her face was wet with tears. We threw ourselves to the floor and gathered around my father's still form. Charity burst into tears. Odinkemmelu and Chikaodinaka, having heard the commotion from the kitchen, also rushed in. I pushed everyone aside and listened for a heartbeat. With relief, I confirmed that my father's life was not yet finished.

'Mummy, what happened?' I asked.

'*Hewu* God help me o . . . God help me *o* . . . *hewu*!'

I pulled myself together and recovered some of that level of thinking that sets man apart from the beasts of the field.

'Godfrey . . . quick! Go upstairs and ask Mr Nwude if he can come and help us drive Daddy to the hospital in his car. Hurry . . . hurry . . . !'

I turned to the rest. 'All of you go out . . . just go out. He needs air.'

I shooed everybody away and closed the door. My mother was still crying. I checked my father's pulse again and again. Godfrey returned from his errand.

'Mr Nwude said we should start bringing him out. He'll meet us downstairs.'

I turned to my mother.

'Mummy, please wear something.'

From the wardrobe, she dragged a *boubou*, which had black stains from unripe plantains covering most of the stomach area, and pulled it over her nightdress. I bent down and held onto my father's arms beneath his shoulders while Godfrey held his legs. We lifted his body from the floor. With his head balanced carefully on my belly, we carried him out. A quick thinker had already opened the front door wide – the main entrance to the house that we reserved for special visitors. That exit would be closer to Mr Nwude's sky blue Volkswagen Beetle.

Mr Nwude rushed out, dressed in an outfit that he ordinarily should have been ashamed of. He was wearing a pair of boxer shorts and bathroom slippers, with his short-sleeved shirt buttoned halfway up. His wife stood beside my mother while we arranged my

69

father into the backseat. I and my mother squeezed into the front passenger seat and forced the door shut. The old car sped off as best as it could, leaving the members of our household staring in distress.

Eight

'What of your card?' the nurse asked.

We were at the Government Hospital Accident and Emergency Unit.

'What card?' I asked back.

'The one they gave you when you made your deposit.'

'We didn't make any deposit.'

'OK, hurry up so I can arrange for a doctor to see him soon.' She pointed her chin at my father, who was lying on a wooden bench with my mother standing beside him. 'Go and pay then come back and fill out the forms.'

What was she talking about?

'Just walk down the hall,' she explained. 'Turn right and walk to the end of the corridor, then turn left, and you'll see a blue door. Three doors from the blue door, you'll see another door that is wide open. Go inside, then look to your left. You'll see where other people are queuing up. That's the cashier. Pay your deposit and bring the receipt back here.'

Deposit? I looked at Mr Nwude. He looked at the nurse.

'Madam, please, this is an emergency,' Mr Nwude said. 'Let the doctor have a look at him now and we'll bring the money by morning.'

She almost laughed.

'Madam,' I begged, 'please, first thing tomorrow morning, we'll bring the money.'

She folded her arms and looked back at me. I wondered if the feminine of brute was brutess.

'Nurse, please . . .'

She patted a pile of forms on all four sides until every single sheet was perfectly aligned. We pleaded and beseeched. She strolled to the other end of her work space and started attending to other

71

matters. We beckoned my mother. Reluctantly, she left her husband's side and leaned on the counter.

'Please, my daughter,' she said in a mournful, motherly voice. 'My husband is very ill and we need to get him some medical attention as soon as possible. As my son was telling you, by tomorrow, we'll bring the money. I can't lie to you.'

Pity clouded the nurse's face.

'Madam . . .'

'Please . . . please,' my mother begged, shedding some tears for emphasis.

'Madam, please. It's not as if the doctors and nurses here are heartless. We've just learnt to be realistic that's all.'

She explained that after a patient was admitted, it became almost impossible to discontinue treatment if it turned out that the patient could not pay. The doctors and nurses were now tired of contributing from their own pockets towards the welfare of strange patients.

We rushed back to my father's side and held a quick consultation. My father did not conceal an emergency stash inside his mattress. All the banks were closed. There was nobody we knew in Umuahia who could afford to loan cash readily.

'What do we do now?' my mother asked. Her face was drenched with worry.

We carried my father back to the car and went searching. The Ndukaego Hospital told us that they were very sorry. The King George Hospital promised us that we were wasting our time. The Saints of Mount Calvary Hospital assured us that there was nothing they could do under the current circumstances. My mother lost her mind.

'*Hewu*! God, please help me! My husband is dying *o*! My husband is dying!'

'Mummy, please.' For the billionth time, I confirmed that my father still had a pulse. 'Mummy, please calm down.'

She continued babbling to God.

'Let's try another hospital,' I said to Mr Nwude.

A light bulb flashed above his head.

'My wife's brother has an in-law whose aunty's husband is a

senior consultant in the Government Hospital,' Mr Nwude said. 'Maybe we can go and ask if they can help.'

We sped to the wife's brother's house. He gave us directions to the in-law's house. At the in-law's house, my mother flung herself against the floor and uttered a cry that shook the louvers. The in-law got dressed and accompanied us to the aunty's house. At times like this, I had no grudges at all about Umuahia being such a pocket-sized town.

After assuring us that the hospital would have no qualms about shoving my father out the next day if we did not produce the cash, Senior Consultant Uncle gave us a signed note addressed to the hospital emergency ward. We sped back to the Government Hospital, flung the note across the desk to the nurse, and got my father attended to pronto. Thank God for 'long-leg'.

'He's had a stroke,' the doctor declared.

He said that my father's blood pressure was too high, that he was in a coma. He could not give any definite prognosis, but gave instructions for my father to be admitted.

The hospital lift was not working, so I and Mr Nwude carried my father up via the staircase to the medical ward on the third floor. After every few steps, we would lean on the wall and pant before continuing.

At the ward, some junior nurses took my father from us, while a militant senior informed us that we could not go in. Visiting time was over.

'You can sleep in the car park if you want to spend the night,' she insisted. 'This is not a hotel.'

Mr Nwude dashed back downstairs, retrieved the senior consultant's note from the nurse at reception, and brought it to the ward. The militant nurse changed her mind.

'You can spend the night, but it would have to be a private room.'

A more expensive alternative, but we did not mind.

My father's room reeked of disinfectant. The walls were stained, the bed frame was rusty, and the lumpy mattress had a broad depression right in the middle. There was neither bedsheet nor pillow.

73

'You're supposed to bring you own bedding,' the nurse chastised.

After my father was secure in bed, oxygen mask clamped over his face, blood samples drawn from his veins, tubes inserted through his nostril and wrist, catheter through his penis, Mr Nwude was ready to leave.

'Thank you very much for all your help,' my mother said to him. 'We really appreciate it.'

'My pleasure, madam,' he replied. 'I'll come again tomorrow to find out how he's doing.'

'Mummy, why don't you go home with Mr Nwude and let me stay the night with Daddy?'

My mother took a seat at her husband's bedside and shook her head firmly. The resolve on her face was as solid as Gibraltar.

I saw Mr Nwude off to the car park. It was not until he drove off that I noticed. Lo and behold, there were people covered in wrappers and lying on mats in many corners. The nurse was not being sarcastic when she suggested that we could sleep there.

All through the night, the mosquitoes came riding in on horseback. The males hummed shrill love songs into our ears, the females sucked blood from our exposed arms and feet. Tired of swatting the air and scratching her limbs, my mother shut the windows against them. Minutes later, we were almost at the point of asphyxiation. She opened them again. The mosquitoes were clearly the landlords. But at some point, we must have set aside our troubles and fallen asleep. A young nurse shook us awake in the morning. I rubbed my eyes and scratched at a red swelling on the back of my hand.

'You should bring a mosquito net for your father,' the nurse suggested. 'And bring a fan for yourselves. Even if NEPA takes the light, as long as there is fuel, the hospital generator is on from midnight till 4 a.m..'

'The doctor who is supposed to see him,' my mother asked, 'what time is he coming this morning?'

'He can come in anytime.'

The nurse handed me a sheet of paper. I studied the handwritten list. The items included a pack of cotton wool, bottle of Izal disinfectant, pack of needles, pack of syringes, roll of plaster, disposable catheter bags, bleach, gloves . . .

'What is this?' I asked.

'Those are the things we need for your father's care,' she replied. 'Any item you don't find at the hospital pharmacy, you'll have to go out and buy it from somewhere else.'

The list even included intravenous fluids!

'Does the hospital not provide these items? Are they not part of the bill?'

'Every patient is expected to buy their own.'

'Let me see,' my mother said.

I gave the list to her.

'So what would have happened if he didn't have any relatives here with him?' I asked. 'Who would have had to buy these things?'

'We never admit any patient who is not accompanied by relatives.'

Irritation had assumed full control of her voice. The last thing I wanted was for someone whom I had entrusted with my father's life to be angry with me over such a minor issue. My mother also seemed to share this thought. She handed back the list and surreptitiously poked my thigh. That was my cue to shut up.

The nurse tugged at some wires and peeked under my father's clothes before exiting the room. As soon as the door clacked shut, my mother turned to me.

'Kings, please hurry up and go to the house and get the cheque booklet for our joint account. It's in my trunk box. Bring it immediately so that I can sign some cheques for you to take to the bank and withdraw some money.'

'I'd like to wait and see the doctor before I go.'

'Please, go now. You know they admitted us on trust.'

On my way out, I walked past a nurse who was pushing a squeaking wheelchair. The wheelchair was stacked with green case files.

The queue at the bank went all the way out the front door and round the back of the building. If only my parents would stop being conservative and transfer their accounts to one of the more efficient

New Generation banks. Thereafter, I went straight to Ola's house. Apart from all the questions I was eager to ask her, she needed to know that my father was ill. Plus, Ola's hugs were like medicine, and every muscle in my body was sore.

As usual, Ezinne was pleased to see me. She unlocked the glass door and hugged me warmly. I waited in the living room while she went inside to inform her sister about my presence. Seconds later, she returned.

'Brother Kings, Ola is not at home.'

I peered at her.

She stood there, pulling at her neatly woven cornrows and twisting her foot from side to side with her eyes fixed on the floor.

'Ezinne, go back inside and tell Ola that I want to see her.'

She obeyed.

Ten minutes later, Ola came out dressed in an *adire boubou* and with an expression on her face like an irritated queen's. She was accompanied by one of her friends from school. The girl bore some coquettish-sounding name which I had forgotten. Either Thelma . . . or Sandra . . . or one of those sorts of names. They greeted me and sat in the chairs opposite.

'My father was admitted into hospital last night,' I said. 'He had a stroke.'

'Stroke? How come? How is he?'

'I'm on my way back to the hospital. I just wanted to see you first. How are you?'

I thought she might offer to come along with me. Suddenly, she became icy.

'I'm fine,' she replied in a voice that was well below zero.

'I was surprised when I went to your school yesterday and they told me that you were in Umuahia.'

'Yes, I am.'

Her answer sounded a bit off point. Nevertheless, I accepted it. She was wearing the same Dolce & Gabbana wristwatch of the other day. The former red strap had been swapped for a brown one that matched her Fendi slippers. Ola looked glum and rigid, like a pillar of salt.

'Ola, are you OK?'

Her companion flicked some dirt – noisily – from one of her red acrylic talons. Ola took a deep breath.

'Kingsley, I think we should both go our separate ways,' she said. 'As far as I'm concerned, there's no future in this relationship.'

She spoke so fast, with her words bumping into each other. Yes, I heard the individual words, but I genuinely could not make out any meaning from what she had said.

'Ola, what are you saying?' I asked.

The other girl hijacked the conversation.

'What essatly do you not understand? She has told you her mind and it's your business whether you assept it or not.'

This tattling termagant, like many of her compatriots from Edo in the Mid-West region of Nigeria, had a mother tongue induced speech deficiency that prevented her from putting the required velar emphasis on her X sounds. They always came out sounding like an S. I ignored the idiot.

'Ola, please let's go somewhere private and talk . . . please.'

Ola tilted slightly forward as if she were about to stand.

'Abeg no follow am go anywhere, jare,' the termagant restrained her in her more typical Pidgin English. 'Abi him hol' your life?'

Ola sat ramrod straight again.

The termagant appeared to be the commandant of this mission. Abruptly, she stood up and nudged Ola. Their task was complete. They had dropped the atomic bomb. Ola stood. I wondered why she was allowing this Neanderthal to control her like this.

'Kingsley, I need to go out now.'

I bent my knees towards the floor and reached out for her hand. 'Ola, please . . . at least let's go into the room and talk . . .'

I thought I saw a twinge of pain in her eyes, but it passed by so quickly that I may have been mistaken. She turned and walked quickly from the living room. Shortly after, she came out dressed in a brown dress, with the termagant following behind her. The scent of their combined perfumes invaded the atmosphere. Each molecule stank of good money. Without looking at me, they walked straight out of the house. I followed like an ass.

'Ola . . .' I called. 'Ola.'

She did not even look my way. Any passerby could have easily mistaken me for a schizophrenic conversing with invisible KGB agents.

'Ola, please just give me a bit more time.'

With me lurking at her side, they stood by the main road and hailed a passing *okada*.

'Empire Hotel!' the termagant shouted.

The daredevil driver did a maniacal U-turn and stopped with his engine still running. Ola climbed on as close to the driver as was physically possible, leaving just enough space for the termagant. When the driver had perceived that they had settled as comfortably as the laws of space would allow, he revved his engine and zoomed off.

Nine

It could have been the sorrowful eyes that she saw.

It could have been the gloomy aura that she perceived.

Whatever it was, as soon as I walked into the hospital with my father's provisions, my mother knew that darkness had befallen her *opara*.

'Kings . . . Kings . . .' she whispered anxiously and jumped up. 'What happened? What's the matter?'

It felt as if a gallon of 2,2,4-trimethylpentane had been pumped into my heart and set alight with a stick of match.

'Ola . . . Ola . . .'

When I was a child, we had watched a documentary on television about an East African tribe who spoke with clicks and gargles instead of real words. I used to imitate their chatter to amuse Godfrey and Eugene. Now I appeared to be talking the same language, the only difference being that I was not doing it to amuse anybody.

'Kings, it's OK,' my mother interrupted. 'Calm down, calm down.'

She led me to the second chair and held me against her chest. I closed my eyes and wept – softly, at first, then louder, with my head and shoulders quaking.

'Kings,' she said gently, after she had allowed me to cry for a while.

I sniffled.

'Kings, look up.'

I wiped my eyes and obeyed. I did not look her directly in the face.

'Kings, what happened with Ola?'

I narrated everything. I mentioned the trip to her school and the visit to her mother, not forgetting the termagant and the Dolce &

Gabbana wristwatch. From time to time, my mother glanced in my father's direction, probably to check if my voice was bothering him.

'Mummy, I don't know what to do.'

I looked at her. She did not say anything. Pain was scrawled all over her face.

'I don't think I can live without Ola.'

'Kings. Kings, if she doesn't want you because you're going through hard times, then she doesn't deserve you. Any girl that—'

'Mummy, what can I do?' I cut in. I was not interested in grammar and grand philosophy.

'Kings, I can't pretend to know what you're going through, but I don't think you deserve the way she's just treated you. If she can do this now, then—'

'I think I should go and talk to her mother again. This is not like Ola at all. I'm sure—'

'Kings . . . Kings . . .'

'If I can just convince—'

'Kings,' she said firmly, 'I don't think you should bother. That stupid woman already treated you like a scrap of paper.'

My mother's advice was definitely biased. She was not a fan of Ola's mother. She claimed that the woman had seen her in the market one time and pretended as if she did not know her.

'It doesn't bother me,' she had said of the incident. 'I'm just telling you for the sake of telling you, that's all.'

Yet she had narrated the same story to my father later that evening and to Aunty Dimma several weeks later.

'But how do you know she saw you?' Aunty Dimma asked.

That was the same question I had asked.

'She saw me,' my mother insisted. 'I even called out to her and she just gave me a cold smile and kept going.'

That was the same answer my mother had given me.

'How do you know she recognised you?'

'Is it not the same woman who came to this house on Kings's graduation day to eat rice and chicken with us?'

'Tell me not!' responded Aunty Dimma, the queen of drama.

My mother got fired up.

'God knows that if not for Kings, there's no place where that woman would see me to insult me. As far as I'm concerned, she's nothing more than a hanging towel. I'm not even sure she went to school.'

'I'll go and see her again,' I insisted now. 'Maybe she didn't think I was serious the last time I went to see her.'

'Kings, I don't think you—'

'In fact, I'll go today.'

'Why not—'

The nurse walked in.

'Have you brought the things on the list I gave you?' she asked.

I suspended my grief and searched around. The carrier bag with the items I had purchased on my way to the hospital was lying beside a deceased cockroach by the door.

Straight from the hospital, I went to the pepper-soup joint. Ola's mother was busy attending to customers. She scowled when she spotted me, but said I could wait until she was free. If I wanted to.

As was usual for that time of evening, most of the white plastic chairs, clustered around white plastic tables, were fully occupied. The place was bustling with the sort of men who liked places like this and the sort of women who liked the company of men who liked places like this. There were giggling twosomes and jolly foursomes, there were debauched young girls and lecherous old men, with a variety of lagers and soft drinks, and cow and chicken and goat pepper soups served on wooden dishes or in china bowls. I recognised one of my father's former colleagues. I wondered if the man had told his wife where he would be hanging out tonight.

My father never ate out. No respectable Igbo married man would leave his house and go outside to buy a meal to eat. It was irresponsible, the ultimate indictment on any wife – '*di ya na-eri* hotel'. Take my Aunty Dimma, for example. Long before she separated from her husband, moved to Port Harcourt, and subsequently became a religious fanatic, she was considered as one of the most incompetent wives to have ever been sent forth from my mother's whole extended family. Generally, she was a lovely woman. She was kind, helpful, always the first to turn up and support us, even if we were simply mourning a wilted plant. But my father once commented to my mother that it was a miracle for anyone to remain married to her and not lose control of themselves.

Where could a husband start in recording matrimonial complaints against her?

She always left home in the morning before her husband and did not return before him.

She had wanted to employ a cook even when he had made it quite clear that he wanted to eat only meals she herself cooked.

She was always arguing with him about what was appropriate for her to wear and what was not. Once, she even insisted on wearing a pair of trousers to accompany him to a meeting of his townspeople.

Aunty Dimma had also been known to openly slight her husband and despise his role as head of the family. Like the time when she had gone ahead and bought herself a car even after her husband had insisted that she should continue using public transport until he was able to afford to buy the car for her by himself.

Despite all this, the most obvious sign that the marriage was in trouble was when the embittered man started eating out. Matters degenerated from that point onwards. Once or twice, my parents and relatives collectively reprimanded him for raising his hand to strike her. But behind closed doors, they all marvelled that he could stop at one or two slaps.

Sixty-five minutes later, Ola's mother was still too busy to see me. Choosing to believe that she had forgotten, I walked up to where she was giving one of her girls an instruction by the counter and gently tapped her.

'Mama . . .'

She looked at me and scowled.

'You can see that I'm busy, eh?'

'Mama, I promise it won't take long.'

She glanced at her silver-strapped wristwatch. It looked brand new. And the stones looked valid, too. She was also wearing a narrow, glitzy bracelet with a matching necklace and pendant.

'*Oya*, go on and say whatever you want to say.'

I wanted to ask for a more private meeting place. Her glare dared me to make any further requests. I stood there – within hearing of any of her girls, any of her customers who cared to extend an ear –

and told her that Ola had informed me that our relationship had no future. I pleaded with her to give me some more time; I was planning to move to Port Harcourt and find a quick job.

She kept looking at me with that curious expression that people have when they are trying hard to understand others who are speaking a foreign language. Then she shrugged an exaggerated shrug.

'Well, me I've decided to remove my mouth. Whatever happens between you and Ola is entirely up to both of you. As far as I'm concerned you people should just go ahead and do what you people like.'

'But Mama—'

'I told you that I'm busy and you said I should listen to you. Now I've listened and told you what I have to say. I have to go back to work now.'

With that, she turned and disappeared into the smoky kitchen, from where all sorts of tongue-tickling scents were proceeding like an advancing army.

Ten

As news of my father's ill health spread, his bedside became a parade of friends and relatives and well-wishers. Every day, somebody new came to express best wishes, to let us know that we were in their prayers. Sometimes I felt like keeping away until all these people had left. But as *opara*, it was my duty to receive them, to share the burden of my mother's faithful vigil at her husband's side. She went home only once a day – to wash and to change and to visit her shop. She always looked drawn. And when she did not have her skull wrapped up in a scarf, her beautiful hair looked as if it had converted completely to grey overnight.

Aunty Dimma had turned up with a flask of *ukwa* and fried plantain, which my mother had barely touched. When I walked in, Aunty stood and unfastened thick, crimson lips in one of her sensational smiles.

'Kings, Kings,' she crooned in C minor. '*Opara nne ya*! My charming young darling, how are you?'

She trapped me in a backbreaking hug that lasted quite long. I felt a gooey substance on my right ear and hoped that it was simply some stray hair gel from her red-streaked pompadour. She tickled my cheeks with her fingers. Aunty Dimma had always been one for histrionics, but this extra zing told me that she had learned that I had been dumped.

My mother heaved a sigh. Aunty Dimma released me and turned to her.

'Are you doubting?' she asked. 'Don't you believe God heals?'

Probably because she was a liberated woman, Aunty Dimma usually spoke in a loud, red-hot voice, even when she was not angry. She also had an opinion about everything – from the second-class status of women in Igbo Land to the status quo in Outer Mongolia. And she always made sure that her voice put the final full stop to every conversation. The only factor hindering Aunty Dimma's complete metamorphosis from liberated woman to full-fledged man was that she had not yet grown a beard.

'Of course I know God heals,' my mother replied softly. 'But I believe that sometimes, God allows sickness to teach us a lesson.'

'If that's the case,' Aunty Dimma said with a smirk, 'why are you even bothering coming to hospital?'

I dived in.

'Mummy, what are we going to do about money? Is there anybody else we can borrow from?'

Both women crash-landed to matters arising. So far, we had borrowed once from Mr Nwude's elder brother while Aunty Dimma had made two medium-sized cash donations that were commensurate with her pocket. All my mother's jewellery and expensive wrappers had already been sold to provide for children's school fees in crises past. Crumbs were left in the bank. Very soon, even if the doctors grabbed each of us by our two legs, turned us upside down with our heads facing the ground, and shook us violently, not a penny would drop.

Aunty Dimma's voice ended the long silence.

'What about your brother?' she asked.

'Which one?' my mother replied.

'Which other one do you think? Boniface is there in Aba spending money on foolish girls and buying new cars every day. Why not tell him that Paulinus is in hospital?'

Terrified, I shot a glance at my father, wondering if he had heard. If he had, he would want nothing more than to rise from the bed and empty his catheter bag into my aunt's mouth. Everybody knew how much he detested Uncle Boniface. I was surprised that my mother did not immediately forbid Aunty Dimma from raising the matter again. Instead, she kept quiet.

I held my breath and watched. She actually appeared to be considering it.

'After all, what's the big deal?' Aunty Dimma continued. 'Other rich people build houses for their relatives and train their siblings' children. One of my friends—'

'Reduce your voice,' my mother whispered.

'One of my friends, her elder brother is paying for her daughter to do a Masters degree in London . . . almost ten thousand pounds. How can you people have a brother who's so rich and you're struggling like this?'

My mother pondered some more.

'These nouveau riche, money-miss-road people,' she responded at last, 'they have a way of getting on someone's nerves. Look at Boniface who lived with us just yesterday. All of a sudden, small money has turned his head upside down. At Papa's burial, didn't you see how he was moving up and down with security guards as if he's the head of state? The boy didn't even finish secondary school.'

Aunty Dimma looked at my mother and laughed. She finished laughing, looked at my mother again, and began another round of laughter.

'Point of correction,' she said, 'his money is not small at all. The cost of his cars alone can pay off all of Nigeria's international debts. You can go on calling him big names like "nouveau riche". You own the big grammar, he owns the big money.'

She laughed some more.

'So what are you suggesting?' my mother asked now, her voice still well below normal speaking range.

'Ozoemena, humble yourself. We're talking about Paulinus's life here. I have his cellular number, but I think it's best to talk to him face-to-face. You don't have to go yourself.' She nodded at me. 'Send Kings.'

'To Aba or to Lagos?' my mother asked.

'He's mostly in Aba. Only his wife and children stay in the Lagos house. I hear she doesn't like Aba.' Aunty Dimma snorted. 'It's probably too backward for her.'

'What kind of marriage is that? How can they live so far apart?'

'Marriage? Hmm. The girl was a professional mistress before she finally settled down. What do you expect? She just generally eats his money and takes care of his children.'

'So do you people think I should go and ask him for the money?' I interrupted, trying to corner them back into action.

'I think so,' Aunty Dimma replied. 'This money that is causing you people sleepless nights is ordinary chewing gum money to some other people. At the end of the day, he's your flesh and blood.'

She gave me more details about where to find Uncle Boniface's office in Aba.

'Just ask anybody,' she said. 'Tell them you're looking for Cash Daddy.'

Eleven

The streets of Aba were flooded with refuse. The stinky dirt encroached on the roads and caused motorists to struggle through narrow strips of tar. Touts screamed at the tops of their voices and bullied commercial drivers into stopping so that they could extort small denominations from them towards bogus levies. A stark naked schizophrenic with a bundle of dirty rags on her head, danced merrily in the middle of a T-junction. As the *okada* snaked through the logjam of vehicles towards Unity Road, I nearly fell off the saddle when we rode past two charred human remains sitting upright by the main road.

'Why are you behaving like a woman?' the *okada* driver laughed.

Next to Onitsha, Aba was the hometown of jungle justice. The people of Aba did not want to depend on their government for everything. They had taken the nobleman's advice literally and asked themselves what they could do for their government instead of what their government could do for them. They had chosen to assist her with the execution of justice. Therefore, when a thief was caught red-handed – whether for picking a pocket or napping a kid – people in the streets would pursue him, overtake him, arrest him, strip him naked, secure him in an upright position, place an old tyre round his neck, saturate his body with fuel, and light a match. The tyre would ensure that the flames continued until all that remained of the felon was charcoal.

My aunty had not been wrong; the *okada* driver had known exactly where I could find Uncle Boniface.

'Oh, you mean Cash Daddy?' he asked. 'Is it his office or his hotel or his house that you want?'

'I'm going to the office,' I replied.

Being something of a celebrity in this part of the country, I knew more about my uncle from the grapevine and from tittle-tattle than

88

I knew from his being my relative. It was still difficult to correlate the stories of immense wealth with the ne'er-do-well lad that lived with us all those years ago. But then, it was not today that Uncle Boniface started making grubby bucks.

Back in the day, my mother had come up with a novel idea. Tired of sending her girls out to buy drinks on behalf of thirsty customers while they waited to have their measurements taken, or to pick up ready clothes that were having finishing touches put on them, she bought a freezer for her shop so she could make soft drinks available for sale whenever her customers wanted. That idea turned into a major source of income since more and more people who lived on the street soon sought her out as their provider of cold drinks. My father then suggested that Uncle Boniface could go down to the shop after school, to help manage these extra customers.

Secretly, the boy soon perfected the art of opening the cloudy-green ginger ale bottles without distorting the metal corks. After selling the real contents to customers, Uncle Boniface preserved the corks and refilled the empty bottles with an ingenious brew of water and sugar and salt. Then he replaced the metal corks and sold the repackaged water. Sales from the improvised soft drinks naturally ended up in his pocket. Whenever the bottles were being served to those who wanted to drink right there in the shop, he yanked the corks with the opener and made a hissing sound from the corner of his lips at the same time.

My mother watched her customers' faces convert to confusion when they took a sip from their drinks. She listened as more and more people started complaining and tried to figure out the mystery. Then, in a moment of passion and infatuation, Uncle Boniface boasted about his exploits to one of the shop girls. This amorous Belle felt scorned when her beloved Beau diverted his attentions to another girl. In a bout of feminine fury, she squealed.

My mother returned home on the day of the shocking discovery and narrated the incident to my father.

'Are you sure this boy is a human being?' he asked with horror. 'Are you sure he's normal?'

'I flogged him in front of everybody in the shop,' my mother said. 'I'm sure he has learnt his lesson.'

'Flogging? Is it flogging that you use to cure evilness?'

'I think it's his age,' my mother excused her brother. 'Young people tend to play a lot of silly pranks.'

'The boy is wicked,' my father said with certainty. 'This is pure, undiluted Satanism. I'm very uncomfortable about him being around our children.'

To this day, the blame for the demise of that aspect of my mother's business had been piled totally on Uncle Boniface's head.

The *okada* stopped in front of an unassuming bungalow that was visible behind a high, wrought-iron gate.

'This is his office,' the driver said.

I dismounted and paid.

Seven men and two women were waiting in front. A security man in an army green uniform was leaning on the wrought-iron bars, with his back towards them. Inside the compound was a line up of five jeeps with uniformed men sitting in the drivers' seats. There were two Honda CR-Vs at each end and a Toyota Land Cruiser in the centre.

One of the waiting women walked closer to the gate and stood directly behind the security man.

'Please,' she begged. 'Please, I came all the way from Orlu. I can't go back without seeing him.'

The security man ignored her.

'I won't spend long at all,' one of the men begged. 'Just five minutes. I and Cash Daddy were classmates in secondary school. I'm sure he'll recognise me when he sees my face.'

The security man did not twitch.

'My brother,' the second woman beseeched him, stretching her hands within the bars and touching the security man gently on the shoulder. 'My brother, please, I've—'

Abruptly, the security man turned.

'All of you should get out and stop disturbing me!' he barked. 'Cash Daddy cannot see you!'

He was about to turn away when I moved forward.

'Excuse me,' I said.

'What is it?'

'Good afternoon. Please, I'm looking for Mr Boniface Mbamalu.'

The plebeian was clearly relishing his morsel of authority. He wrinkled his nose and screwed up his eyes, as if examining a splodge of mucus on the pavement.

'Who?'

'Mr Boniface Mbamalu. I'm his sister's son.'

'Cash Daddy?'

'Yes.'

He looked at me from top to bottom.

'Do you have an appointment?'

'No, I don't. But I'm his si—'

Suddenly, there was commotion. The security man forgot that I was standing there and rushed to unlock the gates. The five jeeps simultaneously growled into action. I turned towards the entrance to the bungalow and identified the reason for the commotion. Uncle Boniface, a.k.a. Cash Daddy, was on his way out.

Like my mother, Uncle Boniface was tall. But now that he bulged everywhere, the distance between his head and his feet appeared shorter. He was wearing a pair of dark glasses that covered almost half of his face. His belly drooped out of the cream linen shirt that he wore inside a distinguished grey jacket. He swaggered, looking straight ahead and swinging his buttocks from one side to the other each time he thrust an alligator skin-clad foot forward. Clearly, fortune had been smiling on him.

Five men in dark suits and dark glasses surrounded him. Two walked ahead, two behind, one beside him. When they were nearing the cars, the man beside him rushed ahead to open the back door of the Land Cruiser. Uncle Boniface heaved his bulkiness through the open door and adjusted himself in the back seat. The same man took his own place in the front passenger seat while the remaining four men hopped into the CR-Vs. The convoy glided through the now wide-open gates. Each car had a personalised number plate. The Land Cruiser bore 'Cash Daddy 1', while the first CR-V was 'Cash Daddy 2', the second 'Cash Daddy 3', and so forth. I watched this display in awestruck wonder.

All of a sudden, as if one driver were controlling all five cars, the convoy stopped just outside the gates. The tinted window of the middle jeep slid down. Uncle Boniface's head popped out. He looked back towards the gate, pointed at me, and shouted.

'Security! Allow that boy to go and wait for me inside my office! Right now!'

'Yes, sir! OK, sir!' the gateman replied.

The others waiting by the gate rushed towards the car. Cash Daddy's convoy zoomed on.

Inside the main building, the receptionist was chomping gum with wild movements of her mouth, as if she had three tongues.

'Please have a seat,' she said, and opened a gigantic refrigerator. 'Would you like something to drink?'

I looked at the assortment of drinks stacked into every single compartment.

'No, thank you,' I replied. I did not want to give the impression that I was from a home where we did not have access to such goodies.

There were four girls and three men waiting inside, some variety of drink or the other on a stool beside each of them. One man was gulping down a can of Heineken while his eyes were fixed on the wide television screen that covered almost half of the opposite wall. The television was set to MTV. Some men, whom the screen caption described as Outkast, were making a lot of noise. Despite the boulder of gum in her mouth, the receptionist was noising along. Incredibly, she seemed to know all the words.

Soon, a fresh bout of commotion heralded The Return of Cash Daddy. As soon as he stepped into the office, one of the dark-suited men produced a piece of cloth from somewhere and started wiping Cash Daddy's shoes. Uncle Boniface used the brief pause to look round at those waiting for him. He saw the man drinking the beer and glared.

'What are you doing here? Haven't I finished with you?'

The man stood up and approached him. Uncle Boniface turned away and pointed at one of the girls.

'Come,' he said.

She rose smugly and stiletto-ed along behind him. My uncle

zoomed through a set of doors which led further inside the office. His jacket had 'Field Marshal' emblazoned in bold, gold-coloured letters on the back. Without looking back or addressing anybody in particular, he shouted: 'Get that man out of here. Right now!'

Three of the dark-suited escorts immediately went into action. On his way out, the man remembered to grab his Heineken and bring it along.

Twelve

Fortunately, it was not a 'first come, first served' affair. The receptionist announced that Cash Daddy was ready to see me right after the girl came out grinning. One of the dark-suited men escorted me to the same doors through which my uncle had disappeared. We walked down a narrow corridor and stopped at the last door on the right. Inside, the man who had sat in the Land Cruiser with my uncle stood up from behind a computer screen, tapped lightly on an inner door and pushed me inside.

The office was vast and uncluttered. There was a refrigerator in a corner, a large mahogany shelf filled with books that looked like they had never been read, a wide mahogany cabinet that housed several exotic vases, various awards that extolled my uncle's financial contributions to different organisations, and a bronze clock. Stealing most of the attention in the room, a large, framed photograph of Uncle Boniface hung centred on the wall. In it, he was wearing a long-sleeved *isi-agu* traditional outfit and a *george* wrapper. He had a beaded crown on his head, a horsetail in his right hand, and a leather fan in his left. Most likely, the photograph was taken during the conferment of a chieftaincy title by some traditional ruler or other who wanted to show appreciation for Uncle Boniface's contributions to his community. Cash Daddy was seated behind the mahogany desk in the centre of the room, which held three telephone sets, a computer, and a Bible.

'Good afternoon, Uncle Boniface,' I said.

'Kings, Kings,' he beamed. 'You're still the same . . . you haven't changed at all. I had to rush out like that because a girlfriend of mine is being chased by a student.'

He swivelled his grand leather chair from one 180-degree angle to the other.

'I heard that he was in her house so I wanted to go and make

94

some noise. Let him know who he's dealing with. Any child who claims that he knows as many proverbs as his father should be prepared to pay as much tax as his father does. Is that not so?'

He swivelled to the left.

'Is that not so?'

'Yes.'

He swivelled to the right.

'Me, I don't play games. I went there with my convoy so that the small boy will be afraid and think twice. Me, I don't believe in film tricks; I believe in real, live action. If he knows what's good for him, he had better clear off. How are you?'

Before I could answer, he stopped swivelling and screamed.

'Aaaaargh!'

I was jolted.

'What is that on your legs?'

Involuntarily, I hopped from one foot to the other and looked downwards. I did not notice anything strange.

'What's that you're wearing on your legs?'

Again, I looked at my feet.

'Are those shoes?' He frowned and looked worried. 'I hope you didn't tell any of the people outside that you're my brother? I just hope you didn't.'

I stared back at him and down at my feet again. The shoes were a gift from Ola for my twenty-second birthday – one of the few items that had come into my possession in a brand new state. As yet, I had never questioned their respectability.

'Protocol Officer!' he yelled.

I was jolted again. It sounded as if he were summoning someone from the next street. The man in the outer office appeared.

'Get this man out of here!'

'Yes, sir,' Protocol Officer replied.

My important mission was about to be botched!

'Uncle Boniface, please,' I begged. 'I just came to talk to you about—

'Get out of my office! Protocol Officer, take this man away.

Make sure he's wearing new shoes before bringing him back. Go!'

The man led me out and handed me to one of the dark-suited men, who accompanied me into a bright yellow Mercedes-Benz SLK with number plate 'Cash Daddy 17'. We drove swiftly to a nearby shop that had a diverse stock of men's shoe brands. After politely declining several of my escort's recommendations, I finally made my pick. They had one of the lowest price tags of all the shoes in the shop, but they were probably the most civilised. Unostentatious, respectable, gentlemanly. I slipped my feet into the pair of black Russell & Bromley shoes. Honestly, there are shoes and there are shoes. As I tried them on, it felt as if dainty female fingers were massaging my feet. A revolution had taken place.

My dark-suited escort paid for the goods while I cast my old pair into the sleek box from whence the new ones had come. Back at the office, my uncle inspected my latest appearance and nodded his approval.

'Didn't you see how your shoes were pointing up as if they were singing the national anthem? Don't ever come to my office again looking like that. A fart becomes a stench only when there are people around. You can afford to be wearing those types of shoes in other places but you can't wear them around me. Do you know who I am?'

I apologised profusely and promised that I would never try it again.

'Have you had something to drink?'

'No, I'm OK, thank you.'

Suddenly, a strange tune pierced the air. My uncle pulled out a metallic handset from his jacket pocket and looked at the screen before answering.

'Speak to me!' he bellowed.

I admired the cellular phone shamelessly. Mere men could not afford any of these satellite devices; they were the exclusive possession of Nigeria's rich and prosperous.

'See you later!' he yelled and hung up.

He indicated for me to sit in one of the chairs in front of his desk.

'How are your parents?'

'My mother is fine,' I replied. 'She asked me to greet you. But my father's in hospital. That's the main reason why I came to see you.'

His face crumpled with concern.

'Hospital? What's wrong with him?'

'He went into a coma a few weeks ago. He's been on admission at the Government Hospital.'

His cellular rang again. He cleared his throat violently after looking at the screen, then allowed the phone to ring some more before answering.

'Hello? Ah! Mr Moore!' he said with excitement. 'I'm really glad you called! I was just about to ring you now! I just finished speaking with the minister for petroleum. In fact, I just hung up when my phone rang and it turned out to be you.'

He listened briefly.

'Calm down, calm down. I understand. But the minister has assured me that you will definitely get that oil licence. He just gave me his word right now on the phone. And one thing about the minister, he might be slow but once he gives his word, that's it. There's no going back.'

He listened. My uncle looked totally committed to the conversation. Perhaps it was the minister he had been chatting so familiarly with a short while ago? Perhaps the phone call with the minister had happened when I went out for the shoes?

'Right now, I'm not too sure when the meeting will hold,' he continued. 'You know the president is currently out of the country so a lot of big things are being put on hold.'

It had been in all the newspapers. His Excellency had tripped on the Aso Rock Villa marble staircase, dislocated his ankle, and had to be flown out to Germany for treatment. There had been a time when things like that did not make any sense to me. But with my recent intimate experience of our hospitals, I did not blame anyone who swam across the Atlantic to get treated for a hangover.

'Tentatively, I would say the sixth,' my uncle was saying. 'I'll go ahead and ask my staff to book your flight and make reservations with the Sheraton.'

He listened. His face showed concern.

'Mr Moore, I know. But the American Embassy clearly advises that any of its citizens visiting Nigeria should stay in American hotels. It's for your own safety. You know Nigeria is a dangerous place, especially for a white man. And one thing about me is that I'm a man who never likes to go against the law.'

He listened with deeper concern.

'I know.'

He listened some more.

'I know. You said so the last time.'

Suddenly, his face sparkled with a good idea.

'You know what I can do? I'll arrange for that same girl you liked very much the last time. How would you like that?'

He smiled. He listened. He laughed.

'Ah, Mr Moore. That's one thing I like about you. You know a good thing when you see it. All right, my good friend. We'll see on the sixth.'

The phone was returned to his pocket.

'So what are the doctors saying?' he said to me, as if there had been no international interruption.

'They said it's a stroke,' I replied. 'They're still observing him but they said his condition is stable.'

He shook his head and went into an extended speech about how much he hated hospitals; how whenever he was sick, he paid the doctors to come treat him at home instead. How the last time he was in France, he had wanted to do a full medical check-up, but when he was told that they could not carry it out right in his château he had bought in the South of France, he had told the doctors to go and jump into the Atlantic Ocean.

I waited patiently for him to finish. My uncle was a hard man to interrupt.

'Anyway,' he concluded, 'I might still try and do the check-up during my next trip to America. You know, in America, there's nothing you can't get as far as you can afford it.'

'Uncle Boniface,' I dived in, 'I'm really sorry to trouble you but I came to ask if you can help us.'

At this point, I wobbled. Asking for money like this felt disgraceful. Even though we had had several relatives suckling from my parents' pockets when times were good, my father refused to allow us to go soliciting help when times became tough. Today was my very first attempt. I remembered my father lying in hospital and summoned the courage to continue.

'Uncle Boniface, my father has been in hospital longer than we expected, and the expenses are rising every day. Right now—'

'What about your father's 505?' he interrupted. 'Do you people still have it?'

I was thrown completely off balance. Did the 505 have anything to do with the issue at hand?

'No, they sold it almost four years ago,' I replied slowly.

'Ah, I remember that car. I used to dream that one day I'll have my own 505 just like that and hire a white man to be my personal driver.'

He laughed a brief, staccato laugh.

It occurred to me that this change of topic was merely the show of light-heartedness that rich people tend to exhibit when presented with a problem they know money can easily solve. I decided to go with the flow.

'And the car was still very strong right until they sold it,' I added with false passion.

'You think that car was strong?' He laughed. 'Honestly, that shows you don't know anything about cars. Have you seen my brand new Dodge Viper?'

Of course I had never seen his brand new Dodge Viper. Still, he silently looked upon me as if expecting an answer.

'No, I haven't.'

He laughed. The same brief, staccato laugh.

'If you see that car . . . turn the key in the ignition, then you'll know what a car really is.'

Then he told me much, much more about his cars. About the ones he used only twice a year and the ones he used once a week. He told me about his frequent trips abroad and how he planned to buy a private jet; about how he was going to take flying lessons so that he could fly his private jet by himself. I sat there, looking and listening without being allowed to contribute a word. Ladies and gentlemen, I present to you a man who loved the sound of his own voice.

I stifled a yawn.

The intercom on his desk bleeped. He stopped talking and leaned forward to push a button.

'Speak to me!'

'Cash Daddy, World Bank is here.'

The lady's announcement was punctuated by the bursting open of the office door. Cash Daddy sprang up like a jack-in-the-box.

'Heeeeeeeeeeee!' he shouted.

'Cash Daddy!' the man who stormed in yelled. 'It's just a matter of cash!'

'Bank! Bank!' Cash Daddy hailed back. 'World Bank International!'

This was obviously one of Cash Daddy's friends who also suffered from elephantiasis of the pocket. He was wearing a cream suit, a diamond-studded wristwatch, several sparkly chains around his neck, and yellow alligator-skin shoes with white, blue, pink, green, and purple strips across the front. He was holding a gold-plated walking stick and had a unique variety of bowler hat sitting on his head. Both men slapped hands, hugged shoulders, exchanged pleasantries, hailed each other's nicknames several times. Finally, World Bank perched himself on the edge of Cash Daddy's desk, with one of his colourful shoes on the seat beside me and the other dangling close to my shin. The navy-blue-suited young man who had accompanied him stood a respectful few paces behind.

'This is my brother,' Cash Daddy said, gesturing towards me.

'Good afternoon, sir,' I said.

'Really! No wonder. He looks like you.'

'Me?' Cash Daddy replied with horror. 'God forbid. How can you say he looks like me? Can't you see how his neck is hanging like a vulture's neck?'

Both men laughed.

'He's a fine young man, he's a fine young man,' World Bank said, 'just that he's too thin.'

'He's a university graduate,' Cash Daddy replied.

'Ah!'

They laughed again. Perhaps it was natural to find all sorts of silly things funny when you had a pocketful of cash.

'I've been meaning to stop by for a long time,' World Bank said, 'but somehow, things kept happening to prevent me. My wedding is on the twenty-third of August. I decided to do everything on the same day.'

'You're a wicked man!' Cash Daddy shouted. 'A very, very wicked man! You have money, yet you don't want to spend it. Why are you running away from throwing three different parties for us? How much is it? Instead, tell me what it will cost, let me pay for everything.'

World Bank guffawed and almost toppled into my lap.

'Cash Daddy, you know money is not my problem,' he said, steadying himself with his walking stick. 'I'm just trying to be wise. I've learnt from my experience with my current wives. I don't want to repeat my mistakes.'

He explained that his first wife always wanted to attend major functions as his companion since she saw herself as the senior wife. She also insisted on being the one to sleep with him in the master bedroom on some nights, when he preferred to have only the second wife in bed with him.

'I don't want any of these ones to come into my house and start giving me trouble about who is the senior wife and who is the junior wife,' World Bank said. 'If I marry three of them on the same day, they'll know from Day One that they are all equals.'

'That's very smart,' Cash Daddy said. 'That's really very smart.'

World Bank looked hurt.

'But Cash Daddy, how can you talk like this? You know I'm a very smart man.'

'Of course, of course.'

They laughed. I wondered how the names of the three brides, the names of their three sets of parents, the names of their three villages . . . would all fit into the traditional wedding ceremony invitation card. World Bank's cellular phone rang. He looked at the screen and hissed.

'These people won't let me rest. One of the girls I'm marrying, the other day, her mother told me she wants a camcorder. Almost every day, she calls to ask when I'm bringing it. I didn't run away when she told me they wanted to renovate their house, I didn't run away when she told me she wanted to open a nursery school. Why should I start running away simply because of an ordinary camcorder?'

'Just be a man and bear it,' Cash Daddy said to console him. 'You know that relatives are the cause of hip disease.'

'Ah. Cash Daddy, you need to see this girl. She's just sixteen, but if you see her buttocks . . . rolling! Just give her another two to three years, that body will become something out of this world.'

I coughed. Honestly, a stray particle had found its way down the wrong passage. Cash Daddy misinterpreted.

'Ah, Kings! That's true. You're going back to Umuahia today.'

'No, no—'

'Protocol Officer!'

I was jolted. The man reappeared through the door.

'Yes, Cash Daddy.'

'Give this man some money.'

He told him how much. My eyes gasped.

'Cash Daddy, what currency?' Protocol Officer asked.

My uncle's phone rang.

'Give him naira,' he said, with eyes on the screen.

'Thank you, Cash Daddy,' I said. The outrageous nickname had slipped out of my mouth very smoothly.

'Greet your mummy for me,' he said and cleared his throat. 'Hello!' he said to the person at the other end of the phone. 'Mr Rumsfeld! I was just about to ring you now!'

In the outer office, I waited by the fax machine near Cash Daddy's closed door while Protocol Officer whisked out a key from his socks and unlocked a metal cabinet. He withdrew some bundles and started counting. I tried hard not to watch. For solace, my eyes turned to the sheet of paper on the fax machine tray.

Professor Ignatius Soyinka
Astronautics Project Manager
National Space Research and Development Agency
(NASRDA)
Plot 555 Michael Opara Street
Abuja, Nigeria

Dear Sir/Madam,

Urgent Request For Assistance – Strictly Confidential

I am Professor Ignatius Soyinka, a colleague of Nigerian astronaut, Air Vice Marshall Nnamdi Ojukwu. AVM Ojukwu was the first ever African to go into space. Based on his excellent performance, he was also later selected to be on Soviet spaceflight – Soyuz T-16Z – to the secret Soviet military space station Salyut 8T in 1989. Unfortunately, the mission was aborted when the Soviet Union was dissolved.

While his fellow Soviet crew members returned to earth on the Soyuz T-16Z, being a black man from a Third World country, AVM Ojukwu's place on the flight was taken up by cargo, which the Soviet Union authorities insisted was too valuable to be left behind. Hence, my dear colleague has been stranded up there till today. He is in good spirits, but really misses his wife and children back home in Nigeria.

In the years since he has been at the station, AVM Ojukwu has accumulated flight pay and interest amounting to almost $35,000,000 (USD). This is being held in trust at the Lagos National Savings and Trust Association. If we can obtain access to this money—

Protocol Officer was relocking the cabinet. He inserted some cash into a brown envelope and handed it to me.

'Thank you very much,' I said, and stuffed the booty into my trouser pocket.

'Thank God,' he replied.

Truly, it is natural to find all sorts of silly things funny when you have a pocketful of cash. All through the journey home, I studied my new shoes and giggled endlessly about the Nigerian astronaut stranded in outer space.

When I showed my mother the envelope's contents, she raised her two hands up to heaven and sang, 'Great Is Thy Faithfulness O Lord.'

Thirteen

The Lord's faithfulness showed up again. Godfrey returned from the post office one morning and started screaming from the kitchen.

'I passed! I passed! I passed!'

All of us rushed out. He had just received his admission letter to study Electrical Engineering at the University of Nigeria, Nsukka.

I became worried.

It was good that Godfrey had written the JAMB and passed, it was good that he had scored enough for admission into one of the best universities in the country. On the other hand, it was not good that a fresh expense had been introduced into our lives when we were still doing battle with the current ones.

I forced myself to see the cup half-full rather than half-empty.

'Congratulations,' I said, grabbing his arm and pumping it up and down.

'Thank you,' he said and grinned.

Charity and Eugene joined in his jubilations. While he waved the admission letter high above his head like the captain of the Brazilian football team at the World Cup finals, they clapped their hands and stamped their feet and skipped about the living room.

I felt sorry for all of them.

Godfrey accompanied me to the hospital that day.

'Why don't you tell your daddy?' my mother suggested. 'I'm sure he'll be very pleased to hear the good news.'

Godfrey rolled his eyes.

'I'm serious,' she said. 'It doesn't matter whether he's awake or not. It would be nice if you told him.'

Surprisingly, Godfrey agreed. Today was probably his day off from rebellion. I could understand my mother's eagerness for her husband to share in the good news. Like all of us, Godfrey was intelligent, but he constantly seemed to have his focus broken by the lesser cares of life such as girls and parties and rap music.

'Come and sit on the bed,' my mother said, indicating a small space at the edge of her husband's mattress.

Godfrey sat. My mother took his right hand and placed it in my father's right palm, careful not to disturb the wires and tubes. Then she returned to her chair and watched.

'Go on,' she said.

'Daddy,' Godfrey began awkwardly. He looked at me helplessly and back at our father in bed. 'I just want to tell you that I've got my admission letter into Nsukka.'

He looked at my mother. She jerked her head and twisted her eyes in encouragement. Godfrey twisted his eyes and jerked his head questioningly.

'Tell him that they gave you your first choice,' she whispered.

'Daddy, they gave me my first choice. They gave me Electrical Engineering.'

Godfrey looked at my mother again. I chuckled quietly. My mother threw me a frown. My chuckling diminished to a loud smile. Godfrey's grace expired.

'Mummy, I need to go,' he said, and stood. 'I want to go and barber my hair before it gets late.'

After he left, I turned to my mother.

'How come you suddenly think he can hear what we say? Does it mean he's been hearing everything we've been saying all this while?'

'I know it might not make sense to you,' she replied with cool confidence, like someone who knew what others did not. 'But I just felt that something like this should not be left to wait.' She paused. 'Sometimes, when I have something very important to tell him, I do it when we're alone in the middle of the night, when everywhere is quiet.'

'Maybe I should try talking to him as well,' I said.

My mother looked searchingly at me. She was not sure whether I was teasing or not.

I sat beside my father on the space that Godfrey had just vacated. I lifted his hand and rubbed the emaciated fingers tenderly. He had lost several layers of tissue, lying there these past weeks. I gazed into his face.

'Daddy, don't worry,' I said, almost whispering. 'We'll manage somehow, OK?'

I massaged the hand some more and entwined my fingers in between my father's own. My mother smiled softly and made a sign. She was going outside, probably to give me some privacy.

'Don't worry about Godfrey's school fees,' I said after she left. 'I know the money will come somehow. I know I'm going to start work very soon. It shouldn't be difficult once I move to Port Harcourt.'

My father continued inhaling and exhaling noisily without stirring. Two days ago, my mother claimed that she had seen him move his right leg sometime during the night, but nobody else had witnessed any other movement.

'Daddy, please hurry up and—'

A nurse walked in.

'I saw your mother leaving,' she said.

'She's just gone out briefly. Is there anything?'

'The doctor wants to see you in his office.'

'Why?'

'It's best if you speak with the doctor directly.'

I hurried out.

When I entered the consulting room and saw the well-dressed, middle-aged physician, my heart started pounding like a locomotive. This particular doctor only made cameo appearances on the ward. Doctors like him had little time to spare on Government Hospital patients who were not paying even a fraction of the fees that the patients in their private practices were. Usually, it was the lesser, hungry-looking, shabbily dressed doctors who attended to us.

'I'm sorry I don't have very exciting news for you,' he began as soon as my behind touched the seat in front of his desk. 'Your father has been here for a while now and we're starting to have some challenges with keeping him here.'

'Doctor, we pay our money and buy all the things you—' I began.

'Oh, certainly, certainly,' he reassured me, nodding his head rapidly. 'I'm glad to say that we haven't had that kind of problem with you people at all.'

'So what's the problem?'

He proceeded to enlighten me. It was a long, sad tale of under-staffing, low government funding, and insufficient facilities. By the time he finished, I felt guilty about us dragging our minor troubles all the way here to compound the hospital management's own.

'I'm sorry, but we can no longer manage your father's care,' he concluded. 'I would suggest we transfer him to the Abia State Teaching Hospital, Aba. That's the only way I can assure you that your father will get the best care he needs at this time. They have better equipment than we do.'

Instinctively, I perceived that this transfer entailed much more than moving my father from one bed to the other.

'How much is it going to cost?' I asked.

'Well, there's quite an expense involved,' he sighed. 'Fuelling the ambulance to transport him to Aba, hiring the specialised person-nel to accompany him on the trip, renting whatever equipment they might require on the journey . . . To cut a long story short, the transfer would cost lot of money.'

He gave me a tentative estimate. The amount nearly shattered my eardrums. I made it clear to the doctor that we could not afford it. He sympathised profusely. Then he assured me that there was no remote possibility of receiving any one of those services on credit.

'I'll give you some time to think about it,' he said. 'Then let me know what you want us to do. I've given you my professional opinion, but at the end of the day, he is your father. It's your call.'

I sat in front of him for a while, staring at the opposite wall without seeing anything, silently marvelling at the gravity of life in general. Then I thanked him for this update and for his sensitivity in choosing to break the bad news to me – first – without my mother present.

Fourteen

This time around, I paid meticulous attention to my appearance. I slipped my feet into my new pair of Russell & Bromley shoes and rummaged through my shirts. Most of them were dead, had been for a very long time. They only came alive when Ola wore them. She used to look so good in my clothes. Back in school, Ola would take my dirty clothes away on Friday evenings and return them washed and ironed on Sunday evenings. One day, while putting away the freshly laundered clothes, I noticed that a shirt was missing. Assuming that Ola had mistakenly packed it up with her own clothes, I made a mental note to ask her to check. Next day at the faculty, she was wearing the missing item. Seeing my shirt on her gave me such a thrill. Since then, she borrowed my shirts from time to time. In fact, she still had one or two with her.

Finally, I made my choice. It would have to be the shirt I wore for my university graduation ceremony. The blue fabric had been personally selected by my mother. She had sewn the shirt herself.

There were nine men and five women waiting at the office gates. Cash Daddy's security man recognised me from my previous visit.

'Cash Daddy has not reached office this morning,' he said.

He advised me to go and seek him at home.

'Please, where is his house?' I asked.

'There's nobody who doesn't know Cash Daddy's house,' he replied with scorn.

'Please, what's the address?'

He snorted with more scorn. He did not know the house number, but he knew the name of the street.

'Once you enter Iweka Street, you will just see the house. You can't miss it.'

I looked doubtful.

'You can't miss it,' he repeated.

I flagged down an *okada* and took off.

Indeed, I knew it as soon as I saw it.

Two gigantic lion sculptures kept guard by the solid, iron entrance. The gate had strips of electric barbed wire rolled all around the top, which extended throughout the length of the equally high walls. Altitude of gate and walls notwithstanding, the mammoth mansion was visible, complete with three satellite dishes on top.

I pressed the buzzer on the wall. The gateman peeped through a spy-slide in the gate. Before he had a chance to question me, a voice boomed from an invisible mechanical device.

'Allow that man to come inside my house! Right now!'

I was jolted. The gateman was unperturbed. He unlocked the gates and showed me inside.

The vast living room was a combination of parlour and dining section. There was a winding staircase that escalated from behind the dining table to unknown upper regions of the house. Everything – from the leather sofas, to the humongous television set, to the lush, white rug, to the vases on the bronze mantelpiece, to the ivory centre table, to the electric fireplace, to the high crystal chandeliers, to the dining set – was a tribute to too much wealth. I almost bowed my hands and knees in reverence.

A well-fed man standing by the door asked me to sit. Then he opened a huge refrigerator. Like the one in the office, this one was stacked with all manner of drinks.

'What would you like to drink?' he asked.

'Nothing. I'm fine, thank you.'

There were two framed photographs of Cash Daddy hanging on the wall above the television screen. One was taken, apparently, while he was playing golf. In the other, he was sitting on a magnificent black horse. How on earth had my uncle managed to manoeuvre his super-size onto the narrow saddle?

There were five young, equally well fed men sitting around the dining table. They ate silently, but eagerly, making sloppy, kissing sounds as they licked their fingers.

Shortly after I sat down, Protocol Officer – the very same one of the other day – descended the stairs.

'Cash Daddy is ready to see you,' he said, and waited.

I stood up quickly and joined him at the foot of the staircase.

'Good morning,' I said to the feeding men as I walked past.

The tantalising aroma of *edikainkong* and *onugbu* soups whispered to me from the huge tureens before them. The men grunted nonchalantly.

Protocol Officer led the way. At the third-floor landing, he opened one of the doors and entered a large bedroom. He continued to where two men were standing beside another open door within the room. The men shifted to create space for me in the narrow doorway.

Inside, Cash Daddy was crouched on the toilet seat. Apart from the boxer shorts rolled around his ankles, he was as naked as a skinned banana. Imagining that I had barged in on a most private moment, I muttered an apology and was turning to leave, when his voice flashed like lightning and stopped me in my tracks.

'Kings, Kings! How are you? How is your daddy doing?'

I ducked my eyes and replied that my father was still in hospital.

'What of your mummy?' he continued. 'I hope you told her that I greeted her.'

'Yes, I told her. She said I should thank you very much for your gift.'

He ignored me and spoke to the other men, apparently continuing with a discussion that had begun before I arrived.

'Don't forget that we're supposed to see Police Commissioner by Monday. Make sure you don't forget. When one sees a dog playing with somebody it's familiar with, it looks as if the dog can't bite. I don't want the type of situation we had the last time to happen again.'

I tried taking advantage of this diversion to make my escape – and bumped into Protocol Officer, who was firmly entrenched in the getaway route behind me. I gave up and stood still. Cash Daddy was still speaking.

'That seven hundred and fifty-five thousand dollars has to be ready before weekend. There are some things I can afford to play with but not things like this. Have you made arrangements with—'

Cash Daddy broke off his speech. He contracted his facial

muscles and made a low, grunting noise. He relaxed his face again and took in a deep breath. I heard the dull thud of solid hitting the surface of water. This process was repeated three more times before he was finally satisfied. Then he stood up, yanked some tissue from the roll strapped to the wall, bent slightly forwards, and wiped. Cash Daddy tossed the used tissue into the toilet bowl and flushed. Before continuing with what he was saying. Starting from exactly where he had stopped.

'. . . with Sonny and Ikem about the government official we'll need for the Japan transaction?'

The man on my right confirmed that the arrangements had been made. From the corners of my eyes, I looked at each man standing beside me. None of them appeared to be the least bit discomfited.

The stench had started disorganising my brain cells, when Cash Daddy pulled up his shorts and made his way towards the door. Honestly, it is such a pity that some people just never learn. The number of times my dear mother had berated Uncle Boniface in the past for using the toilet without washing his hands. We parted to let him through and followed into the bedroom.

The bedroom had the exact same personality as the living room. A wide canopy bed, plush sofas, humongous television, huge refrigerator, crystal chandeliers, exotic vases, elegant photographs of him taken in different poses and at different grand events. A closed-circuit television screen that showed coverage of several different parts of the house, in different segments of the large screen, stood directly opposite the bed. Cash Daddy planted himself on the thick mattress, lifted a handset from the bedside stool, pressed a button, and yelled into the mouthpiece.

'Bring my food! Right now!'

A fat man on one of the CCTV screen segments went into action in what looked like the kitchen. Another one of the screens clearly showed the front gate and everybody coming in or walking past. Aha! Via his CCTV, Cash Daddy must have sighted me coming into the house and then yelled his instruction to the gateman, using this same handset.

Cash Daddy stretched out his chunky legs and slapped a harmonious tempo on his belly with his hands.

'I'm so hungry,' he announced. 'Kings, sit down.'

I sat in the chair directly in front of him, while the other men remained standing by the bed in silence. Suddenly, he stopped the music he was making with his belly and looked as if seeing me for the first time. He frowned.

'Kingsley.'

'Yes, Uncle?'

'What is this you're wearing?'

I scanned myself in utmost terror. What could it be this time?

'Kingsley, am I not talking to you? What is this thing you're wearing?'

My brain was as blank as an empty bottle.

'Kingsley.'

'Yes, Uncle?' I whispered.

'Are you sure it's not a carpenter that constructed your shirt? You'd better be careful.' He raised his index finger and wagged it at me. 'Be very, very careful. One day you'll be walking down the street and the police will just arrest you because of the way you dress. It's only the fly that doesn't have advisers that ends up in the coffin with the corpse. Don't say I didn't warn you.'

The fat man arrived with a tray of food which he placed on one of the side stools. He readjusted the stool to suit Cash Daddy's position on the bed.

'Do you want to eat anything?' Cash Daddy asked. He did not wait for me to answer. 'Cook, bring this man some rice, chicken, goat meat, beef . . . Just bring him everything you have in the stew.' He turned to me. 'I want you to eat well. You're too skinny.'

I did not bother telling him that there was nothing he could do for me in that area; I was destined for perpetual skinniness.

Cash Daddy plunged into his meal.

'Go,' he said to the waiting men.

His rice bowl, as large as a bathroom washbasin, was filled to the brim. The rice was served with a bowl of tomato stew, a separate bowl of assorted meat, and a one-litre packet of Just Juice. He held his spoon like a shovel and clanged his teeth against the steel each time he shoved food into his mouth. While he chewed, I could look right into his mouth and watch the entire process of the solid rice granules being crushed. With his free hand, he pushed the pieces of meat to the very back of his mouth and tore them apart with his molars. Then he spat the unconquerable bones straight into the tray with such noise and force that no doubt was left that his upbringing had definitely been lacking.

'How is your daddy?' he asked, after a particularly loud belch.

In a few sentences, I told him everything the doctor had said and the reason for my visit.

As I was speaking, my uncle continued giving full concentration to his feeding without looking at me. At some points, I wondered if he was even listening at all.

It turned out that he was, because when I finished, he started relating his comprehensive thoughts about how he was sure the nurses intentionally kept a patient in a coma for longer than necessary so that it would look like they were busy earning their wages. While he was talking rubbish, my eyes strayed to the array of shoes somewhere on the other side of the room. I was mesmerised for just five seconds. Still, he caught me.

'What are you looking at?' he asked.

I panicked. Had he realised that I was not really listening to him? How was I going to escape from this latest trouble?

'Are you looking at my shoes?'

I felt as awkward as a cow on ice. I did not reply.

'You haven't even seen anything.' He laughed. 'If you go into the next room, every single thing there is just shoes. And not one pair of them costs anything less than a thousand dollars.'

I kept looking at him.

'Go on. Go out and look. I know you're hungry, but after looking, you can come back and finish your rice.'

I put down the tray with my half-eaten meal on it and left. My uncle was right. The entire space was covered from wall to wall with racks. Each rack harboured shoes of a different shade and different make. There were green shoes and yellow shoes, and red shoes and turquoise shoes. Every single member of the class *Reptilia* must have been represented in that collection. I finished looking and returned to the bedroom.

'Have you finished looking at my shoes?'

'Yes, I have.' Then as an afterthought, 'Thank you.'

He nodded heartily and began another marathon monologue about his footwear. From there, he extended to the topic of his wristwatches and then to his designer clothing.

When his three bowls had nothing left in them but stubborn bones and fingerprints, my uncle lifted the Just Juice packet and poured the liquid directly into his mouth, pausing from time to time to spread his mouth open and belch out a noise that sounded like a frog in heat. I half-expected him to gobble up the empty packet as well. Instead, he flung it onto the tray. Then he shouted for Protocol Officer, who came and doled out some money retrieved, this time, from inside the wardrobe. I received the naira notes thankfully and left.

The next day, my father was transferred to the Abia State Teaching Hospital, Aba. A week later, he awoke.

Fifteen

To think that one person's waking up from sleep could cause the sun to rise and the stars to shine in so many hearts. I was especially glad for my mother, whose constant night-and-day vigils had paid off. She had been right there when it happened.

Contrary to what soap operas have taught us to believe, a person who wakes up from a coma is first disoriented and confused. So my mother could not say exactly how long it was that my father's eyes had been open.

'It was around II a.m. or so that I raised my head from a brief nap and saw him staring at the ceiling,' she said.

Like people who dream without ever expecting their dreams to come true, at first she had dismissed what she saw as the wishful thinking of a desperate wife who had spent the past many nights sleeping on a raffia mat on the floor of her husband's hospital room.

'Next thing, his eyes just turned and started looking at me,' she continued.

Then he opened his mouth and said something in Igbo.

'*Ha abiala?*'

My mother became worried. The only times she heard her husband speak Igbo were when he was dealing with the villagers. He never spoke it to her, he never spoke it to us, he never spoke it in our house. Even the house helps from the village were banned from speaking vernacular. In due course, though, my mother realised that it did not matter what language he was speaking. The fact was, her man was awake and talking.

'I started jumping about and screaming for the nurses to come,' she laughed. 'Honestly, you should have seen me. You would have thought I'd gone mad.'

But she was afraid to touch him. When the nurses came in to investigate, she hovered around the bed and waited with her hands clasped against her chest. Finally, one of them noticed her reticence and assured her that her touch would not push him back into oblivion. My mother then sat beside him on the bed and stroked his hand until I arrived.

The rest of the day, my father stared as if seeing for the very first time. He stared at the ceiling, at the nurses, at me, and at his wife. Apart from one or two insignificant phrases in Igbo, he did not speak and did not acknowledge anyone when he was spoken to. His breathing was also not much different from when his eyes had been closed. The doctor confirmed that his left side was slightly paralysed and that he might not be able to regain his communication skills for some time. He also explained that it was common for patients just waking from a coma to speak languages that had been relegated to the archives of their minds.

'The most important thing,' the doctor said, 'is that there has been some major progress.'

Each day brought some new improvement. The catheter was removed. He could walk to the bathroom while he leaned on my mother's shoulders, taking one slow step after the other. He was able to eat some solid foods which my mother fed to him with a small plastic spoon as if he were a baby. She never complained. Not even when he spat unwanted food onto her clothes.

Time and time again, my mother said that she owed everything she was in life to my father. Prior to his arrival, tradition had placed her as one of the least important members of her family. But when this most eligible bachelor asked for her hand in marriage, her ranking increased overnight. Her elder brothers even sought her opinion regarding arrangements for their father's burial. Her union with my father, despite having suffered its own unique variety of roughness, had created a warm, secure environment for her because one thing had remained constant: her husband loved her and she enjoyed loving him in return.

I made quick arrangements for Godfrey, Eugene, and Charity to visit the hospital to welcome their father back to our world. One by one, they walked up to his bed and held his hand.

'Daddy, how are you?' Godfrey said.

'Daddy, we miss you,' Eugene said.

'Daddy, when are you coming home?' Charity said.

As soon as they touched on his daughter, a faint glow seemed to light in our father's eyes and the right side of his lips appeared to twist slightly upwards. That was when we knew for sure that he was aware of us being there.

Owing to the distance from Umuahia to Aba, my siblings could no longer pop into the hospital as casually and as regularly as before. Neither could my mother come home as often for a change of clothing or to inspect her shop. She packed some personal items and became a permanent resident of the hospital. Depending on the kindness of the nurses on duty, she had her daily shower in one of the hospital bathrooms. Regarding family visits, we agreed on an arrangement where the less significant participants in the hospital drama would sort of take it in turns. That particular morning, it was Charity's turn and I took her along with me to Aba.

My mother was dozing off on the bedside chair when we arrived. With an excited yelp and a fervent shoulder shake, Charity woke her up. They hugged and kissed and cuddled as if they had not seen each other in months. I observed my mother's eyes casting their spotlight on Charity's armpit. The hair had overgrown again. My mother removed her eyes and let the matter pass.

Charity sat beside my father on the bed, holding his hand tenderly, as if she were afraid that it might fall on the bed and crack.

'Daddy,' she said, 'we've started reading *Macbeth* in school and we had a test last week. I made the highest score because I was the only one in class who knew the main significance of Lady Macbeth's sleepwalking scene.'

She paused and smiled. The blank expression on my father's face did not change.

'We've also started Organic Chemistry,' Charity went on, 'but I'm not really enjoying it. No matter how hard I try, I can't seem to tell which one is a straight chain and which one is a compound chain.'

My sister looked distraught. I was tempted to tell her that I would teach her how to work it out later, but decided that now was not the time. Charity continued chatting – about school, about her test scores, about a documentary on the Nigerian/Biafran civil war which she had watched on television – without bothering that he was not responding. Watching her evoked memories of when I was a child, when my days were never complete until my father had carried me in his lap and told me a folktale.

While Charity was still talking, my mother got up. She gestured discreetly with her eyes, like a crook, indicating for me to follow. I allowed some seconds to pass before leaving.

My mother had stopped somewhere just outside the ward. I walked over and stood beside her.

'Mummy, is something wrong?'

'No *o*, nothing is wrong. Just that Boniface was at the hospital this morning.'

'Really?'

'Hmm. I was equally surprised.'

She said that she had been cleaning my father's teeth when the nurse on duty informed her that a visitor was waiting in reception. Without checking the clock, she knew that visiting time did not begin until about five hours later. Apart from my siblings and me, any other visitor who ventured near the ward before visiting time received a bark and a bite from the nurses. This time, the nurses did not seem to mind.

'When I came outside, I saw a group of nurses whispering with excitement.'

They kept quiet when they saw her. The nurse who had come to inform her pointed with a significant smile. Uncle Boniface was standing there in the corridor with five men in dark suits and dark glasses.

'He apologised for not coming earlier,' she said and smiled.

So many different things had been taking up his time, but he had determined that he must come today. In fact, he was supposed to travel out of the country this morning, but had postponed his foreign business meeting to visit my father instead.

'I was quite touched,' she concluded.

'I hope Daddy didn't get upset about him coming,' I said.

'I don't think so. At first, I wasn't sure how your daddy would react to seeing him, but I felt it would be wrong to leave him standing in the reception. He didn't stay for too long before he left. But while he was there, your daddy didn't really show any emotions.'

'On second thoughts,' I said, 'maybe it would have been better if he had been upset. That might have been what he needs to finally force him to say something intelligible.'

To my relief, my mother laughed at my morbid joke. These days, her face looked less tired. I had not heard her laugh so heartily in a very long time.

'The nurses have been treating me differently since Boniface came,' she continued. 'He seems to be quite popular here in Aba. They kept telling me that they had no idea he was my brother. Some were asking if he's my real brother or just a relative. When he was leaving, he even dashed them some dollars for lunch and told them to make sure they took care of his brother-in-law.' She smiled like a happy child. 'He wanted to lodge me in his hotel so that I can go there and be spending the night instead of staying here, but I refused.'

I could understand my father's point of view, but, in truth, I was beginning to appreciate my uncle more and more. He had been so kind, so generous, so helpful. Right now, it did not matter where he got the money from. How would we have made it this far without him?

'You should have agreed to go to the hotel,' I said to my mother.

'No, no, no. I'm fine. I want to be here whenever your daddy needs me.'

If only I had been there when Uncle Boniface made the offer, I would not have minded taking it up for myself. Truth be told, this daily travelling to and from Umuahia was quite debilitating.

'Anyway,' my mother continued. 'He asked me to tell you to come and see him before you go back to Umuahia today.'

'What does he want to see me about?'

'He didn't say. He just said I should tell you to stop at his house before you go.'

'Maybe he wants to give me some more money.'

'I thought so too,' she agreed quickly. 'He's really been very kind to us during this difficult period. I only wish his money were not so filthy.'

'His money might be filthy, but at least it's being used for a good cause.'

My mother paused and thought.

'Well, I suppose you're right,' she agreed eventually.

'What about Charity? If I'd known I'd be going to see Uncle Boniface from here, I wouldn't have come with her today.'

My mother considered.

'It doesn't matter. You can take her along. I don't think there's anything wrong with that. After all, we'll eventually have to tell your daddy where we got most of the money for his treatment from and he would probably want to thank Boniface personally.'

That would be the marvel of all marvels. The word 'probably' was the most active part of that sentence.

Sixteen

'Open my gate now!' Cash Daddy bellowed.

Charity jolted like a firecracker. By now, I was unperturbed by these outbursts, but as we walked into the mammoth mansion, I worried about my sister's tender sensibilities. Cash Daddy's environment was not really the place for a lady.

We sat in the living room, and the well-fed sentry of the other day opened the refrigerator. I declined his offer while Charity threw her mouth open in amazement. Expecting to hear a response from her, the man left the cooling machine open.

'No, thank you,' I responded on her behalf. I knew Cash Daddy was likely to offer us food when we went upstairs.

The man had just slammed the refrigerator door shut when Protocol Officer came downstairs.

'Kingsley, Cash Daddy is ready to see you,' he said.

I held Charity's hand and stood.

Upstairs, Cash Daddy was lying spread-eagled on the bed. Two striking ladies with dazzling light skin and ample mammary glands were with him. One was sitting at his feet with her eyes glued to the vast MTV screen, the other was pressing a pimple on his face with her fingers. Thankfully, all three of them were fully clothed. The girls were in short dresses. Their knees and knuckles were black where the bleaching cream had refused to work. Cash Daddy was wearing a white linen suit and a pair of oxblood shoes that looked as if they had been crafted in the Garden of Eden.

Cash Daddy saw Charity and sat up straight. He pushed the pimple-presser away. A smile struggled through the mass of fat on his face and finally shone through.

'Ah! Is this not Charity?' He beamed. 'I didn't recognise her at first. Look at this little girl of yesterday. You've already started growing breasts.'

Charity blushed. He reached out a chunky arm and swept her close to his chest. Suddenly, the smile seeped back into his face.

'Be careful,' he said seriously, wagging a chubby finger at her. 'Be very, very careful. Very soon, all these stupid boys will start chasing you up and down. Make sure you don't allow them to deceive you. That's all they know how to do – to deceive small, small girls. Do you hear me?'

She turned her eyes to the floor and nodded coyly. Actually, I had never had cause to worry about my sister going astray. Charity had a good head on her shoulders.

Cash Daddy asked us to sit. He lifted the headset by his bed and shouted for his cook. I asked the man for pounded yam and *egusi* soup. Charity asked for fried rice and goat meat. The food arrived just as Cash Daddy's cellular phone rang. He lifted the gadget and shouted into the mouthpiece.

'Speak to me!'

After several minutes, he concluded his deafening conversation with someone called Long John Dollars. Then he dialled another number. The second phone call, about some money in his Barclays Bank Docklands account, kept him occupied until we finished our meals. Then he leaned over and opened the refrigerator by his bed. He pulled out a packet of McVitie's milk chocolate biscuits and a tub of Ben & Jerry's vanilla ice cream. He dumped the items casually on the stool in front of Charity.

'Stay here and demolish these goodies,' he commanded her.

My sister's face lit up. When we were children, my father usually returned from work with these sorts of imported treats. Gradually, they had gone out of reach of the common man. I could not remember the last time I had eaten any McVities biscuits.

'We're going upstairs but we're coming back now,' Cash Daddy continued.

He headed out of the room.

'Kingsley, follow me,' he said without looking back.

I obeyed.

We went on to the fourth floor. He removed a key from his trouser pocket and opened a door. He stood aside to let me pass, then locked it behind us. It was the first time I had seen him open a door – or perform any other minor task, for that matter – without assistance from his numerous attendants. It was a weird sight, like seeing a United States president, say Bill Clinton, leaning over the bathroom sink and washing his socks.

This room was similar to his office. It had a mahogany desk with a budget of papers on top, and a worktop lined with fax machines, computers, and telephones. I spied a Nigerian National Petroleum Corporation letterheaded sheet amongst the pile on the table. There were several other letterheaded sheets that I could not make out.

I sat in front of the desk. Cash Daddy dragged a chair beside mine and sat with his knees massaging my own knees. He looked serious, like a doctor about to inform me that I was in the last stages of colon cancer.

'I was at the hospital to see your daddy,' he began. 'I'm happy that he's getting better.'

'Thank you very much, Uncle,' I replied. 'We're really happy, too. And we're also very grateful for all your financial support. Thank you very much.'

He scrunched up his face as if I had just looked him up and down and called him a blob of fat.

'Kings, what do you mean by thanking me? What do you mean by that? There's no need for you to thank me for anything. When the eye weeps, the nose also weeps. After all, you're my brother. We're family. Is that not so?'

There was a pause.

'Is that not so?'

I nodded. There was a longer pause.

'Kings,' he said at last, 'you must be wondering why I asked you to come and see me, is that not so?'

I nodded again. He nodded as well.

'You see all these boys here . . . all these boys around me?'

I did.

'They're all working for me.' He thumped his hand on his chest. 'I put food on their tables, I put clothes on their backs, and I make sure that they're well sexed. And guess what? None of them, not

124

one single one of them, is related to me in any way. Kings, I've been thinking about it and I've decided to help you.'

Wow. Perhaps he knew someone who was a top shot in the Petroleum Corporation. Perhaps the person was his very close friend. Perhaps the person had told him that he was looking for suitable employees and had asked him for a personal recommendation. Once again, 'long-leg' was about to work in my favour.

Cash Daddy leaned forward.

'You see, there are two main things people like me have used successfully in business. One is the love of money. The other is a good brain. I can see that you're the sort of person that will do very well in business. You, you're a smart young man. I don't know if you love money but I know . . . I can see . . . that you need it. I want you to come and work for me.'

He paused and stared as if expecting me to say something. I decided to tell the truth.

'Cash Daddy, please, what do you mean? I'm not sure I understand you.'

He threw back his head and laughed.

'Kings, I know you're a smart boy, I know you understand me. Tell me, what do you think about what I just said?'

'What sort of work do you want me to do?' I asked, rephrasing my thoughts.

'Oh . . . different things. At the beginning stage, some minor errands. There are one or two basic things you'll need to learn. No matter how big some of us look today, all of us started from somewhere. I don't know if you've heard about Money Magnet? He was my godfather in this business. I started by driving him around in his cars before I hit it and decided to launch out on my own.'

He leaned even closer and placed his hand on my shoulder.

'You see, I have other urgent things to focus on in the near future and I need a smart person who can watch over things for me. Kings, I need you. I'd like you to move into my house as soon as possible and start.'

At that moment, a giant fly could have flown into my mouth, laid her eggs on my tonsils, and I would still not have noticed. The way he was talking so casually, you would have thought that he was simply asking me to run down to the shops and buy a packet of Nasco biscuits.

'Uncle Boniface, are you actually asking me to join you in 419?'

He laughed.

'You're saying it as if I asked you to kill somebody.' He slapped my thigh playfully. 'Relax. One doesn't refuse the food being offered without first opening the pot. I've been in this business for many years now and I can tell you there are two things I will never do. I will never take another person's life and I will never follow another man's wife. Those two things . . . never. You can call it whatever name you want, all I'm saying is that you should come and work for me.'

At times like this, I wished I was well versed in the art of using swear words. I remembered my visit to the church – the sermon and the way The Rich Man had spoken to Lazarus. I became angrier. Did Uncle Boniface think that because he gave my family crumbs from his massive fortune, he could think of me in such an insulting manner?

'Uncle Boniface, I'm sorry,' I replied, bolder than any man had the right to be in the presence of his benefactor. 'I'm not cut out for this sort of business. I'm a graduate, and I intend to get a good job and later further my education. I've always wanted to study as far as PhD level and that's what I'm—'

I stopped talking when Cash Daddy upgraded his laughter to a guffaw.

'Kingsley,' he asked, struggling to regain his breath, 'what was it you said you studied in school?'

'I read Chemical Engineering.'

'Very, very good. That means you must know a lot of mathematics.'

I did not dignify him with an answer.

'Are you good with numbers?'

I continued saying nothing.

'Go on, tell me. Are you good with numbers?'

'Yes, I am,' I answered as a matter of fact. 'I'm very good with calculations.'

'Do you know how to write one million naira? Do you know how many noughts it has at the end?'

'It has six zeroes,' I rattled off without even thinking.

'Apart from when you were using a calculator in your classroom, have you ever written down one million naira in any single trans-action before? Have you ever calculated money you wanted to spend and it came to a total of one million naira?'

He did not wait for me to respond.

'So, after all this your education – the one you've done so far – what have you gained from it? With all the big, big calculations you did with your calculator in school, has it made you to calculate those same amounts of money in your own pocket? Or in your own bank account? Or in different currencies?'

He hissed. The sound was a fine blend of disdain and amuse-ment.

'You know something? Me, I don't have a problem with poverty as far as it's a choice somebody has made for himself. But look at you. Very soon you'll be standing by the street with a tin cup in your hand – begging. Mind you, no one gets a mouthful of food by picking in between another person's teeth. All your book . . . is that why you were wearing headmaster shoes the other day? Is that why your sister looks like somebody who hasn't eaten since Christ-mas Day? Is that why your mother is wearing the cloth that other women were wearing in the sixties?'

He hissed again.

'Just look at my sister. Today at the hospital, she was looking almost thirty years more than her age. Has all your book put food on your table? How many people are you feeding every month? How many people's salaries do you pay every month? Eh? Tell me.' He sneered. 'See your mouth. You say you don't eat rats but you just want to taste only the tail. Please don't close my ears with all this your rubbish talk about education. Me, I don't believe in film tricks. I believe in real, live action.'

The more he spoke, the more I found myself sitting straighter in the chair. He sounded almost as convincing as the multiplication table.

My father was learned and honest. Yet he could neither feed his family nor clothe his children. My mother was also learned, and her life had not been particularly improved much by education. I thought about my father's pals, most of whom were riding rickety cars . . . about most of my university lecturers with their boogie-woogie clothes and desperate attempts to fight off hunger by selling overpriced handouts to students. Yet Uncle Boniface – our saviour in this time of crisis – had not even completed his secondary school education. However, my father's hallowed words of time past rose up and sounded a piercing siren in my head.

'Uncle Boniface, you can make all the fun you want, but in the long run, even the Bible says that wisdom is better than silver and gold.'

This time, he guffawed so long that it seemed as if the fat on his face might melt and start dribbling onto the floor. He started choking and struggled to catch his breath.

'Ah, you think, me, I don't know Bible myself? Or haven't you heard the story of the poor wise man?'

I had no idea what he was talking about. Was this part of his infinite repertoire of Igbo proverbs, or was this a story from the Bible? Did he mean the story about The Rich Man and Lazarus? As far as I could remember, it never said anywhere that Lazarus was wise.

He saw the confusion on my face.

'Ah, ah? I thought you're the one who went to school. You're the one who knows everything, including Bible? OK, wait.'

Using my knees as leverage, he pushed himself up. He strode confidently to the bookshelf and pulled out a leather-bound Bible. He returned to his seat and dropped the holy book in my lap.

'Open Ecclesiastes,' he instructed.

I did.

'Turn to chapter nine.'

I did.

'Read from verse fourteen to sixteen.'

I obeyed.

'There—'

'No, no, no. You don't need to read it out. Read it to yourself.

Me, I already know it. It's you with all your book that needs to hear it.'

I closed my mouth and read with my eyes only.

There was a little city, and few men within it; and there came a great king against it, and besieged it, and built great bulwarks against it: Now there was found in it a poor wise man, and he by his wisdom delivered the city; yet no man remembered that same poor man. Then said I, Wisdom is better than strength: nevertheless the poor man's wisdom is despised, and his words are not heard.

Unimpressed, I finished at verse sixteen. Was it not Shakespeare who said that even the devil can cite scripture for his own purpose?

'People like you can go to school and finish your brains on book, but it's still people like us who have the money that feed your families.'

He laughed. His laughter was beginning to gnaw at my nerves.

'Uncle Boniface, please. My father would never approve.'

'Kings, we're talking about money,' he said with irritation. 'Let's leave poor men out of this conversation.'

With that, Uncle Boniface had exceeded the speed limit in his derogatory comments. He had no right to talk about my father in that manner.

'Uncle Boniface, my father might be poor,' I said with rising anger, 'but at least he will always be remembered for his honesty.'

'Is honesty an achievement? Personality is one thing, achievement is another thing altogether. So what has your father achieved? How much money is he leaving for you when he dies? Or is it his textbooks that you'll collect and pass on to your own children?'

I sat staring at this braggart in disbelief. My father once said that people who did not go to school were perpetually angry with those who did. This man was a barrel of bile. An authentic devil in disguise. I decided to leave before a thunderbolt would come and strike the building. I rose and tossed the Bible on the executive desk.

'Uncle Boniface, I'm sorry but if you've finished, I'm going.'

He laughed gently, like an apostle who was under persecution by people who understood very little about his life-transforming message.

'Take your time. Don't be like the grass cutter who likes eating palm nuts but doesn't like climbing palm trees. I might be a very rich man, but from time to time, I can also exercise patience.'

I stomped out of the room and slammed the door behind me. I rushed downstairs and into the bedroom where Charity was still chomping on the chocolate biscuits. She had polished off the ice cream.

'Let's go!' I ordered.

Charity opened her eyes like an astonished kitten. Then she must have seen the urgency in my face because she stood up hurriedly, still clutching the remaining biscuits. The other two girls did not remove their eyes from the MTV screen. I grabbed Charity's arm and fled.

Seventeen

At last, the doctor decided that my father could go home. He said that his condition was stable, that he would regain the use of his muscles and speech gradually, even though it might take as long as two years for him to fully recover. Since we could not afford additional physiotherapy, the hospital educated us on the sort of exercises he could do at home. They also advised us to get him a walking stick.

Two days before he was due back home, my mother called me aside in the hospital.

'Kings, I don't think you should bother coming tomorrow.'

I was surprised.

'Why?'

'I want you to stay home and make sure everything is ready.'

She proceeded on a long list of microscopic instructions, and the next day I ordered Odinkemmelu and Chikaodinaka on a cleaning spree. They went about sweeping and scrubbing, dusting and polishing. I gave Charity some money to go to the market. She stocked up on unripe plantains, vegetables, and some other low-carbohydrate foods. From our parents' bedroom to the living room, Eugene cleared the pathway of obstructing buckets and dusty storage cartons; my father would need as much space as possible to manoeuvre his faulty left limb. Godfrey changed the sheet on their bed and plumped the cushion on my father's chair. I adjusted the television tripod stand so that it would be easier for him to watch without straining his neck. Then I went to the carpenter whose shop was close to my mother's and collected the walking stick I had ordered a few days before.

That night, I found it hard to sleep. For the billionth time, I trembled for my life that no longer included Ola in the picture. I felt as if, like my father, I would have to start learning the basic skills of living all over again. But there was still hope. Ola's mother might allow her to take me back once I moved to Port Harcourt and got a job.

I dug my head under my pillow and forced my mind to be quiet. Tomorrow would be a busy day; I needed all the rest I could get.

When sleep finally came, I dreamt about my father.

I was standing directly in front of him while he was sitting on his hospital bed.

'Kingsley, do you want to be useful to yourself in this world?'

I answered in the affirmative.

'Do you want to make me and your mummy proud?'

Again, my answer was the same.

'Do you want people to know you and respect you wherever you go?'

Yes, I did.

'Do you want to end up selling pepper and tomatoes in Nkwoegwu market?'

At that point, I woke up sweating.

Sometime in the early hours of that morning, my father died.

When I walked into the hospital ward in the morning, that strange instinct that tells a young man that he no longer has a father took over. I knew what had happened without being told. Right from the reception area, the nurses stared at me in a strange way, as if I had strapped a bomb to my abdomen and mistakenly left my shirt unbuttoned. Then I heard my mother.

'*Hewu o!*' she screamed. 'You people should leave me, let me die!'

The sound of her voice seemed to be coming from her intestines instead of from her throat. She was engaged in physical combat with some of the nurses. Whenever she managed to break free from their hold, she flung herself to the floor or bashed her head against the cement wall. She was writhing and gnashing her teeth like someone burning in hell. I stood in silence for a while, watching this apparition. Then I walked past them and opened the door to my father's room. Two male nurses walked in with me and stood within arm's length.

Someone had covered him from head to toe with a white sheet

that had a huge circle of ancient brown dirt right in the middle. Interesting that they had sheets for the dead but none for the living. I shifted the cloth aside. I lifted his hand and squeezed his fingers in my palm. They felt cold and stiff. I placed my ear against his chest and listened. I checked for a pulse. Lastly, I lifted his eyelids and stared. My father stared back.

When I finally understood that I would never again hear the shuffling of my father's feet as he came to the dining table, I sat down heavily beside the bed. I gripped my head. The two nurses came closer and stood beside me like sentinels. Then, as with a person in the very last moments of death by drowning, several scenes from my life flashed before me. They came one after another, awakened from the dormitories of my mind like a parade of supernatural characters in a Shakespearean drama.

In the first scene, I was sitting on my father's lap, while my mother was lighting a kerosene lamp. NEPA had taken the light.

'Kings,' my father said suddenly, 'do you know how the tortoise broke his back?'

I had seen the tortoise several times on television. His shell was in patches, as if several pieces had been glued together to make the one. I shook my head. I did not know.

'Once upon a time,' he began, 'there was a famine in the land of the animals.'

The animals decided that they would each kill their mothers and share the meat. They started with Squirrel, and went on to Fox, then Elephant, Antelope, Tiger . . . Finally, it got to Tortoise's turn.

'But Tortoise was very tricky,' my father said.

He decided to hide his own mother. He made a very long rope, used it to climb up into the sky with her, then came back down and hid the rope. Afterwards, he started weeping and wailing. When the animals asked what the matter was, Tortoise told them that his mother had died.

My father mimicked each animal saying 'sorry' to Tortoise.

Every day, Tortoise would bring out the rope from where he had hidden it, and climb up to the sky to give his mother some food to eat. One day, Fox noticed that Tortoise was always going out with some food. He became suspicious and followed sneakily behind him. He watched Tortoise climbing up to the sky.

When Tortoise finished feeding his mother, on his way down, he saw the other animals gathered at the bottom of the rope, waiting for him. In panic, he started climbing back up. The animals noticed that he was trying to escape and started pulling the rope. They pulled so hard that the rope broke and Tortoise crashed to the ground.

'Tortoise landed on his back,' my father concluded. 'Till today, his shell is still cracked in several places.'

The scene faded. Another took its place.

I was having breakfast with my parents. My father went to check who was thumping our front door so loudly on a Saturday morning, like a landlord being owed a year's rent. Five of his sisters poured in, each of whom aspired to a higher standard of obesity than the previous one. As soon as they were seated and all the pleasantries over, the eldest sister began.

'Pauly, we're very unhappy with the way things are. How can we come into our eldest brother's house, and instead of the noise of children running about the place, everywhere is so quiet?'

My father did not respond. The second eldest sister took over.

'Like Ada was saying, we're very worried. You're not getting any younger. You don't have to wait until all your hairs have turned grey and all your teeth have fallen out before you decide to do something about the situation.'

She handed the baton back to Aunty Ada.

'Pauly, we understand that you're busy with your job at the Ministry. You might not have the time to sort things out for yourself, so we've decided to help. We've found two girls in the village that you can choose from. They are chubby and have very strong bodies. We want you to come down to the village with us and have a look at them so that you can decide which one to choose.'

My mother received the pronunciamento with silence. A woman who could not produce children deserved whatever treatment she received from her in-laws. So far, her only saving grace had been that my father was standing firmly by her. My father, on the other hand, reacted with ferocity. He slammed a fist on his knee, sprang up from his chair, and clenched his teeth till the two white rows almost merged into one thin, white line.

'I've heard what you people have to say,' he said. 'Now would you please get up and leave my house.'

He spoke in a low voice that still managed to startle everybody. But Aunty Ada recovered quickly. She jumped out of her chair, stationed her hands on her waist, and poked her face into his nose.

'Paulinus!' she barked. 'It's not today you started allowing this, your education, to confuse you. No matter what, every man needs children to carry his name. Every man! God forbid, but what if something was to happen to Kingsley? That means your name vanish forever. Is that what you want?'

My father roared like King Kong.

'Leave my house right now! All of you . . . get up and leave! Get up and leave! Now!'

Another scene.

I had accompanied my father to inspect the work-in-progress on our village house. The workmen were laying the foundation. Towards evening, he took me on a stroll down the dusty village path. It was the same route he had trekked daily to the mission primary school as a child – barefooted because, back then, children were not allowed to wear shoes.

'This tree is called Orji,' he said, pointing at a tall one with a mighty trunk. 'That's from where we get our kola nuts. This one is Ahaba. It makes the best firewood. This one is called Udara.' He smiled. 'Whenever it was *udara* season, I and my friends used to wake up much earlier than usual so that we could pick the ripe fruits that had fallen to the ground at night, on our way to school. We always had to wait for the fruits to fall by themselves because they are never sweet when you pluck them.'

Soon, it was time for us to go home. I was disappointed.

'Don't worry,' my father said. 'When our house is completed, we'll come and spend a whole week here so that I can show you the river and the farms and the forests.'

Several other images came and went.

My graduation day. My father was smiling and watching me

135

pose for a photograph. He raised his hand and asked the cameraman to wait. Then he walked up to me and adjusted the tassel on my cap.

'This is a picture you're going to show your children and your grandchildren,' he said. 'You have to make sure that everything looks perfect.'

How was I going to tell Godfrey and Eugene and Charity that their father would never be coming home, that he would never switch off the television abruptly and order them to study? Their father would never witness their matriculation ceremonies into university, tell them what courses to choose or what schools to fill into their forms? I wished I had died instead.

My mother let out another sharp scream. Then I remembered Ola, and that she was not there to hold me. I crumbled into tiny pieces.

Eighteen

Our house was brimming with condolers. Some I recognised, others I did not. Some came in the morning, some came in the evening. Some brought food items, some cooked what others had brought. We borrowed chairs from our neighbours to accommodate the rising numbers. Those who still did not have places to sit either squatted on the linoleum floor or stood behind the circle of variegated chairs. Each night, there were bodies snoring on the floors and limbs dangling over chairs in the living room.

Every morning, my mother dressed in her dark-coloured wrappers and sat in the living room to accept condolences. Her eyes were always wet and swollen. With each new person that came, she retold the story.

'I usually don't wake up at that time of morning,' she would begin, 'but for some reason, I woke up around four-thirty that day. Then, I noticed that I was feeling a bit cold.'

Her first thought was that her husband would probably feel the chill. She rose from her raffia mat and turned off the table fan. Then she returned to the floor and almost fell back into sleep, but something was nagging. The silence was unusual. At last, it dawned on her. Her husband's respiratory orchestra had stopped playing. There was no rattling, no laboured breathing. My mother sprang up from the floor and crawled towards his bed. She leaned on the edge and tore at the mosquito net.

'I started calling his name and shaking his shoulders.'

Those listening struggled to hold back their tears.

When he did not stir, she repeated his name and shook him again – more violently – hoping that he might even yelp. When he still refused to respond, she flicked on the light and saw the open mouth and half-shut eyes.

'I didn't even know when I started screaming.'

Those listening started crying and wailing.

After my mother narrated this story to my father's sisters, his brothers, her brothers, her sisters, our neighbours . . . Aunty Dimma instructed that it was enough.

'You can't use all your energy to keep telling that story,' she said. 'When another person asks you how it happened, just tell them that you can't talk now.'

Almost all the people who came proceeded on an undeclared competition to see who could wail longer and more bitterly than the other.

'*Hewu o!*' one woman chanted. '*Onwu, chei! Elee ihe anyi mere gi o?!*'

A man staggered into the living room and let out a fearsome yelp.

'Paulinus!' he called. 'Paulinus!' he called again.

The man shook his head and sat while a wrinkled man took his place and launched into the milestones of my father's lifetime.

'Do you remember the day he first came back from London? How his face lit up when he sighted us waiting for him on the dock?'

'Are you telling me?' resumed another male voice. 'How about the day he came to tell us that his wife had had their first son? Do you remember the big smile that was covering his face?'

'Where is the *opara*?' the elderly man asked.

They all turned and looked at me.

'*Hewu!*' the man cried. 'He looks exactly like his father. In fact, carbon copy.'

He was lying. I had my father's hairline and my father's eyebrows, but everything else belonged completely to my mother. Except nobody was sure where I got my small nose from.

'Paulinus was the most intelligent man in our class,' another man said. 'He used to take first position all the time.'

'Do you remember how he used to ask questions about everything as soon as the teacher finished teaching?'

'And he never stopped reading; he always had a book in his hands. Truly, I've never met a more intelligent man in my life.'

The eulogy continued. Ola walked in.

The sun broke through the clouds. For the first time in these series of grievous occurrences, I began to feel that God was truly in His heaven and that all was right with the world. She came over to me.

'Kings.'

I stood.

Two big tears fell from the corners of her eyes to the corners of her pretty lips. I reached out and held her hand. She squeezed it. Suddenly, grief tasted different, as if some saccharine had been stirred in to make it less bitter.

'Let me greet your mummy.'

She knelt on the floor in front of my mother and whispered into her ears. My mother nodded as she had been nodding to everyone else who had been whispering into her ears. From there, Ola went to Godfrey and Eugene and Charity, who were seated around the dining table with a flock of relatives surrounding them. Then she came over to where I was waiting by the kitchen door.

'How are you?' I asked.

'I'm fine. How are you, how are you doing?'

A surge of love overwhelmed my grief. I felt as if everything was almost all right now that she was here. Indeed, it must be true what someone said about love being the cure for everything. Everything except poverty and toothache.

'It's all been quite a shock,' I replied. 'I had no idea he was going to die.'

I retold my mother's story word for word. She cried in all the right places while I squeezed her hand.

'What of plans for the burial?' she asked.

I sighed.

It was vital for every Igbo man to be buried 'well'. The amount required to give my father the sort of send-off that would be deemed suitable for a man of his untitled status would total ten times more than what we had expended on bills for the duration of his hospital stay. Apart from the entertainment of guests for the wake-keeping and funeral, there was a certain amount of live-stock and liquor that tradition required us to present to each of the different age grades in our village. There were the expenses for the obituary, the mortuary, the embalmment, the grave, the coffin, and the welfare of guests that would come from far and near. To make matters worse, our house in the village was not yet complete. It was extremely embarrassing for our guests to see my father being buried in a compound with a building that was mere carcass.

'We're waiting to see how much our relatives can contribute,' I replied. 'But whatever the case, the burial has to be very soon because we don't want to spend too much on mortuary fees.'

'Won't there be—'

An elderly woman stepped in and broke into a glum song about how dead bones shall rise again. As she sang, she swayed from side to side and cried. Most of the other mourners joined in with the singing.

'Okpukpu ga-adi ndu ozo, okpukpu ga-adi ndu ozo, okpukpu ga-adi ndu ozo, okpukpu ga-adi ndu ozo . . .'

I wished they would all just shut up and allow us to mourn in peace. Besides, the competition was settled. No one would ever outdo my father's sisters in drama and intensity of mourning.

'I need to go,' Ola said.

'No, stay a little bit longer. I really need you now.'

'I really need to go. I can't stay too long.'

I followed her outside. We walked round to the front of the house. I dragged her into the vestibule that led up to the other three floors of our building. The place was quiet.

'Ola, you probably don't know how glad I am to see you. I've not stopped thinking about you for one single day.'

She threw her eyes to the floor. I touched her cheek with my hand and told her how much I loved her. I told her I understood the pressure she must be under from her mother. I told her that I was moving to Port Harcourt, that I was definitely getting a job soon even though it might not be with an oil company. I told her that she would certainly not regret her decision to wait a little bit longer for me. She may have been listening, she may not.

'Kings, it's too late,' she said when I finished.

'What do you mean "too late"?'

She looked up, she looked sad, she looked afraid.

'I'm sorry,' she said.

'Sorry for what?'

'Kings, I'm getting married.'

Consternation struck me dumb.

'I'm getting married to someone else. Everything has been fixed.' She paused. 'I'm really sorry.'

At what point would Ola smile and confess that this was all part of some expensive joke? Perhaps another side effect of her being a citizen of Venus. Then I stared into her eyes and knew it was no joke. I felt as if I had been stabbed in the back, punched in the eye, struck on the head with a pestle, and bitten in the ankle, at the same time.

'I'm sorry,' she said again.

'What do you mean "everything"? Do you mean the wedding?'

She nodded.

'They've taken wine to my father and he's given them a date.'

I was quiet and kept quiet and continued keeping quiet. But, sooner or later, the ugliness of life loses its power to shock. I became ready to hear the rest.

'So how long have you known this man?'

She sighed, as if she was relieved that we had finally scaled the highest hurdle.

'I met him a while ago,' she said. 'But it wasn't until recently that things became serious.'

Aha! The Dolce & Gabbana wristwatch and the Gucci slippers and the Fendi handbag. The man was clearly very serious.

'Who is he?'

'There's no need—,'

'Just tell me . . . Who is he?'

'What are you doing with that information? Are you going to plant a bomb in his car?'

Aha. The man even had a car. All my feelings rolled up into one tight ball of anger.

'I'm just curious. What's the point keeping it secret? After all, it's not as if you're going to have a secret wedding.'

She shrugged.

'I guess you're right. His name is Udenna. I don't know if you've heard of Ude Maximum Ventures. He's the one that owns it.'

Of course I had heard of UdeMax. His logo was branded on several buses that carried passengers from Eastern Nigeria to Northern Nigeria and back again. His logo was on several of the *gwongworos* that transported palm oil and tomatoes and onions. Suddenly, my mind stubbed against a rocky thought.

'Ola, did he go to school?'

She refused to answer. I panicked. Most Igbo entrepreneurs of his kind never completed any formal education.

'Wait! You're planning to get married to somebody who didn't even go to school? Ola, what's the matter with you?'

'You know what, Kingsley? I have to leave now. I need to go before it gets dark.'

I was about to bark something else when she pressed something into the palm of my hand. I looked. It was a wad of naira notes.

Haha.

Back in school, Ola often shared whatever little pocket money she had with me whenever I was broke, which was almost always. The difference was that then, the money was not from Udenna's pocket. I pushed the wad back into her hand.

'Please take it,' she insisted.

I shook my head vigorously. Never.

'Kings, please . . .'

I continued shaking my head. She forced the notes back into my palm. I flung them away. She looked hurt. She abandoned the notes on the ground and started walking away.

'Olachi, take that money away!'

She was jolted and stopped in her tracks. She picked up the notes and hurried off. I stared into her back as piercingly as I could without committing homicide.

Two days later, the familiar sounds of grief in our living room were dispelled by the sudden din of commotion outside. Through the open louvers, I saw that a throng of neighbours and passers-by had gathered to watch. It was not often that a convoy of Land Cruisers and CR-Vs blared horns and rumbled engines on Ojike Street.

With Protocol Officer's help, an aqua green shoe protruded into view. Cash Daddy poured out of the car.

I was ashamed to sense how relieved I felt to set my eyes on him.

Nineteen

My father was buried in grand style.

A few days before the funeral ceremony, Cash Daddy took out full-page obituary announcements in three of the most widely read national newspapers. At the bottom of each page, it was mentioned in bold print that he was the sponsor of the announcement. My father's photograph took up three-quarters of the page. Uncle Boniface's mug shot was inserted in a corner, just beneath my father's own.

'When people see my photograph with your father's own,' he said, 'it'll catch their attention immediately and they'll want to read the whole thing. When they find out that I'm related to your father, they'll make sure they attend.'

He also paid for obituary announcements on radio and television. Each one ended with the announcer declaring: 'This burial announcement was signed by Chief Boniface Mbamalu a.k.a. Cash Daddy, on behalf of the Ibe family.'

There were cloth banners hung in strategic places from our village all the way to the express road, and large obituary fliers posted on walls and trees. We hired a fifty-eight-sitter commercial bus to transport my mother's relatives all the way from Isiukwuato to Umuahia. Food and drink were very plenty, more than enough for the villagers to scuffle over and for the opportunistic to smuggle away in their inner garments.

During the funeral Mass, when I saw how smart my father looked in the brand new Italian suit my mother and his younger brother had dressed him up in, I could not help the tiny smile that crawled out onto my lips. My father had always preferred Western fashions to traditional African clothes. He said they were less cumbersome. Quite unlike most men of his generation, my father had no quarrel with the white man. He also preferred his climate;

he said that the more temperate weather conditions made it easier to think creatively. And he preferred his diet; he said their food did not contain too much spice, which made it easier to enjoy the original taste of the ingredients. Several people mockingly referred to my father as *onye ocha nna ya di ojii*, the white man whose father is black, but he never cared.

From church, we accompanied the coffin back to our compound, where four of my father's male relatives heaved it into the open grave that had been dug a few inches from our brand new building. After more than eleven years of the structure being a monument to our hardscrabbling, in just a few months the village house had been roofed, painted, and furnished in time for the burial ceremony.

The priest sprinkled some holy water over the grave and began the committal rites in an unhurried and solemn voice.

'Our brother, Paulinus Akobudike Ibe has gone to his rest in the peace of Christ, may the Lord now welcome him to the table of God's children in heaven.'

I stared into the grave and tried not to think that my father was lying in there, about to be concealed from me, from all of us, forever. My mother tottered beside me. Her relatives gathered closer around her. They all wore dark blue ankara fabric. My father's relatives wore the same design, but in dark green. The younger men in the immediate extended family wore white T-shirts with my father's photograph printed on the front. My mother, my siblings, and I wore outfits made from expensive white lace. Every category of cloth had been provided free of charge for the various groups of people.

'Because God has chosen to call our brother Paulinus Akobudike Ibe from this life to Himself, we commit his body to the earth, for we are dust and unto dust we shall return.'

My mother fell to the ground and had to be dragged up by two of her sisters and Aunty Dimma. Cash Daddy sniffed very loudly. He was dressed in the same ankara fabric as my mother's other relatives, but there was just something about having money. Cash Daddy stood out from all of them.

'Merciful Lord,' the priest continued, 'You know the anguish of the sorrowful, You are attentive to the prayers of the humble. Hear

Your people who cry out to You in their need, and strengthen their hope in Your lasting goodness. We ask this through Christ our Lord.'

'Amen.'

Aunty Dimma held on tightly to prevent my mother from rocking into the six-foot hole. My mother looked like a ghost, like a dead person mourning another person who was dead. The only signs that she was alive were that her eyes were red and flooded, and her face was dripping and contorted. Godfrey and Eugene stood beside me on the other side, both weeping like three-year-olds who had received a severe spanking. Godfrey was holding Charity's two hands tight. She was wailing at the top of her voice and struggling to jump into the grave.

Because I was the *opara*, after my mother shook a handful of soil into the open grave, it was my turn. I bent and grabbed a handful of the freshly dug-up soil. As I rose and looked into the grave again, I felt the tears welling up. Trying to be a man, I blinked and looked straight ahead while the dust crumbled from my fingers. My eyes landed on my young cousin's chest, and on the photograph of my father printed on his white T-shirt. My father had posed for the shot during his graduation from Imperial College, London, probably hoping that he would show it to his children and to his grandchildren. The tassel from his cap was hanging over his right eye. And he was grinning with the confidence of one who knew that he was about to conquer the world. Ha.

I took my eyes away from the photograph and dislodged the last crumbs of sand into my father's grave. My mother swooned and passed out.

Afterwards, my father's female relatives were ready to perform the next phase of the bereavement rites. It was time to shave my mother's hair. Knowing how much my father loved my mother's long hair and how strongly he detested backward customs, I vehemently opposed it. Even when Aunty Ada scolded me for hindering my father's smooth passage to the spirit world, I refused to budge. It was my duty to honour my father and to protect my mother. I was the *opara*.

In the end, it was my mother who told me to step out of the way.

'What's the point?' she asked. 'The person for whom I've been wearing the hair is no more, so what do I care?'

Right there and then, a switch flipped inside my head. Indeed, my father was no more. And it was my responsibility to start caring for the people who were still here. There was nothing stopping me now.

By the time the women finished their task, my father could have looked down from the spirit world and seen his reflection gleaming on his beloved wife's skull.

Part 2

Chịnchị sị na ịhe dị ọkụ ga-emechaa juo oyi.

The bedbug said that whatever is hot would eventually become cold.

Twenty

At first, it was difficult. Composing cock-and-bull tales, with every single word an untruth, including 'is' and 'was'. Blasting SOS emails around the world, hoping that someone would swallow the bait and respond. But I was probably worrying myself for nothing. They were just a bunch of email addresses with no real people at the other end anyway. Besides, who on this earth was stupid enough to fall prey to an email from a stranger in Nigeria?

Then, someone in Auckland replied. And another one in Cardiff. Then a lady in Wisconsin showed interest. Soon we were on first-name terms. It was almost like staying up to watch a dreadful movie simply to see what happened at the end. I continued stringing the sucker – the mugu – along. Then a Western Union control number arrived. Unbelievable. I, Kingsley Onyeaghalanwanneya Ibe, had actually made a hit!

No oil company interview success letter had ever given me a sharper thrill of gratification. Like an addict, I was eager to recreate that thrill again. And again, and again, and again. Gradually, it occurred to me that I had discovered a hidden talent. Over the past year, I had adapted and settled into my new life.

At the office, I went through my emails, deleting messages, typing out some new ones. I spellchecked the document on my screen, making double sure all information was correct. To make a clear distinction between my mail and any subsequent replies, I changed the document to uppercase. Most people tended to write in sentence case, but once in a comet-across-the-sky while, I encountered some of the world's weirder people who wrote regularly in all caps. In that event, I switched back to sentence case.

I read the letter one last time.

SUBJECT: REQUEST FOR URGENT HUMANITARIAN ASSISTANCE/BUSINESS PROPOSAL

DEAR FRIEND,

I DO NOT COME TO YOU BY CHANCE. UPON MY QUEST FOR A TRUSTED AND RELIABLE FOREIGN BUSINESSMAN OR COMPANY, I WAS GIVEN YOUR CONTACT BY THE NIGERIAN CHAMBER OF COMMERCE AND INDUSTRY. I HOPE THAT YOU CAN BE TRUSTED TO HANDLE A TRANSACTION OF THIS MAGNITUDE.

FOLLOWING THE SUDDEN DEATH OF MY HUSBAND, GENERAL SANI ABACHA, THE FORMER HEAD OF STATE OF NIGERIA, I HAVE BEEN THROWN INTO A STATE OF UTTER CONFUSION, FRUSTRATION AND HOPELESSNESS BY THE CURRENT CIVILIAN ADMINISTRATION. I HAVE BEEN SUBJECTED TO PHYSICAL AND PSYCHOLOGICAL TORTURE BY THE SECURITY AGENTS IN THE COUNTRY. MY SON, MOHAMMED, IS UNDER DETENTION FOR AN OFFENCE HE DID NOT COMMIT.

THE TRUTH IN ALL THIS IS THAT THE CURRENT PRESIDENT OF NIGERIA WAS JAILED FOR PLANNING A COUP AGAINST MY LATE HUSBAND'S GOVERNMENT. HE WAS ELECTED AS THE PRESIDENT OF NIGERIA WHEN HE WAS RELEASED. I AND MY CHILDREN WERE NEVER PART OF MY LATE HUSBAND'S REGIME. YET, THE NEW PRESIDENT HAS SUCCEEDED IN TURNING THE WHOLE COUNTRY AGAINST US, AND IS TRYING DIFFERENT WAYS TO FRUSTRATE US.

THE NIGERIAN GOVERNMENT HAS GONE AFTER MY FAMILY'S WEALTH. YOU MUST HAVE HEARD REPORTS OVER THE MEDIA AND ON THE INTERNET, ABOUT THE RECOVERY OF VARIOUS HUGE SUMS OF MONEY DEPOSITED BY MY HUSBAND IN DIFFERENT

COUNTRIES ABROAD. MANY OF MY LATE HUSBAND'S REAL ESTATE HAVE BEEN SEIZED AND SOME AUCTIONED. ALL OUR BANK ACCOUNTS IN NIGERIA AND ABROAD, KNOWN TO THE GOVERNMENT, HAVE BEEN FROZEN. THE HUNT FOR OUR MONEY IS STILL ON. THE TOTAL AMOUNT DISCOVERED BY THE GOVERNMENT SO FAR IS ABOUT $700 MILLION (USD) AND THEY ARE STILL TRYING TO FISH OUT THE REST.

MOST OF OUR FRIENDS HAVE EITHER ABANDONED OR BETRAYED US. I AM DESPERATE FOR HELP. AS A WIDOW WHO IS SO TRAUMATISED, I HAVE LOST CONFIDENCE IN ANYBODY WITHIN THE COUNTRY. OWING TO MY PREVIOUS EXPERIENCES, I AM AFRAID THAT IF I CONTACT ANYBODY WHO KNOWS US, I MIGHT BE EXPOSED. PLEASE DO NOT BETRAY ME.

SOMETIME AGO, I DEPOSITED THE SUM OF $58,000,000.00 CASH (FIFTY EIGHT MILLION USD) OF MY LATE HUSBAND'S MONEY IN A SECURITY FIRM WHOSE NAME I CANNOT DISCLOSE UNTIL I'M SURE THAT I CAN TRUST YOU. I WILL BE VERY GRATEFUL IF YOU COULD RECEIVE THESE FUNDS FOR SAFE KEEPING. FOR YOUR KIND ASSISTANCE, YOU ARE ENTITLED TO 20% OF THE TOTAL SUM.

I NEVER REALLY INTENDED TO TOUCH THIS MONEY WHICH IS VERY SAFE AND SECURE IN THE VAULT OF THIS SECURITY FIRM. BUT OWING TO OUR PRESENT SITUATION, I DO NOT HAVE ANY OTHER OPTION. WE ARE BADLY IN NEED OF MONEY. MY SON MOHAMMED IS VERY SICK IN PRISON AND HIS LAWYERS ARE RIPPING US OFF. THE PROBLEM IS THAT I CANNOT LAY MY HANDS ON THIS MONEY OWING TO THE FACT THAT ALL INTERNATIONAL PASSPORTS BELONGING TO THE MEMBERS OF MY FAMILY HAVE

BEEN SEIZED BY THIS GOVERNMENT, PENDING WHEN THEY FINISH DEALING WITH US.

THIS ARRANGEMENT IS KNOWN ONLY TO YOU, MY HUSBAND'S YOUNGER BROTHER (WHO IS CONTACTING YOU) AND I. AS SURVEILLANCE IS CONSTANTLY ON ME, MY HUSBAND'S BROTHER WILL DEAL DIRECTLY WITH YOU. HIS NAME IS SHEHU. SHEHU IS LIKE A BROTHER TO ME. THE NIGERIAN GOVERNMENT DOES NOT KNOW ANYTHING ABOUT THIS MONEY, NOBODY ELSE KNOWS ANYTHING, SO THERE IS NOTHING TO FEAR.

IF YOU ARE NOT WILLING TO HELP ME, PLEASE DO NOT EXPOSE ME. JUST ASSUME WE NEVER DISCUSSED THIS MATTER. BUT I WILL BE MOST GRATEFUL AND WOULD SHOW MY APPRECIATION IF YOU CAN HELP TO RESTORE LIFE AND HOPE IN MY FAMILY AGAIN.

ADEQUATE ARRANGEMENT HAS BEEN MADE FOR RECEIVING THE FUNDS. IT IS TOTALLY RISK FREE.

I AWAIT YOUR URGENT RESPONSE. PLEASE REPLY THROUGH THIS EMAIL. SHEHU WILL RESPOND ON MY BEHALF.

YOURS SINCERELY,
HAJIA MARIAM ABACHA

I watched my cursor hover on the Send icon. Out of the thousands of messages I blasted out every day, very few were replied to. But once an initial contact was established, there was a seventy per cent chance that I would make a hit. Even after all this while, I still felt a slight apprehension about the sudden changes my emails could bring about in a stranger's life.

The lady in Wisconsin had gulped down my story about a businessman client of mine who had died suddenly of a heart attack while vacationing in the South of France. My businessman client had not listed any next of kin. His domiciliary account fixed deposit balance currently stood at $19 million (USD). If she agreed to bear the huge burden of next of kin, we would share the proceeds 60/40. But she must first sign an agreement promising to send my sixty per cent as soon as she received the money into her account. After a few email exchanges, the kind lady granted me permission to doctor some documents that would qualify her to claim the money. Then, I went for the hit.

DEAR MIRABELLE,

THANK YOU FOR YOUR KIND ASSISTANCE AND YOUR AGREEMENT TO PARTNER WITH ME OVER THIS VERY DELICATE BUSINESS. I HAVE ALREADY INITIATED PROCEEDINGS FOR THE TRANSFER OF THE FUNDS. COULD YOU PLEASE SEND FOUR THOU-SAND FIVE HUNDRED DOLLARS ($4,500 USD) FOR THE PROCESSING OF THE DEATH AUTHORISATION FORM? ALSO SEND ALONG FOUR COPIES OF YOUR RECENT PASSPORT PHOTOGRAPH. PLEASE DO THIS IMMEDIATELY TO AVOID DELAYS. THE DEPOSIT WILL BE RELEASED TO YOU WITHIN SEVEN WORKING DAYS.

I AWAIT YOUR URGENT RESPONSE.

YOURS SINCERELY,
OSONDIOWENDI

She played volleyball.

When the Western Union official removed his five percent silencing fee and handed me the rest, I clasped the bundle and shut my eyes tight. I am not sure for how long I stood there. Eventually, I regained consciousness and opened my eyes. The money was still there. I wanted to jump, to shout, to run through the streets crying, 'Goal'! At last, the Book of Remembrance had been opened and Fortune had called out my name. The sun peeped in through the windows of the dank collection office and flashed me a smile. I counted the cash two more times before I left.

After Protocol Officer had removed Cash Daddy's sixty percent, I counted the bundle again. Several times throughout the rest of the day, I hauled the notes from my pockets and recounted. That night, I lay in bed with the wad cradled neatly under my pillow. At 2 a.m., I woke up and recounted. I did the same thing at 4 a.m.. By 7 a.m., I had scrambled out of bed and confirmed that the money was still there.

Two thousand dollars had not been enough to buy my mother a brand new car. I bought her a jar of cooking gas, some new wrappers, and a bag of rice instead. For a change, I was giving. Not taking.

I felt like a real *opara*.

Over a period of two months, Mirabelle sang dough-re-mi to the tune of about $23,000. For processing of a Death Authorisation Certificate, Next Of Kin Affirmation, Bank Recognition Form, and Deceased Demise Declaration. Then I sent another email explaining that $7,000 was required for the Fund Transfer Repatriation. This, I promised, would be the very final payment before she received the $19 million. Her reply shocked me.

Dear Osondiowendi,

I'm so sorry to cause delays but I've spoken with a close friend who's promised to lend me the $7,000 but he says he won't be able till next weekend. Don't worry, I didn't breach your confidence. He's my ex-boyfriend and I told him some BS story about how the money was to start IVF treatment before my partner will be ready with the money at the end of the month. He didn't ask too many questions when I promised to pay him back double :).

Could you also please let me know when exactly the money is going to be in my account? The reason is I've been taking out of the money me and my partner are putting together to move into our

*own home and I want to be sure to replace it before he notices it's
gone.*

> *Yours,*
> *Mirabelle*

This note caused my heart to crack. The poor woman would find
herself in a cauldron of debt and disaster when the money she was
expecting did not show up. Who knows what comforts the couple
had forfeited in saving up to buy a house? What if she was actually
hoping to start IVF treatment? Here was a real life happening
behind the curtains of an email address. It was a bit unrealistic
refunding what we had eaten so far, but I thought, at least, we
could shred the job. I spoke with Cash Daddy about the unique
problem on our hands.

'Kings,' he said when I had finished explaining.

I waited.

'Kings,' he called again.

'Yes, Cash Daddy?'

'This woman . . . what's her name?'

'Her name is Mirabelle.'

'No, no, no . . . what's her full name? Her surname?'

'Winfrey. Mirabelle Winfrey.'

He sighed deeply and shook his head remorsefully.

'Kings.'

'Yes, Cash Daddy?'

'Is she your sister?'

I did not reply.

'Go on . . . answer me. Is she your sister?'

'No.'

'Is she your cousin?'

'No.'

'Is she your brother's wife?'

'No.'

'Is she your mother's sister?'

I got the point.

'Go on . . . answer me.'

'No.'

'Is she your father's sister?'

'No.'

He shrugged. Then as an afterthought: 'Is she from your village?'

'No.'

'So why are you swallowing Panadol for another person's headache?'

'Cash Daddy,' I persisted. 'The woman borrowed the money she's been using to pay her bills. Her life is going to be ruined.'

He laughed.

'Kings, with all the school you went, you still don't know anything. These *oyibo* people are different from us. Don't think America and Europe are like Nigeria where people suffer anyhow. Over there, their governments know how to take good care of them. They don't know anything about suffering.'

He leaned closer.

'Do you know that as you are right now – thank God you already have a job – but if you were a young man without a job abroad, the government will be giving you money every week? Can you imagine that? So you could even decide never to work again and just be collecting free money. They'll even give you a house.'

I was not pacified. He must have seen it on my face.

'OK,' he continued. 'You, you went to school. Did they not teach you about slave trade?'

'They did.'

'Who were the people behind it? And all the things they stole from Africa, have they paid us back?'

'But Cash Daddy, can you imagine what will happen when her . . . ,' I knew about husbands and boyfriends and sugar daddies, but the word 'partner' was alien to my vocabulary, '. . . when her man finds out? At least let's leave her with the one we've eaten so far and try and—'

'Kings, sometimes I get very worried about you. Your attitude is not money-friendly at all. If you continue talking like this, soon, whenever money sees you coming into a room, it will just jump out through the window.'

He had glared for a while, then shrugged, as if finally willing to concede.

'OK. Since you don't appreciate this opportunity God has given you to abolish poverty from your family once and for all, continue worrying about one *oyibo* woman in America. Be there worrying about her and leave off your own sister and your mother.'

Cash Daddy was right. Not being able to take care of my family was the real sin. Gradually, I had learnt to take my mind off the mugus and focus on the things that really mattered. Thanks to me, my family was now as safe as a tortoise under its shell. My mother could finally stop picking pennies from her shop and start enjoying the rest of her life. My brothers and sister could focus completely on their studies without worrying about fees.

Mirabelle had her problems, I had mine.

Suddenly, I heard a mouth-watering sound. My head snapped up from the computer screen. In this business, the ringing of a phone – whether cellular or land – was the sound of music. It was also a call for order. Buchi, who was sitting at the desk with the five phones and the fax machines, removed chewing gum from her mouth, pasted it onto her wrist with her tongue, then clapped her hands quickly to catch everybody's attention.

'Shhhhhhh!' she shouted.

All talking ceased.

There were five of us who shared this room that Cash Daddy had called the Central Intelligence Agency. The receptionist, the menial staff, the dark-suited *otimkpu* whose main duty was to herald the arrival of their master and to make sure his presence was well-noticed, all stayed in the outer office. Buchi received all incoming calls before passing them on. At different points in time, depending on who was calling, she could say she was speaking from the Federal Ministry of Finance, the Nigerian National Petroleum Cooperation, the Central Bank of Nigeria . . . Now, after ensuring that the noise in the office had reduced to a more conducive level, she cleared her throat and lifted the receiver.

'Good morning. May I help you?' she asked in a clear, professional voice.

Buchi was a graduate of Mass Communication from the Abia State University, Uturu.

'Yes,' she said. 'Yes,' she said again.

While listening, she nodded and scribbled diligently in a jotter. Buchi took her job quite seriously.

'All right if you could just hold on for one second, please, I'll pass you on to the person in charge of that department.'

She pressed the mute button and extended the appliance in my direction.

'Kings,' she whispered as an extra precaution, 'it's Ben's Port Harcourt Refinery mugu.'

Ben was one of our office cleaners. As well as those of us in the CIA, everybody else – the *otimkpu*, gatemen, drivers, cleaners, cook, receptionist, the boys who lived in Cash Daddy's house – was entitled to compose their own letters and blast them out to whomever they pleased. Like Cash Daddy always said, there were more than enough mugus to go round. But as soon as contact was established and it looked like money was on the way, whoever had initiated the correspondence was supposed to let me know. Only I and Protocol Officer had keys to the cabinet where we stored the letterheaded sheets, death certificates, bank statements, call-to-bar certificates, proof of funds, money orders, cheques, and any other documents that might be required to prove the authenticity of a transaction. Only I and Protocol Officer could make the phone call to authorise our Western Union official to look the other way.

Some weeks ago, Ben had sent out letters claiming that he was the head of a committee that tendered for and recently completed some construction work on the Port Harcourt Refinery. The project, he stated, was purposely over-inflated by $40 million and he needed help to smuggle the money out of Nigeria. All the recipient had to do was to claim that his business had been awarded the $40 million contract and provide a bank account detail for the transaction. For that, he would keep twenty-five per cent for himself – as long as he transferred the remaining seventy-five per cent to Ben's bank account. This mugu had agreed and was told to fax his business details so that his business could be registered in Nigeria. He had sent the $6,000 required for the process last week.

The Corporate Affairs Commission registration documents had been faxed back to him yesterday. I took in a deep breath as I grabbed the receiver from Buchi.

'Good afternoon,' I said after letting out the air from my lungs, 'This is Mr Odiegwu on the line. How may I help you?'

'Hello,' the Englander replied. 'I have a document here that shows my business has been registered with the Nigerian Corporate Affairs Commission, and I just wanted to confirm my registration details.'

Naturally, he had rung the number on the CAC letterheaded sheet.

'May I have the registration number, please?'

He read it out slowly, careful not to miss any slashes or hyphens. I repeated after him without making record anywhere. What he did not know was that the registration certificate had been faxed from this same office. Dibia, our document expert, was quite good. All the logos and stamps on the documents he supplied were authentic, and so were the signatures.

'Could you please hold on while I go through our records?'

While waiting for a plausible length of time to elapse, I admired the Atilogwu acrobatic dancers on the wall calendar in front of me. I had seen their energetic and entertaining dance on television several times before. Their uniforms were remarkably colourful.

'Is that Mr Del B. Trotter?' I asked at last.

He confirmed his name eagerly.

'Yes, we have the documents here,' I said. 'The registration was processed on the 12th.'

I could almost hear the splashes of the grin that swam out onto his face. After all, every Homo sapiens – whether Englander or Burkinabe – had the natural right to grin over the prospect of colliding with $10 million for doing almost nothing.

'Thanks for your kind assistance,' he said.

I returned the phone to Buchi and made a mental note of the fact that I would still need to speak with this same mugu soon. If Ben successfully convinced him to send another $9,000 for the contract documents to be drawn up, Mr Trotter would probably want to ring the Port Harcourt Refinery office to make some further enquiries.

The clicking of gum and the talking resumed. I was about to return to my screen when Wizard let out a high-pitched cry.

'My lollipop is awake o! My lollipop is awake!'

All of us recognised this as our daily call to amusement. We rushed over to Wizard's desk. The words he typed onto the screen sent everybody quaking with laughter.

'Oh lollipop,' he had written, 'am really scared, hun. Am really scared that I ain't gonna see you again no more, my darl. These people are really threatening me. You know how wild these Africans can be.'

My laughter became the loudest of all.

Wizard had been conducting several online relationships with randy foreigners he met in chatrooms. His romance with this particular American had been going on for six weeks. When their loooove blossomed to the point where the man proposed to 'Suzie' that she travel from East Windsor, New Jersey to visit him in Salt Lake City, Utah or vice versa, she informed him that she was just on her way to Nigeria on a business trip. She was a make-up artist, you see, and had an offer to transform girls strutting down the catwalk for an AIDS charity in Lagos. She had arrived in Lagos two days before, and had her American passport stolen in a taxi. Now, she had no way of cashing her traveller's cheques and the proprietor of the hotel was threatening arrest.

'Oh babe,' the man replied, 'what you gonna do now? Ain't there no way of taking it to the police?'

'Sugar pie, all they gonna want is bribes,' Wizard replied. 'Hun, I'm gonna really need your help right now. I wanna see if you can show me that you really love me and that what we share is real. Can you do me a real big favour?'

Wizard must have been watching a lot of American movies. His gonna-wanna American-speak was quite fluent.

'Sure, babe,' the man wrote. 'Anything I can do to help.'

'Honeybunch, I wanna send the traveller's cheques to you to pay into your bank account. Can you do that and send me the cash?'

Wizard broke off typing and turned quickly to us. 'How much should I write? Is $2,000 OK?'

'That's too small,' Ogbonna said. 'Double it.'

'Yes, double it,' we concurred.

Wizard resumed.

'What I've got in cheques is about $4,000. Honey, I gotta have some help real quick. Can you be the one to help me out here?'

Suzie went on to explain to her beau that the cheques would arrive within three days; she would send them by DHL. He should deposit the cheques as soon as he received them, and then send her the cash by Western Union. Since her own passport had been stolen, she would send him the name of one of her colleagues at the charity event so that he could send the Western Union in the colleague's name. The lover boy, swept away by the current of true love, wasted no time in responding.

'Anything for you, sweetie. I ain't got that much in my cheque account right now but I could get some from my credit card and replace once I've cashed the cheques.'

All of us screamed the special scream. Wizard had made a hit.

It would take about eight days for the bank to process the documents, before the man realised that the cheques that had been paid into his account were fakes. I looked in a corner of the chat box and saw the photograph of the bearded, voluminous Caucasian. Then I looked in Wizard's own box and saw the photograph of the trim, buxom blond who had no resemblance whatsoever to the V-shaped eighteen-year-old clicking away at the keyboard. My heart went out to the lonely man, but Wizard was untroubled.

'Thanks honeysuckle,' he wrote. 'I knew I could really count on you. Please get it done ASAP cos I ain't got nothing left on me no more.'

'Sure, Suz,' the man replied. 'By the way, babe, you gotta take good care of yourself and watch out, OK? Maybe I should've warned you when you said you were going. I saw on CNN sometime that the folks in Nigeria are real dangerous.'

'No problem, love,' Wizard replied. 'I've learnt my lesson and I'm gonna take real good care of myself from now.'

'I love you babe,' the man wrote. 'I really can't wait to meet you.'

'Me, too,' Wizard replied. 'I promise we're gonna have a swell time and you're not gonna wanna let me go.'

Wizard wrote something vulgar. The man replied with something equally vulgar. Wizard topped it with something much more vulgar which Azuka had suggested, and then added one or two more unprintable things that he was going to do to the man when they met.

'By the way, hun,' the man added, 'while you're out there, you'd better watch out for diseases, especially HIV. I hear almost all of them over there have got it.'

All of us standing round the screen stopped giggling. In the ensuing silence, I could almost hear the whisperings of our National Pledge.

I pledge to Nigeria my country
To be faithful, loyal and honest
To serve Nigeria with all my strength
To defend her unity
And uphold her honour and glory
So help me God

Wizard seemed to have heard it as well. The faint voice of patriotism must have ministered to the young Nigerian.

'It's not like that in Nigeria,' he replied. 'It's in South Africa that they've got it so bad.'

'Is it? Anyway, you still be careful. All them places are all the same thing to me.'

Suddenly, I stopped feeling sorry for the mugu and remembered something I had to do. I went back to my desk, clicked the Send icon, and wished my urgent email Godspeed.

Twenty-one

This business of being a man of means had taken me quite a while to get used to. Sometimes, I even forgot that my circumstances had changed. I was about to pass out on the floor the day my first cellular phone bill arrived, when I remembered that I could afford to pay it. I was storming my way out of an Aba 'Big Boys' shop in protest at the obese price tags, when I remembered that I had nothing to quarrel about, went back in and bought my Swatch wristwatch. My mother was also having a hard time getting used to the better life.

She had been delighted the day I visited home with the cooking gas and the wrappers and the rice, she told me how much I reminded her of my father when I brought a variety of McVitie's biscuits and Just Juice for my siblings, but when I presented her with a bundle of oven fresh notes, her feelings took on a different shape.

'Kings,' she asked with fear, 'how did you get all this money?'

'Mummy, I told you I've been doing some work for Uncle Boniface. This is from my salary.'

'What sort of work do you do?'

I had told her before.

'I help out at his office. I take phone calls. I run small errands. I help him organise his business meetings . . .'

'So how much is this salary he gives you for running errands?'

'Well, it varies,' I shrugged. 'It's all done on a commission basis.'

'Commission – on errands?'

I fumbled with my shoelaces, pretending I had not heard.

My mother continued staring at the bundle in her lap without touching it, as if she expected the cash to rise up on its two feet and bite. She was about to ask another question when I laid firm hold of her Achilles' heel and twisted.

'Don't worry, Mummy. I know how much you miss having Daddy around, but I'm your *opara* and I'm really going to take care of you. Very soon I'll get my own house and all of you can come and be spending time with me.'

My mother smiled. For the first time since the money took up residence in her lap, she invited it into her fingers for a proper welcome. My dear mother had probably never handled so many notes at any one time in her entire life. Her smile grew very fat.

'But make sure you keep looking for a proper job,' she said. 'You know this work for Boniface is only temporary.'

'Mummy, don't worry. I'll keep looking.'

'OK, come let me bless you.'

I knelt on the floor in front of her. She placed her right palm on the centre of my head. Legend had it that her own father had done the same thing when she brought him an envelope containing half of her very first salary. The other half had paid obeisance to her husband.

'You will have good children who will take care of you in your old age,' she began.

'Amen,' I replied.

'You will find a good wife.'

'Amen.'

'Evil men and evil women will never come near you.'

'Amen.'

'You will continue to prosper.'

'Amen.'

'Wherever this money came from, more will continue to come.'

'Amen.'

My mother's prayers worked. A few weeks later, I made a $27,000 hit and moved from Cash Daddy's mansion into a rented four-bedroom duplex in Aba.

Shortly after, I travelled to Umuahia.

My family rushed out when I arrived. Eugene and Charity hovered around my brand new Lexus. They stroked the body, sat inside, took turns at pretending to steer the wheel. My mother admired the car briefly and stood by the front door watching them.

Odinkemmelu and Chikaodinaka peeped from behind the living room curtains. When my cellular phone rang, the excitement was just too much for my siblings to contain. They squealed like toddlers being tickled in their armpits and navel.

It was my Lufthansa airline pilot mugu whose $27,000 had rented my new house and contributed towards my Lexus. I asked my family's patron saint to please ring back later. Under the best of conditions, I required superhuman faculties to unravel his guttural accent; with my mother standing beside me, I was certain not to extricate a word. My mother was staring at the cellular phone and then at the car. She looked slightly disturbed. There was no need for me to worry too much about her mood. Wait until she saw the surprise I had in store for her.

'Are you people ready?' I asked.

My mother and siblings threw their bags into the car boot. They were spending the weekend with me.

'Mummy, sit in the owner's corner,' I said.

'Yes, sit in the owner's corner,' Eugene and Charity chanted.

With a modest smile, my mother went round to the back right of the car where people who could afford chauffeurs usually sat. Eugene held the door open for her.

'Mummy,' I said, looking up at her image in the rearview mirror as we sped off, 'I forgot to tell you. Please can you arrange for some relatives – at least two – to come and live with me? It's a big house and I'll need help.'

'OK. I'll ask Chikaodinaka's mother. I think she has some younger ones.'

'No, no, no. I don't want people that are too young. I'll prefer people who're older. Or people who've already lived with someone before. I don't have the time to start teaching anybody how to flush the toilet and turn on the gas.'

Everybody laughed. Once, we had a help from the village who mistook the china teapot as an exotic drinking cup. And another one who blocked the toilet with sheets of my father's *Statesman* newspaper which she had ripped out to clean up herself. These helps were as useful as oxen, but they came with their own variety of headaches.

'How big is the house?' Charity asked.

'You mean the one we're going to or the one I'm planning to build?'

'The one we're going to.'

'Don't worry. You'll soon see it.'

She bounced about on her seat and beamed. Charity was such a big baby. She leaned forward on the back of my headrest and played with my ears. I felt like a real elder brother.

'OK, how about the one you're going to build?' Eugene asked. 'How big is it?'

'It's double the size of the one you're going to see now.'

'Wow! I'm so glad my school hasn't yet resumed,' Eugene said. 'I wrote to Godfrey to tell him that we were going to your house this weekend. Once he gets the letter, I'm sure he'll go straight to Aba.'

Eugene was in his first semester at the University of Ibadan. My mother had tried persuading him to choose a university that was closer to home, but he remained adamant that the medical department in Ibadan was the best. Nobody had any argument with that; it was the distance that troubled us. Plus, Ibadan was a favourite hotspot for trouble. As soon as the elections gained momentum, the place would be boiling with bloody riots. My father would never have allowed Eugene to go, but then, there were so many other things my father would never have allowed if he were alive.

My mother reminded me to drive carefully about five hundred times before we finally arrived. When I honked, my gateman opened. I parked in the middle of the compound, some distance from the closed garage door.

'*Aboki*, come and take these bags into the house.'

The man rushed to the boot and started manoeuvring the bags. I went ahead and unlocked the front door. After taking my mother and siblings on a tour of the exquisitely furnished living room, the ultramodern kitchen and the four en suite bedrooms, I led them back outside.

'I have a surprise for you,' I announced.

I unlocked the garage. Inside was a brand new Mercedes-Benz V-Boot.

'Mummy, this is for you.'

168

Charity burst into tears. Eugene's eyeballs popped out of their sockets and bounced off the shiny, grey body of the car. My mother used her two hands to cover her face. Gradually, she dragged the hands down towards her mouth. I tucked the keys between her fingers and hugged her.

'Mummy, whatever it is you want, just let me know. I'll buy it for you.'

Charity and Eugene were jumping all over the garage, but my mother just studied the car in silence. Eventually, she hugged me back.

The rest of the day was almost like the good old days. My mother cooked, we ate together on the dining table, we sat in the living room and watched television. Back in Umuahia, the only channels we received were NTA Aba and IBC Owerri. Both commenced daily broadcasting at 4 p.m. and usually ended at about 10 p.m.. Their primetime serving largely consisted of government-sponsored documentaries and repeats of locally produced sitcoms. But now that I could afford the pricey satellite TV subscription, I and my family laughed loudly to *Fresh Prince of Bel Air*.

'I'm going to bed,' my mother announced during the commercial break.

We tried persuading her to stay. But since my father passed away, she hardly stayed up to watch television once the seven o'clock news was over. Not long after she left, I heard her voice from the top of the stairs.

'Kingsley!'

'Yes, Mummy!'

'Please come.'

I ran upstairs with the television remote control still in my hand. I did not want to miss what would happen to Will Smith when his uncle found him performing in the strip club.

'Yes, Mummy?'

'Come and sit down,' she said softly.

I was tempted to tell her that I would come back later. Instead, I sat beside her on the wide, sleigh bed. First class design, imported from Italy.

'Dimma has been complaining that Ogechi doesn't read her books,' my mother began. 'She hasn't been doing well in school.'

'Really?' I said with false shock.

'Please try and call her from time to time to encourage her to read.'

That could never be the reason why my mother summoned me to this closed-door session. I continued playing along.

'Tell Aunty Dimma not to worry. I'll talk to Ogechi.'

We chatted more about Aunty Dimma, but soon, that bogus topic had certainly come to the end of its lifespan. My mother adjusted her feet in her bathroom slippers and scratched the back of her head.

'By the way, Kingsley,' she said as if it had just popped into her mind for the first time when her fingers jogged around her scalp, 'what type of work is it you say you're doing for Boniface?'

'I told you I help him run his office.'

'What type of business exactly is it that . . . that you help him out with?'

'With contracts and investments.'

'Contracts and investments? What type of contracts and with whom?'

I fiddled with the remote control and laughed without looking at her.

'Mummy, why are you asking all these funny questions?'

'Kingsley, they're not funny questions. I want to know exactly what it is you do for a living . . . how you get all this money.'

'Mummy, I've told you what I do. And you know Uncle Boniface is very generous. He gives me money from time to time. Just relax and enjoy yourself. Let me spoil you.'

'Kingsley, that's another thing,' she said quietly. 'I don't want the car.'

I felt as if I had noticed a trickling of blood running down my leg right after giving her a hug. My mother saw my face and withdrew her knife.

'I don't really think I need a car right now,' she said. 'You know that at my age, I need exercise and the only exercise I get is by walking about.'

'Mummy, what does that mean?'

She took a deep breath.

'Kings, I don't want the car.'

'But—'

'Whatever work it is you say you're doing for Boniface, I think you should just get a proper job and leave that place. Don't forget you're from a good home. Don't forget where you're coming from. And you promised your daddy before he died that any other job was just temporary. You promised him you would get a Chemical Engineering job.'

That conversation with my father could certainly not count for a deathbed promise.

'All right, I've heard you,' I finally said. 'Come, let's go downstairs and watch TV.'

'No it's OK. I'm a bit tired. I want to rest.'

The sound of my siblings' merry laughter rose from downstairs. At least, some of my efforts were not in vain.

Twenty-two

Dear Shehu,

Thank you SO MUCH for your email. I'm HAPPY to say that I CAN HELP! I'm SO SORRY to hear of the persecution of your relatives, the General's wife and son. It must really be HORRIBLE for you all.

Please let me know how I can be of assistance in HELPING you obtain the funds.

Best,
Edgar Hooverson

PS: You mentioned you were going to give me 20% of the total sum. Does that mean I get $11.6 MILLION (eleven million six hundred thousand dollars)? Please clarify. Thank you.

It was not stem cell research or landing a man on the moon, but packaging a mugu was a science of its own. Whenever I did not handle things properly, my mugus became sceptical and vanished into thin air.

I had to explain the transaction in terms Edgar Hooverson could easily understand. I had to convince him that it was risk free and transparent at the same time. I had to make him feel that I was someone he could trust. I had to make him think that he was special, that Fate had recognised his significance in the universe and had decided to reward him at last. I had to make him see how vulnerable I was. I had to make him know how desperately we needed his help, how grateful we would be for any action he took on our behalf. I had to finetune him into believing that every word of my story was true. And then, of course, I had to emphasise my access to a lot of funds which I would gladly share with him as soon as our temporary predicament was resolved.

DEAR FRIEND,

THANK YOU VERY MUCH FOR YOUR RESPONSE TO MY DEAR SISTER'S EMAIL. YES, MR HOOVERSON. IF YOU HELP US WITH THIS TRANSACTION, WE WILL GIVE YOU 20% WHICH COMES TO $11.6 MILLION (ELEVEN MILLION SIX HUNDRED THOUSAND DOLLARS). I HOPE THIS AMOUNT IS SATISFACTORY.

MR HOOVERSON, FROM NOW ON, BOTH OF US MUST WORK AS A VERY CLOSE TEAM. I HEREBY SUGGEST THAT WE CHOOSE A CODE WHICH SHALL PRECEDE EVERY ONE OF OUR CORRESPONDENCES. ALUTA CONTINUA, IS MY SUGGESTION, UNLESS OF COURSE YOU HAVE ANOTHER PREFERENCE.

THIS IS MY CODE NAME OF CHOICE OWING TO THE FACT THAT MY FAMILY IS CURRENTLY ENGAGED IN A STRUGGLE AGAINST INJUSTICE. BUT WE SHALL CONTINUE FIGHTING, FOR TRUTH MUST ALWAYS PREVAIL IN THE END. AS THE LATE UTHMAN DAN FODIO, ONE OF OUR GREAT LEADERS, SAID, 'CONSCIENCE IS AN OPEN WOUND; ONLY TRUTH CAN HEAL IT.' THIS CODE NAME MUST BE CONTAINED IN ALL OUR CORRESPONDENCES AND PHONE CONVERSATIONS. THE ESSENCE OF THIS MAY NOT BE IMMEDIATELY EVIDENT TO YOU, BUT MY DEAR FRIEND, UNFORTUNATELY, THERE IS A LOT OF CORRUPTION IN NIGERIA AND PEOPLE GET UP TO ALL SORTS OF DEVIOUS THINGS.

YOU MUST UNDERSTAND THAT IT IS OWING TO FRUSTRATIONS AND BETRAYALS FROM PEOPLE VERY CLOSE TO MY FAMILY THAT WE ARE THROWING CAUTION TO THE WIND AND TRUSTING YOU DESPITE THE FACT THAT WE HAVE NEVER MET. BUT

AS THE SAYING GOES, SOMETIMES, STRANGERS ARE EVEN TRUER THAN FRIENDS. AFTER ALL, THE GOOD SAMARITAN WAS A STRANGER TO THE MAN HE HELPED. I WILL BE MOST OBLIGED IF BOTH OF US HAVE TRUST AND CONFIDENTIALITY AT THE BOTTOM OF OUR HEARTS.

MY SISTER DEPOSITED THE SUM OF US$58,000,000.00 WITH A SECURITY COMPANY IN EUROPE. THE GOVERNMENT OF MY COUNTRY IS UNAWARE OF THE WHEREABOUTS OF THIS MONEY, IF NOT THEY WOULD HAVE CONFISCATED IT ALONG WITH THE REST. HENCE, THE REASON WHY CONFIDENTIALITY IS NECESSARY IN ENSURING A SMOOTH COMPLETION OF THIS DEAL.

FURTHERMORE, I SEEK YOUR ASSISTANCE TO TRAVEL DOWN TO EUROPE AND ACT AS THE BENEFICIARY OF THE MONEY, SECURE THE MONEY IN CASH, AND THEREAFTER, OPEN AN ACCOUNT IN EUROPE TO LODGE THE FUNDS IN AND SUBSEQUENTLY TRANSFER IN BITS TO YOUR VALID ACCOUNT IN YOUR COUNTRY OF ABODE.

HOW DO WE PLAN TO ACHIEVE THIS? MY PERFECT MODALITIES TO ENSURE A RISK AND HITCH FREE COMPLETION OF THIS DEAL ARE AS FOLLOWS:

1. I WILL SEND TO YOU AN AGREEMENT WHICH MUST BE RETURNED VIA EMAIL/FAX, INDICATING THAT AFTER YOU MUST HAVE SECURED THE FUNDS IN EUROPE, IT WILL BE SAFE IN YOUR CUSTODY AND SOME USED FOR FURTHER INVESTMENT.

2. AFTER I RECEIVE THE AGREEMENT FROM YOU, I WILL THEN INSTRUCT MY SISTER'S LAWYER TO DRAFT A POWER OF ATTORNEY, CHANGING THE BENEFICIARY'S NAME TO YOUR NAME/COMPANY, AND I WILL SEND YOU A COPY WHICH YOU WILL

SIGN AND SEND BACK TO ME. I WILL IN TURN SEND IT TO THE SECURITY COMPANY IN AMSTERDAM, NOTIFYING THEM OF THE CHANGE OF BENEFICIARY FROM ME TO YOU.

3. THE SECURITY COMPANY IN EUROPE WILL NOW TAKE CARE OF ALL THE PAPERWORK DOWN THERE AND IN DUE COURSE, YOU CAN BOOK AN APPOINTMENT WITH THEM WHENEVER YOU ARE READY TO TRAVEL TO EUROPE. I WILL ALSO BE IN ATTENDANCE AT THIS MEETING, SO THAT I CAN HAVE IMMEDIATE ACCESS TO SOME OF THE FUNDS.

4. WE HAVE AGREED TO GIVE YOU 20% OF THE TOTAL MONEY AS YOUR COMMISSION FOR YOUR ASSISTANCE AND COOPERATION.

5. YOU ARE ALSO REQUIRED TO SEND ME YOUR COMPLETE NAME AND ADDRESS WHICH I WILL USE TO REFER YOU TO THE SECURITY COMPANY IN EUROPE, AND ALSO A PHOTOCOPY OF YOUR INTERNATIONAL PASSPORT OR DRIVERS LICENSE TO ENABLE US TO KNOW YOU, THE PERSON WE ARE DEALING WITH.

I AWAIT YOUR URGENT RESPONSE. AS YOU MUST BE AWARE, TIME IS OF EQUAL IMPORTANCE AS CONFIDENTIALITY IN THIS TRANSACTION.

PLEASE FEEL FREE TO CONTACT ME AT ANY TIME TO ASK QUESTIONS.

REGARDS,
SHEHU MUSA ABACHA
ALUTA CONTINUA!

Mr Hooverson would probably need a little bit more time to chew and swallow – or spit. This was the crucial point. Many keen mugus swiftly lost interest as soon as they learned about their expected role in the whole affair. Did they really expect to receive so much money without doing anything substantial? Thankfully, there were the few who made all the efforts worth it, the true believers who swallowed hook, line and swindler.

I strolled across to give Wizard the list of names I had copied out while watching television last night. He was our cyberspace harvester. Using software that could crawl through hundreds of servers, he fetched thousands of email addresses in one go. I encouraged him to always be on the lookout – in movies, newspapers, magazines – for rarer names. At some point or another, the average John or Peter or Smith had probably been blasted by a great number of 419ers, which is why all we were likely to receive for our effort was hate mail filled with four-letter words and clear directions to hellfire – one mugu had even assured me that I would share a stall in hell with Jack the Ripper. But a Wigglesworth or an Albright or a Letterman would most likely be receiving their first ever email blast of all time.

'Kings, please come and tell me what you think,' Ogbonna called out from his desk.

I went and studied the letter on his screen.

DEAR FRIEND IN CHRIST,

CALVARY GREETINGS IN THE NAME OF OUR LORD.

I AM FORMER MRS MARIAM ABACHA AND NOW MRS MARY ABACHA A WIDOW TO LATE GENERAL ABACHA. I AM NOW A CHRISTIAN CONVERT. I INHERITED ALL MY HUSBAND'S WELTH WHICH I INTEND TO SHARE OUT PART OF IT AS MY CONTRIBUTION TO EVANGELISATION OF THE WORLD BECAUSE I KNOW NOW THAT WELTH WITHOUT CHRIST IS VANITY UPON VANITY.

YOUR CHURCH WAS SELECTED TOGETHER WITH OTHER—

The grammatical errors stood up from the page and punched me right in the middle of my face.

'Please, move,' I said.

Ogbonna shifted away, allowing me space to take over his keyboard. Unlike Azuka and Buchi, he had never made it to university. The level of language in our emails did not matter, though. It was probably just the purist in me. Apparently, mugus were never really surprised to see an African emitting dented English.

When I finished with the corrections and returned to my desk, Mr Hooverson's reply was waiting. Perhaps it would simply be a 'Get lost, you orangutan! What a load of balderdash!' Well, life would simply go on to the next mugu. A new one was born every minute. With heart pounding against my teeth, I opened the email.

Dear Shehu,

ALUTA CONTINUA!

My heart REALLY goes out to you people. I'm not going to pretend that I know what you're going through, though, but it's at times like this that I'm THANKFUL for the USA being such a free country where JUSTICE and the RULE OF LAW prevail. Like I said before, I'm WILLING to do whatever it takes to HELP.

You could not have made a BETTER CHOICE. I am a business EXPERT and can give you some PROPER ADVICE on how to invest your money. Along with copies of my passport and driving license, in my next email, I'll also send an attachment with some IDEAS I've come up with for INVESTING your money right here in the USA. I have INSIDE INFORMATION about a few business deals that should interest you especially if you have your eyes on REAL ESTATE. Let me know what you think after reading the document.

I do some business traveling, but I don't get to go to Europe very often. I am a part owner of LUMMOX UTILITIES and our offices are in Mississippi. It shouldn't be a problem for me to take some time off and do a SPECIAL TRIP to Europe on your behalf.

Don't forget to have a look at my business ideas and LET ME KNOW what you think.

Best,
Edgar

Each word was as pleasant as the clinking of dishes on a tray. A fresh rush of that good old thrill coursed through my veins. No one could accuse me of being dishonest when I addressed Edgar Hooverson as 'my dear friend' in my next email.

MY DEAR FRIEND EDGAR,

YOU SOUND LIKE A VERY TRUSTWORTHY FELLOW AND I'M HAPPY THAT I MADE THE RIGHT CHOICE. HOWEVER, I WANT YOU TO FURTHER ASSURE ME THAT YOU WILL NOT DEPRIVE ME OF MY SHARE OF THE FUNDS WHEN THE MONEY GETS INTO YOUR ACCOUNT. ON THAT NOTE, I HAVE ATTACHED AN AGREEMENT FORM. A SOUND BUSINESSMAN SUCH AS YOURSELF MUST KNOW THE UTMOST IM-PORTANCE OF CONTRACTS, EVEN IN BUSINESS DEALINGS BETWEEN TWO CLOSE FRIENDS.

AS SOON AS I RECEIVE THE AGREEMENT, I SHALL IMMEDIATELY INSTRUCT MY ATTORNEY TO PERFECT THE CHANGE OF BENEFICIARY, AND WITHIN 4 WORKING DAYS, YOU SHALL BE CONTACTED BY THE SECURITY COMPANY FOR COLLECTION OF THE CONSIGNMENT IN AMSTERDAM.

THANKS ALSO FOR THE BUSINESS PROPOSALS. I WILL GO THROUGH THEM AS SOON AS POSSIBLE AND LET YOU KNOW WHAT I THINK.

PLEASE CALL ME ON MY CONFIDENTIAL CELLULAR

178

PHONE FOR A BRIEF DISCUSSION (090 893456). I
DON'T HAVE ENOUGH CALL TIME TO CALL YOU.

GOD BLESS AMERICA! GOD BLESS ALL OF US!

I AWAIT YOUR IMMEDIATE RESPONSE.

REGARDS,
SHEHU MUSA ABACHA
ALUTA CONTINUA!

I was finetuning the email for the billionth time, when my intercom bleeped.

'Kings, Cash Daddy wants to see you,' Protocol Officer said.
'Now.'

I clicked Send before I went.

Cash Daddy had recently taken an excessive interest in newspapers.
He had a vendor deliver ten different dailies every morning, which
he perused page by page. He ran a commentary on and generated
fresh topics from the headlines. He asked me to read lengthy
opinion-editorials and give him a verbal summary of whatever the
writers had said. Unlike my father, instead of throwing tantrums
when he read something outrageous, he nodded his head and saw a
new perspective on life.

'Well,' he once said after reading about a reform-minded gubernatorial aspirant who had been assassinated in Ekiti State, 'at
least it will always be remembered that he died for the cause of
democracy.'

Now, his eyes remained transfixed on whatever he was reading
on the front page while I sat beside Protocol Officer and waited. At
last, Cash Daddy snapped up his head.

'Government,' he said. 'That's where the real money is. Do you
know how much money Nigeria makes from oil? Billions and
billions of dollars. And it belongs to all of us. There's no reason
why people like me should not be able to taste some of it. After all,
we're all Nigerians.'

He tossed the newspaper on top of the thick, black Bible that was open to the book of Ecclesiastes on his desk. I glimpsed the bold front-page headline of the story he had been engrossed in.

SCOTLAND YARD ARRESTS NIGERIAN STATE GOVERNOR IN LONDON WITH £2 MILLION CASH

'Kings, you're no longer a little bird,' Cash Daddy continued. 'It's time for you to fly out of the nest. I'm having an important meeting with a mugu next month. Ask Dibia to start sorting out the documents for your UK visa. You're travelling to London with me.'

My heart jumped twice and somersaulted thrice. My intestines started tying themselves up into tight knots. I had always wondered what England, the celebrated land of my father's traveller's tales, was like. But for the first time ever, I was going to be face-to-face with one of our mugus.

'Why is your face like that?' Cash Daddy asked.

I must have looked as if I wanted to run up a tree and hide, then uproot the tree and pull it up after me.

'Kings, there's nothing to be afraid of. What can a white man do to you? *Oyibo* people are harmless. It's not today I started dealing with them. There's no reason why you should be afraid.'

Yes, I had reason to be afraid. The Columbine murderers and the Unabomber and Dr Harold Shipman. I forced my face to look less terrorised.

'Where are those documents?' Cash Daddy asked.

Protocol Officer whipped out a sheaf from a folder in front of him. This one must be big. Cash Daddy had boys working for him in Amsterdam, Houston, London. As a godfather, he hardly ever got directly involved in a job unless the dollar prospects were colossal – large enough to require a foreign bank account. He was the only one who knew the details and locations of these foreign accounts, the only one who dealt directly with the bankers.

'Kings, read them,' Cash Daddy said.

I started with the business proposal on top of the pile. The left corner of my mouth twitched slightly.

'What is it?' he asked.

'No . . . nothing.'

'Why were you laughing?'

'I wasn't—'

Protocol Officer chuckled. That gave me the confidence to tell the truth.

'Is that his real name?' I asked.

'No, no, no, no,' Cash Daddy reprimanded in a soft, serious voice. 'You people shouldn't laugh at him. Do you know that this is the man whose money is going to feed your children and your children's children and your children's children's children?'

On that note alone, the mugu could be forgiven. After all, his money was all that really counted. But what on earth had the man's ancestors been thinking when they took a name like Winterbottom upon themselves?

Twenty-three

Satellite TV bought me my freedom from the national prison sentence of having nothing else to watch at 9 p.m. every day, when all the local TV stations in the land switched to Lagos for the Network News. Occasionally, however, it made sense to touch base with home, irrespective of how doctored the local news might be. I reached for the remote control and flicked from BBC to NTA.

A disgruntled Senator from the thirty-third largest political party had decamped to form a brand new party of his own. Another billionaire had declared his intentions to join the presidential race. Exactly as I and my mother had warned Eugene, the Wild, Wild Western Nigeria was a-boiling. Apart from the usual riots and disruption of the voters' registration process, this morning, yet another House of Assembly aspirant in Oyo State had been assassinated. This recent killing brought the total number of politically motivated assassinations in the country to twenty three. Within this election period alone.

Different public awareness campaigns had been encouraging people to turn out for the voters' registration process. The posters, the announcements on radio and television, insisted that it was a civic responsibility and the only opportunity to make a change. Apparently, the public were responding well. A reporter had turned up at one of the voters' registration centres in Enugu and was interviewing the masses.

'How long have you been waiting here?' she asked.

In the background, a multitude was buzzing around.

'I've been here since 6 a.m.,' the man replied.

'That means you've been waiting for about ten hours.'

'It's my civic responsibility,' he replied proudly. The haggard man had my father's Nigeria-is-a-land-flowing-with-bottled-milk-and-jarred-honey tone of voice. 'This current regime has done nothing for us and it's time for change. I'm ready to pay any price to vote.'

Pity that such a well-spoken man had been taken in by all that hogwash. The only power to change anything that needed changing was the power of cash.

My cellular rang. I reached across the vast mattress and grabbed it from the edge of my sixth pillow. Real feathers. John Lewis, House of Fraser.

'Where are you?' Cash Daddy bellowed.

'I'm at home.'

'I'm just coming from the golf club,' he said. 'You know it's not everybody who wants to join that they allow. I'm going to see one girl . . . that beautiful girl from Liberia who's been begging to have a baby for me. Today's her birthday.'

He paused. I knew he could not have finished.

'Honestly, I won't mind allowing her to have a baby for me, but Liberia's too far. You know how these women behave. One day she'll just wake up and tell me she's taking my child back with her to Liberia and I don't want that type of rubbish. You know they all have one kind of funny accent. I won't spend long at the birthday. I just want to show my face and dash her some small pocket money. From there, I'll go straight home. Come and see me.'

At Cash Daddy's mansion, the gateman threw open the gates before I honked the horn. I parked my Grand Cherokee Jeep beside Cash Daddy's latest Acura. I strode inside and headed for the stairs. The four young men seated at the dining table greeted me fervently. I mumbled a reply and marched up, taking the stairs three at a time.

In Cash Daddy's bedroom, I glanced around. Then I pushed the door of the bathroom. He was scrubbing himself in the shower.

'Kings, Kings! How are you?'

'I'm fine, tha—'

'Have you heard from Dibia about the documents for your UK visa?'

'Yes. He said they'll be ready soon.'

'Very good, very good.' He looked me over from top to toe and

183

wagged his finger at me. 'Make sure you buy some proper clothes before we go. You can't follow me around looking like this.'

Cash Daddy paused to scrub under his arms while I surveyed my shirt – new, but obviously not good enough. Well, truth be told, despite my Swatch and my Lexus, I had not yet completely relaxed into the habit of lavishing things like clothes on myself. Some of Wizard and Ogbonna's shirts could have funded my siblings' tuition for two whole semesters.

'As soon as we come back,' Cash Daddy continued, 'tell him to start working on documents for your US visa. Those ones might take a little longer. You know the Americans are much more difficult.'

I nodded. I had heard that the American was the one embassy where no officials agreed to have their palms greased in exchange for visas or for keeping closed eyes about spurious documents. Even booking an interview date with either of their embassies, in Abuja or Lagos, could take several months. But Dibia's skill was truly a gift from God. It had never failed.

'Honestly, America's the place,' Cash Daddy said. 'Not just that the people are very generous, you can't even say you've ever been abroad until you've been to America. *Kai*!'

He stopped scrubbing and jerked his head as if trying to contain the weight of the memories that had just come upon him.

'Is it the houses . . . is it the food . . . is it the roads . . . is it the women . . . ? You'll see all types of women with all types of complexions; you won't even know which one to choose. In America, you'll understand why it's good to have money, because you'll keep seeing things to spend it on.'

He stepped out of the shower and yanked a large towel to start drying his body. Once again, I wondered how the scrawny urchin who had lived with my family all those years ago, had metamorphosed into this fleshy edifice. Cash Daddy's cheeks were puffy, his neck was chunky, his five limbs were thick and long. I half expected his bloated belly to wriggle free of his body and start break-dancing on the tiled floor in front of us. It seemed to have a life of its own. He dropped the used towel on the floor and grabbed one of the many toothbrushes in a glass mug on the washbasin.

'Come and put some toothpaste for me,' he said.

I reached out for the tube of Colgate. Despite my extreme carefulness, his belly still brushed against my hand. He held out his toothbrush while I squeezed the white paste. When I had finished my task, I withdrew to a less discomforting distance.

'By the way,' he continued, in a more subdued and official tone. 'I have an emergency meeting with the police commissioner tomorrow and I want you to be there.'

'Do we have any problems?' I had never accompanied him to see the commissioner before.

Cash Daddy grated his throat twice and spat.

'One should remove the hand of the monkey from the soup before it becomes a human hand. The main reason for the meeting is for us to make sure that there's no problem. He didn't tell me much, but it looks like there are some places where we've made one or two mistakes and he wants us to take it easy.'

His cellular phone rang. I rushed to pick it up from the bathroom mat and held it out to him. Cash Daddy glanced at the screen and made a quick sign of the cross like a priest being pursued by the devil. I knew immediately that it was his wife calling. Something to do with the children. Conversing with his wife was one of those uncommon occurrences when Cash Daddy did more listening than talking.

When he finished, he chuckled, and asked if I had seen the latest photographs of his children. I had not.

'Ah. I just got them. Come let me show you.'

He led the way out of the bathroom, stopping briefly at the door to scratch the inside of his thigh. He opened his bedside drawer and extracted some photographs. He handed them to me with the sort of smile that you have when presenting a beloved friend with a priceless surprise gift. I tried to appear commensurately keen.

In the first one, the five cherubs and their mother were all dressed up – the two girls in long, flowing frocks, the three boys in black dinner jackets and red bow ties, their mother in a clingy, sparkly red dress that made her look like a tall goldfish. He explained that they had all attended some ceremony in the eldest child's school. This eldest son was enrolled in an exclusive boarding school in Oxford.

'He even won an award,' Cash Daddy beamed proudly. 'Anyway, I'm not surprised. Whatever the python gives birth to must eventually be long. I know that boy is going to be great in this world. Greater than me even.'

The children all looked like distant cousins of Princes William and Harry. Graceful and illustrious. There was not the slightest trace of that untamed look on their faces, the look that neither diverse currencies nor worldly comforts had quite erased from their father's countenance. I tried to imagine the distinguished accents that would come forth when they spoke.

Interesting – these offspring of Uncle Boniface, the money-miss-road, were the aristocrats of tomorrow.

Cash Daddy's voice smashed into my musings.

'I've told you to hurry up and get married,' he said. 'I don't know what you're waiting for. The advice I always give young men is: once you start making money, after buying your first set of cars, your next investment should be a wife. You should have been married long ago.'

He was right. I should have been married a long time ago. I should also have been working in Shell or Mobil or Schlumberger and coming home to Ola every night. Unfortunately, that was life.

He inspected his physique in the full-length mirror. While he squeezed into a pair of Versace jeans and a silk Yves Saint Laurent shirt, he talked about business and some new ideas.

'I'm also thinking of employing some more of these young boys who know more about the internet. The only person we have is Wizard. He's good, but the boy is a thief. He can even steal from inside a woman's womb without anybody noticing. And two things I can't stand are people who steal and people who are disloyal.'

He turned away from the mirror and looked at me.

'What of your brother?' he asked.

I blinked.

'I mean Godfrey,' he clarified.

'Never.'

'But he appears quite sma—'

'Never.'

He must have understood that the matter was very closed. He stopped talking and looked back at his image in the mirror.

My phone rang. It was my father's third sister's son.

'Ebuka, please call me back later. I'm in a meeting.'

'Kings, go on and take your call,' Cash Daddy said.

'No, it's OK, I can—'

'Take your call.'

Ebuka needed some money to buy his GCE forms.

'But I sent you money to buy forms a short while ago,' I said.

'Brother Kings, that one was different. That one was for my SSCE. I've already bought the form and filled it. If you want, I can bring the receipt for you to see.'

'OK, come and see me in the house tomorrow evening and collect some money.'

There was no need giving him my address. All my relatives from far and near now knew where I lived. There seemed to be a benevolent fairy whose job it was to pass on my contact details to any two-winged insect that flew past.

'Brother, thank you very much,' he said.

Cash Daddy was brushing his eyebrows and flashing his teeth in front of the mirror. His grooming was always lengthy before he got satisfied.

'Kings,' he said suddenly, 'has it occurred to you that I'm now too big to be chasing dollars around? Come.'

He held me by the upper arm and escorted me to the window. He walked very close, almost leaning his chest against my shoulder. For a while, we stood and stared out of the glass panes without speaking. The window overlooked his front gate.

Almost all the buildings on Iweka and on farther streets were in total darkness. NEPA had struck. In the distance, I made out the bright lights of World Bank's humongous house. Like Cash Daddy, he had a power generator. After a while, I peeped at my uncle. He had a faraway gaze on his face, like an emperor wondering by how much more he should reduce his subjects' taxes.

'Kings,' he said suddenly, 'do you sometimes feel as if God is talking to you?'

I gave it some thought.

'No.'

He turned away from the window and looked at me.

'Kings, don't you read your Bible?' He did not wait for a reply. 'You should read your Bible often and memorise passages,' he said, shaking his head slowly and wagging his finger at me. 'It's very, very important.'

Sermon over, he returned his eyes to the window and took in a deep breath.

'Kings,' he exhaled, 'each time I stand and look out through this window, I feel as if God is talking to me. It's as if I can hear Him saying that He's given me the land as far as my eyes can see, just like He said to Papa Abraham.'

He paused and looked at me.

'Kings, I've decided to run for governor of Abia State in the coming elections.'

The fact that I did not drop to the floor with shock was simply supernatural.

Twenty-four

My regular visits to Umuahia came with mixed feelings. A blend of nostalgia about the good old days – the times spent there as a child – and anger about the hard times – our poverty and my father's illness and premature death. These days, a new feeling had been stirred into the concoction – apprehension about facing my mother.

Heads turned as my Lexus sped through the streets. Eyes followed in wonder and admiration. Without braking, I honked at some pedestrians occupying the better part of a pothole-riddled road. The three men jumped away in fright. My windows were up and the air-conditioning was on full blast, so I could barely make out their invectives.

I noticed that the scallywags had now gone beyond traffic signs and dustbins. There were election posters on the face and torso of the bronze statue in the Michael Opara Square. To think that Cash Daddy's face would soon be joining them. He had not yet made his gubernatorial aspirations publicly known, so none of his posters were out. If not for the potbellied, important-looking strangers with whom he had been holding endless meetings at the office, I would have assumed he had changed his mind.

I parked beside Mr Nwude's blue Volkswagen. The back wind-screen of the faithful car was completely gone and had been replaced by a cellophane sheet. I made a mental note to greet his family before I left. As usual, I would pretend it was a gift for the children and give them some cash.

As soon as I switched off my engine, Charity screamed. Nano-seconds later, she dashed out of the house.

'Kings, I didn't know you were coming today!'

We hugged.

'How's school?'

'We're closing soon,' she said with excitement. 'Kings, I'm coming to spend my holidays with you. I've already told Mummy and she said it's OK.'

My siblings could go in and out of my house anytime they pleased without giving me notice. I had reminded them several times.

'But that means Mummy will be at home alone,' she said with concern. 'Eugene is not likely to come back till after Easter.'

'Don't worry. We can both drive down to visit her often. What of your JAMB forms? Have you bought them?'

'Since last week.'

'OK, we'll fill them together before I leave.'

I gave Charity the McVities biscuits and the pair of high heels I'd bought for her. She accompanied me to my mother's bedroom.

'Mummy, Kings is here,' she chimed.

As I was about to open the door, Charity held back my hand.

'Kings,' she whispered with tilted head and pleading eyes, 'can I use your phone? Please?'

Two of Charity's friends had land phones in their houses. Each time I was around, she wanted to ring them with my cellular, never mind that she saw them in school almost every day. I handed her the phone and she scampered back to the living room, gleeful as a fly.

My mother was lying in bed – staring – with her upper body propped up on two pillows. For a widow whose first son had come to visit, her smile appeared some seconds too late.

'Mummy.'

'Kings.'

I sat beside her and entered her embrace. Even that was not as cosy as it should have been. Her face appeared more furrowed than on my last visit. She was wearing one of her old dresses stained with the sticky fluid from my father's unripe plantains. Maybe it was her age, maybe it was her grief, but the hair on my mother's head was taking its time in growing back. And I could see her scalp clearly through the grey strands. Unlike the former, the new growth was scanty.

'Mummy, how have you been getting on?'

'I'm fine.'

With cheeks pressed against her face, I scanned the room with my eyes. Everything was exactly as it had been when my father was alive. His jumper was still hooked to the wardrobe door. His bathroom slippers were arranged neatly at the foot of the bed, as if he were about to step right into them. A half-empty bottle of Old Spice aftershave lotion was sitting beside a half-empty Vaseline hair cream jar on his side of the dresser. In a corner of the room, I sighted the machines I had recently purchased for my mother's shop. The large, brown cartons were sealed and unopened. I pulled myself away from her and walked towards them. My suspicions were confirmed.

'Mummy,' I asked wearily, 'what about these machines? Haven't you started using them yet?'

My mother bent her eyes to the floor. She was composing another lie.

When I replaced the television in the house, came back to visit, and saw the old one back in its place, my mother had said it was because she could not figure out how the new one worked. When I mentioned repainting and refurbishing the flat, she had said she preferred if it remained the exact way it was when my father was alive, never mind that I had promised not to tamper with his favourite armchair. When I bought a generator to supply electricity when NEPA took the light, she had said it made too much noise. I hated seeing her put herself through all this just to make a point. Now I watched her struggle to make up another excuse.

She raised her eyes.

'Kingsley, the only thing that can make me happy is if you get a proper job. You know I'm very uncomfortable with whatever work it is you say you're doing for Boniface.'

'Mummy, I'm working and I'm doing this for all of you.'

'Kings, if you really want to make me happy, you'll stop it.'

She said the 'it' with force. My mother was a person who could provide a euphemism for every embarrassing word that existed. Her cache included at least fifty different replacements for sex and for the various private body parts. She had more for single mothers and divorcees. But when it came to 419, this ability had completely failed her. She never had a name for exactly what it was that she wanted me to stop.

I was tempted to change the topic by telling her that her brother was planning to be the next governor of Abia State, but that would simply be kindling another inferno. On behalf of her absent husband, my mother would probably explode with outrage. It was better to just go straight to the point of my visit.

'Mummy, I came to let you know that I'm travelling abroad next week. I'm going to London for a meeting.'

'Is it with Boniface you're going?'

'Yes.'

She sighed.

'How long are you going for?'

'About a week.'

'So how do we contact you if there's something urgent?'

I told her that I would ring Aunty Dimma to check in. My mother had also refused a land phone.

'Kings, whatever it is you people are doing, please be very careful. Be very, very careful.'

Aha! We were making progress. If she wanted me to be careful, that meant she accepted I was in the speed lane. It was only a matter of time before she completely came around.

'Of course, Mummy,' I said.

She sighed the world's deepest sigh.

Twenty-five

It was my first trip on a plane. I waited for Cash Daddy to settle down into his first class seat and left him with Protocol Officer. Then I walked towards the back to find my own place.

'Don't worry,' Cash Daddy said as I left. 'Very soon, you'll be able to join other big boys and fly in style.'

Had I not already seen what first class looked like, I might have thought nothing of it. But when I swept the separating curtain aside, I was startled. The people in economy were packed tight together, like a set of false teeth. After much probing, I found my seat in between two men and settled down to enjoy this new experience. But one of my neighbours refused me the enjoyment. Every few minutes, he would release a silent dose of effluvium, powerful enough to disperse a civil rights protest march. It became worse after the elegant, blond air hostess served minor portions of rice with a suspicious-looking green sauce that tasted like nothing I had ever eaten before. Bland, raw, and chalky. Could this really be the sort of Western diet that my father preferred over African food?

At Heathrow Airport, the immigration queue did not recognise first class or economy so, once again, I was reunited with Cash Daddy and Protocol Officer. The stern immigration officers were scrutinising passports, interrogating coldly, and whispering amongst themselves. Some from our queue were asked to stand aside and wait while an immigration officer took their passports and disappeared. I wondered what they had done wrong. I had heard all sorts of gory stories about desperate immigrants who had their hopes demolished right here at Heathrow – escorted onto the next plane back to Nigeria without even as much as a glimpse of the greener pastures beyond the airport. What if the same thing happened to us? What if they suspected that we were 419ers? I shuddered.

Finally, it was our turn. Protocol Officer quickly stepped forward and handed over Cash Daddy's passport.

'How long do you plan to stay in the United Kingdom?' the officer asked. His teeth were brown and misaligned.

'Two weeks,' Protocol Officer replied on Cash Daddy's behalf. 'He's here on holiday.'

The immigration officer stared back into Cash Daddy's passport. Then he stared directly into Cash Daddy's face. Cash Daddy glared back. The man shrank and took his stare away. He looked back at the passport and flipped the pages. He cleared his throat, brought out a pair of glasses from his shirt pocket, and looked through his glasses and over them. He cleared his throat again and looked over his glasses again, then through them once more.

He opened his mouth to ask another question.

Cash Daddy stared right into his face.

The man withered.

'Welcome to the United Kingdom,' he said.

Cash Daddy ignored him and strode past. The man spent some extra time staring at Protocol Officer's passport and asking questions. Many of Protocol Officer's answers missed the truth by about five kilometres. For some reason, the officer did not think I deserved too much scrutiny. He welcomed me without much ado.

'Nonsense,' Cash Daddy said, when I caught up with him. 'Witches and wizards fly in and out of any country they want to without going through immigration. Why should I be harassed?'

The important thing was that we had made it through.

'Anyway, by the time I become governor,' he continued, 'I'll have a diplomatic passport so nobody will be able to talk to me anyhow.'

I knew that we were in the white man's land. Still, I felt a slight shock at seeing so many white people walking about in one place at the same time. It was extremely rare to see a white person on the streets of the average, small Nigerian town. So rare, in fact, that sometimes in Umuahia, people would stop and stare at a white person, some chanting 'Oyibo', hoping that the white person would turn and wave.

When I was in primary four, there was a German girl in my class whose father was an engineer with the Golden Guinea Breweries. Several children spent their spare time surreptitiously running their fingers through her hair just to taste the straight, blond strands. Being the cleverest pupil, I was assigned by my teacher the prized sitting position right next to her. Standing up to answer a difficult question one day, I pressed the heel of my shoe against her toes. I just wanted to hear what it sounded like when she screamed.

The driver of the hired limousine also had brown and misaligned teeth. And so did the hotel concierge. My father had not mentioned any such anomaly in his traveller's tales. How could English people have such bad teeth? Or perhaps these were just immigrants, and not real English people.

After settling into our different rooms, we converged in Cash Daddy's suite for a final briefing. I and Protocol Officer stood by the bathroom door while Cash Daddy addressed us from the bathtub.

'Like I told you people, this one is not the type of job that you chop and clean your mouth and shit and it ends there.'

He shot one leg out of the soapy water and draped it over the tub.

'We have to package this mugu very well so that we can keep chopping him for a very long time. Once things start off well, Kings can just be talking and meeting with him regularly. That's all.'

Sometime ago, Cash Daddy had instructed Protocol Officer to send letters to foreign businessmen who might be interested in investing in Nigeria. Protocol Officer wrote that, as the CEO of Ozu High Seas Construction Company, he had a strong government contact who could guarantee access to juicy contracts. All he needed was a foreign partner with a muscular bank account to act as guarantor. Mr Winterbottom had responded. He was the director of Hector Bank International and the CEO of Changeling Development Cooperation, Argentina. Because he had partnered extensively with South African businessmen, Mr Winterbottom was willing to peep into Nigeria. He and Protocol Officer had had several discussions over the phone before agreeing on this meeting in London. Protocol Officer told him that the current Nigerian minister for aviation was attending an economic summit in London over the next two days. The minister was, he said, his former boss, and Protocol Officer wanted both men to meet. Because of his limited time, the minister had asked them to join him for breakfast at his hotel tomorrow morning.

I nodded calmly as Cash Daddy went through each person's script line by line, also giving instructions about body language and general demeanour.

'Kings,' he said, pointing at me, 'all that big grammar they taught you in school, this is the time to speak all of it.'

But a riot had begun in my endocrine, nervous, and digestive systems. Not only was tomorrow going to be my first, real, live episode with a mugu, I had a few other worries. For example, the real Nigerian minister of aviation was actually attending an economic summit in London. It had been on the news.

'Cash Daddy,' I said, shifting my weight from one foot to the other to conceal some embarrassment I felt at my cowardice, 'what if he sees the real minister on TV?'

Both men laughed as if I had just cracked a splendid joke. Cash Daddy cleared his throat and wriggled the toes of the foot dangling over the tub.

'Let me tell you something,' he said. 'Me, I really like these *oyibo* people. They're very, very nice people. See how they came and showed us that the ground where we've been dancing Atilogwu has crude oil under it. If not for them, we might never have found out. But Kings,' he dragged in his dangling foot and sat up in the tub, 'white man doesn't understand black man's face. Do you know that I can give you my passport to travel with? Even if your nose is ten times bigger than my own, they won't even notice.'

It was my turn to laugh.

Twenty-six

Despite the plush beddings of my five-star hotel room, I had a turbulent night. My slumber was besieged with nightmares about officers from Scotland Yard chasing me in and out of dark alleys. Most of the officers were female. All of them knew my name. One who had a striking resemblance to Margaret Thatcher had just made a wild leap at me, when I woke and saw that it was morning. My heart was throbbing like a drum warning a village against danger. I sat up in bed and pondered.

What was the best way to break the news to Cash Daddy that I had changed my mind? Should I tell him the truth or just lie in bed, pretending that the airplane diet had turned my digestive system upside down?

Slowly, I threw the bed covers aside and went to the bathroom. After a cold shower, I dressed in the Armani suit and Thomas Pink shirt that Wizard had accompanied me to purchase from an Aba 'Big Boys' boutique. It would be idiotic and cowardly for me to back out now. Plus, my uncle would be enraged.

When we stopped by his room, Cash Daddy swept his eyes over every inch of my body.

'Keep it up, keep it up,' he said, nodding.

Walking with Protocol Officer towards the elevator, I could not help but smile. Cash Daddy had actually given me sartorial approval.

The hotel restaurant was quiet, with just a few people sitting at the dainty tables. Sitting alone, sipping from a teacup and darting his eyes about like a pickpocket, our mugu was easy to identify. He waved his hand shyly and eagerly, like a man who had just spotted his thirteen-year-old bride disembarking at the bus station. He stood as we approached. A chubby, well-dressed man with brown hair, Mr Winterbottom had glittering dollar signs stamped all over him, even his smell.

'Good morning, Mr Winterbottom,' Protocol Officer said.

'Hello, Mr Akpiri-Ogologo,' the mugu replied.

We shook hands. Protocol Officer introduced me.

'This is engineer Lomaji Ugorji,' he said. 'He's the liaison officer in charge of our international operations. He's our point man in all foreign transactions.'

'It's my pleasure to meet you,' he said.

I wondered for how long the pleasure was going to last. We sat and ordered tea. There was something about Mr Winterbottom's total comfort in our company that made my fear flee.

After we had exhausted the topic of the London weather and completed a comprehensive analysis of the climates in Argentina and Nigeria – apparently, Argentina was at its winter peak in July, while the sun came all out in December – Mr Winterbottom asked us about the minister's arrival.

'Why don't you give him a call to let him know we're waiting?' I suggested to Protocol Officer.

'Yes, why don't you?' Mr Winterbottom seconded.

The minister had given us an 8 a.m. appointment. It was 9 a.m. and he had still not appeared. Protocol Officer dialled, spoke briefly and snapped the phone shut.

'He said he'll see us in five minutes.'

Mr Winterbottom nodded happily.

Half an hour later, the minister entered. In his flowing, white, embroidered *agbada* and grey cap, Cash Daddy looked like the man who was in charge of formulating key policies for some major oil-producing economies of Africa. He smiled at us and sat at a different table. We abandoned ours and hurried over to him, with Protocol Officer leading the stampede.

'Good morning, Alhaji,' we all said in greeting. I and Protocol Officer genuflected for emphasis.

'Alhaji, this is Mr Winterbottom,' Protocol Officer said. 'Mr Winterbottom, this is Alhaji Mahmud, the Minister of Aviation of the Federal Republic of Nigeria.'

'I don't like that place you were sitting because anybody passing can see me,' Alhaji Mahmud said.

Arriving late, no apologies, it was typical. Ladies and gentlemen, I present to you a bona fide Nigerian top government official.

'And once people know I'm in town,' he continued, 'they start disturbing me for one favour or the other. Government is a heavy burden. Sometimes one needs to rest.'

When we were all seated, Cash Daddy looked at the menu with disdain.

'Rubbish,' he declared.

'Sorry?' Mr Winterbottom queried.

'Rubbish. You white people eat all sorts of rubbish. There's nothing like Nigerian food. Anywhere I am in the world, I look for a Nigerian restaurant where I can go and eat real food. It's just because of you people that I agreed to eat here.'

All three of us apologised.

'It's not everybody that I can make this sort of sacrifice for,' the minister said. 'You know Mr Akpiri-Ogologo here used to work under me in the ministry long ago, before I became Minister of Aviation. He's very close to me.'

Mr Winterbottom looked at Protocol Officer, his eyes shining with a new kind of respect.

'Thank you very much, sir,' Protocol Officer said humbly.

Cash Daddy proceeded to order almost everything on the menu, and shocked me with the genteelness of his feeding process. He took slow, small bites like a well-bred little girl and chewed without enlarging his mouth.

Over breakfast, we chatted about the wind and the waves and about life and times. Throughout, the minister was jolly as a shoe brush. He told anecdotes and cracked jokes and laughed with all his might. The white man consumed several cups of coffee without touching his food. He kept hopping about on his seat and giggling long before the minister's punch lines. Clearly, he had other things on his mind. At the end of the meal, the mugu offered to pay the bill. Nobody tendered a word of argument.

'So let's get on with business, shall we?' Alhaji Mahmud began.

Protocol Officer got on.

'Alhaji, like I was telling you, Mr Winterbottom is very interested in the development of Africa. His company has invested in several projects in South Africa and Uganda.'

He went on to elaborate on Mr Winterbottom's sound qualities, speaking humbly and sparingly like a man who knew that he had limited time to make his case. He had started mentioning the bid for the Akanu Ibiam International Airport project, when Cash Daddy truncated his speech.

'Where did you say you're from again?' Alhaji Mahmud asked. 'Czechoslovakia, was it?'

'I'm Argentinian,' Mr Winterbottom replied. 'My parents were originally English and then they lived in Uganda where I was born. But I moved to Argentina in the seventies.'

'Unbelievable!' exclaimed Alhaji Mahmud. Three diners and four waiters shot glances at our table. 'I'm very excited to hear this! A real international citizen! And you're also one of our African brothers. Unique. We don't only have black Americans, we also have White Africans.'

Mr Winterbottom giggled. We smiled.

'With our young democracy,' the minister continued, 'Nigeria is ripe for huge foreign investors like you right now. And we're trying as much as possible to diversify. Most of the big contracts my department has awarded recently have all been taken by the Germans. I don't want them to start thinking that Nigeria belongs to them. If it took so long to chase out the British, who knows how long it will take with the Germans?'

It sounded like a joke. I and Protocol Officer laughed. Mr Winterbottom did as well, after looking round to make sure that nobody was eavesdropping.

'It's time to open up our country to others,' the Minister continued. 'What better place to start than with a white man who is even our own African brother?'

Cash Daddy slapped Mr Winterbottom on the back. The giggling and smiling resumed. Abruptly, the minister sobered up.

'Mr Winterbotom, let me tell you something. This Akanu Ibiam Airport project is very close to my heart. The Igbos have been advocating for their own international airport for a long time, and

I'm delighted that in my tenure as Minister of Aviation of the Federal Republic of Nigeria, their dream is being fulfilled.' He turned to me and Protocol Officer. 'You're Igbo, aren't you?'

'Yes, Alhaji,' we said.

'Ah.' He shook his head with pity. He kept on shaking his head. 'Mr Winterbottom, do you know what a nigger is?'

The white man recoiled, as if a viper had briefly flicked its tongue out of Cash Daddy's mouth. He shifted his eyes to me and shifted them to Mr Akpiri-Ogologo, then back to the minister again. He seemed unsure as to whether this was a trick question, whether he was supposed to admit knowing what the dirty word meant.

'Do you?' Cash Daddy insisted.

'Oh, it's a term that never finds its way into my vocabulary,' Mr Winterbottom replied.

'But you know what it means?'

'Errrrrrrrrrrrr . . . Yes.'

'The Igbos are the niggers of Nigeria,' Cash Daddy declared, pointing at us. 'They've been maltreated and marginalised.'

He stopped and drew a valiant breath.

'Ignored,' Protocol Officer quietly added.

Cash Daddy glanced quickly at me.

'Forgotten,' I mumbled quietly, too.

'Do you understand that they live in the only geopolitical zone in Nigeria without an international airport?' Alhaji Mahmud continued, still pointing. 'This one is going to be their first.'

'Thank you very much, Alhaji,' we said.

'I'm not Igbo,' Alhaji Mahmud lowered his voice modestly, 'but I feel so honoured to be part of this historical event.'

The white man opened his mouth and swallowed the noble proclamation like a seasoned ignoramus. How could anybody look at Cash Daddy and imagine that his name could ever be anything like Alhaji Mahmud – a name that was more likely to belong to a Hausa person from the northern part of Nigeria? Cash Daddy had the unmistakable thick head and chunky features of the Igbos. Plus, a concrete Igbo accent. It did not matter whether it was a three-letter word or a five-letter word, each came out with its original number of syllables quadrupled, and with so much emphasis on the consonants that it sounded as if he were banging on them with a sledgehammer. The Hausas had more delicate and slender facial features, and the phonetic structure of their mother tongue gave them an accent that sounded almost Western.

Cash Daddy was right! The white people did not know such things.

'I might be a Hausa man,' the minister continued, 'but I have always believed in One Nigeria. That's why I'm so glad that Biafra didn't succeed.'

He went on to narrate details of the Nigerian civil war with tears filling his eyes. How, as a child growing up in Kano, Northern Nigeria, he had watched a Hausa man slit open the belly of a pregnant Igbo woman with a dagger. The woman had lain there in a pool of blood while the baby wriggled about and gasped for air.

'Why?' he asked with tears in his voice. 'After all, we are all one. One flesh, one blood.' He sniffed. 'Why?'

'Oh dear,' said the mugu.

'They are our brothers and sisters. Why must we treat our own people that way?'

I could hardly restrain my admiration for Cash Daddy. His tongue must have been made of silver. If this was a rehearsal for his live performance as politician and future governor, my uncle was sure to win rave reviews. And there was something about his voice. It had a certain irresistible attraction like the smell of fried chicken. He could probably even talk a spider into weaving silk socks for him. The same magic was in his face. Under his gaze, you felt like the most important figure in his life. From Mr Winterbottom's face, I could see that his soul was being thoroughly converted to mugu.

'The time for unity has come,' Cash Daddy proclaimed. 'Allah has given the call. Unity amongst Igbo and Hausa, amongst Hausa and Yoruba, amongst Yoruba and Igbo. One Nigeria! My dear friend, it's at times like this that I understand why America had to fight the Cold War. You understand what I mean?'

I did not. The white man, on the other hand, was several scales ahead of me in the evolutionary process. He understood perfectly.

'I'm with you,' he replied.

Cash Daddy speechified some more. By the time he stood up, ready to leave, even I was convinced that we had been breakfasting with the minister of aviation of the Federal Republic of Nigeria.

'I have a meeting with the British transport secretary later this morning,' Cash Daddy said, 'to finalise discussions on the Nigerian-British Bilateral Air Services agreement. I need to make some phone calls before then. Mr Winterbottom, it's been nice meeting you.'

The minister departed in a whirl of good humour. We were left sitting around the table in silence.

'Quite a remarkable man,' Mr Winterbottom finally said. 'I like him. I like him very much. Very friendly and down-to-earth.'

Mr Akpiri-Ogologo reminded Mr Winterbottom of something.

'Oh yes! I almost forgot.'

Mr Winterbottom leaned under his seat and brought out a carrier bag. It contained the two Rolex watches, one Sony camcorder, and two Nokia handsets Protocol Officer had told him that the chairman of the Contracts Award Committee had specifically requested as part of his bribes. Thanks to Wizard's online search, Protocol Officer knew the exact high-tech models to ask for.

'I hope I got the right ones,' Mr Winterbottom said.

Protocol Officer dug his hands into the carrier bag and inspected each item.

'I won't know for sure until the Chairman sees them,' he replied. It was always wise to make allowance for future requests.

Back upstairs, Cash Daddy flung one of the Rolex watches at me.

'Throw away that toy on your wrist,' he said.

I switched watches immediately. My new Rolex was as fabulous as Aladdin's ring. But instead of throwing the Swatch away, I would pass it down to Godfrey.

That was one thing everybody liked about Cash Daddy. He was not a cheat. Unlike some godfathers who reversed tongues when good things came in, Cash Daddy always made sure that each participant in a job received his fair share.

In his own special way, my uncle was an honest man.

Twenty-seven

Everybody poured outside to look. Ben, the office cleaner, had bought his first car. It was a *tokunbo*, secondhand, Mercedes-Benz V-Boot. Smuggled across the border from Cotonou. He had driven it to work that morning, dashed into every room in the office and invited us out to see, declaring that he was hosting the whole office to free lunch.

'Well done,' Wizard said.

We all stood around, admiring the car and congratulating Ben. But there was no way he could maintain such a car on his cleaner's salary. He had been working in this office for the past three years and the Port Harcourt Refinery mugu was his first ever hit – a very humble one, for that matter. Unless he made another one pretty soon, he might have to exchange his wife and nine children for spare parts and fuel to keep the V-Boot running. But then, who was I to worry about how another grown man had chosen to spend his hard-earned dollars?

'You need to see how everyone in my estate came out to look when I parked the car in front of my house,' he said. 'From now on, they'll all be calling me "Yes sir!"'

We laughed. Everybody except Azuka. He declined the free lunch expedition, and so did I. Finally, both of us were all alone in the Central Intelligence Agency.

'Azuka, are you OK?'

He sighed.

'What's the problem? You've been moody all morning.'

He hissed. The sound was thick with regret.

'Kings, my brother. I don't know what is happening to my life. Ben has already bought a car. Me, I'm still here writing letters and receiving insults from white people. Anything I touch . . . *kpafuka!*'

Actually, Azuka's history was pathetic. He added a more

unfortunate detail each time he narrated it. In his final year of studying Law, he had been rusticated from the University of Calabar for involvement in secret cult activities. He migrated to Spain. Two years later, he got stopped for a driving offence, and was arrested for not having a valid visa on his passport. He was deported to Nigeria after spending months being tortured in a Spanish prison. He resumed work with Cash Daddy and, in the past four years, he had not made a single hit.

'Azuka, listen. This thing is out of your hands. You have no control over whatever mugu comes your way. All you need to do is just pray that whichever one falls into your hands is the right one.'

He snapped his head abruptly.

'Kings, this thing is not about mugu or no mugu. It's not. Just before I started work with Cash Daddy, I managed to hit four hundred dollars from one mugu I met in a chat room. As I was coming out of the Western Union office, the police stopped me and collected all the money from me, as if they were just standing there waiting for me. This happened on two different occasions.'

It did not require any special kind of bad luck to have had such an experience. It was for such reasons that people sought refuge under godfathers like Cash Daddy. Cash Daddy had enough clout to keep the police eyes closed and the Western Union mouths zipped. Such services were incorporated in the sixty per cent he scooped from every dime we made. His percentage also covered the expenses for forged documents, phone bills, internet connection etc. This business of ours was expensive to run. You had to have the financial ammunition to keep the cannon booming.

'That could have happened to anybody,' I replied.

'But there are some people who never have problems. Why do you think Cash Daddy takes you along on big jobs? He knows you have good luck.'

I laughed. Cash Daddy had once told me that I had an honest face. He said it was good for business. Pity that my supposed good luck and honest face had not done much for me in all the oil company interviews I had attended.

'Kings, you're finding it funny but I'm not joking.'

'OK, let me see the replies you received today.'

He shifted to allow me to view his screen. Each email was more vitriolic than the other. Finally, I came across one that was mild.

> Dear Sheik Idris Shamshuden (or whatever your real name is),
>
> Your letter is a classic 419 scam. I can smell these things a mile away.
>
> I love Africa and Africans. Please stop harming your economy by causing any more people to distrust Africans. I know this is a way you can make some quick money, but the long-term effects to the African economy are terrible.
>
> I am not against you. If we met in person, we probably would have a wonderful conversation. I really do hope that you turn from your illegal ways. Please use your obvious talents and creativity for things that will count 1,000 years from now and throughout all eternity.
>
> God bless you,
> Condoleezza

'Please, move,' I said to Azuka.

He allowed me more space to take over his keyboard. I hit reply and typed. This woman was clearly not the greedy type, but she had another human weakness. She was caring.

> DEAR CONDOLEEZZA,
>
> PLEASE FORGIVE ME. YOU MIGHT NEVER KNOW WHAT YOU'VE DONE FOR ME. YOUR EMAIL HAS CHANGED MY LIFE AND FORCED ME TO RECONSIDER MY WAYS. I KNOW I HAVE THE POTENTIALS TO DO THE RIGHT THING IF ONLY I COULD BE GIVEN A CHANCE.
>
> CONDOLEEZZA, PLEASE IS THERE ANY WAY YOU CAN POSSIBLY ASSIST ME TO START SOMETHING USEFUL? I WOULD BE VERY GRATEFUL FOR ANY HELP

YOU CAN GIVE. I LOOK FORWARD TO HEARING FROM YOU. THANK YOU FOR TAKING TIME TO WRITE ME THAT LIFE-CHANGING EMAIL.

GOD BLESS YOU.

YOURS,
DAVID

On second thoughts, I deleted 'David' and wrote Azuka's real first name. After all, there was absolutely nothing irregular about an African begging for foreign aid.

I definitely had the Midas touch. This 419 thing was my calling. Condoleezza sent him $600 the very next day and a letter full of advice on how to turn his life around. Dollars were hard currency, no matter how small.

Azuka was overjoyed.

'Make sure you keep in touch with her,' I advised him.

'But, of course,' he replied, still grinning.

Condoleezza would be delighted to receive updates on how much progress her African mentee was making down the straight and narrow path. If her delight translated into Benjamin Franklins once in a while, none of us would complain.

The chain of good luck seemed to have been unleashed. An Iranian mugu replied to another one of Azuka's emails some days later, and soon Azuka received $10,000 for initialisation fees.

'Kings, maybe it's your good luck that rubbed off on me,' he said.

We were still laughing when my phone rang. It was Charity. Sobbing with all her might.

'Charity, what's the matter?' I asked without much panic.

In between thick sobs, she told me that she had just seen her JAMB score.

'I scored 198.'

Fortunately, she did not hear me gasp. No university in this world was going to give her a place with such a malnourished score. For once, I agreed that my sister had a valid reason for shedding tears.

'Charity, stop crying,' I said. 'You know they have a funny way of marking this JAMB. Even the most intelligent people sometimes make low scores.'

She continued crying until the customers waiting in the business centre grumbled loud enough for me to hear. She hung up, rejoined the queue, and rang back an hour later. Her sobs had not subsided.

'Charity, stop crying. Failing JAMB is not the end of the world.'

'Mummy said I'm not allowed to hang out with my friends again,' she wept. 'I can't imagine staying at home for a whole year, waiting to take another JAMB.'

Could my sister's poor score have had anything to do with the weeks she had spent in my house prior to her exams? Charity had watched quite a lot of Nollywood movies on my VCD player. There was a corner shop at the end of my street which stocked these movies that were released in hundreds every week. Each featured the same yellow-skinned, abundantly chested actresses and the same dreadlocked men, and each had a Part 1, a Part 2, and Part 3 – at least. Too bad that the JAMB exam did not test knowledge of Nollywood.

'Charity, don't let it worry you, OK? Just go home and relax and forget about it. I'll talk to Mummy later.'

But it was hard to forget my sister's sobbing. My mother must be in great distress and my father must be revolving in his grave. The following day, I spoke to Buchi about it. I had once overheard her telling Wizard where he could purchase expo GCE question papers a week before the exam date.

'Is there no one you know?' Buchi asked me.

I had never needed to know someone for things like this.

She gave me the name of one of the faculty deans in her former university.

'He helped one of my friends get into Accounting,' she said. 'He might be able to help.'

But my visit to the professor would have to wait. Mr Winterbottom was coming to town.

Twenty-eight

Abuja was different from other Nigerian cities. There were no hawkers in the streets, no *okadas* buzzing about like flies, no overflowing bins with unclothed schizophrenics scavenging in them for their daily sustenance. None of the roads had potholes and all the traffic lights were working. And unlike in our parts, where a flashy car was the ninth wonder of the world, most of the cars here were sleek, many with tinted windows.

I and the hired driver waited at the entrance to the arrival lounge. Mr Winterbottom soon appeared, sweating like a hog. I strode across and welcomed him with a handshake. The driver rushed out and grabbed the handle of his suitcase.

'It's so terribly hot,' the mugu groaned.

The Nnamdi Azikiwe International Airport was even fully air-conditioned. Fighting for space high up on a prominent side of the arrival lounge wall were massive portraits of the president of the Federal Republic of Nigeria, of the minister of the Federal Capital Territory of Nigeria, of the minister of aviation of the Federal Republic of Nigeria, and of the chairman of the Nigerian Federal Airports Authority. I placed my hand on Mr Winterbottom's shoulder and steered him away from the incriminating view. Just before leaving the hotel, I had remembered to take off my Rolex.

'Thanks a lot for coming to get me,' he said.

The pleasure was all mine.

A few weeks after the London meeting, Ozu High Seas and Changeling Development Cooperation were awarded a $187 million contract for the upgrading of the Akanu Ibiam Airport, Enugu, to an international airport. The government officials had insisted on a $10 million bribe before the contract documents could be released.

Mr Winterbottom sent the money in four instalments. The

arrival of the first batch threw me into a massive shock that left me in a species of trance for days. Two and a half million dollars! In one transaction. Just like that. Did such amounts actually exist in real human beings' accounts?

And from what I had seen, Mr Winterbottom was a normal human being like me. He did not have two heads.

I tried to imagine a life with access to that kind of money. Glorious. All my problems solved forever. But how? By what means? Not even the oil companies paid enough to give anyone that much. Many Nigerian superbillionaires I knew of had attained their wealth after stints in high public office but such an opportunity was not likely to come my way anytime soon, even if I had the heart. Siphoning from foreigners in parts of the world where the economy was sound was one thing, but stealing from your own brothers and sisters who had entrusted you to serve was the abyss of wickedness, especially when you had the firsthand opportunity to witness their daily sufferings and struggles. I was not hurting anyone by taking a little of what the Winterbottoms of this world had. There was much, much more where those millions had come from.

When the subsequent three instalments arrived, I received them without flinching a single muscle.

Now that everyone had received their due bribes, Mr Winterbottom had come to finalise things at the Ministry of Aviation and to sign the memorandum of understanding. Since it was his first time visiting the Lion of Africa, as an act of goodwill I reserved his ticket, booked his hotel room, and picked him up from the airport.

'Your country is beautiful,' he said on the way back to the hotel. 'Everywhere looks so well organised. This isn't what I expected.'

No need telling him that this was all film tricks; our beautiful Abuja was a Potemkin village. Mr Winterbottom would probably never have to cross the River Niger to Igbo land, where poverty and disarray would stare him eyeball to eyeball. Not only was Abuja the Federal Capital Territory and the new seat of government, it was probably the most expensive city in Nigeria. Whenever the masses complained about the astronomical costs of living, the government reminded them that Abuja was not for everyone. The journalists and opinion-eds were still debating who the 'everyone' was. Meanwhile, it was probably time for me to speak to an estate agent about buying some nice property here.

The meeting took place in the Ministry of Aviation complex. The real complex. World Bank's wife number two's cousin had risen to the level of having a somewhat fancy office in the building, and for a fee, he had agreed to lend it to us.

Cash Daddy was sitting in the executive chair when we entered. He was in a hurry to attend a meeting with the president, he said, but granted us a brief chat before handing over the necessary documents.

'We're still expecting the National Assembly to OK the budget,' the minister said. 'So, we can't give any mobilisation fees to any contractors right now.'

Mr Winterbottom assured him that we were loaded enough to go ahead, and he was happy to wait and collect all the outstanding payments later.

'That might even mean waiting till the completion of the project,' the minister warned. 'We might just end up paying the $187 million in full at the same time.'

The sound of $187 million arriving in full does a certain something to the human brain. Mr Winterbottom giggled and hopped about in his seat.

Back at the hotel, I brought out Ozu High Seas letterheaded documents and handed Mr Winterbottom his copies. I guess the Englishman from Uganda and Argentina was not such a mugu after all. He perused each piece of paper intensely, asking me questions from time to time before he was satisfied and finally willing to sign. Then he brought out a sleek pen from his jacket pocket and inserted a signature that looked as if it was in the habit of endorsing billions.

Afterwards, Mr Winterbottom said he wanted to go sightseeing. He had travelled along with his camera. The hired driver said he knew the best places we could see. I agreed to accompany Mr Winterbottom on the tour.

The driver showed us the modern mansions of Asokoro and the

scenic streets of Maitama. He pointed out former Head of State General Ibrahim Babangida's mansion, former head of state General Yakubu Gowon's mansion, former head of state General Abdulsallam Abubakar's mansion. He even showed us a house that was built in the shape of an aeroplane. But Mr Winterbottom was not impressed.

'Where can I get some real good shots?' he asked. 'I want some real photos of real Africans.'

I apologised that Abuja was not the right place. There were no bare-bottomed children running around with flies in their nostrils. The driver of the hired car overheard our conversation and chipped in.

'*Oga*, e get plenty villages wey dey for around Abuja, If you want, make I take you. Them no dey far at all.'

He took us just fifteen minutes away, to Kikaokuchi village. What I saw was beyond belief. The slum was teeming with real Africans living in real African houses. How could such sordidness be juxtaposed with so much affluence? The villagers gathered and stared at the white visitor in their midst. Mr Winterbottom went around patting shoulders.

'*Bature, bature,*' they whispered excitedly amongst themselves.

After about three hours of babbling with awestruck natives, listening to a bare-bottomed lad playing a bamboo flute, and taking photographs of men drinking *fura da nono* on raffia mats in front of their shacks, Mr Winterbottom was thirsty for new wine. The driver suggested yet another village that was just twenty minutes away.

'No, I think we should go back to the hotel,' I said. I had seen more than enough of Africa for one day.

'I don't mind visiting a few more places,' Mr Winterbottom said. 'This is really very exciting.'

'I think we should go back to the hotel,' I insisted. 'You know Nigeria is a dangerous place.' I paused. 'Especially for a white man.'

That did the trick. He entered the car without another word of protest.

Back at the hotel, the driver nearly zonked out when Mr Winterbottom recompensed him with $100 – a likely approximate of his monthly income in just one day. The man genuflected at least a gazillion times, chanting 'thank you, Master, thank you, Master' each time his head arched towards the floor.

I shook Mr Winterbottom's hand, wished him a good evening, and left him by his room door. Someday, he would look back and understand why I had been so shy throughout the African tour, why I had declined every one of his fervent invitations to feature in his photo shots.

Twenty-nine

On the day that Cash Daddy publicly declared himself as one of the Abia State gubernatorial aspirants, there was not a single tout left roaming the streets of Aba. All of them had been paid in advance and transported in fifty-eight-sitter buses to the National Advancement Party (NAP) headquarters in Umuahia, where they were gathered and waiting when our convoy of brand new jeeps arrived. As soon as they sighted us, the crowd chanted and cheered with naira-fuelled gusto.

'Cash Daddy na our man! Cash Daddy na our man!'

Their man descended slowly from his carriage and waved with a straight face. Protocol Officer, his bodyguards, some of his new political friends, and yours truly accompanied him into the building, where Protocol Officer presented a seven-figure naira cheque in exchange for the nomination form. The crowd hollered another loud cheer when they saw us emerge from the building. They grew more deafening when Cash Daddy waved the form in the air. Major newspapers and television stations in Abia State had been paid good money to cover the event, so the cameras flashed and the microphones popped out. When Cash Daddy raised his right hand, the crowd fell silent.

'People of Abia State,' he began. His voice was deep and calm, like a defence counsel in a murder trial closing his case. 'I appreciate that you've turned out to show your support as I declare my intention to contest for governor of this great state. I thank you very much. I promise you will never regret it.'

The crowd cheered. He dimmed his eyes and scanned the multitude as if taking personal note of each person's face.

'I've been very, very blessed in Abia State, and all I want is an opportunity to be a blessing in return.'

He told them of his plans to provide free education at primary

214

school level, about his plans for agriculture and for development of roads and other infrastructure. He promised to attract foreign investors to ensure that Abia was given its rightful place on the map of the world. Once again, I could not restrain my admiration for this Boniface Mbamalu of a man. I had composed this speech two days ago and spent most of the previous night rehearsing it with him. But I was the mere architect; Cash Daddy had infused the words with real life. The touts gathered might not be equipped to appreciate all these wonderful promises, but the television and radio audiences would understand.

Cash Daddy concluded.

'My brothers and sisters, God bless Abia State, God bless all of us.'

The crowd burst into a flood of cheering and chanting.

Cash Daddy smiled, waved, kept on waving, and continued waving for about ten more minutes, before we finally returned to the jeeps and drove off.

Back at the office, I waited for Cash Daddy to finish conferring with his political cronies. He wanted to meet with me afterwards. Meanwhile, I was delighted to see that my good friend Edgar was still very much in the flow.

Dear Shehu,

ALUTA CONTINUA!

I received another phone call from Jude at the security company and he ACCUSED me of causing unnecessary delays. I assured him that it WASN'T MY FAULT that things were taking SO LONG. I had NO IDEA about all the FULL REQUIREMENTS before I sent him the other documents, if not I would have waited. I would APPRECIATE if you or your sister could give him a call and assure him that all the delays haven't been any fault of mine.

I know you and your sister already have A LOT you're dealing with, but DON'T WORRY, I'm right here to HELP you get this thing sorted out. You REST ASSURED that I'm COMMITTED to helping you TILL THE VERY END.

Best,
Your friend, Edgar

Oh, I had no doubts at all about his commitment. For an $11.6 million cut, Goering would have been willing to save Anne Frank.

So far, Mr Hooverson had sent money to Nigeria for the change-of-beneficiary certificate and lawyer's fees. In exchange, I had given him all the receipts and other documentation necessary to claim the money at the security firm. He was now in the hands of our associates in Amsterdam who would carry on milking him until he became unbearably desperate.

There was also an email from my Lufthansa airline pilot mugu, threatening me with the FBI. Haha. Unfortunately, the FBI could not do much to stop us. We had fictitious companies registered with the Corporate Affairs Commission and the Chamber of Commerce. We had account details that had been given to us by several different mugus over time, and we had carried out transactions from thousands of ghost accounts in banks around the globe. Anybody hoping to follow our trail would simply be throwing away their precious time.

My phone rang. It was Charity, calling from a business centre in her school.

'Kings, they've fixed the date for our matriculation. It's on the twenty-ninth of November. Are you going to be in the country on that day?'

I smiled. My sister probably added that last part to let the keen eavesdroppers know that she had a brother who could afford to travel abroad.

At first, the professor Buchi had recommended scoffed at Charity's score when I went to visit him at the Abia State University. Then I told him how much I was willing to pay and he agreed to 'see what I can do'. Three weeks later, Charity's admission letter to the Department of Philosophy was ready, complete with deputy vice chancellor's signature.

'That's the best I could do,' he explained. The Law list was already jam-packed and overflowing.

My father would never have allowed his daughter to enrol on such a worthless course, but studying Philosophy was far better than staying home for a whole year, doing nothing. Plus, even though she did not comment on the process, my mother had been pleased. For an additional amount, the professor had assured me that he would switch my sister over to the Law Department by next session.

There was no way I was going to miss her matriculation ceremony. I told my sister so.

'Thank God,' she sighed. 'I was afraid you might be in London again.'

'Just make a list of everything you require for that day, then call me later and we can discuss it.'

Simple. Education without tears.

I went back to making a living.

'I'm relocating my campaign headquarters to my building on Mbano Road,' Cash Daddy announced. 'It's not good to mix business with pleasure. So, Kings, I want you to keep an eye on things here.'

It was becoming clearer to me by the day that God must have been speaking to him about this governorship thing for a long time, probably as far back as the day he summoned me into his private office and made me the offer to come and work with him. Somehow, I was touched that he had chosen me. And proud.

'I'm too big to chase dollars up and down the world,' he continued. 'Money should be chasing me instead.'

He went on to explain that life is in stages, that each person must learn to make changes to accommodate each new stage. He said that he had paid his dues in life and it was now time for life to treat him well.

Protocol Officer's entrance truncated his speech.

'Cash Daddy, I've just been speaking with Grandma,' he said. 'She said someone at her bank was warning her about our account.'

As Protocol Officer gave further details, Cash Daddy grew wilder.

'What do they mean by that?! What type of rubbish is that?!'

Protocol Officer's 'Grandma' lived in Yorkshire. He must have dabbed a very potent mugu potion on his lips the first time he spoke to her, because Grandma was totally consumed with faith in whatever Protocol Officer told her. For centuries, the elderly lady had been trying to help him get his mother out of Nigeria for cancer treatment in the UK. But over time, Grandma's more perceptive children had cautioned her. Each time, she had disregarded their advice – and now a staff member of the bank had tried. She had once again brought the matter to Protocol Officer's attention for advice. This Grandma woman was every 419er's dream.

'Can you imagine this rubbish?' Cash Daddy barked. 'Call the bank for me right now!'

Protocol Officer unlocked a cabinet and whipped out a file. He flipped through and found the number he was looking for, dialled, and asked to speak with the manager before passing the cellular on.

'Do you know who I am?!' Cash Daddy bellowed.

Maybe the bank manager did, maybe he did not.

'Is that the way you treat your big customers? Look, I'm taking this matter to the press! You hear me? You have no right to give out information about what goes on in my account to anybody!'

The bellowing went on and on and on. I could only imagine what was happening at the other end.

'Is it because I'm black? That's what it is, is that not so? If I was a white man, you wouldn't treat me with such disregard. Look, let me tell you. I might be black, but I'm not a monkey and I deserve to be treated with respect!'

Haha. Cash Daddy need never worry about being mistaken for a monkey. With the right diet and the right tutoring from superior brains, a monkey could probably learn how to program computers, pen great works of literature, make scientific discoveries. But no monkey born of creation or evolution could swipe cool millions of dollars with such ease. I could not vouch for the entire black race, but the niggers of Nigeria were certainly not monkeys.

'You'd better be very sorry!' Cash Daddy ranted on.

Then, he handed the phone back to Protocol Officer, who spoke to the manager before hanging up.

'They said they'll send a formal apology,' Protocol Officer said. 'They said they're very sorry, that they'll investigate which staff member spoke to Grandma and take disciplinary measures. They promised it won't happen again.'

No bank wanted to be publicly accused of having issues regarding clients' confidentiality.

'Imagine the rubbish,' Cash Daddy continued. 'Confidentiality. It's a simple word. What's so difficult about that? English is not my father's language. Yet I understand what it means.'

'He promised it won't happen again,' Protocol Officer said consolingly.

'How can they be telling people stories about my account?' Cash Daddy hissed. 'Just because I'm black.'

He continued frowning.

'Where's that form? Who has it?'

'Cash Daddy, I have it with me,' Protocol Officer replied.

He brought the sheet of paper we had just purchased from the NAP headquarters, extended it across the table, and sat beside me. Cash Daddy did not even touch the form with his eyes.

'Kings, you have a good handwriting,' he said. 'Fill it.'

Protocol Officer repositioned the form in front of me. I removed a pen from my shirt pocket and started filling while Protocol Officer stuck out his neck and clung his eyes to my hand. Quickly and efficiently, I filled out the section for name, address, and marital status. In the section for date of birth, I wrote July 4 and paused. I looked up at Protocol Officer and tapped my pen in the space for year of birth. He considered the matter briefly before looking up at Cash Daddy.

'Cash Daddy, what year of birth do you want us to put?' he asked.

'What are they doing with my year of birth?' Cash Daddy asked gruffly, 'Do they want to throw a birthday party for me?'

'Cash Daddy, it's because of the age,' Protocol Officer replied. 'You know they have a minimum age for people who want to contest.'

Cash Daddy dimmed his eyes and made a humming sound in his throat, as if he had been asked to recollect the year when, for ease of administration, Lord Lugard amalgamated the Northern and Southern protectorates of the British Colony, and bundled them up into one country which Lady Lugard had named 'area around the Niger' – Nigeria.

'What's the minimum age?' he asked eventually.

None of us was sure. Protocol Officer placed a phone call to someone he was sure would know and confirmed that the minimum age was definitely thirty years.

'Then let's make it thirty,' Cash Daddy said. 'You know, in this life, it's always better for one to start out early. It has many advantages.'

I did a quick calculation and arrived at a year of birth which placed Cash Daddy and me within the same age bracket. I ignored this water-to-wine category of miracle and continued with my task. When I arrived at educational qualifications, again I tapped my pen and looked to Protocol Officer for assistance. I already knew that the minimum requirement for governorship candidates was a GCE certificate. Protocol Officer considered the matter and arrived at another roadblock.

'Cash Daddy,' he asked, 'what do we put for your GCE?'

'I don't know,' he snapped. 'Put whatever you like. When Dibia's preparing my birth certificate, tell him to get me a GCE certificate as well.'

In moments of great stress, it is usually the most implausible fib that comes to mind. I filled in my own straight-A result for Cash Daddy. But that was not the end. I still needed help to know what secondary school he wanted me to state. Protocol Officer drew another blank and turned to his master for help. His master banged one hand on the desk and flailed the other in the air.

'What's wrong with you people? Can't you fill a simple form without asking me stupid questions? If you have to ask me about every single thing before you fill a simple form, then I don't know why I'm paying you so much money. You might as well go and work in a bank!'

'Cash Daddy, we're sorry,' we both apologised.

'Get out of my office and go and fill that thing somewhere else. You people are starting to annoy me.'

On my way back to the Central Intelligence Agency, I was about to turn the door handle when the air suddenly filled with a sensuous, luxurious scent. I looked back and saw that a majestic frown had walked in through the connecting door to the reception area. In its train was Cash Daddy's wife.

Thirty

Mrs Boniface Mbamalu was the most beautiful wife that money could buy. Each of her facial features was perfectly sculptured. Every item on her lithe, six-foot frame could be considered a fortune. From the flaxen hair extensions, to the chunks of metal around her throat and wrists, to the lace fabric of her *buba* and *iro*. And her skin shone with a glorious luminosity that had nothing at all to do with nature; it could only have come from inside an expensive cosmetic jar.

'Good afternoon, madam,' I said.

She ignored me and swished past. Red-hot fumes were smoking out of her ears and nostrils.

Instinctively, I retraced my steps. Protocol Officer was frozen to the spot, as if he had just spied a three-headed python while taking a stroll in the garden behind his house. Mrs Mbamalu had swept into Cash Daddy's office, and from where we stood, we could hear the sparking of her wrath and the thundering of her rage. Glass was smashing, wood was crashing, and her voice was at topmost volume. Everybody else in the building must have heard. Yet not even the tough-looking *otimkpu* dared to intervene.

'Useless idiot!'

Crash! Smash! Bang!

'What sort of rubbish is that?!'

Bang! Smash! Crash!

'Whatever you do with your private life is none of my business, but I will never have you flaunt it in my face. Are you hearing me?!'

Smash! Crash! Bang!

'If you know what's good for you . . . better relocate that stupid girl . . . my next trip!'

Slap! Slap! Slap!

Within minutes, she had finished delivering her message and

vamoosed. From what I could gather, she apparently had discovered that Cash Daddy was renting a flat for one of his girlfriends on the same street in London, Belgrave Square, where she, his wife, had her own private apartments. From all indications, this woman had flown all the way from Lagos to Port Harcourt, taken a taxi to Aba, stopped at her husband's office, and afterwards headed directly back to Lagos. The straightforward purpose of the trip had been to communicate some slaps.

After she left, I went into Cash Daddy's office with Protocol Officer. The place looked as if a tornado had dropped by to say hello. The exotic vases were smashed to smithereens on the floor, the wall cabinet was lying facedown like an Islamic worshipper, every single item on his executive desk had been transferred to the ground. Interestingly, the only thing in the room that seemed untouched was the photograph of him in a traditional chieftaincy outfit. The image looked down on the dishevelled room from its position high up on the wall.

Cash Daddy was sitting on his swivel chair, with head bent and hands folded on the executive desk. That desk, I noticed, was now in a slanting position. Protocol Officer started picking things up off the floor with the morbid efficiency of one who had seen it all before. I stood, marvelling at the effects of this ironic sort of rage that immoral single women suddenly develop against immorality as soon as they get married. Was this not the same woman who they said had been a professional mistress in her time?

Abruptly, Cash Daddy looked up. A drop of blood escaped a cut on his lower lip. He licked it, like a reptile capturing its dinner.

'Kings, do you believe in love?'

'Yes, I do,' I answered slowly. I knew for sure that I had once loved a certain woman.

He laughed.

'Let me tell you something. Women are like babies. Just give them whatever they want and they'll keep quiet. Don't mind all their *shakara*. The only time a woman becomes dangerous is when there's nothing else she wants from you.'

I said nothing.

'Did you know that?'

'No, I didn't,' I lied.

He laughed and shook his head.

'Kissing may be the language of love, but it's money that does the talking.' He paused. 'By the way, when are you planning to get married?'

I had not thought about marriage since Ola.

'I'm waiting for the right woman to come along,' I replied.

'Stay there and continue waiting. If that's the case, you'll never get married. All you need to do is fix a date for the wedding, book the venue, pay for the catering . . . just plan everything. As soon as you've done that, you'll see that the woman will just appear on time and fill in the slot.'

I knew that he meant every word of what he was saying.

'What about your current girlfriends? Is there none of them that you can marry?'

'I'm not in any relationship right now.'

'Do you mean you don't have any relationship with any girls you want to marry or that you don't have any girlfriends at all?'

He often referred to the female gender in plural form, as if they did not exist except in batches.

'No, I don't have any girlfriend.'

'Kings, stop trying to make me laugh. I have a cut on my lip.'

'Cash Daddy, I'm not joking. I don't have a girlfriend.'

It took a while for the disbelief to cover the whole region of his vast face. Then he uttered a scream that rattled the pieces of glass on the floor.

'Are you serious?! Are you really serious?!'

I smiled. What was all the fuss was about?

'Come to think of it,' he said meditatively, 'I've never seen you with any women. I thought there might be some you left behind in Umuahia who were taking care of you from time to time. So what's the problem? What's wrong with you?'

Now it was my turn to laugh.

'I'm serious. Tell me the problem. What's wrong with you?'

'Nothing is wrong with me.'

He turned his voice into a whisper.

'Are you having some problems with your machete?'

'Cash Daddy, I'm fine. Nothing is wrong with me.'

'Or are you a homo?'

Accusing another man of such a thing could easily lead to a mouthful of broken teeth. I let the insult pass.

'Cash Daddy, I'm not.'

'Kings, I beg you in the name of God. I know that relatives are the cause of hip disease, but right now, I have enough problems on my hands. I don't want to add the one of having a homo brother.'

'Cash Daddy, I'm certainly not gay.'

'So what's the problem?' He had turned the volume of his voice up again. 'If a man is denying that he has a swollen scrotum, the place for him to prove it's a lie is by the riverside. Why don't you have any women?'

'I was in a relationship that ended a long time ago. Since then, I've not really—'

'A relationship!' He screamed louder than ever. 'Your head is not correct! Are you trying to tell me that you don't have regular servicing from women? Are you normal at all?'

'Cash Daddy, it doesn't really matter to me. I believe that true love is more important than sex in a relationship. After all, sex isn't one of the basic physiological—'

'Come on will you shut up your mouth! I don't believe it. How can I have somebody on my staff who is not being taken care of? Please leave off that your big grammar and just shut up. Your head is not correct.'

He paused thoughtfully. Then looked up with face aglow, as if he had just discovered fire.

'Kings, when is your birthday?'

What had that got to do with the price of fish?

'Am I not talking to you? I said, when is your birthday?'

'It's on the sixth of November.'

'Good. I know what to do. I'm going to give you an early birthday present.'

He brought out his phone and ordered someone at the other end to meet us in the VIP section of his hotel bar later that night. I marvelled at this man who had just been smashed by his wife, and who was now trying to vivify my sex life.

The Bon Bonny Hotel was a popular hangout for people in our line of business. The car park was jammed with all manner of exotic cars and the lobby was equally jammed. Men in dark glasses and dark suits waited as their masters dined or womanised. There were also yellow-skinned, scantily clad ladies who had probably come to see if they could get their hands on some of the International Cake.

On my way to the bar, I spied Azuka disappearing into the elevator with a luscious lady entwined around his arms. Her bright yellow back was bare. Clearly, his newfound good luck was still a-flowing.

The writer of an opinion editorial I read recently in *This Day* had blamed the proliferation of bleached skin amongst young ladies on the average 419er's preference for yellow women who went hand-in-hand with his flashy lifestyle. Another editorial, written by a Roman Catholic priest, blamed the 419ers and their 'promiscuous lifestyles' on the recent 'rise in materialism' amongst young girls and their tendency to dress in 'Babylonian apparel'. Yet another writer blamed the 419ers for importing the AIDS virus to Nigeria.

Blaming problems on 419ers had turned into a national pastime, but then, it all depended on which part of the elephant you could feel.

I knew, for example, that Cash Daddy was personally responsible for the upkeep of the 221 orphans in the Daughters of St Jacinta Orphanage, Aba. He tarred all the roads in my mother's local community. He dug boreholes, installed streetlights, built a primary health care centre. Just two days ago, I received a letter from the Old Boys' Association of my secondary school requesting my contribution towards a new classroom block. I replied immediately to say I would fund the whole project. I knew what it felt like to endure classrooms that had no windows, no doors, and no tiles on the floors, just because the complete funds pledged towards the project had not yet been collected.

So, no matter what the media proclaimed, we were not villains, and the good people of Eastern Nigeria knew it.

In the bar, I sat at an inconspicuous table and waited. Cash

Daddy was the Patron Saint of 'African Time'; he would be at least an hour late as usual.

A waitress strutted over with a priceless smile.

'Good evening, *Oga*,' she beamed, and jiggled her waist to one side.

'Good eve—'

'What of *Oga* Cash Daddy?' she beamed, and jiggled her waist to the other side.

'He's coming later,' I replied.

I asked for a bottle of Coke and tipped her enough to compensate for the beaming and jiggling. As I sipped, I peered around the room.

There was Kanu Sterling. Both he and Cash Daddy had worked under Money Magnet. I had heard that Kanu lit his cigarettes with one-dollar bills.

There was Smooth. A chromosomal criminal, unlike some of us. Well educated, extremely cultured, he had been familiar with the good things of life since birth. But while he was schooling in Stanford, USA, the sweet lure of illegal money had been like a siren to him.

There was Amarachamiheuwa. He was personally responsible for the death-by-cardiac-arrest of one of the most prominent businessmen in Brazil, after duping the man out of 115 polo horses.

Cash Daddy arrived exactly two and a half hours after the time he had given me – without Protocol Officer, which meant that he probably had a high-maintenance adulteress waiting in one of the rooms and would spend the night at the hotel. He went from table to table, slapping hands and exchanging wild laughter. These men were not necessarily his friends, but they were all united in the brotherhood of cool cash.

'Pound Sterling!' Cash Daddy said to Kanu. 'The only currency with a surname! I haven't seen you in a long time. I was wondering if the white people had carried you away.'

'Me?' the man replied and beat his chest repeatedly. 'Cash Daddy, me? How? They no afraid to carried me away? *O bu na ujo adighi atu fa?* Does they knows who I am?'

227

Amarachamiheuwa's subsequent phone conversation eclipsed every other sound in the building.

'Go to my house right now!' he screamed. 'No, not the one on Azikiwe Road! Go to the one on Michael Opara Crescent! Ask my gateman to show you where I parked my Mazda! It's inside my garage, the one that's very close to my swimming pool! Between my Volvo and my Navigator! Inside the boot, you'll find three briefcases! One contains pounds! One contains dollars! One contains naira! Bring the briefcase with naira for me! Hurry up and come back now!'

Finally, Cash Daddy finished his rounds, sat at a table of his choice and beckoned me to join.

'The usual,' he said to the waitress who sauntered across. She was different from the one who had attended to me earlier.

I ordered oxtail pepper soup to go with another bottle of Coke. Our orders arrived in a jiffy.

'Kings,' Cash Daddy said after jawing the first chunk from a piece of fried meat in his saucer, 'have you noticed that I never fall sick? Even if I go to a place where mosquitoes drink blood with straws, I can never catch malaria.'

He leaned closer and whispered.

'Have you also noticed that my women are always coming back for more? No matter how many times they're with me, they still want more. It's because there's nobody who satisfies them the way I do.'

He laughed.

'This is my secret.' He pointed at the meat he was chomping on. '404 works wonders in the body. You see all those funny diseases that women carry around in their bodies? With 404 you won't catch anything.'

I was aghast. 404 was dog meat. I had heard of certain parts of Nigeria where dog meat was a delicacy, but this was my first time watching someone eating it.

'And another thing . . .' he continued, '404 protects you from your enemies. No one of them can touch me if I keep eating it regularly.'

He took a sip from the wine in his glass.

228

'Should I tell them to bring some for you?' He grinned. 'You'll need it against tonight. You know you have to sharpen your machete very well before you set off for the farm.'

'No, thank you,' I replied quickly.

Recently, I had done several things of which I had never thought myself capable, but eating the body parts of a dog was way beyond my league.

'OK, don't say I didn't warn you,' Cash Daddy said. 'Camille is a very dangerous girl.'

While we were eating, an enchantress stiletto-ed over to our table in a short red dress that clung dangerously to her derriere. Her knees and knuckles were black where the bleaching cream had refused to work. Her hair extensions went all the way down to her waist and curled at the tips. Cash Daddy patted her behind and introduced us.

'This is Camille,' he said. 'My jewel of inestimable value. She's a law student at Abia State University.' He grabbed my shoulder and shook. 'This is Kings. The latest millionaire in town. After all, our elders say that a dirty hand will eventually lead to an oily mouth.'

I realised too late that the misapplication of this popular Igbo proverb was supposed to be a joke. My laughter joined in when theirs was already at an anticlimax.

Camille bubbled with goodwill to all mankind. She gazed attentively at Cash Daddy, and winked at me from time to time. She wiped some grease from his upper lip, and straightened my shirt collar. Eventually, she reached over and kissed me briefly on the lips. I worried that some of her rouge might have stayed behind, but resisted the urge to wipe my lips with my hands. Then she transferred herself to my lap and smiled like someone used to turning scrawny sonnies into world heavyweight boxing champions. I was not sure where to keep my hands; I left them dangling awkwardly by my side.

Camille's instructions from Cash Daddy were simple.

'Collect the key to room 671,' he said. 'Take him inside and deal with him. It doesn't matter how much it costs. By the time you're through, I don't even want him to remember his father's name.'

*

It was not until about noon the following day that I was finally able to lift myself out of bed and answer my phone. It was my mother.

'Kingsley!' she said with fire in her voice.

'Mummy.'

'You're still sleeping?'

'I'm a bit tired,' I mumbled.

'Kings, are you well?' she asked with concern.

'I'm fine.'

'What's the matter? Are you sure—'

'Mummy, I'm fine.'

She paused. She remembered why she had called. Her voice resumed its initial fire.

'Kingsley, why didn't you tell me?'

'Why didn't I tell you what?'

'I saw on the news last night that Boniface is contesting for governor. Is it true?'

Agreed, the Nigerian media were experts at conjuring headline news out of incidents that never happened, but surely my mother must have seen Cash Daddy declaring his good intentions to the world with his very own mouth.

'Yes, he's contesting.'

'Why didn't you tell me in advance?'

'I didn't? I thought I did.'

'No, you didn't.'

'Oh.'

There was a pause.

'Kings, have you started looking for another job?'

'I'm working on it.'

'That's what you told me the last time.'

'Mummy, I'm working on it.'

'Where and where have you applied to?'

'Different places.'

'Does it mean not one of them has called you in for an interview yet?'

'Mummy, you know how Nigeria is.'

'Kings, please, please, please. Find a proper job. I don't understand this so-called work you say you're doing for Boniface. You know Nigerian politics is very dangerous.'

'Mummy, I'm not in any way involved in his campaign. Stop worrying yourself unnecessarily.'

'There's no way you can be working with him and not—'

'Mummy, I need to go now. I'll talk to you some other time.'

'Remember you promised your fa—'

It was only a matter of time before she would come round. I returned to Camille. In a short while, I forgot everything about my dead father and my worried mother. I was transported to another galaxy.

Thirty-one

Mr Edgar Hooverson's was a typical case of gambler's fallacy. Every additional payment had simply increased his commitment, the need to win money had kept him going.

But at last, all the mind-bending was taking its toll. After paying $16,000 for lawyer's fees, $19,000 for a Change of Beneficiary Certificate, $14,500 for Security Company Tariff, $21,000 for Transfer of Ownership, $11,900 for courier charges, $23,000 for Customs Clearance, $17,000 for Hague Authorisation, $9,000 for ECOWAS Duty, and $18,700 for insurance fees, his enthusiasm had started waning. The time was ripe to release the $58 million into his care.

My friend, Edgar, then sent me an email.

Dear Shehu,

ALUTA CONTINUA!

I've spoken with Jude and arranged to be in Amsterdam on TUESDAY THE 27th. Is that date CONVENIENT for you? Please let me know so I can go ahead and book my ticket and accommodation. I intend to be at THE AMSTERDAM AMERICAN HOTEL which Jude told me is not too far from the security company.

I'll send the $4,000 for your travel ticket and hotel accommodation BEFORE the day runs out.

I'm quite EXCITED and LOOKING FORWARD to meeting you after all this correspondence. My regards to your dear sister.

Best,
Your friend, Edgar

PS: Something just occurred to me! I'll also email you a RECENT PHOTOGRAPH of myself. The one on my driving license and international passport is a bit OUTDATED and I want to avoid the risk of you coming to the hotel and MISTAKING me with someone else. I know it's not very likely that would happen, but as an EXPERIENCED business man, I've learnt to always take ADDITIONAL PRECAUTIONS.

I had no reason to doubt Mr Hooverson's experienced-ness as a businessman. He might even have been one of the most brilliant. After all, there were people renowned for their ability to remove tumours from tricky crevices in the human body, who were useless at changing their car tyres. Others could interpret every formula that Newton and Einstein had come up with, but could not tell the beginning or the end of the stock market. Any intelligent, experienced expert could become a mugu. It was all about the packaging.

The date that Mr Hooverson had chosen – just a few days before Charity's matriculation – was actually not convenient for me. But our associates in Amsterdam advised that it was risky to postpone the meeting; Mr Hooverson's desperation was dead ripe. Pity, I would have to rush back so soon. It would have been nice to check out all the outlandish stories Cash Daddy had narrated about the Red Light District in Amsterdam.

In Amsterdam, after checking into my hotel, I met my associates in a nearby cafe. Either of them could have been the Jude who had been in touch with Mr Hooverson.

They laughed when I would not take off my coat.

'You should have worn a lighter coat,' Amuche said. 'This one you're wearing is meant for the peak of winter.'

'Anybody seeing you would know immediately that you're a Johnny-just-come straight off the boat,' Obideozor added.

'I don't think you people understand what I'm going through here,' I said and shivered.

Both men laughed without control.

After a life of sweating it out in the blazing heat of tropical West Africa, nothing could have prepared me for the plummeting temperatures of this, my very first winter on earth. Suddenly, bits of puzzling information started making sense. At last, I understood the necktie – an item of clothing that had never previously made the slightest sense. I now knew that boots were more than a fashion statement. They were a lifesaver. And as the cold November air charged through the broad entrances to my nostrils, I remembered something my father had once said.

'The white people's narrow nostrils and pointed noses are not just to help them speak with a nasal accent,' he had said. 'It's to help protect them against the cold.'

I rubbed my palms vigorously and wished that my nose was more pointed. My two associates continued being amused. I and Obideozor finished our cups of tea and headed out.

'I'll be waiting for your call,' Amuche said.

We had planned everything right down to the smallest detail. I was the one to knock. The face that peeped out of the narrow space beside the open door when I did was exactly the same as the one in the Jpeg that Edgar Hooverson had sent.

'Mr Hooverson?'

'Yes?' he replied sternly, like a female post office clerk.

'*Aluta Continua!*'

His smile opened up like an umbrella. He pulled the door all the way. In his neat, old-fashioned suit, Mr Hooverson could easily have passed for a Baptist minister. He was a tall, handsome man who looked as if he had recently started feeding too often and too well. I was not quite sure about his age. He looked slightly older than a secondary school principal, but much younger than a grand-father. I noticed that his fingernails were bitten halfway down to the cuticles.

'I'm Shehu Musa Abacha. This is Dr Wazobia. He was my late brother's trusted chemist.'

Mr Hooverson's smile flickered. He looked unsure of this new character. His mouth opened to ask a question; I grabbed him into a tight embrace.

'Thank you,' I said with tears in my voice. 'Thank you very, very much for all your help towards my sister and my family.'

It is amazing the things we never know about ourselves, the skills that situations and circumstances drag out of us. In all my six years of secondary school, nobody had ever considered me for a single part in the yearly Inter-House Drama Competition. They said I was too set in my personality, they said I could not act. Now, here I was giving a performance that was on a par with any of Denzel Washington's.

'It's my pleasure,' he replied and hugged me back.

We remained in each other's arms for several seconds. The whole thing had a certain United Nations touch.

'My sister Mariam asked me to apologise for not being able to meet you herself,' I said, as we went into the room.

'Oh, I perfectly understand. I understand about the horrible situation in your country. It's really very sad.'

I moved on to stage two.

'When my sister rang the security company yesterday just to make sure that everything was in order, they told her that the only thing remaining is an anti-terrorist certificate.'

'What! They never told me anything about that!'

'I think it's something new they just started implementing,' Dr Wazobia said.

We told Mr Hooverson that we had raised $5,000 of our own money for the anti-terrorist certificate, and would pay the remaining $10,000 when the consignment arrived.

'Oh, great,' he sighed.

'But they said we can only have part of the delivery until I pay them the remaining.'

'How much would that be . . . Part of the delivery?'

'It's one of two trunk boxes,' I replied. 'That comes to exactly half of the $58 million.'

I could see the mathematics going through his head. Half of $58 million dollars was still over $25 million.

'That seems like a perfect idea to me,' he said and nodded. 'Once we have the first trunk, we can then pay from that for the second trunk . . . Everyone is happy!'

I dug into my pocket and brought out an envelope of cash. I counted out fifty $100 bills in full view of everybody and handed them to Dr Wazobia, who then left to pay the anti-terrorists. He was supposed to return with the certificate, which we would then take to the security company. Then we would receive our trunk of millions.

Mr Hooverson and I were now alone.

'How's your sister doing?' he asked in a tone of utmost concern.

My reply painted as pathetic a picture as I could conjure. Grunts of different shapes and sizes escaped from Mr Hooverson's lips. By the time I finished, he was clutching his chest with grief. Did I say Denzel Washington? Make that an Eddie Murphy or an Al Pacino.

'How sad,' he said. 'How very, very sad, I would have loved to pop over to Nigeria quickly and see her, but I need to be back in the US as soon as possible. I left him at home.'

While speaking, he reached into his wallet, extracted a photograph, and passed it on to me. I stared at the muscular, jet-black creature.

'Is this your dog?' I asked.

Mr Hooverson glared at me as if I had just called his mother a hermaphrodite. The skin on his face changed from the colour of boiled chicken to the colour of a baboon's buttocks.

'Don't call him a dog!' he howled with uncharacteristic, un-good-Samaritan-ish vexation. 'His name is Kunta Kinte!'

My heart went pit-a-pat. Rapidly, I calculated how many leaps and bounds would get me to the door.

'Kunta Kinte's been through a lot,' he said in a much softer voice. 'He gets very agitated when I'm not at home. My new wife is really mean to him. She never lets him sleep in our bed.'

I was still clutching my heart between my teeth. My mind was already halfway down the valley of the shadow of death. I recalled all those stories about Americans who suddenly whipped out guns from grocery bags and started shooting everyone in sight. And from what I had seen on television, every American had at least one firearm. What if Mr Hooverson had come along with his gun? Would he shoot me if he happened to find out right here that all this was a scam? Would he shoot himself afterwards or live to tell the story? Would the shooting event make it to CNN or BBC? Would it be on the NTA 9 o'clock news?

What would my mother say when she saw it? I started losing weight right there in my seat.

Mr Hooverson went on to narrate several stories about the dog, describing Kunta Kinte's good qualities, remembering with tears in his eyes the day he lost him and later found him in the garden shed. I listened on with sweet patience, but in my mind I had started throwing huge boulders at him. At long last, I could take it no more. I had never been one to shine at small talk, but I decided to try.

'Do you have any children?' I asked, hoping that this would lead to a more tolerable topic.

'Kunta Kinte is my only child,' he replied tenderly. 'One of the reasons why I'm looking forward to this money coming in is so I can leave him something to live comfortably on even if something was to happen to me. I'm thinking of a trust fund in his name.'

God being so kind, right then, Dr Wazobia rang my cellular phone.

He informed me that the person at the anti-terrorist office was insisting on the complete $15,000 before he could issue the certificate. I threw a tantrum over the phone.

'What sort of rubbish is this? Mr Hooverson has come all the way from America to help us and now this! Can't you explain to them that we'll give it from the one in the trunk?'

I continued the heated talk while Mr Hooverson looked increasingly worried.

'Let me see what I can do,' he finally said.

He rang someone in the USA and asked them to wire money, quick. The person appeared reluctant. Mr Hooverson insisted that it was an emergency. After a brief argument, the savage in him burst through the Caucasian coating.

'Just do it!' Mr Hooverson howled, punching the arm of his chair until it groaned.

That was one thing I loved about these Yankee Doodles. They had a way of getting things done.

The next few hours were a rush of dramatics. I accompanied the mugu to a nearby cash machine and stood respectfully aside while he punched in his pin. When would this sort of technology reach my dearly beloved Nigeria? These cash machines were like gods standing right there in the streets, answering the cries of the needy at the press of a button.

Dr Wazobia met us up at the hotel lobby. He collected the cash, dashed out again, and returned shortly after with the anti-terrorist certificate. Now we could officially pick up our trunk of millions. We hailed a taxi to the security company. Mr Hooverson knew the address by heart.

The security company office was complete with signboard, reception, and inner office. There was even a Caucasian man and woman in charge of things. Cash Daddy had exhumed this setup from where-I-do-not-know, but it looked perfectly authentic.

Shortly after we arrived, the receptionist ushered us into the inner office.

'Which one of you is the beneficiary?' the white man asked.

'I am,' the mugu replied.

Mr Hooverson whipped out his navy blue American passport. The white man examined the photo and stared up into Mr Hooverson's face. He did this at least three more times before he was finally satisfied. Then he unfolded some documents that had been tightly clamped inside his armpit.

'Could you please sign here,' he said.

The mugu signed – after perusing carefully – and handed back the documents. The white woman collected the documents, took them away, and returned.

'Everything seems alright,' she said. 'I've just spoken to the courier. He'll be here very soon.'

Indeed, soon, Amuche arrived dragging a trunk box that looked exactly like the one where my mother kept her precious belongings in Umuahia.

'The second one will arrive in about an hour,' he explained. 'For security purposes, we deliver one at a time.'

He unlocked the box with a great deal of panache, making a show of removing the bundle of keys from his pocket, choosing the right one, and sticking it into the lock. He turned the key and paused some extra seconds before opening the lid. The trunk box appeared jammed with dollar notes. All of them stained black.

Thus, we moved to Stage three.

In a corner of the box, was a dark brown 150cl bottle. Mr Hooverson was speechless. Elation and confusion were fighting for space on his face.

'What's this?' he asked at last.

'That's where Dr Wazobia comes in,' I replied. 'He's a professional chemist who'll help us wash the money.'

'Wash the money?'

'For security purposes,' Dr Wazobia explained, 'we had the dollar notes invalidated with a fluid known as phosphorus sulphuric benzomate. It turns them black. All we have to do is wash them in the lactima base 69% contained in that bottle.'

Dr Wazobia raised the bottle from the box.

'Ah!' he exclaimed.

'What?' Mr Hooverson and I replied simultaneously. Our voices had equal degrees of curiosity.

'The chemical has congealed,' Dr Wazobia said. 'It was left in here for too long. But there's a little left in it.' He swished the leftover liquid in the bottle about. 'Let's see how much we can wash with this. I'll need to dilute it with some water.'

We followed him to the bathroom. Dr Wazobia put the bottle to the mouth of the running tap, placed some black notes in the sink, and poured from the bottle onto the notes.

'Wow!' Mr Hooverson gasped.

The black paint had washed off, leaving gleaming dollar notes behind. Only the first row of notes in the trunk box were real. The rest were old newspapers, painted black and cut to dollar size. Pray tell, who was that 419er who first thought up these serpentine scams? Men and women had received the acknowledgment of History for displaying less ingenuity in other fields.

239

After Dr Wazobia had washed about $1,000, the liquid in the brown bottle finished.

'Sorry, this is all I can do for now,' Dr Wazobia said. 'You'll have to order a fresh batch from the chemical plant. A full bottle of this size is about seventy thousand dollars. That should be more than enough to wash all the money in that trunk.'

From the corner of my eyes, I watched Mr Hooverson, in case he actually had a gun. I expected that he might wake up at the mention of yet another payment.

But no, the money he had seen was scattering his thoughts. In front of my eyes, Mr Hooverson became a mental case. He started shivering and pacing like someone sleepwalking. All his ten fingers went into his mouth.

'We have to get that chemical. We have to get that chemical,' he muttered. His head shot up. 'How long does it take?' He blew a crumb of fingernail into the air. 'The chemical. The chemical for washing the money. How long does it take to arrive?'

'Oh, the lactima base 69%. Almost immediately. They usually have it permanently in stock. It's mostly reserved for use by the FBI and Interpol, but I have my contacts at the plant.'

'We need to get that chemical. We need to get that chemical,' Mr Hooverson repeated over and over again.

Out of the blue, Dr Wazobia came up with a smart plan.

'Why don't we leave this with the security company until we're ready with the money for the chemical?'

Mr Hooverson's face did not seem to like the idea. For a moment, he left off chewing his nails.

'So, next time, after we get the chemical, all we have to do is come here, collect the keys, and take the two trunks?' Mr Hooverson asked.

'Then you can take your share and keep the rest for them,' he nodded at me, 'in your account. But you have to get that chemical first.'

Mr Hooverson was pacing again. Then he stopped abruptly.

'I'm not sure how long it will take,' he said. 'But I'm pretty sure I can raise the funds.'

I gasped. I considered clutching my chest, but restrained myself. No need to take the acting too far.

'Mr Hooverson, I can't let you do this,' I said. 'You've done so much for my sister and her family already.'

'The sooner we get this money out, the better it is for all of us,' he replied matter-of-factly. Clearly, the time of pretence was over.

We parted outside the security company, but not before I drew Mr Hooverson towards me and gave him another United Nations hug.

Cash Daddy was right. These white people were harmless.

Thirty-two

Too drenched in sleep, it was not until the passengers broke into a loud cheer that I jolted back to reality and realised that the plane had landed in Port Harcourt. Nigerians always clap when an international flight touches on home soil. Who could blame us? With the number of tribulations that were lurking out there, to have gone and returned in one piece was worth celebrating.

I had spent my last few hours in Amsterdam looking over my shoulders for Interpol and the FBI. It was not until the plane lifted off the tarmac that I finally relaxed.

The air hostess smiled and thanked me for flying with them. Having flown first class, I was entitled to their free limousine service to convey me from the airport to wherever I was going, but I had declined. I preferred for my driver to pick me up. That way, I could make personal phone calls on the journey home without worrying about being overheard.

On my way to immigration, I switched on my phone. It rang almost immediately. It was my father's sister.

'Kings, I'm in serious trouble here. I've been trying to reach you for the past two days.'

She sounded very anxious. She gave me a number and asked me to ring her back on it immediately.

'Kings, I don't know what to do. NEPA has been giving us low current and my fridge has broken down. I don't know for how long I'll have to keep cooking fresh food every day. It's not easy for me at all.'

'Aunty Ada, relax . . . relax. Have you asked them how much it will cost to repair the fridge?'

'Hmm. Kings, it's a very old fridge. I don't know if anybody can repair it. Most people don't use this type of model anymore.'

I got the message.

'Aunty Ada, how much will a new one cost?'

She told me. I promised to send the money before the week ran out.

'Only God knows how I'll be able to do without a fridge till the weekend but thank you, anyway. I'll try and manage somehow.'

'OK, Aunty. Don't worry. I'll try and send the money by tomorrow.'

'You really are your father's son. God bless you my dear child. You're such a blessing to this family.'

The officer at immigration beamed a broad smile and lifted his right hand in amateur salute.

'Welcome, sir!' he shouted.

Poverty had a way of sharpening the sense of smell. These sorts of people could sniff out a prospective heavy tipper. I smiled and gave him my passport.

'Is there anything you'd like us to do for you, sir?' he asked.

'No, thank you,' I replied.

The last time I travelled with Cash Daddy, he had required the immigration officer's assistance to adjust their stamp so that his passport could read as if he had entered Nigeria on a previous date. These minor peccadilloes were necessary to keep the people at the embassies happy.

The immigration officer finished and held my passport towards me. I took the dark green booklet and sneaked him some Euro notes. Hopefully, the tip was heavy enough to ensure that my face was stamped in his memory for eternity, just in case I needed his help someday.

On my way to baggage collection, I dialled Camille.

'Kings, Kings! You're back! I really missed you!'

Camille and I had spent several more nights together since our first meeting. I would ring when I needed her, we would meet at the hotel, and she would leave the following morning. The girl had special ways of helping me forget my sorrows. Come to think of it, I did not even know her surname. But what was the point getting to know everything about a girl, only for her to dump you in the end? With Camille, I was free – free to extract as much pleasure as I wanted from our relationship whenever I wanted. That was the most important thing.

'Can you meet me later tonight?' I asked.

'Sure. What time?'

'I'm still at the airport. I'll ring you when I get to Aba and let you know.'

'I'm really looking forward to seeing you, Kings. I hope you brought back something from Amsterdam for me.'

Even her voice had something mesmerising about it. Was there a certain school where these types of girls went to master their art or was it an inborn talent? No wonder she charged so much. I rammed into someone who had been walking too slowly. He turned. I was about to apologise.

'Kingsley Ibe!' he exclaimed.

'Andrew Onyeije!'

We shook hands.

Andrew and I had competed in a science quiz back in form five. After a tough battle, I had won. Fresh complexion, robust cheeks . . . he looked very well.

'So what are you up to these days?' he asked.

'I'm based in Aba.'

'Oh, really? Where do you work?'

'I'm sort of doing my own thing. I'm into business. Importing and exporting.'

He laughed.

'What happened? Didn't you always say you wanted to read Engineering?'

'Actually, I read Chemical Engineering.'

He laughed again.

'And now you're importing and exporting. What was the point of going into sciences if you weren't intending to use it in the end?'

I tried to smile, but I was not doing it very well.

'And you?' I asked. 'What do you do?' Perhaps he had developed a contraceptive pill for men.

'I'm into IT,' he replied contentedly. 'I'm based in the States.'

That explained his fresh complexion. The wicked Nigerian sun had not smiled on him for a long time.

'You know IBM, don't you?' he continued. 'I'm with the head office in New York. I just flew in for my sister's wedding. I'll be in Nigeria for just about a week. Then I've gotta be back in the States for an important meeting.'

No wonder he could afford to open his mouth and make all sorts of stupid comments. He was so busy munching frankfurters in America, he had probably not yet seen any of the engineers and lawyers and medical doctors who were wearing hunger from head to sole.

'I'm soooo glad to be back home,' he went on. 'The last time I was in Nigeria was ages ago. There's nothing like being back in your own country, amongst your own brothers and sisters. It's such a wonderful feeling.'

Together, we stood by the sluggish conveyor belt and waited. Some lackeys promptly arrived beside us with trolleys.

'I've missed Nigeria so much,' Andrew said.

I pointed out my first suitcase. The lackey rushed to grab it.

'What and what did you do your Masters in?' he asked.

'I haven't yet done a Masters.'

He gasped.

'Kingsley Ibe! You don't have a Masters? I don't believe it! These days, you can't move forward in this world without one. I have a Masters in Cyber Informatics from Rutgers, a Masters in Tetrachoric Correlations from Cornell, a Masters in Data Transmogrification from Yale, and next fall, I'll be starting my PhD with Harvard.'

'That's wonderful,' I said, still struggling to smile.

'Wonderful?' He laughed. 'You're really cracking me up. My brother at Princeton has seven postgraduate degrees. My cousin at Brown is starting her third PhD soon. Honestly, there are so many great minds in this country. Yet once you mention you're from Nigeria, all they think about in the States is 419. It's sad.'

His voice had turned burgundy with nationalistic fervour. I felt like tipping him over a cliff. Were the minds of the 419ers any less great than the minds of the Masters degree and PhD holders? It would have been interesting to see what would have become of his great IBM mind if he had remained here in Nigeria.

Andrew reached for his suitcase. The lackey leapt forward and did the rest.

'I love Nigeria soooooo much,' he belched on. 'Whatever happens, I'm gonna come back here and settle someday. With my family.'

I pointed out my second suitcase. Held hostage by his effusion of nationalism, I could not immediately take my leave. His second suitcase arrived. The hot air merchant was still talking. He talked and talked and talked and talked. With each new word, my dislike for him increased. My guardian angel flapped a wing and caused my cellular to ring. It was Camille.

'Kings, I'm sorry but something urgent just came up. I won't be able to see you tonight.'

No way. I really needed her tonight.

'OK, how about tomorrow? How early can you come over?'

'I'm sorry, I'm not available tomorrow. I'm not going to be available for the rest of the week.'

I was about to ask where she was going.

'But I can send you someone else,' she said.

What? I felt as if I was being rudely awakened from a long and pleasant dream.

'Kings, would you like me to send someone else?'

Gradually, I came out of my swoon. I hung up. The smoke screen cleared from my mind. Unlike my cellular phone, which belonged to me and me alone, Camille was like a public telephone – available for use as far as it was free. Andrew's third suitcase arrived along with his fourth. He gestured to let me know that those were the last. Together, we headed out of the airport with the lackeys pushing along behind us.

Andrew screamed.

'What is it?' I asked.

He was feverishly shoving his hands in and out of his trouser pockets like someone having a convulsion.

'My passport! My US passport! I'm certain it was in this pocket!'

'When last did you see it?'

'I had it stamped right there at immigration, then I put it back in

246

my pocket. I remember vividly. It was right here with my boarding pass.'

He convulsed through his pockets again. Still, no passport.

'It's gone!' he announced three times. 'I had it in this pocket,' he cried two times. 'I'm quite certain of that.'

'You'd better go and report it immediately,' I advised. If not, a desperate immigrant could be out of the country with that passport on the next flight to the US.

Suddenly, his patriotism changed colour.

'This country is unbelievable! I haven't even come in yet and they've already stolen my passport!'

His American accent had also vamoosed.

'Someone probably saw you putting it back in your pocket,' I said.

'I just don't believe this! I've been looking forward to coming back home after all these years. I haven't even been here up to an hour already, and now this!'

How could I abscond when he was in such dire straits? Besides, the petty enmities that exist between one man and another suddenly disintegrate when they are linked with the bond of affliction. Now that Andrew had been initiated into the brotherhood of motherland mishaps, I found myself hating him less. I accompanied him to the security office to make a preliminary report.

'Ha!' a potbellied security officer laughed. 'How could you have done such a thing?'

'Done what?'

'Are you stupid? How can you put your passport inside your pocket? American passport for that matter. Why didn't you put it inside your trousers? Don't you wear underwear?'

'Fuck you!' Andrew exploded.

'Hey!' A more gaunt security man threatened him with a raised baton. 'Do you know who you're talking to?'

'Andrew, cool down, cool down,' I said, hiding my Schadenfreude away.

'I know my rights! He can't do anything to me.'

I almost laughed.

Quickly, I stepped in and apologised on his behalf. He was from

America; he did not understand. Twenty minutes later, the security officer kindly agreed to forgive.

'Talk to them politely so that you can get it sorted out soon,' I said to Andrew. 'You'll need a report from them to take to the police.'

Despite all his Masters degrees and PhDs, Andrew took my advice and explained his predicament in meeker tones. The pot-bellied man assigned a female officer to attend to him. She brought out a form, which Andrew was supposed to fill in.

'*Oga*, what did you bring for us from America?' the female officer tweeted, her fingers still super-glued to the form.

Andrew turned to me with bulging eyeballs and soaring eyebrows. My father never gave bribes, no matter for how long the police detained us at their checkpoints, but what did my father know about survival?

'Just give her a small tip so that they can treat your matter as urgent,' I whispered.

'I can't believe this . . . I just can't. Man, this country is seriously fucked up.'

No, this country was not fucked up. It was also not a place for idealising and Auld Lang Syne. Once you faced the harsh facts and learnt to adapt, Nigeria became the most beautiful place in the world.

Thirty-three

If there was a world record for brevity of time spent on grooming, I had just broken it. I sped a comb through my hair while racing downstairs. I was panting when I reached my BMW. Before jumping into the car, I paused and inspected my appearance in the window. I straightened my jacket and adjusted my shirt collar, but all that did not matter. Any outfit that cost an arm and two legs could speak for itself, whether neatened or not.

My cellular phone rang while I was reversing out of the gate. It was Charity.

'Charity, I'm on my way. I'm on my way. I'm just leaving the house.'

She was relieved.

My sister had rung several times the previous day. She wanted to make sure I would be there early. She wanted to remind me to bring my camcorder along. She wanted me to know where we should all meet up afterwards, just in case we did not get to see her before she went into the school auditorium for the matriculation ceremony. This morning, her phone call had woken me from sleep.

'Kings, you're still sleeping!'

'No . . . I'm awake.'

'Kings, please wake up and start getting ready. By the time you get here, the ceremony would have already gone halfway.'

She obviously did not know the abilities of my latest BMW 5 Series. Anyhow, my sister had a right to be anxious on this special day of her life. I had felt the same way on my graduation day.

I remembered everything about that great event as if it had happened just yesterday.

My mother spent the evening before supervising the slaugh-tering and plucking of three grown chickens, putting the finishing touches to four adult male shirts and plaiting her thirteen-year-old daughter's hair. Yet by the time the rest of us woke up on my graduation day morning, she was already in the kitchen and the whole house was consumed with the smell of good things. While washing the odour of kerosene fumes off her body, my mother sang the first two stanzas of 'There Shall Be Showers of Blessing' at top volume.

Ordinarily, I would have expected that my mother would be the one to cry. But from what she said, as soon as I rose to collect my certificate, her only response was to stand and clap. My father, on the other hand, sat in his seat and wiped his eyes. I was the very first of the second generation of university graduates from the whole Ibe extended family.

After the ceremony, I left the auditorium and went to meet them at a prearranged location, under the mango tree by the university health centre. Aunty Dimma was waiting with them. She had insisted on coming to the school as well, instead of just turning up at the house later in the day like our other invited guests. As soon as they saw me approaching, all of them rushed towards me.

'Congratulations,' my father said, shaking my hand.

'Congratulations,' my mother said, giving me a hug.

'Congratulations,' Ola said, placing her hands on my shoulders and giving me a holy kiss on the cheek.

Ola had worn a smart blue skirt suit which my mother later told me was too short.

'Congratulations,' Charity said, hugging me around the waist and refusing to let go.

'Congratulations,' Godfrey and Eugene said, with their eyes on the coolers of food that would soon be opened.

'Mr Chemical Engineer,' Aunty Dimma said, locking me inside her arms and pecking my cheek.

We ate. Some people I knew and many people I did not came round, and my mother dished out some food from the coolers for them. The total expenditure for the day's celebration had seriously head-butted my parents' budget and broken its two legs, but they did not mind. My graduation from university was supposed to be the dawn of a new day in their lives.

Fortunately, things were different this time around. I had made sure of that. Finances were the last thing my family had had to worry about while preparing for Charity's matriculation.

We would never have found Charity in that crowd. There were human heads everywhere. After the ceremony, I and my mother and Aunty Dimma proceeded to the designated meeting place by the car park and waited. It was not long before Charity joined us. She and my mother and Aunty Dimma did their hugging routine.

'Hmm . . . Charity, you're now a big chick!' Aunty Dimma said. 'You look so beauuuuutiful.'

'Thank you,' Charity said and blushed.

In her dark green River Island skirt suit and black Gucci heels, Charity definitely looked sharp. I had purchased the top-to-toe outfit specially for this day. No stupid man would ever jump out of the hedges and turn my sister's head upside down because of Gucci.

'Did you people see me?' Charity asked.

We had seen her sitting amongst the matriculating students, but at the end of the ceremony, she had disappeared amid the sea of tasseled caps.

Eugene could not make it. He had exams coming up soon and the nine-hour journey from Ibadan would have been too much of a distraction.

Godfrey eventually arrived. Accompanied by three of his friends. Dressed like a drug baron. Pierre Cardin shirt unbuttoned almost to his navel, white Givenchy, silver-capped shoes, and texturised hair. Two gold chains dangled from his neck, a gold bracelet danced around his wrist. No wonder he was constantly running out of pocket money and ringing me to send some more. Often, I succumbed. I wanted to be as much of a father to him – to them all – as possible. I wanted to be there for them in ways that my father had never been there for me. The few clothes I had in school – the ones that were not gifts from Ola – had come from the 'bend-down' boutiques, where different grades of secondhand clothing that the people in Europe and America no longer wanted to wear were displayed on waterproof sheets on the ground and sold. I made sure that my siblings wore the latest styles and the best quality.

'Sorry I'm late,' Godfrey apologised. 'Our car had to keep

stopping because one of the passengers had a running stomach. If I had known, we would have just paid for all the seats and had a taxi to ourselves. Kings, where are the things you bought for me?'

'I wasn't able to do much shopping on this trip,' I said.

'You didn't buy the CD?'

'I really didn't have the time.'

He frowned.

'Kings, that CD is the hottest thing right now. They haven't yet started selling it in Nigeria so just a few people have it.'

'I'm sorry. But don't worry, I'm travelling again soon.'

We posed for several photographs. Godfrey put the camcorder to work and attracted quite a few stares in the process. For the first time in a very long time, I missed having my father around. I could perfectly imagine him on a day like this. Proud, emotional, optimistic. Matriculation was not such a grand event as graduation from university so my mother had not done any cooking for today. But Charity had made me promise that I would take her and her friends out to a fancy restaurant. It was Godfrey who had given her the suggestion.

Charity went off to find her friends. My cellular rang. It was Protocol Officer.

'Kings, Cash Daddy said I should tell you to look out for him on TV on Monday night. He's appearing on *Tough Talk*.'

'Oh, really?'

'He said you should also make sure everyone in the office watches it. It's at 10 p.m.'

'OK, I will.'

I noticed Aunty Dimma staring at me in a funny way, as if she had been trying to read my lips. As soon as Protocol Officer hung up, my aunty miraculously found herself by my side.

'Kings,' she said quietly, 'what are you doing the Friday after next?'

'I'm not sure. Why?'

'I want to invite you to a special programme we're having in my church. It's a one-day deliverance session.'

'Deliverance from what?'

252

'All types. Deliverance from enemies, from your past . . .' She paused. 'Deliverance from demonic influences and evil spirits.'

'Ah. Aunty, I just remembered. I don't think I'll be free on that day. I have some things I planned to do.'

'You can still try and make it. Honestly, it'll be worth it.'

I promised her that I would try. I knew that I would not. Charity returned with her friends. About seventeen of them.

'Aren't they too many?' Aunty Dimma rebuked Charity in a red-hot whisper.

'Aunty,' I cut in, 'there's no problem.'

My pocket was more than equal to the task.

Thirty-four

The American Embassy officer scrutinised my documents. She scanned the pages of my passport and saw evidence of my frequent trips to and from the UK and the Schengen region. She saw written evidence that I had my own importing and exporting business. She observed my bulging bank accounts and knew that I could not be planning to remain illegally in her country, flipping burgers in McDonald's or bathing corpses in a morgue.

Still, the scowling brunette on the other side of the glass partition grilled me belligerently, as if it was my fault that she had found herself in such a lousy job.

'What are you going to the United States to do?'

'Let me see your tax clearance certificate.'

'Fold it!'

'How long do you plan to stay?'

'Why aren't you going with your wife and children?'

'Don't interrupt me when I'm talking!'

'Have you ever been involved in any terrorist activity?'

'How do I know you're planning to return to Nigeria?'

After about forty-five minutes, the inquisition was over. The Gestapo officer instructed me to return to the embassy by 2 p.m. the following day for collection of my stamped passport. Hurrah. My journey from Aba to Lagos had not been in vain.

'Thank you very much,' I replied. It was always best to repay evil with good. Besides, it could not have been any easier for Columbus; what right did the rest of us have to complain?

'Congratulations, my brother,' several panic-stricken visa seekers mumbled as I walked past.

I left the building elated. An American neuroscientist was very willing to invest in a Ministry of Education contract, and this new mugu sounded like another long-term dollar dispenser. The packaging was getting to a stage where I would need to schedule a meeting with him in Amherst, Massachusetts.

I walked past some other embassies on my way to the car park at the end of the crescent. Even the embassy of Bulgaria gates were besieged with long queues. The US and the UK – and perhaps Ireland – were understandable, but why on earth would anyone want to run away from Nigeria to Bulgaria? As I reached the car, I heard someone shouting my name.

'Kings! Kings!'

I turned. In that instant, I forgot all the sinister plots I had devised in murderous daydreams. All the diabolical strategies I had composed in midnight moments of pain and anger vanished from my mind. I beamed like a little boy lost who had just been found by his mother.

I ran screaming towards the sweet sound of my name.

'Ola! Ola!'

We rushed into each other's arms. We hugged like old friends. I looked her over from head to toe.

'Wow! Ola, you look . . .'

I stopped. She was as fat as a dairy cow. There were light green stretch marks tattooed into her swollen cleavage.

'You look lovely,' I said, and that was the truth.

'I had two babies, that's what happened,' she replied with a satisfied smile. 'You, how are you?'

'I'm fine.' I could feel myself still grinning stupidly. 'Honestly, you're the very last person I imagined I would bump into today. I just came for my American visa interview.'

She nodded.

'I came to renew our British visas – me and my children.'

'Wow. Ola, it's so good to see you. Why don't we sit somewhere and have a proper chat. I hope you're not in a hurry.'

She agreed. We walked around in search of somewhere to hang out. The complex housed a number of shops, business centres, and eating places, but most of the restaurants were dingy – obviously designed with only the waiting drivers in mind. Suddenly I remembered that times had changed. Ola and I did not have to put ourselves through this.

'Why don't we go somewhere nice in town?' I asked. 'We could go to Double Four or Chocolat Royal. Or wherever else you want.'

I was bold to throw the offer open. Unlike those days, now I could afford it.

'No, I'm OK with anywhere here,' she said and smiled. 'I'm not that hungry, anyway.'

We chose the least dingy restaurant of them all. The air smelt of a mixture of fresh fish and locust beans. Large and small flies buzzed and perched about with alarming sovereignty and audacity. A sweaty, matronly waitress who looked like she knew all the flies by name galumphed to our table. Eating anything in that place would have been like signing a treaty for the invasion of my digestive system.

'I'll have a Coke,' I said.

'Diet Coke for me,' Ola said.

I handed the matron the highest denomination naira note I had in my wallet. She grumbled and dug into her belly region in search of some change.

'You can keep the change,' I said, loud enough for Ola to hear just in case she had been distracted.

'Thank you, *Oga*!' the matron beamed. '*Oga*, thank you very much!'

'Kings, Kings,' Ola joked. 'You're now a big boy.'

I smiled. The drinks arrived immediately, served directly from the bottles, with a suspicious-looking straw sticking out from the neck.

'But Kings, if anybody had told me that somebody like you would ever do 419,' Ola continued, 'honestly I would have said it's a lie.'

Strangely, this was the first time someone who knew me, someone whom I did not work with, had told me to my face that I was a scammer. Nobody ever mentioned it. Even my mother, despite all her misgivings, was still in the realm of hunting for euphemisms. There was something emancipating about the way Ola had put the elephant right on top of the table. I would not have to spend our time together being furtive.

'I wonder who's been telling you these things,' I said with mock shock.

Ola laughed.

'How won't I hear? You know Umuahia is a small place. When a maggot sneezes, everybody hears, including people outside the town. Anyway, I hear you're still humble and level-headed. Unlike many of these other loud 419 guys.'

I sniggered.

'Ola, the things that change us are quite different. I always find it funny when people say that money makes people proud. If you check it, poor people are some of the proudest people in this world.'

My father, for example.

Ola kept quiet. Then she nodded.

'I agree with you, you know. Poor people can be soooo proud. There was a time back in school . . . that time I joined the Feed the Nation people . . . I don't know if you remember?'

Like almost everything else about her, I remembered it clearly.

'When we used to go out every Sunday to feed poor people in the streets. One time, there was this man who came and asked us for his own pack of rice and sachet of water. We gave him. Then he asked us to give him another one for his wife.'

They asked the man to go and bring his wife; they were only supposed to feed those physically present. He explained that his wife was ill. They asked him to imagine what would happen if everybody collected an extra portion for a spouse who was ill. There would be nothing for those who actually came.

As Ola spoke, a huge fly came and took up residence on her left ear. I wanted to stretch out my hand and frighten it away, but for some reason, I did not.

'Do you know that the man got so angry with us?' The fly ran away but returned almost immediately. 'He told us that we were insulting him, that we were calling him a liar. That did we think it was a big deal that we were giving him food?'

Then he flung the rice and water on the floor in front of them and stormed off.

'Can you imagine?' she concluded.

She had narrated the story to me the very same day it happened.

Still, I shook my head and tut-tut-ed in all the right places as if I were hearing it for the first time.

'Like I said before, I'm quite surprised that somebody like you is doing 419. You used to be so soft and innocent. How do you cope with swindling all those white people of their money? Don't you feel guilty?'

I shrugged. The fly left her ear at last.

'Well, I guess I just don't think about it too much,' I replied.

'But how can you not feel guilty?'

She appeared truly bemused. What was there to be guilty about? Was anybody feeling guilty about the artefacts and natural resources pilfered from Africa over the centuries? My mugus were merely fulfilling their role in the food chain.

'So how's married life?' I asked, changing the topic.

'Oh, everything is fine,' she replied quickly. The smile that should have accompanied her voice came some nanoseconds after she had spoken. 'My husband opened a new headquarters in Enugu, so we moved from Umuahia almost immediately after we got married.'

She paused.

'The kids and I will be leaving for London by next weekend.' Her face lit up with excitement; emotion had now returned. 'We'll be there for about two weeks and then we'll go on to America.'

She rhapsodised some more about the forthcoming holiday trip. I asked her what she was doing at present. All the excitement left her voice in a deep sigh.

'My husband doesn't want me to work. He wants me to just stay at home and take care of the kids and it's really frustrating. Everybody has tried talking to him but he's been adamant.'

Apparently, the man's decision had taken her by surprise. I could have warned her for free. His actions perfectly fitted the profile of the average, uneducated Igbo entrepreneur.

'What type of job would you have wanted to do?' I asked.

'I'd like to work in a large organisation . . . Something related to my degree. Or maybe just get one of these bank jobs that everybody seems to be getting these days. Anyway, I've already made up my mind. As soon as my youngest child starts school, I'm going to look for a job.'

'What if your husband says no?'

She frowned.

'Kings, leaving my brain to lie fallow is too high a penalty to pay for maternity. God knows I won't allow that to happen.'

Good luck to her. The best the man would probably ever allow her was a boutique where his friends' wives could go and purchase expensive shoes and bags.

'How old are your children?'

She smiled.

'Ah, I have some pictures here.'

She dipped into her Louis Vuitton handbag and whipped out a batch of photographs.

'These are from the birthday party of my first child.'

I inspected each photograph. There was a shot with the two children sitting in front of a huge Spiderman birthday cake with their mother and a man who, by the proud smile on his face and the way his hand was clasped around Ola's ribs too close to her breasts, appeared to be their father. Hopefully, my face did not betray my shock. Poor Ola – her husband was unpardonably ugly, as if he had done it on purpose. As if he had gone to a native doctor and asked for some juju that would make his face hideous. Where was I to start? Was it the square eyes or the spacious nostrils, or the puckered face or the quadruple chin? The man was a veritable troglodyte.

Fortunately for the children, their mother's genes had won the battle. The outcome could win a Nobel Prize for Nature. Ola's children were all quite handsome – saved, delivered, from their father's DNA. At that moment, I decided that if losing Ola to this man meant that the human gene pool had discontinued some frightful traits and produced a better-looking hybrid, then I was glad to have made my noble contribution to the advancement of humankind. I handed back the photographs.

'You have very lovely kids,' I said.

Like all proud mothers, she smiled as if she had been waiting all the while to hear me say just that.

'And they are American citizens,' she added. 'They were born in the US.'

I smiled louder, to prove that I was happy for her.

I asked about Ezinne, about her other sisters, and about her mother. She asked about my mother and my siblings:

'How's your uncle . . . Cash Daddy? I still find it difficult to believe that he's actually contesting for governor.'

I smiled. She laughed. Then, we were silent for a while. Sitting in front of her like that reminded me of old times, of how much I used to love being with her.

'So are you seeing anyone?' she asked suddenly.

I could not look her in the face.

'Not really.'

'Not really, how?'

'I'm not in any serious relationship.'

'How come?'

'How come not?' I forced a smile.

How was I supposed to tell her that while she was busy popping babies and growing fat, I was paying dollars for sex?

'I don't really have the time,' I lied.

'Time? Why? Are you burying your head in your books again? What? Are you doing a postgraduate course?'

Haha.

I sighed.

'Ola, right now, I'm not thinking about any of that. I look at my siblings and I'm satisfied that they're doing well and it makes me content with being the sacrificial lamb. I don't mind setting aside—'

'Kings, it's not worth it.'

The force of her words, though quietly rendered, could have smashed a hole right through the Great Wall of China.

'Kings, you can't set aside your goals and convictions just for the sake of your family or any other people. Take it from me, I know what I'm talking about.'

We went back to silence again, both of us deep in thought. I had spent my childhood daydreaming about my future as a scientist. Ola knew this. My name was going to appear in my children's science textbooks. I was going to be known all over the world because of my inventions. Top on my list, I once told her, was an electric fan that also ran on batteries so that the mosquitoes would not bite even if NEPA took the light in the middle of the night.

A wave of depression came over me. Ola was right. This was never the life I had planned.

Suddenly, it struck me. Inside all those layers of fat, the Ola I loved was still there. She had a way of getting to me, of making me think differently. She had seen me at my lowest and at my highest, at my best and at my worst. And I had not been able to talk to any other person with such easy freedom in a long time – with honesty, with confidence, without apprehension. Ola was my soul mate. Unlike my mother, she understood without being judgemental.

'Ola . . .' I paused. 'Maybe if I had you by my side, things would be different. Maybe you're what I need.'

She remained quiet. Abruptly, she stood and said that it was time for her to leave. She had not touched her Diet Coke. I had not touched my Classic Coke.

'Ola,' I said.

I reached out and held her hand. The warmth of her soft palm was as delicious as a forbidden fruit. I felt a slight tingling run down my spine. Still holding her hand, I asked if we could arrange to meet some other time. She did not respond.

'Even if it's just to talk,' I added. 'Even if it's just for a meal. You know I always dreamed of taking you out to somewhere nice and expensive but I never had the chance.'

Ola continued being quiet. After a while, she pulled her hand away and shook her head. In desperation, I cast off all restraint and said it.

'Ola, I still love you.'

She did not appear startled or repelled.

'I've never stopped—'

'Kings, let's not start something that neither of us can finish,' she said quietly.

'Ola, there's nothing to be afraid of. Things are a lot different now. I can make you happy. I have a lot of money and I can buy anything you want for you. Whatever your mother wants, I'll give it to her.'

Udenna was the least of my worries. His only merit was his money. I was educated, certainly did not look like a troglodyte, and my bank account could now do fair battle with his. I reached out for Ola's hand again. She drew it away and averted her eyes.

'Ola, please. We can both start our lives afresh. Please, just give me another chance. Please.'

She looked into my eyes.

'Kingsley,' she said softly, 'I've made enough mistakes in my life already. I think it would be extremely foolish of me to start making any fresh ones at this stage.'

She patted me twice on the cheek with her fingers. I continued staring long after she walked away into the car park. When my mugu's phone call rammed into my misery, inquiring about his payment for the completed Akanu Ibiam International Airport project, I almost asked him to take his millions and shove them up his Winterbottom.

Thirty-five

There were many possible explanations for the atrocious traffic in Lagos – population explosion, insufficient mass transit, *tokunbo* vehicles going kaput, potholes in the roads, undisciplined drivers, random police checkpoints, and fuel queues. But in Cash Daddy's opinion, the go-slow started whenever the devil and his wives were on their way to the market. I think he was right. Certainly, today's traffic looked as if the devil was behind it. Car bumpers were locked in French kisses. The masses, crammed into *molues* like slaves for sale, hopped out of the geriatric yellow buses and continued the rest of their journeys on foot. At this rate, I would be lucky not to miss my flight back home.

I had been granted leave to travel in and out of the United States of America for as many times as I pleased over the next two years. Hallelujah. Yet my mind was still troubled. Dear Ola. She seemed to hold some magical power over me. She could take over the steering wheel of my life anytime she pleased, drive me in whatever direction she chose, and then abandon me to navigate from there. Since yesterday, I had not stopped replaying my conversation with her.

Was the sacrifice I was making in 419 worth it?

Did it make sense to set my dreams aside in keen pursuit of cash?

I could do without the eight-bedroom house and the driver and the gardener and the cook, but how about the welfare of my family? My sister could do without McVities biscuits and Gucci shoes, but how about a good education? I sensed some motion by my window and turned. It was a muscular boy dangling a string of seven rats.

'Rat poison! Rat poison!' he shouted.

He rattled a row of red sachets in his other hand. Two of the rats twitched. I ignored the hawker until he got tired and left. I also ignored the ones that came with toilet seats, standing fans, cold drinks, gala sausage snacks, plantain chips, handkerchiefs, curtain rails, Irish potatoes, and apples. Then along came the boy selling books. When was the last time I read a book? The boy noticed my interest and clung to the body of the jeep when the traffic appeared to be moving a little bit faster. I wound the window halfway down.

'*Oga*, which one you want?' he asked.

I browsed the titles on display: *Rich Dad, Poor Dad*; *The Richest Man in Babylon*; *God's Plan for Your Financial Increase*; *Why God Wants You Rich*; *Wealth Building 101*; *Cracking the Millionaire Code*; *Talent is Never Enough*; *Nine Steps to Financial Freedom*; *Think and Grow Rich*; *Money Making for Dummies* . . . Then I noticed a colourful series of booklets.

'Let me see that,' I said.

The boy tossed four of the miniature books onto my lap: *Prosperity Scriptures*; *Healing Scriptures*; *Marriage Scriptures*; *Wisdom Scriptures*. I flipped through the prosperity booklet and chuckled at the first scripture that caught my eyes: 'A feast is made for laughter, and wine makes life merry, but money is the answer for everything.'

'How much is it?' I asked.

I paid the hawker for one copy. Then on second thoughts, I asked for another one. And one of the marriage ones, as well. Cash Daddy would probably find these books very helpful – an easy way to memorise yet more scriptures without wading through the entire books of the Bible.

Mr Winterbottom's patience was wearing thin. After disbursing several million-dollar instalments through different foreign bank accounts to cover the Akanu Ibiam International Airport project, he had every right to be upset. He had been ringing almost daily. It was time to pacify him. Straight from the airport, I went to the office. I switched on my computer and went to work.

The Contracts Review Panel
Central Bank of Nigeria
Abuja
Nigeria

Dear Mr Winterbottom,

PAYMENT OF OUTSTANDING DEBTS TO FOREIGN
CONTRACTORS

Following a recent review, it has come to our notice that
you have duly executed contract number (FMA/132/019/
82) awarded by the Federal Ministry of Aviation. The contract sum for the first, second, and final phase of the contract is $187,381,000 (USD). This excludes an interest of
$13,470,070 (USD) which has accrued owing to delays in
payment by the Central Bank of Nigeria. Therefore, the
amount due to you currently stands at $200,851,070
(USD).

Our office will immediately process this outstanding
$200,851,070 (USD) funds as soon as we receive fluctu-
ational charges of $6,730,000 (USD).

We apologise for any inconvenience caused by previous
delays. As soon as we receive the above sum, we shall
forward your outstanding $200,851,070 (USD).

Yours faithfully,
Mr Joseph Sanusi
Governor of the Central Bank of Nigeria

I printed the letter on CBN letterhead and put it through the fax
machine.

There was no dial tone.

I pressed on and off; still no dial tone. I sat at my desk, stood,
pressed again and again. Still nothing. With my cellular, I dialled
Camille.

'Is there anybody you can send to me this evening?' I asked.

'What time?' she replied.

'As soon as possible. I'm leaving work soon.'

'The notice is quite short but I'll see.'

Over time, Camille had done quite well for herself. She was now the recognised mistress of one of the state governors. Last time I spoke with her, she was on her way to Paris to shop for her birthday party. But she still made some extra income on the side by being helpful with organising girls for busy men like us as and when needed. Even when it was impromptu, like now.

'Is it the same place as the last time?' she asked.

'Yes. Same place, same room number.'

As a personal policy, because my siblings popped in and out of my house from school whenever they pleased, I never brought any strange girl back home. I had a permanent reservation at Cash Daddy's hotel. On his advice, for security reasons, I switched rooms after every few weeks.

'OK. I'll get back to you,' she said. 'I'll let you know if there's any problem.'

I knew there would be no problem. There never was with Camille.

Ninety-five minutes and some hgs of blood pressure later, the fax eventually went.

Afterwards, the girl had started watching *The Jerry Springer Show*. So far, I had stomached the transvestite dwarf and the ragamuffin playboy. But now, the 400kg black American woman was yanking the brassiere off the anorexic peroxide blonde.

'Could you please change the channel?' I said to her.

'Oh, sure, sure,' she chanted, and reached for the remote control. 'What channel do you want?'

'Anything else,' I replied.

She started flicking through. She hovered too long on MTV.

'Put it on CNN,' I suggested. *The Daily Show* should be on about this time.

It turned out that I was wrong. Instead of *The Daily Show*, Christiane Amanpour was telling the story of yet another man-made calamity that had erupted somewhere in East Africa. My cellular phone rang.

'Kings, hurry down to the house,' Protocol Officer whispered urgently. 'Come quickly.'

'Is everyth—?'

He hung up.

As I turned the doorknob, the girl switched back to Jerry Springer.

My driver was making the turn into Cash Daddy's street when I noticed the police cars parked in front of the gate. It was not the usual nonchalant policemen that hung around checkpoints extorting money. This posse patrolled decisively, like they actually had some work to do.

'Reverse!' I yelled. 'Turn! Quick! Quick!'

My driver obeyed and fled so fast that anyone would have thought the car was running on rocket engines.

'Just keep driving,' I said. I did not care if we went as far as Ouagadougou.

When I was certain that we were far away enough from danger, I collected myself and resumed the normal thinking processes that set man apart from the beasts of the field.

'Find somewhere to park the car,' I said.

We had found ourselves on the kind of street that was largely populated by dried maize husks, torn pure water wrappers, and straggling youngsters. My driver parked in front of an uncompleted building with a bold warning painted in red on the front wall: 'BUYER BEWARE OF 419! THIS BUILDING IS NOT FOR SALE!'

My driver looked at me in the rearview mirror.

'*Oga*, the policemen there were plenty,' he said.

He looked in the rearview mirror again.

'There must have been about twenty of them,' he added.

I was not in the mood for chin-wagging. This could be the very end of me. I could just imagine my mother's face when she heard that I had been arrested. What would happen to Godfrey and Eugene and Charity if I went to jail? I rang Protocol Officer and insisted.

'Tell me. What exactly is going on?'

'They're taking Cash Daddy to the station for questioning,' Protocol Officer whispered. 'But I just spoke with Police Commissioner and he said it's just routine. Hurry up because we'll be leaving soon.'

Back at Cash Daddy's house, some policemen who wore pot-bellies beneath their black uniforms were sitting with an almost empty bottle of Irish Cream and some wine glasses. I greeted them and strode past to join Protocol Officer, who was standing by the staircase in the dining area. He was flanked by the *otimkpu* and about seven of Cash Daddy's campaign team bigwigs, all muttering indignantly.

'Where's Cash Daddy?' I whispered to Protocol Officer.

'He's having a bath.'

I jerked my head furtively in the direction of the police officers.

'Do they know he's upstairs?'

'He told them to wait,' Protocol Officer replied impatiently, and returned his full attention to the group.

I turned to go upstairs and saw Cash Daddy on his way down. The policemen all stood and greeted him.

'I hope they took care of you people?' he asked.

'Yes, sir,' replied the officer who looked like he was in charge.

'Very good, very good.'

'Are you ready to go, sir?' the same man inquired.

'Let's go,' Cash Daddy replied.

The policemen allowed him to walk ahead and followed at a respectful distance. One of them rushed to open the back door of one of their vans. We watched Cash Daddy settle uncomfortably into the backseat before we jumped into our different cars and followed behind. On the way, my cellular rang. It was my house phone.

'Kings, are you back to Aba, yet?' It was Charity.

'Yes. I'm still at the office. I'm working a bit late today. I didn't know you were at home.'

'I just came in today. I'll be going back first thing tomorrow but there's something important I want to discuss with you.'

'What's the matter? Is everything OK?'

'Everything is fine. It's just something we need to discuss face-to-face.'

Face-to-face? I died with fear. Was she having problems in school? Were her girlfriends gossiping about me seeing strange girls? Had my mother been complaining about my lifestyle? It would be very unfair if she transferred her misgivings to my siblings. Whatever my mother felt about me was her business alone.

'Charity, I'll see you soon, OK? I'm just finishing up something urgent at the office.'

Cash Daddy's campaign manager was waiting at the police station, muttering into a cellular phone. Cash Daddy's lawyer was with him. The notable human rights activist accompanied his client inside for questioning. On the way, Cash Daddy stopped suddenly.

'Ah!' he said. 'I almost forgot.'

He removed the watch from his wrist, the phone from his pocket, the belt from his trousers, and handed them to Protocol Officer.

'Kings, let me give you some advice,' he said. 'Never take anything with you into the police station if you're not ready to part with it forever.'

God forbid. I, Kingsley Onyeaghalanwanneya Ibe, was being given advice for a trip to jail.

Soon, the lawyer emerged from the bowels of the station. Without Cash Daddy.

We panicked.

'Where's Cash Daddy?'

'They decided to keep him,' the lawyer replied. 'But they can't hold him for too long because they don't really have any evidence.'

'Evidence of what?' one of the campaign team asked.

'Money laundering. The allegation was made at the Zonal Command in Calabar, so the police here have to pretend as if they're really doing something serious about it.'

'Who made the allegation?' I asked.

'It's politics,' the campaign manager answered. 'They just want to get Cash Daddy out of the way. They know he's definitely going to win the elections.'

'These are the dangers I warned him to expect right from the beginning,' the human-rights-activist lawyer added. 'Nigerian politics is a dirty game.'

'They're wasting their time,' Protocol Officer said with flames in his voice.

'They've been writing all sorts of rubbish about Cash Daddy in the newspapers,' another one added indignantly, 'but thank God the people of Abia State are not foolish enough to believe everything they read.'

'No matter what they do,' yet another one added, 'Cash Daddy is still going to win.'

'Of course,' they all responded.

'Cash Daddy is our man.'

Back at home, I saw that in my absence Charity had once again arranged my shoes according to their colours. Wondering for how long I would be able to maintain the order this time, I unbuckled the Prada shoes I was wearing and placed them carefully in the caramel row. Then I sat beside her on the bed, where she had been waiting for me. Seeing the gravity of her facial expression, I became more deeply immersed in dread.

'Kings,' she began. 'There's this very close friend of mine I met through one of my friends in school.'

I swallowed a hard lump of fear.

'Kings,' she looked up at me with shy eyes, 'he asked me to marry him and I told him yes.'

Because of how serious she looked, I immediately resisted the temptation to burst out laughing. Truly, the idea of marriage makes girls suddenly behave strangely. I had never seen my sister like this before.

'What's his name?' I asked, strictly for want of speech.

'His name is Johnny,' she replied. 'But he's Igbo,' she added quickly. 'His Igbo name is Nwokeoma. Nwokeoma Nwabekee.'

Naturally, I would not want my sister to marry someone who was not Igbo, but right now, that was the least of my concerns. Throughout that night, I tossed and turned in bed, tormented by various fears. What would become of my family – what would become of my sister – if anything were to happen to me? Losing a father was bad enough. But losing their source of life and sustenance would bring unimaginable disaster.

And what would happen to me, their source of life and sustenance, if anything were to happen to Cash Daddy?

It was not until five in the morning that I remembered the girl waiting for me at the hotel.

Thirty-six

Cash Daddy was released by 9 a.m. He came out of the police cell looking dishevelled and disoriented, like a hermit who had just been discovered in a cave. On his way out of the station, he took some cash from Protocol Officer and distributed the hundred-dollar notes amongst the officers on duty. They thanked him profusely and saw him off to the waiting car. Protocol Officer had arrived in a Jaguar that bore 'Cash Daddy 47'. He came alone, with just a driver and without the usual convoy. Cash Daddy chatted briefly with his political cronies, dismissed them, and turned to me.

'Enter my car,' he said.

From the backseat of my Audi, I took the carrier bag with the books I had purchased in Lagos and instructed my driver to ride behind us. Protocol Officer took his usual position in the front passenger seat, I sat next to my uncle in the back.

We drove past a police checkpoint without stopping. This checkpoint had not been here yesterday. As usual, when the men-in-black saw the number plate on the car, they shifted from the roadblock, genuflected, and waved. Sometimes Cash Daddy threw cash out of the window at them. Today, he did not even look in their direction.

Before long, his verbalomania kicked into action and Cash Daddy, once again, became as talkative as a magpie.

'These people don't know who they're dealing with,' he began. 'Of course I know it's Uwajimogwu that arranged this police trouble for me. The eagle said that it wasn't a child when it started travelling long distances. I've been getting in and out of trouble since I was this small.' He indicated a distance from the floor to the air that was not higher than a toilet seat. 'Honestly, he doesn't know who he's dealing with.'

Uwajimogwu was his co-contender for the gubernatorial ticket of the National Advancement Party. It was general knowledge that even though there were at least thirty others who had collected forms and indicated their intention to contest, the fight was really just between both men. Whichever of them won the primaries was fairly certain to become the next governor of Abia State. The NAP was currently the strongest party, the one with the most billionaires and the highest concentration of reincarnated politicians whose histories went as far back as Nigeria's first democratic elections in the 1960s.

'He knows I have the police here under my control, that's why he went and lodged his complaints with the Zonal Command in Calabar. But they still don't have any proof. Money laundering of all charges. He wants to get me into jail and the only thing he could come up with is money laundering.'

Cash Daddy laughed. This tactic of digging into a co-contender's past to unearth crimes was proving quite effective in many states around the country. Just last week, a House of Representatives candidate in Delta State had been disqualified for spending four years in an Italian jail for drug trafficking. The man had kept denying the allegation until his opponents published the twenty-year-old records, which they had obtained from the Italian police, in five national dailies.

'At first, I tried to be considerate,' Cash Daddy continued. 'I had planned to allow a few delegates to vote for him in the primaries, but now he has made me very angry. I'm going to make sure that not a single vote goes to him on that day. He'll see that they don't call me Cash Daddy for nothing. If a person bites you on the head without being concerned about your hair, then you can bite him on the buttocks without being concerned about his shit. Is that not so?'

Fortunately, I was not required to answer.

Cash Daddy tucked his hands beneath his T-shirt and started slapping a rhythm on his belly.

'I'm very hungry,' he announced. 'I don't think I slept more than five minutes last night. Mosquitoes were singing the national anthem in my ears. I have to make a complaint to Police Commissioner. At least they should have put a fan in my room.'

From what I had heard of our police cells, the facilities in a horse stable were supposed to be better.

Cash Daddy stretched his upper jaw to the North Pole, his lower jaw to the South Pole, and yawned. A billion mosquitoes must have lost their lives in the malodorous fumes from his mouth. Cleaning his teeth must have been the very last thing on his mind this morning.

'I'm sure the whole of Nigeria has been trying to reach me,' he said, switching on the cellular phone Protocol Officer had returned to him.

His face split in another yawn. He peered through his tinted window. A blue Bentley was coming from the opposite direction.

'Is that not World Bank?' he asked excitedly.

Protocol Officer had already seen the oncoming car and confirmed that it was.

'I haven't seen him in a long time,' Cash Daddy said. 'Stop!'

The driver stopped. Exactly where the Jaguar was in the middle of the road. He wound down Cash Daddy's window from the control panel in front, and Cash Daddy stuck his head out. World Bank noticed his pal and must have commanded his own driver who stopped directly beside us. Also in the middle of the road.

'Your Excellency!' World Bank hailed. 'Long time no see!'

'My brother,' Cash Daddy replied, 'you know it's not my fault. I've been very busy with the campaigns. Every day it's one meeting after another.'

'It's a good thing I saw you now. Very soon, we'll have to fill forms and go through all sorts of protocol before we can see you.'

'That's the way life is,' Cash Daddy replied apologetically. 'From one level to another. Anyway, we shall survive. How are things with you?'

'Cash Daddy, let me give you notice. I'm throwing a party for my parents' fiftieth wedding anniversary in August. And I'm celebrating it big! Even my sister in Japan is coming back with her family. It'll be a good opportunity for a family reunion. The last time we were all together was during my father's burial. It's such a pity that he's not alive to witness the anniversary.'

By this time, there was a pile up of cars in both directions of the busy road, a road made even narrower by erosion and debris. The accommodating drivers waited for what they assumed would be a brief chat. When it went on for longer than was acceptable by highway etiquette, many of them started honking. Some stuck out their heads and yelled earnest invectives. Cash Daddy and World Bank were unperturbed. They continued their chitchat to its natural conclusion before saying goodbye.

While the driver was pressing the control to slide Cash Daddy's window back up, a man who was about four cars behind World Bank's Bentley, leaned out of a Datsun Sunny that looked as if it had been stuck together with chewing gum and tied up with thread.

'Thieves!' he shouted. '419ers! Please get out of the way! Was it your dirty money that built this road?'

As we drove on and past the Datsun Sunny, the irate driver stretched out a fist and punched the body of the Jaguar viciously. Protocol Officer took this action personally. He cursed loudly and started winding down his window.

'Don't mind him, don't mind him,' Cash Daddy said calmly, like the elephant who had just been told that the spider was coming to wage war against her. 'Just ignore him. You don't blame him, his problem is just poverty. Can't you see the type of car he's driving? If you were the one driving that type of car, wouldn't you be angry? That's why I don't like poor people around me. They're always looking for someone to blame for their problems.'

Reluctantly, Protocol Officer wound his window back up. Cash Daddy wagged his finger at me.

'But that doesn't mean you should cut off all the poor people you know,' he warned. 'They don't have to be very close to you, but it's good to keep them within reach, because they can come in handy once in a while. Me, I know enough pepper and tomato sellers who can start a riot for me any day I want.'

As we drove on, there was silence for a while. But not for too long.

'How did it go at the American Embassy?'

'I collected my visa yesterday.'

I gave brief details of the stressful interview.

'Don't worry about all that,' Cash Daddy said. 'By the time you reach America, you'll see that it was worth it. That's the same way they'll stress you at the point of entry, but it still doesn't matter. They'll even bring big, big dogs to sniff your whole body, but that's how they treat every other Nigerian, so there's no need for you to start thinking you've done something wrong. The only way you can avoid all that stress is to get an American passport.'

He yawned again.

'You're lucky that you're not yet married,' Cash Daddy continued. 'If I'd thought about it early enough, I would've married a woman who's a British or American citizen. By now I would have had my own full citizenship.'

He tossed his head back onto the headrest.

'By the way, Kings, have you decided when you're getting married?'

I snorted.

'You think it's funny, eh? Listen, let me tell you something. When a warrior is involved in a wrestling bout and has his eyes both on the fight and on his surroundings, even a woman can defeat him. That's why it's good to marry early. Better hurry up. Even Protocol Officer is getting married.'

'Ah! Protocol Officer? Congratulations.'

'Thank you,' he replied without looking behind. Years of sitting in the front of Cash Daddy's vehicles had taught him the art of turning his ears around without turning his head. I tried to imagine all that his ears must have soaked in while sitting there all these years.

When we drove through the gates of the mammoth mansion, nine men ran out of the house to welcome Cash Daddy. As soon as he stepped out of the car, almost all of them struggled to be the ones to clean his shoes. That was when it occurred to me just how much all of us loved him, how much he meant to us. What would become of all of us if he went to jail? Then I remembered the gifts I bought for him. I grabbed the carrier bag from the floor of the car before climbing out after him.

'Cash Daddy, here's something I got for you in Lagos,' I said, stretching the bag out to him respectfully, with my two hands and with a slight stoop.

'What?'

'Here's something I got for you.'

For once, Cash Daddy was as speechless as a stone. He kept looking at my hands without touching the bag. Finally, the shock covered the whole acreage of his face and passed. He shook his head slowly and took the bag from me.

'This boy, your head is not correct,' he said quietly. 'There's something wrong with you. Why didn't you use the money to buy *garri* for one old woman in your village? How can you be spending your money buying me things?'

He started walking towards the house. After a few paces, he stopped and turned.

'I was just thinking about it,' he said. 'Do you know that this is the first time in almost fifteen years that anybody has bought anything for me? Just like that . . . for no reason?'

He smiled like a delighted child and continued towards the house.

Thirty-seven

Charity had taken the weekend off school for the special occasion. Her suitor was paying me a courtesy call this Saturday afternoon. From my bedroom window, I saw that Johnny a.k.a Nwokeoma was not infected with the 'African Time' epidemic. He had arrived a whole seven minutes before his 2 p.m. appointment. To make sure that nobody mistook his brand new Honda for a *tokunbo*, Johnny had left the protective cellophane wrappings on the seat covers and on the headrests. Like many people, he would probably never tear the covers off but leave them to wear out with time.

My sister rushed outside to welcome him. With fury, I watched them embrace. I was daring the man to take their body contact any further when they held hands and sauntered happily into my house. Charity had him seated comfortably in the living room, then came upstairs to announce his arrival. I had been pacing up and down in my bedroom for the past thirty minutes, wondering what to say to him when he turned up. Still, I allowed an extra forty minutes to pass before coming downstairs. I did not offer any apologies for keeping him waiting.

Johnny presented some 'wine' to formally initiate me into his intentions. I received the two bottles of Rémy Martin cognac and placed them on the stool beside me. Since I was not particularly desperate for my sister to leave the house, I was not going to ask for a wineglass and sip from the drink immediately.

'I'm delighted to finally meet you,' he said. 'Charity holds you in such high regard. Very soon, you'll meet my family as well. They've all met Charity and they're also looking forward to meeting you.'

The man greatly amused me. He was tall, thin, slow, hairy, with heavy linear eyebrows that looked as if they had been cut out of a thick rug and pasted onto his face with cheap glue. Each time he shifted his head, I half-expected the eyebrows to drop onto the floor. His look was stiff and sluggish, like all his mannerisms. When he began a five-word sentence, I could have walked up the flight of stairs, gone to the bathroom in my bedroom, turned on the tap, washed my hands, turned off the tap, descended the stairs, sat down, and he would still not have finished speaking.

But there is some good in everybody: beneath his burdensome eyebrows, Johnny was quite handsome.

'I hear you're a banker,' I said.

'Yes, I am,' he replied as if each word had a phobia of the next one coming after it. 'I'm head of operations at the Standard Trust Bank in Okigwe.'

For a second, I relished the many advantages of having an in-law who worked in a bank. In our line of business, it always helped to have a banker on your side.

He went on to say that he had a degree in Business Administration from the Nnamdi Azikiwe University, Awka. He was Roman Catholic, his parents were civil servants, and he was desperately in love with my sister of course. Plus, he was thirty-four years old!

At that moment, Charity walked in with a tray of refreshments. The corners of the man's mouth expanded to his ears in a smile. He stopped speaking while she adjusted the centre table and deposited her offering in front of him. He fixed gleaming and delighted eyes on my sister from the moment she entered the room, while she was opening the bottle of soft drink, till she twisted her tiny behind and left. There was a strong possibility that his eyeballs would have popped out of their sockets if she had not left when she did.

I felt like bruising his handsome jaw with my fist.

'If everything goes according to plan,' he continued, 'we would be married by August.'

He was a British citizen, you see, and had enrolled at the London School of Economics. The postgraduate course would be starting in September. He wanted Charity to come along with him as his wife.

I listened to him broadcasting his well-calculated plans and thought to myself, what a fool.

He kept talking. His voice started sounding as annoying as a toddler crying on the plane during an all-night flight. I stopped listening and started wondering. Finally, I reached a conclusion. There could only be one reason why my young, intelligent, beautiful, naive, unassuming, impressionable sister would want to marry this cradle-snatching slug. He had a British passport. This Anglo-Nigerian was her ticket to a better world – a marriage proposal attached to a magic carpet.

The whirring noise in my ears suddenly ceased. The man had finished his ditty. Out of curiosity – strictly out of curiosity – I asked him one last question.

'What about her education? What will happen if she gets married now and has to leave the country?'

Of course he had that all planned out, too.

'That's not a problem. She can transfer to some schools in London. Or she can just start right from the beginning. It all depends how long we'll remain in the UK.'

I nodded. The man was not such a fool, after all.

'I plan to go and see your mother in Umuahia by next week,' he said.

Because I was *opara* – and in my father's absence, the head of the family – he had come to see me first.

When he was ready to leave, Charity accompanied me in seeing him off. As his brand new Honda slid out of my gates, she took my hand in hers and looked up shyly. She was anxious to know what I thought of her beau.

'He's OK,' I replied as we walked back into the house. 'He's quite OK.'

'Do you know that he's a British citizen?' she asked, her eyeballs swollen with visions of a magnificent future in El Dorado.

'Yes. He told me.'

We sat in the living room, pretended that we had both forgotten about Johnny, and watched a Nollywood movie about a girl who was engaged to a boy that she did not know was the child her mother had abandoned by the riverside twenty-three years ago. Just as Charity was slotting in Part 4, I invited her into my bedroom. We sat side by side on the bed.

'Charity,' I began, 'how did you say you met Johnny?'

'I met him through a friend at school,' she began excitedly, almost out of breath. 'In fact you even know her. Thelma.'

Who on earth was Thelma?

'She was one of those who came with us on my matriculation day. The one that sat next to you at the restaurant.'

Ah! The girl whose breasts were as big as if she were nine months pregnant with twins, who had kept digging her foot into my calf. And winking each time I looked up, oblivious to Godfrey slobbering across the table. The only reason why I did not follow up was because she was not my type and I did not want to just fool around with my little sister's friend.

'Oh, yes. I remember her,' I said.

'She's known Johnny's people for a very long time and she says they're from a good family.'

In other words, his family were neither *osu* nor *ohu*. None of their ancestors had been dedicated as slaves to the pagan gods of any shrine, none of their ancestors had been slaves to other families. And so we *nwadiala*, freeborn, were not forbidden from marrying amongst them. The first thing my father's sisters had wanted to know when I told them about Ola was whether or not she was *osu*. But with Johnny, I had other concerns.

'How long have you known him?' I asked.

'We've known each other for four months,' Charity replied. 'He's reeeeally nice.'

She placed an emphasis on the 'really', as if to distinguish between his own and the other types of niceness that exist. I nodded to show that I understood.

'Do you like him?'

'I love him,' she answered swiftly and confidently.

I nodded again. Something caught my eyes. Her matriculation photograph in a silver picture frame on the dresser beside my bed. She was wearing the mauve gown and cap that she had hired from the university. She was smiling in a juvenile way that showed her dazzling white teeth like a crescent moon in the sky. Charity had eventually misplaced the cap and I had had to pay a ridiculous amount to the school for its replacement. She told me that my unrestrained expense at the fancy restaurant had been the talk of her friends at school for days.

'Why do you want to get married now?' I continued.

She frowned.

'Because . . . because I've met someone I love,' she answered stupidly.

'You're not even up to twenty.' I did not wait for her to answer. 'Charity, there's no need to make any rash decisions that you may later regret. Look at you. You're bright, beautiful, and you have your whole future ahead of you. Even if you say you love him, it doesn't matter. You'll definitely find another person that you can also fall in love with. Life goes on and you won't die.'

The attentiveness on her face did not alter. Neither did she look like she was going to cry. I decided it was safe for me to push ahead.

'Charity, remember that you don't have to be as desperate as so many other girls are. There's nothing for you to escape from.' I paused. 'Charity, look at me.'

She lifted her gaze and stared into my eyes.

'Charity, you know I have money. OK? Plenty of it. Just focus on your studies and forget about a husband for now. OK?'

She nodded.

'I have nothing against Johnny,' I lied. 'But no matter how far you want to go . . . if it's Harvard or Cambridge . . . there's no problem. My money can take you there . . . and you'll be able to make better choices. Do you hear me?'

Charity sat frozen, so I took her in my arms and squeezed her tight. She placed her head against my chest and folded her arms into my embrace.

Right there and then, I realised that Ola was wrong. My sacrifice was worth it.

'OK?'

Her head moved up and down against my chest. We were silent for a while.

'Charity, do you want to go to London next summer?'

She looked up at me with awestruck eyes.

'I'll arrange a visa for you. We can travel together.'

She stretched her arms around my torso and hugged me.

Suddenly, I noticed that the matriculation photograph in the silver frame on the dresser was starting to swim in front of me. Then a drop of water tapped my cheek. I had not realised I was crying.

By two o'clock in the morning, I was still awake. I got out of bed, went quickly to my dressing table, and flipped open my wallet. I wavered. After a long glance, I removed the photograph. That Kingsley whose arms were once wrapped around Ola at the Mr Bigg's eatery on Valentine's Day had been standing guard in my heart for too long and preventing a successor from taking his place. It was now time for him to give way. Henceforth, he did not exist.

Before climbing back into bed, I tore the photograph into shreds.

Thirty-eight

I had tried to keep track of their names. After Camille, there was Jackie. Then Imabong, then Chichi, Precious, Amaka . . . These days, I no longer bothered to ask. Today's girl was getting up to go to the bathroom when I noticed that her right foot had a big toe that was much, much smaller than all her other toes.

The one thing these strange girls had in common was that they were all undergraduates of the neighbouring universities and poly-technics. They were forced to exchange their bodies for cash in order to bear the burdens of survival in school. Interestingly, of the girls that Camille sent, the ones drenched from head to toe in Fendi and Gucci and Chanel, were usually the ones who carted off all the soap and shampoo and body lotion from my bathroom, and the Cokes and bottled water from my fridge, on their way home. One particular girl had even stolen the pack of toothpicks, and the roll of tissue paper from the holder on the wall.

My cellular rang. It was Aunty Dimma.

'Kingsley Ibe! What kind of child are you?'

Her voice singed my ears.

'Aunty, what do you mean?'

'What do you mean by what do I mean? I find it difficult to believe that you, of all people, have turned out like this. Men! You people are all the same.'

'Turned out like how?'

'So you think your lifestyle is normal? You actually think your lifestyle is normal? That's the problem with money. It's an evil spirit. Kingsley Ibe, I don't like the person you've become!'

What made her think I liked the person she had become? She used to be less opinionated and less aggressive. If Aunty Dimma so badly wanted to be a man, she could at least try being a gentleman.

'Aunty, why are you shouting at me?'

'Kingsley, when last did you visit your mother?'

Her question threw me off balance.

'Errrr . . . I've . . . She . . .'

'Kingsley, I'm asking you. When last did you visit your mother?'

'Aunty, I've been very bu—'

She detonated.

'Busy doing what?! What is so busy about your life that you can't travel down to Umuahia and see your mother regularly? Is that too much to ask of a first son?'

I was defeated.

'OK, Aunty, I'll go and see her this weekend.'

'You can't wait until weekend. Go today! Your mother hasn't been feeling well.'

I swung my feet to the floor. The girl came out of the bathroom wearing nothing. My heart slammed against my chest. It had nothing to do with the temptation in front of me.

'Not feeling well? What's wrong with her?'

'You should be ashamed of yourself.'

'Aunty, please.'

'You should have been the first person to know. You should have been the one calling to tell me. But you're too busy. Busy making money for that criminal.' She paused to suck in a breath. 'She's been having eye trouble. I'm just coming from Umuahia. I spent the past two days with her.'

She ranted some more. I apologised. She terminated the call halfway through my apology. I sprang up from the bed.

'Is everything OK?' the naked girl asked.

I had actually forgotten that she was there.

'Get dressed,' I replied. 'I need to go out now.'

'Would you like me to wait for you?'

Never. Apart from the Cokes and toilet paper, it had taken a pair of Prada slippers, 100mls of Issey Miyake perfume, a pack of Calvin Klein boxer shorts and $3,500 cash for me to learn. These strange girls were never to be left alone.

'Get dressed,' I said.

I jangled my car keys and waited for her to gather her clothes. When she was through, I removed five $100 bills from my wallet and pushed them into her palm. She stuffed the money into her Ferragamo handbag and walked out ahead of me.

My mother was lying flat on her back. I held her hand and stroked her face. Her eyes were red and swollen.

'Kings, how was your trip?'

My trip to America had gone very well. It was my neuroscientist mugu's turn to visit Nigeria next. America was all that Cash Daddy had said it would be and more, but I was glad when my stay eventually came to an end. With the mighty portions of food they served in American restaurants, it would only have been a matter of time before my bathroom scale started reading to-be-continued when I stepped on it. No wonder many shrivelled Nigerians who visited yonder returned massive overnight.

'Mummy, how are you? How are you feeling?'

She sighed.

'They gave me some eyedrops at the hospital, but it doesn't seem to be helping much. The eyes have started swelling again and they're aching me right inside. I've booked to see the specialist next Thursday.'

I hissed.

'Mummy, don't worry. I'll come tomorrow and take you to the Specialist Eye Hospital in Port Harcourt. I hear they have the best ophthalmologists there. I'm sure someone will be able to see you immediately.' It was just a matter of cash.

My mother closed her eyes.

'Mummy, did you hear me? I'll come and take you tomorrow morning. First thing in the morning. OK?'

'Don't worry. I'll wait for my turn at the General Hospital.'

'But they ca—?'

Realisation struck me dumb. I continued staring at her in disbelief.

'Mummy, please,' I said quietly. 'We're not talking about a car or a house. This is a matter of your health. Please don't make a fuss over anything.'

Her sore eyes caught mine and held onto them with as much strength as they could muster.

'Kings, I'm not going with you to Port Harcourt,' she said calmly.

I stood up from the bed and paced up and down the room. I stopped abruptly in front of her with arms akimbo.

'Mummy, are you trying to kill yourself just to make a point? This is your health.'

'Kings, I've told you that I'm not going. Just forget it.'

Her voice was soft and steady, betraying neither stubbornness, nor resentment, nor contempt. I sat back on the bed and kept quiet. Then I pretended as if I had taken her seriously and started chatting about different trivial things. After a while, I left.

Before she had even woken from sleep the next morning, I turned up again at the house. Her eyes were so swollen that she could hardly open them. When I touched her, she sucked in air and grunted with pain.

'Mummy, get up.'

She raised her hand and shook it from side to side. No.

'Mummy, please get up,' I insisted.

This time, she did not even bother raising her hand. I cajoled some more, she remained silent. Finally I lost my temper.

'Well, if that's what you want,' I scolded, 'if what you're trying to do is punish me, you can have it your way. God knows I'm doing—'

'Kings,' she interrupted, speaking in the same soft and steady of yesterday, that betrayed neither stubbornness, nor resentment, nor contempt, 'the only way you can make me happy is to leave this thing you're doing and get a job and settle down. It's not your money, it's not your cars, that can make me happy. You know it really worries me no end.' Her voice became less soft. 'The way it is now, there's no time I think about you and I'm happy. No time at all. It's always worry and fear. And with Boniface and his politics, I'm terrified each time I think that you're—'

'Mummy, I've told you. I'm not involved in the campaign. I work strictly in the office while Cash . . . Uncle Boniface has other people working on the elections.'

She forced her eyes as far open as they would go. Her look seemed to ask if I genuinely thought she believed anything I told her any longer.

'Kings, please . . . Your father would be miserable seeing you like this.'

I slammed the door on my way out.

My car was parked beside Mr Nwude's blue Volkswagen. One of the back tyres of the faithful car was missing and had been replaced by a cement block. Some children were gathered around my jeep. They caressed the body and peered into the rear lights. One stood beside the driver's door, mimicking the whirr of the engine and pretending that the deflated football in his hands was the steering wheel.

Quietly, I retreated into the vestibule and watched. The likelihood that any one of them would ever grow up to own a car like that was low. Very low. I was one of the lucky few. And my own children would be bred from birth with cash. The good things of life would be natural to them.

Alas, with the kind of girls I had been hanging out with, the prospect of marriage and children was still very far away.

Thirty-nine

The place looked like a carnival. There were elegant and haggard, wrinkled-faced and fresh, respectable and uncouth. Many of these guests at Protocol Officer's wedding had probably strayed in from the highways and the byways. Most likely, many of them had never set eyes on the bride and groom before.

But the assessment of this wedding would depend on how well the hosts incorporated these unexpected guests into their planning. If the food ran out, the wedding was a failure. If there was still food for the inevitable latecomers who would arrive after the bride and groom had gone off to live happily ever after, the wedding was a success.

I experienced a moment of disorientation on seeing the colourful orange banner that ran from one end of the hall to the other: 'NWAEZE WEDS NKECHI'. Of course, the name on his birth certificate could not possibly have read 'Protocol Officer', but it had never occurred to me that he actually had a name and a life of his own, a life that was not attached in some way to Cash Daddy's welfare.

Three hours after the wedding reception began, right after the bride knelt in front of her husband and fed him with the cere-monial first meal – a piece of the wedding cake – the emcee put the ceremony on hold.

'Ladies and gentlemen,' he announced, 'right now, I would like us to acknowledge the presence of a very special guest in our midst. Ladies and gentlemen, please put your hands together to welcome the sponsor of this wedding. Chief Boniface Mbamalu alias Cash Daddy.'

The ladies and gentlemen put their hands together. Cash Daddy entered slowly, accompanied by his *otimkpu*.

'Cash Daddy, we would like to request the honour of your presence at the high table,' the emcee added.

Two female ushers escorted Cash Daddy to join the bride and groom at the table where they sat with both sets of parents. The *otimkpu* followed and stood behind.

The rest of us who went by the euphemism 'special guests of the groom', had our own special tables right beside the platoon of bridesmaids. Excluding those of us from the CIA, these special tables were occupied by people who had worked under Cash Daddy and had left to set up their own offices. They still saw Cash Daddy as their godfather, and still paid obeisance to him as and when due, like now. In my cream suit and brandy-coloured leather shoes, I was easily the most conservatively dressed of them all. Azuka, for example, was wearing a satin tuxedo and red bow tie. He spent a good deal of time throughout the ceremony chatting on his cellular phone. Clearly, his Iranian mugu had been taking good care of him.

When it was time for the couple's dance, all of us stood to join them and to paste currency notes on the couple's foreheads. In recent public awareness campaigns, the government had included this tradition of 'spraying' as one of the ways by which the naira became so badly mutilated. Rather than placing money on celebrants' foreheads and trampling on the money while dancing, the public was being encouraged to present their monetary gifts in envelopes instead. Although no Nigerian citizen was happy about the wretched and smelly naira notes, who could forestall all those young men who looked forward to opportunities like this to show off the fruits of their hard labour? I brought out the bundles of crisp notes I had prepared for the occasion. Some others on the special table unwrapped their bundles of dollar notes.

When the spraying was over and the couple seemed ready to return to their seats, Cash Daddy rose.

The live band noticed his advancement and quickly switched to a more titillating tune that allowed them to slot his name into the lyrics. Knowing that something good was about to happen, the couple intensified their gyrations once again.

Cash Daddy was not in a hurry. He took slow steps towards the couple while one of his *otimkpu* followed, carrying a small Ghana-must-go bag in one hand. Apparently, the Ghanaian economic immigrants had needed lots of the waterproof check bags when the Nigerian government sent them packing sometime in the eighties. Rather than pasting the naira, dollar, and pound notes individually on their foreheads, the dark-suited *otimkpu* handed Cash Daddy bundle after bundle. Cash Daddy ripped the paper bands off each bundle and split it into three, then flung each portion into the air nonchalantly, allowing the notes to shower down upon the couple in an avalanche.

The hall fell silent with fascination.

'Disgusting,' a disenchanted voice close to my ears hissed softly.

I turned sideways. One of the bridesmaids, the one sitting closest to me, had turned her seat towards the dance floor and was frowning violently at the show. I was turning away when something struck me. I swung my head back for a second look. The girl was quite pretty. Her skin glowed flawless ebony. She looked innocent, too. I must have turned to look at her at least five more times during that dance.

The last time I turned, she was already looking at me.

'Hello,' she said.

'Hi,' I replied and faced front, feeling like an idiot.

'Are you here on behalf of the bride or the groom?' she asked the side of my head.

I turned.

'The groom.'

There was an awkward pause.

'My name is Merit. What's yours?'

'I'm Kingsley. Pleased to meet you.'

We shook briefly. Her palms tasted nice.

'Kingsley? That's quite an interesting name. Is it Igbo or English?'

I thought that to be a very dumb question. Nevertheless, I indulged her. After all, who was I to complain when I stank so badly at small talk?

'It's English.'

'So how come I hardly ever see anybody who's not Igbo bearing the name?'

'Errr . . .'

'One of my cousins who grew up in America said all the people she met in America called Kingsley were Igbo. She said she kept asking people what the name meant in Igbo without knowing it was actually English. You, have you ever met or heard of any non-Nigerian called Kingsley?'

I laughed. The girl was right. I also had never encountered any non-Nigerian, any non-Igbo, whose name was Kingsley. We seemed to have hijacked the name.

'There're quite a few names like that,' she continued. 'Like Innocent . . . like Goodluck . . . like Merit.'

Both of us laughed at the same time. I wanted to add 'Boniface' to the list but restrained myself.

'Maybe they're Engli-Igbo,' I said.

She laughed at my dry joke!

This girl was really sweet. She was of medium height, slightly chubby, and had a fringe of hair which gave her a juvenile look that contrasted sharply with her voluptuous figure. She wore a peach flower in her hair. It matched her orange ball gown. While she spoke, she leaned slightly towards me and stared confidently into my face. Her voice was confident, too, and she gesticulated graciously when emphasising a point.

Merit proceeded with a running commentary on everything that was going on in the hall. She commented on the way people were going for third and fourth helpings and the way some people should have known that they were too fat to be eating so much; on the way the guests were laughing too loudly and the way nobody was listening to the bride's father's speech; on the way the elderly people were frowning disapprovingly at the young people's fashion sense each time any of the young people walked past them.

Wit came easily to Merit, like money from America. I found myself laughing a number of times. Camille and her crew were excellent in unprintable ways, but none of them had ever captured me with such humour.

'How do you know Nwaeze?' Merit asked suddenly.

The question was so out of the blue that I was taken aback. It took me a long moment to remember that she was referring to Protocol Officer.

'We both . . . He . . . He works for my uncle,' I stammered. For some reason, I was ashamed of the truth.

'Cash Daddy is your uncle?'

'My mother's younger brother.'

'No wonder.' She sighed, apparently with relief. 'All the while, I've been wondering how someone like you knew Nwaeze. So what do you do?'

'What do I do?'

'Where do you work?'

'Oh, I do my own thing. I'm into contracts and investments.'

'Where—?'

'How do you know Nkechi?' I asked, shifting the spotlight from me.

'Nkechi and I were best friends when we were ten. Even though we attended different universities, somehow we managed to keep in touch over the years.'

'Merit.' One of the other bridesmaids tapped her. 'Let's go.'

Merit stood.

'Are you leaving?' I asked, alarmed.

'Not yet. We're going to distribute souvenirs. I'll be back.'

She strutted off with the other bridesmaids. I noticed that Cash Daddy had left. Soon, the bridesmaids were going from table to table with huge sacks, distributing plastic bowls and buckets. There were also jugs and trays and mugs, and towels and notebooks and calendars. The souvenirs had smiling faces of Protocol Officer and Wife plastered on them, with names of the family members or friends who had donated these gifts. All of us at the CIA had contributed towards the notebooks and calendars.

Merit skipped several tables and hurried round to mine. She gave me two of each item in her sack and hurried off again.

Long after my colleagues at the special tables had left, Merit reappeared. The peach flower was missing from her hair. Her fringe was standing on end.

'Have you people finished?' I asked.

'Can you imagine?' she sulked. 'These people wanted to tear off my dress just because of souvenirs. Some people had up to ten trays in their hands, yet they were scrambling for more.'

'At least, when they get back home, they'll have something to boast with to those who didn't bother coming for the wedding.'

She laughed.

'You're so funny,' she said. 'Anyway, I just came to tell you that I'm leaving. All of us bridesmaids have to accompany Nkechi to her husband's house. They're expecting more guests there.'

I stared. I knew what I wanted to say but did not know how to. Truly, shy men suffer a serious disadvantage in this world.

'Take care,' she said and turned to leave.

'Merit.'

She turned back.

I was starting to feel like an idiot again. I forced the words out of my mouth.

'Is it OK for me to give you my number so you can call me sometime?'

She shrugged.

'OK.'

Delighted, I fished in my wallet for a complimentary card. My fingers had just caught one when I came to my senses. This girl might see beyond the Investment Coordinator of Bon Bonny Capital Investments appellation on my complimentary card to the real situation of things. She was smart.

'Sorry, I don't have any of my cards here,' I said. 'I'll just write down the number.'

I tore a sheet from one of the souvenir notebooks and scribbled. She took it from me and looked at it.

'Talk to you soon,' she said and smiled, then sashayed away.

Forty

Once again, Mr Winterbottom was getting out of control. I was tempted to end the show, pull back the curtains and allow the mugu to see the brick wall at the back of the stage, but that would be premature and cowardly. And I, Kingsley Onyeaghalanwanneya Ibe, had nothing to fear from any mugu in any part of the world.

I decided to press another button. Hopefully, more dollars would come forth.

The Contracts Review Panel
Central Bank of Nigeria
Abuja
Nigeria

Dear Mr Winterbottom,

PAYMENT OF OUTSTANDING DEBTS TO FOREIGN CONTRACTORS

We apologise for the delays in payment of $200,851,070 (USD) owed to you by the Nigerian government for the execution of Ministry of Aviation contract number (FMA/132/019/82). The delay was due to an ongoing restructuring within our organisation.

Please be informed that, owing to interest accrued over the extra delay period, the amount owed to you currently stands at $374,682,000.15 (USD). This outstanding amount will be paid into your designated bank account as soon as the additional fluctuational charges of $4.5 million (USD) are received by our office. Once again, we

apologise for any inconveniences caused by the delays on
our part.

Yours faithfully,
Mr Joseph Sanusi
Governor of the Central Bank of Nigeria

Now that the debt had ballooned to $375 million – almost double
the initial contract amount – it would be very stupid of Mr
Winterbottom not to keep playing along, especially when he had
already invested so much.

My phone rang. It was Protocol Officer.

'Cash Daddy said I should tell you that he's going to be on TV
on Saturday night,' he said. 'It's a phone-in so make sure you call.
Tell the others in the office as well. Write out some questions for
them. I'll ring again later so that you can tell me what the questions
will be.'

I went into action on the assignment immediately. When it came
to running errands for Cash Daddy, Protocol Officer was as brisk as
a bailiff. His 'later' could expire within the next thirty minutes, and
then he would be at my throat again for the list. I had gone as far as
the seventh question when, suddenly, Azuka screamed.

'Hallelujah! Hallelujah!'

Everybody else rushed over to his desk. I looked up from my
screen.

They all joined in the screaming.

It turned out that Azuka's good luck had reached its very peak.
So far, his Iranian mugu had dropped about $70,000. He was eager
to invest another $150, 000 and had just sent an email inviting
Azuka to a business meeting in Tehran. The Iranian businessman
wanted Azuka to meet some of his businessmen friends who were
also willing to invest more tons of dough.

'Congratulations!' I shouted across.

'Thank God!' Azuka replied.

Knowing Azuka, he would probably want to move out and
establish his own office as soon as he received his booty. Not that
I minded anyway. I preferred working with Wizard and the two

new recruits. There was a youthful passion they brought to the work that was almost beautiful to watch, a pure zeal that was not tinged by desperation. Unlike for most of us, who were nudged into this business by circumstances, 419 was a choice they had made simply by aspiring to be like their role models.

Azuka declared free lunch for everyone in the office, then came over to discuss the documents for his Iranian visa.

'How easy is it to get a visa to Iran?' I asked. I had never known anyone who went to Iran.

'It shouldn't be a problem,' he replied. 'It's almost the same as any other embassy.'

I started putting together the list of documents that Dibia would need to produce.

'Let me see the letter he sent to you so that I don't make any mistakes.'

Azuka went to his desk and forwarded the document. The passport would bear the name Sheik Idris Shamshudeen, all other documents would show that he was a contractor for the Zamfara State government. Zamfara was the first state in Nigeria to fully implement Sharia law; the Iranians would definitely fall in love with Azuka.

I read the letter twice to make sure that there was no vital information I had missed. Suddenly, I felt strange. I had this nagging feeling that something was wrong. It was a simple letter of invitation to meet with the mugu's Iranian partners, but something was amiss.

'Let me see the other letters he's been sending you,' I said to Azuka.

He forwarded many of the previous ones. I had just started reading through, when my cellular rang.

It was Merit!

'Kings, call me back on this number,' she said. 'It's my office phone.'

I scrambled to obey. Since Ola, I had not woken up in the morning and gone to bed at night with the same girl on my mind, but Merit had stayed with me. There was something about a girl who was not afraid to make the first move. I was never impressed by hard-to-get games. Saying hello when she noticed me staring at her at the wedding was obviously a come-hither gesture, and she had not feigned disinterest when taking my phone number either. Plus, I had not laughed so freely with any woman in a long time. Merit seemed to appreciate my sense of humour as well. Every human being deserved at least one person to laugh at his jokes, no matter how dry.

After a brief chitchat, we agreed that I would pick her up from home later in the evening. My heart started playing a new song.

Merit's house was not difficult to find. It was on a quiet street with humble buildings that were numbered in an orderly way. The residents might not have had too much money, but they were respectable and tidy. I found a space across the road from Merit's gate and parked. A young boy materialised by my car and tapped frantically on the window. I jumped. He said something which I did not hear.

'What?'

I still did not hear. He was super skinny, with a plantation of pimples on his forehead, but he did not look like a mugger or a psychotic, so I took a chance and wound down my window.

'Good evening,' he said. His pubescent voice was just beginning to crack. 'Please, is it Merit you're looking for?'

How was it his business? Nevertheless, I answered.

'Yes.'

'Merit said I should ask you to wait for her. She's coming. Let me go and tell her you're around.'

He took off at the rate of seven miles per hour, and dashed back out to tell me that Merit would soon be on her way. Soon, she appeared and trotted to the car. She looked and smelt like a rose.

'Please drive off quickly,' she panted.

Instinctively, I hit the accelerator.

'What was all that about?' I asked when we had left her street.

'Oh, it's my parents. They're usually quite meddlesome about my visitors. That's why I had to ask my brother to look out and tell me when you arrived.'

The skinny lad was her brother? Perhaps it was true that the most attractive girls seem to have the least attractive brothers. Anyway, he was young, so there was still hope for him.

'Aren't you old enough to hang out with whom you please?' I asked.

'My parents are deacons in Jehovah the King Assembly. They're quite strict about certain things.'

It was too early in our relationship for me to express opinions about a full-grown adult sneaking in and out of her house. I let the matter be.

'Where would you like us to go to?' I asked. 'Is there anywhere in particular you have in mind?'

It had been so long since I was on a proper date. I had no clue about where best to spend the evening. She suggested somewhere that I was supposed to know.

'You don't know it?'

'No, I don't.'

'I don't believe it. There's nobody in Aba who doesn't know where it is. That's the place everybody goes these days.'

She gave directions. I drove. As soon as we arrived, I understood why Merit had been so eager to come here, why this was the place where everybody went these days. There was a white couple and child sitting at one table and two white men sitting at another. These ones were not real white people like Britons and Americans, though. They looked more like Lebanese or Syrians or one of that type of people, but it did not matter. I had observed the same phenomenon in every Nigerian city I had visited. Any joint that was frequented by any category of white people automatically shot up in ratings amongst indigenes. The place was jammed. As Merit and I searched for a free table, someone called out to me.

'Graveyard!'

I turned.

'Graveyard! Longest time!'

It was my roommate from university.

'Ah! Enyi. How are you?'

We shook hands. I had not seen him since my father's burial.

'Graveyard, you look good. You look really good. I hear you're now a big—'

I cut him off.

'Merit, this is Enyi. We were roommates on campus.'

I asked her to go ahead and find somewhere to sit.

'I'll join you soon,' I said.

'Graveyard, you look really good,' Enyi continued after Merit left. 'I hear you're now a bigger boy in Aba. I hear you're doing very, very well. And you've put on weight!'

Who would ever have imagined? When they came to spend time with me during their last holidays, I had handed down a mountain of tight shirts to my brothers. I would probably have to pass on yet another batch when next any one of them was around.

'Honestly, Graveyard, I'm so glad I saw you today. The other day, I was telling some people that both of us were very good friends in school and they thought I was lying.'

I smiled some more. He dipped into the messenger bag strapped across his chest and extracted a book.

'Graveyard, I just wrote my first novel. Honestly, I'll be very honoured if you can attend my book launching.'

He handed me the book. *From Morocco to Spain in 80 Days*.

I was impressed.

'I didn't know you were a writer. That's great. Who're your publishers?'

'My uncle owns a printing press in Ngwa. They published it for me.'

I flipped through the uneven, poorly printed pages and paused to read. At least nine muscular typographical errors rose from the page and gave me a slap across the face.

'This book is just too much,' Enyi continued. 'I'm sure it's going to be a bestseller. It's about my experiences while travelling across the Sahara to Europe.'

I had heard of several Nigerians ready to risk wind and limb by making this treacherous journey across the desert in search of greener pastures. Some died or were arrested along the way, some were captured and kept in detention camps the moment they arrived. I considered myself lucky for the opportunity to sit at my desk and reach across to greener pastures with my keyboard.

I handed back the book.

'No, keep it. This one is your own copy. You can give me the money for it even if you're not attending the launching.'

I asked him how much it was; he told me.

'But that's the official price,' he added, then smiled and winked. 'A bigger boy like you, you can't just pay the official price. You have to put something good on top.'

'I haven't got much with me here,' I smiled back. 'I just came out with enough for our meal.'

'It doesn't matter. I can stop over at your office and collect it some other time. Is it not that building behind Bon Bonny Hotel?'

I handed him a complimentary card, anyway – as an act of noblesse oblige. He assured me that he would see me soon.

I joined Merit at the obscure table she had chosen in a far corner of the room. A waiter came round and took our orders. With Ola, we always requested that the waiters go and come back later to allow us calculate what aspects of the menu our pockets could handle. Merit made her choice of appetizer, main meal, and dessert without restraint. I felt like a real man.

We laughed and talked while we ate. She was an Accountancy graduate and worked with her father's friend's private firm in Aba. She was a year younger than I. She had an elder brother, an elder sister, and three younger ones. Her father had a private law practice, her mother was a civil servant. Her elder brother was doing a Masters in International Law, her elder sister had finished university two years ago and was now doing a course at Bible School.

'You know, you're very different from the first impression I had of you when I saw you at the wedding,' Merit said.

'What first impression?'

'Hmmmmm . . . ?'

'Was it the way I looked?'

'No, not the way you looked. I'm not really sure what it was. Maybe it's the people I saw you sitting with. I was a bit confused because you looked different from them, but at the same time I was wondering why you were sitting with them. It was after you told me Cash Daddy was your uncle that I understood.'

I shifted about in my chair. Perhaps I should hint at the truth.

'But I work for my uncle, though.'

She stiffened.

'Work for him doing what?'

'I help him with some investments . . . sort of like consultancy. He didn't like the way other people were handling some of his business deals, so he decided that he wanted a relative to do it for him.'

'Oh.' She relaxed. 'I hear he has a lot of businesses on the side.'

On the side of what? Like my mother, Merit was using euphemisms. Probably to spare me the embarrassment of having an uncle who was a 419 kingpin. The nice girl.

'Anyway, be careful about first impressions,' I said. 'The mind's construction is not written on the face.'

'Or in the clothes,' she added.

I laughed. She laughed. My cellular rang. It was Mr Winterbottom. I stood hastily.

'Excuse me, let me take this call,' I said to Merit and moved some distance away.

'It was really tough trying to convince some of the senior bankers,' Mr Winterbottom said. 'We've been arguing about it all day. They agreed to release this last $4.5 million dollars under the condition that the CBN will pay the full amount before the end of next month.'

I smiled.

'But I'm definitely not paying any more fees,' he continued. 'The bank has decided that this is the last.'

No need for Mr Winterbottom to take his bank's words too seriously. If given another good enough reason, they would cough out more.

I hurried back to Merit. We talked some more about false appearances, about life and current affairs.

'Do you have my house land phone number?' she asked at the end of the evening.

'No. You only gave me your office number.'

'OK, I'll give it to you. But whenever you call, please, if it's my dad or mum who picks up, pretend that you want to speak to my older brother. His name is Mezie.'

Forty-one

There was something suspicious about Edgar Hooverson's email. I read it several times even though it was very brief. My suspicion grew with each reread.

Suddenly, it hit me. I realised what had nagged at my mind when Azuka showed me the email from his Iranian mugu. I rang his cellular phone immediately.

'Azuka, where are you?' I asked.

'I'm at the airport. We're just about to board.'

'I've been thinking about that email from your Iranian mugu. Something doesn't sound right.'

'How?'

The Iranian mugu's email was similar to Mr Hooverson's.

After the meeting in Amsterdam, Mr Hooverson had started trying to raise the $70,000 for the lactima base 69%. When it was taking too long, Dr Wazobia asked him to send an initial instalment of $15,000 to see if the people at the chemical plant would be persuaded to give us at least quarter of a bottle. Mr Hooverson made the payment in three instalments. Afterwards, the chemical plant said it was impossible to sell quarter bottles. Fortunately, Dr Wazobia also had a friend who had a contact at the chemical plant who could arrange half a bottle. If Mr Hooverson could come up with at least half of the outstanding amount.

No reply from Mr Hooverson.

This was the first I had heard from him since then. After ignoring all my emails and voice messages, he had now written to say that he had the rest of the money for the lactima base 69%. He was eager for another trip to the security company and would prefer bringing the raw cash all the way to Amsterdam rather than wiring it. In his email, he spent too much time emphasising all the cash he was bringing along. Plus some extra in case we needed unexpected funds.

'Azuka, your mugu spent half of the email talking about the money he was going to give you and the plans for your trip to Iran. He didn't even talk much about the business proposal and his own cut from the deal. Are you sure he's not trying to bait you?'

Azuka laughed.

'Seriously. That's what it looks like to me.'

'Kings, don't worry. I've cooked the man very well in my pot. This is a clear deal.'

'Azuka, why not tell him you couldn't make it? Schedule another date.'

'Nooooo! *Hei*! Don't you know that he's already told all his partners I'm coming tomorrow? If I cancel, it might look as if I'm unserious. Especially after all the trouble he went through to help me with my visa. Don't forget we're talking about 150,000 dollars here – US dollars, not Taiwan dollars. Kings, after all my years of suffering, God has remembered me. This is my time.'

'You don't get it. It's not about the money. What's the point goi—'

'Kings, don't forget that I'm older than you,' he said testily. 'I'm old enough to know when something is not good for me and when it is. Relax. I have this thing under control.'

I sighed.

'Look. Kings, relax.'

'OK. But please ring me as soon as you get into Iran, so that at least I'll know that you arrived safely.'

'No probs. See you next week.'

I sat looking at my phone for a long time. Then, I went back to work. It was not always sensible to jump to conclusions, so I created a fresh email account.

Dear Edgar Hooverson (Mr),

Re: INTERNATIONAL COLLABORATION AGAINST AD-VANCE FEE FRAUD

I am writing to inform you that the FBI has forwarded us

your complaint and we are treating it as a very serious matter from our end. Please rest assured that our government is committed to doing all it can to curb this menace of fraudsters that are tainting our image around the globe, and to tighten the loopholes that make it easy for them to operate.

We would appreciate any assistance you can render us to catch these men and put them behind bars. Once they are captured, we would ensure that any monies seized would be returned to their rightful owners.

Yours faithfully,
Dr Nuhu Ribadu
Director, Economic and Financial Crimes Commission
Abuja, Nigeria.

I hoped the email was vague enough to keep Mr Hooverson singing my tune even if my suspicion turned out to be wrong. But his reply, which was almost instantaneous, settled the whole matter.

Dear Dr Ribadu,

Thank you SO MUCH for your email. I am HAPPY to say that I CAN HELP! We can work TOGETHER to get these WICKED men into police custody where they belong!

I was pleasantly SURPRISED to hear from you. I reported my case to the FBI but they did not APPEAR to take it SERIOUSLY—

I went on to read about how he got to know that he was being scammed through a co-worker whom he had asked for a loan and how he had been in and out of hospital ever since; how his therapist had suggested that he contact the *Oprah* and *Montel* shows for an opportunity to tell the world what he had been through.

As usual, Cash Daddy had been right. Mr Hooverson, described me as 'a YOUNG MAN in his twenties who looked and sounded

WELL-EDUCATED and who had a very HONEST FACE'. He had even attached copies of all our email correspondence. Honestly, these white people were so funny. Did they really think that everybody else had the energy to expend on all sorts of fanciful troubles like they did? Dr Ribadu was too busy running after the billions of dollars that were going missing from the national and state coffers every day. When would the poor man have time to read all this?

But letter writing was my source of income, so I had all the time in the world to reply.

Dear Edgar Hooverson (Mr),

Re: INTERNATIONAL COLLABORATION AGAINST ADVANCE FEE FRAUD (VICTIMS REIMBURSEMENT)

Thank you for your prompt response. I am happy to inform you that, right now, we have in our custody a number of gangs of scammers who have been operating from Amsterdam for the past few years. We have seized all their assets and frozen all their accounts. We are currently working with the FBI to ensure that all the monies recovered are returned to their rightful owners.

From your story, it appears that you might have been one of their victims. I am glad to see that we have your full cooperation. The millions of dollars contained in their accounts will be used to refund as many victims as we can contact. We promise to do our best to ensure that all your stolen funds are returned to you.

Please send us any documented proof of whatever payments you made to the scammers. This should help us calculate exactly how much to refund you.

To facilitate the process of retrieving your funds, we would require a payment of $5,000 US dollars for the International Collaboration fees. This payment should be received within the next two weeks. Your stolen funds will be ready for clearance four days after payment.

I hope this unfortunate encounter will not prevent you from doing business with Nigerians in future. There are many great Nigerians helping to move the economies of the world forward.

Yours faithfully,
Dr Nuhu Ribadu
Director, Economic and Financial Crimes Commission
Abuja, Nigeria.

Forty-two

We never saw Azuka again. Four days after he was due back in Nigeria, I rang the Tehran hotel and confirmed that he had not come back to his room since his first night. I rang the airline and was informed that his return ticket had not yet been used. I rang his mugu's contact numbers and was greeted by a polite female voice who responded in Arabic from beginning to end. Or maybe the language was Iranian. After a week of searching and trying, the whole Central Intelligence Agency was bleak with despair.

'Kings, do you think he's been arrested?' Buchi asked.

'I have no idea.'

'But had he seen the mugu by the time he called you?' Wizard asked.

'No. They had spoken, but he was just leaving the hotel for the meeting. The hotel said he hasn't come back since. All his stuff is still in the room.'

'Can't we go to the Iranian Embassy and make a report?' Buchi asked.

'How can?' Wizard and Ogbonna replied at the same time.

'Even if we pretend to be his relatives,' I explained, 'that means we'll have to give them our contact details to get back to us when they find him. That could just be a neat trap for them to catch all of us.'

The two new recruits flashed wide open eyes, their faces flooded with dread.

'How about the Nigerian Embassy in Tehran?' one of them asked.

'Who will we tell them we're looking for?' Ogbonna asked back. 'Sheik Shamshudeen or what?'

'What do you think they could have done to him?' the second one asked.

'Ah,' Wizard replied. 'You know in Iran they use Sharia law. They can either cut off his two hands or just behead him. Simple.'

There was a deathly silence.

'Kings, maybe you should let Cash Daddy know,' Buchi suggested quietly.

'Let's wait a little and see what happens,' I replied. 'I'll try to think of something.'

After all, it was all my fault. Why had I changed Azuka's mind about his bad luck? His pessimism might have been his salvation. Perhaps, I did not present my misgivings strongly enough. He might have been dissuaded from going.

'We're here worrying ourselves,' Wizard said with an attempt at cheer in his voice. 'For all we know, they might have given him seventy virgins to keep him busy. That might be why he's forgotten to call.'

Nobody laughed.

I went through the rest of the day's tasks like a zombie. All my colleagues looked as if they had been sautéed in a deep fog. I thought, kept thinking, and continued thinking, but no solution came to mind. This 419 thing had always been like a game to me – hooking mugus, making hits, returning to the scene of the crime and making more hits. For the first time, I was seeing a chill wind in our game. My sang-froid was in ribbons.

Eventually, I rang Merit. Thankfully, her evening was free.

'I'll be at your house around six,' I said.

'OK, I'll ask my brother to watch out for you.'

At least there was something cheerful to look forward to after all this gloom. Merit's company was a true delight. She could discuss any topic intelligently, her opinions always made sense, but unlike Ola, she was quick to say whatever she thought. At first, I was concerned that she might be an Aunty Dimma in training, but Merit knew the limits of womanhood. On one of the evenings we were out together, I got tired of wincing each time she leaned towards me and finally told her what I thought of her new hairdo.

'You look much better with your natural hair,' I said. 'I don't think you need to use hair extensions.'

Plus, the hair reminded me too much of the Camille crew. There was never any of them who did not have someone else's hair stitched into her scalp.

For almost thirty minutes after my comment, Merit made her strong arguments for hair extensions. At a point, I just kept quiet and let her talk.

'And who says it's someone else's hair?' she concluded. 'After all, I paid for it with my own money.'

Nevertheless, she had taken off the extensions the very next day.

After all was said and done, I preferred a girl who was forthright from the beginning to one who was coy and submissive when things were good and who ended up shutting you out coldly when things went bad.

And best of all, since meeting Merit, I had never once rung Camille.

Days later, I was still worrying about Azuka. I acknowledged defeat at last. Cash Daddy's phone rang out the first time. The second time, he answered after seven rings. His environment sounded rowdy.

'Cash Daddy, please, there's something I'd like to discuss with you.'

'What is it?'

'It's about the office.'

'What type of rubbish is that?' he yelled. 'Why didn't he sign the document?'

I heard a cowering response from someone in the background and was relieved to realise that my uncle had not been talking to me.

'And so what if it's not their policy?' he yelled on.

The beneficiary of his tirade said something.

'What car does he drive?' Cash Daddy asked.

I did not hear the response.

'Burn down that old car and resurrect another one for him within three days,' Cash Daddy replied. 'Then take that document back for him to sign.'

Cash Daddy then returned to me.

'Kings, what's the problem? How can you be disturbing me with office matters now? I'm beginning to get very suspicious of you. Do you want me to be the next democratically elected executive governor of Abia State or not? You'd better tell me now.'

'Cash Daddy, we haven't heard from Azuka since he went to Iran. He was due back more than a week ago.'

He was silent for a very long while.

'I have meetings lined up the whole of today,' he said at last, in a mellowed voice. He was silent again. 'Anyway, no problem. Come and see me tonight. I'll be at my hotel.'

If anybody had any doubts before, Cash Daddy was clearly now a very important man in Abia State of Nigeria. Four policemen were standing outside the seventh-floor elevator. There were several more policemen and men in dark suits lining the corridor. And they were not the usual noise-making *otimkpu*; these ones were fully armed to the toenail. My uncle's head of security identified and passed me, but I was still stopped and searched three different times before finally reaching his suite. Obviously, Cash Daddy had heeded the warnings of his lawyer about the dangers of Nigerian politics. He was not taking any chances on his enemies sneaking up on him while he slept.

Protocol Officer was sitting with Cash Daddy's campaign manager in the outer room. He asked me to go inside.

The ticket holder of the NAP gubernatorial ticket was sitting on the bed with a towel wrapped around his waist, shouting into his cellular phone. There were three Indian girls in exotic Indian wear, massaging different parts of his body. Apparently, the local market was no longer sufficient; my uncle was now hiring expatriate genitalia.

'Kings, what did you say happened to Azuka?' he asked as soon as he finished his call.

I leaned forward in my chair.

'Cash Daddy, honestly, I don't even know where to start.'

'Make up your mind quickly,' he replied, and lay flat on his belly in bed. 'My eyes are almost closing.'

I told him everything, not forgetting to mention my warning to Azuka and all my efforts to trace him so far. All the while I was speaking, Cash Daddy's eyes were closed and the girls continued moving their hands up and down his body. He remained like that for a long time after I finished. Just when I had concluded that he had fallen asleep, he spoke, still without opening his eyes.

'Kings, tell me what you think. If a man is standing on the rail track and a train comes and knocks him down. What would you say killed him?'

I did not say anything.

'Kings.'

'Yes, Cash Daddy.'

'What will you say killed him?'

'Azuka?'

'Noooo. The man standing on the rail track.'

'The train?'

He laughed.

'It's not the train. It's his stupidity that killed him. Or his deafness. One of the two. Did he not hear the train coming? I'm disappointed. I'm very, very disappointed. I knew Azuka had bad luck, but I didn't know he was this stupid. I can't believe I had such a stupid person working for me. How can he carry his two legs and go to Iran?'

Listening to him was somehow a relief. Cash Daddy was right. Azuka had been stupid, and there I was thinking it was my fault. There I was worrying that this business of ours was more dangerous than I had previously thought, that I might someday fall into unforeseen troubles. It was all about sense and craft. And I was certainly not as stupid as Azuka. Like the spider spinning her web and knowing which threads were safe for her to tread on and which were the sticky ones meant to trap her meals, I was quite a master at the work of my hands. One of the Indian girls started cracking the knuckles of Cash Daddy's toes.

'The thing about our business is that one has to be smart,' Cash Daddy continued. 'There are mugus in America, Britain, Germany, Russia, Argentina, France, Brazil, Switzerland, Spain, Australia, Canada, Japan, Belgium, New Zealand, Italy, Nether- lands, Denmark, Norway . . . Kings, remind me. What other countries?'

'Spain.'

'No. I've already mentioned that one.'

'Japan.'

'I've also mentioned that one.'

'Errr . . . Israel.'

'Good! Even Israel. There are mugus all over the world. Yet it's the one in Iran that Azuka went to look for. Doesn't he know that those ones are not real *oyibo* people? Their level of mugu is not as high. In fact, they are almost as smart as we are. Me, I'm not afraid of anybody, but I know where to put my leg and where not to put my leg. That's one of the secrets of my success. Azuka was just stupid.'

He hissed and kept quiet.

'But, Cash Daddy, isn't there anything we can do?'

'Of course, there is. Why not? First thing tomorrow morning, you can go to the Iranian Embassy and tell them you're looking for one of your brothers who went to Tehran to collect from a mugu. Tell them that both of you do jobs together, that your brother hasn't yet come back and you're missing him at the office.' He paused. 'Or, you can go all the way to Iran and try and find the mugu. You have the man's address, don't you?'

I sat there, gripping the arms of my chair. My head was woozy, my palms were sweaty, my heart was thumping fast. Azuka was gone. Vanished. Just like that. And there was nothing any of us could do about it. Not even Cash Daddy who usually had a solution to every problem.

To think that Azuka had been so gay and confident on his way to doom, like the moth as it dances into the flame. What if disaster suddenly overtook me while I was feeling safe and smug? What if the FBI or Interpol were waiting when next I turned up at an airport? What if a disgruntled mugu somehow traced me back to Nigeria and did my family harm? I could almost feel my hair whitening with fright.

'Don't you?' Cash Daddy repeated.

I jumped.

'Yes, I do,' I replied slowly.

'Good. You can go tomorrow. If you leave for Lagos tomorrow

morning, you should be able to catch the first flight to Iran. But before you go, make sure you tell me what story you want me to tell your mother when you don't come back. Which reminds me. Why have you been having problems with your mother?'

'What problems?' I asked, surprised. I had never discussed anything about my mother with him.

'This woman phoned the other day. What's her name? That mad woman who left her husband's house.'

'Aunty Dimma?'

'Yes, that's the one. I couldn't talk to her, but she left a message with Protocol Officer on my phone. She said your mother is very worried about you, that I should leave you alone to go and find a job. What's the problem? What's happening?'

Aunty Dimma and her uninvited opinions yet again. But there was something about the atmosphere, something about the realisation that Azuka might be gone forever and Cash Daddy's swift change of subject beyond that problem, that made me gush. Like a geyser, I vented everything, complete with my mother refusing my gifts and better medical treatment when she was ill.

'Sometimes when I go to visit her,' I concluded, 'I wonder if all the money I'm making is worth it. I think she was even happier when she had nothing except the hope that I would one day get a job and start taking care of her. Honestly, I don't know what to do. Sometime ago, I was considering maybe going back to school to do a postgraduate or something. I really don't know.'

'There's a pimple on my cheek,' Cash Daddy said. 'Press it.'

'Sorry?'

'There's a pimple on my cheek,' Cash Daddy said again. 'Press it.'

I realised that he was talking to his Indian girls. Apparently, none of them expected that talking or listening would be part of the job description. They ignored his instruction.

'Kings, I don't think these girls understand English. Explain to them what I'm saying.'

I reached out and tapped one of the girls. With fingers on my face, I puffed out my cheek, and showed her what Cash Daddy wanted.

'Ahhnnnnnnnnnnnn,' she said and smiled, then went to work.

'So how is your mother's health now?' Cash Daddy asked. 'Is she feeling better?'

'Yes, she's a lot better. She eventually saw the eye specialist and they did some tests. The medicine he gave her seems to be working.'

He nodded.

'Kings, I don't believe that at this stage in your life you're still talking about going back to school. Look, don't burn down your whole house because of the presence of a rat. You know what we shall do? Just hold on for a while. Just hold on. Once I become governor, I'll find you one small political appointment that will keep her happy.'

He flapped his right hand in the air like someone flicking through a bulky file.

'Maybe something in the Ministry of Education or Ministry of Finance,' he said, arriving at the page he wanted at last.

'How about the Ministry of Works and Transport?' I asked. Since my father had worked there, my mother would definitely be thrilled.

'If that's what you prefer,' Cash Daddy replied. 'But it has to be something small that won't take too much of your attention. Because as soon as I become governor, I'll have even less time for business than I have now.'

It was understandable for Cash Daddy to be concerned about the future of his business. He had spent years building things up to this level – the local and foreign contacts, the staff, the expertise. He had also taken great pains to recruit and groom me. His suggestion made sense.

'The problem with you is that you don't know how to think,' Cash Daddy continued. 'Too much book has blocked your brain. You see all these problems you're having with your mother? They will all disappear as soon as you get married. Can you imagine how happy she'll be if you brought a wife for her? Once your mother starts seeing grandchildren all over the place, she'll forget about your job.'

Hmm. This sounded quite attractive. And Merit had the sort of appearance that my mother was likely to fall for. She looked like a utensil, not an ornament.

'Even me,' Cash Daddy continued, 'I'm thinking of picking an extra wife. Because of my new status. You understand?'

He asked the question solemnly, like a humble man struggling to cope with the greatness that had suddenly been thrust upon him. I nodded.

'After my first term in office, when I'm campaigning for second term, I want to have a beautiful young woman who'll be following me around. I hear that's the way they do it in America. I hear they even carry their children around with them sometimes. Maybe, I'll bring my boy to join me, too. You know he speaks very, very good English. His English is even better than yours.'

How would his current Mrs react to the concept of her husband bringing in a second wife who would be the face of her husband's campaigns? I could only imagine.

'But Kings, sometimes you make me wonder.'

He shook his head out of the pimple-presser's grasp and turned to me.

'Look, there are many different ways to kill a rat. You just need to forget all the books you read in school and learn how to think smarter. A person who doesn't know how to dance should look at those who know and imitate their steps. Look at me for example. You know I have my car showrooms and my filling stations?'

I nodded.

'You know I have my hotels and my rented properties?'

I nodded.

'That's being smart. That way, when people ask, I can always point and say, this is what I do that brings in my money, that's what I do that brings in my money. Do you understand what I'm saying?'

I nodded.

'You need to look for ways to invest the money you have loaded in your account. There are so many business opportunities for you to choose from. Take telecommunications for example. With this new GSM technology, soon, everybody is going to be able to afford cellular phones. What stops you from getting involved in that? Then there's the Internet. From what I hear, very soon, even poor people won't be able to do anything without using the internet. What stops you from importing equipment and starting your own business centre?'

He waited for me to answer.

'Nothing.'

'You see? Kings, use your brain. If the cow makes its tail beautiful, it will be useful for swatting flies; if it makes its horn beautiful, it will be useful for drinking wine. Learn how to make your money work for you.'

As usual, Cash Daddy was making a great deal of sense. The best thing was just to put Azuka out of my mind and move on with my life.

Forty-three

The documentary was called *Chief Boniface Mbamalu – The Politician, The Man*. All his years of living on stage, of playing the parts of ambassadors and business moguls and top government officials, were definitely paying off. Cash Daddy sat composed in a knee-length *isi-agu* outfit and red cap. With legs spread slightly apart and hands folded on his knees, my uncle stared the viewers straight in the eyes and repeated his original promises. He had mapped out strategies to attract foreign investors for the development of infrastructure. He was determined to eliminate corruption from Abia State, starting from the grass roots. He knew he had enemies who did not want him to be governor because they were afraid of his planned reforms, but he was undeterred. It was all about the people of Abia. He was willing to lay down his life for us.

The producers had also interviewed his mother, people from his local community, and people who had benefitted from his various works of charity. I was shocked to learn that, for the past five years, my uncle had been giving scholarships to every single law student from Isiukwuato Local Government Area who was studying in a Nigerian university. He had boasted to me about almost every work of charity he was engaged in. Why had he never mentioned this?

'Why did he choose only the law students?' Eugene asked.

'We're the learned profession,' Charity replied.

'Please, shut up,' Eugene said. 'You make so much noise about this your law. What do you then expect us doctors to do?'

This was one of those rare times when all my siblings were back home on school holidays at the same time. Godfrey had made my house his permanent base for the past year or more; Eugene and Charity had come from Umuahia a few days ago. All universities had thought it wise to take a break and reopen after the elections.

No school wanted to bear the burden of quelling any tempests that might arise from polling day turbulence.

My mother's niece's daughter came out of the kitchen.

'Brother Kingsley, your food is ready.'

I left my siblings to their teasing and went over to the dining room. They had already eaten. I realised how hungry I was when I got a whiff of the thick paste of *egusi* soup that had huge chunks of chicken, *okporoko* fish, and cow leg protruding from the exotic china bowl.

The front door opened and there was a noise as if a riot had just started in the market.

'Hey, Kings!' Godfrey shouted on his way upstairs.

'Hello,' I responded.

Godfrey was hardly ever without his party of friends. Each day, he appeared with a new set. The two chaps he had come in with also greeted me and followed him upstairs. They were having a rowdy conversation about a European Champions League football match and making almost as much noise as the supporters who had gathered in the stadium for the match must have made. Recently, my brother had bestowed his life on the Arsenal football club. He never missed watching any of their matches, knew the names and birthdays of all the players, and had their face caps, mufflers, T-shirts . . . If only my brother could be more responsible with his time and money.

My cellular rang. It was Merit.

'Did you remember to watch the documentary on Cash Daddy?' I asked.

'No.'

'Oh, you really should have. It was quite interesting. His villagers even have a special song they composed to extol his good works.'

I sang a bit of it and laughed. She may have laughed, she may not.

'*O dighi onye di ka nna anyi* Cash Daddy, *onye Chineke nyere anyi gozie anyi,*' I sang some more.

I laughed; she certainly did not.

'Merit, is everything OK?'

'Kingsley, why did you lie to me?' Her tone of voice could have slain Goliath.

'What do you mean by that?'

'I'm so upset with you. I don't believe you had me fooled. Did you really think I wasn't going to find out? Kingsley, what do you do for a living?'

Her question struck me like thunder.

'What do you do for a living?'

'I'm into contracts and investments,' I replied calmly, though sirens were blaring in my head. 'I already told you that before.'

'Kingsley, stop! How long were you going to keep lying to me?'

'Merit, honestly, I don't know what you're talking about.'

She was silent.

'Merit, I've—,'

'I'm not that type of girl, OK? I'm not into guys like you. Just stay out of my life. Please.'

She hung up.

I was numb. I kept staring at my phone screen and replaying Merit's words and wondering when this latest nightmare would end. How could a relationship that seemed to be going so well suddenly turn awry?

I sank back in the chair. It was all my fault. I should have known that, sooner or later, she would hear something. Merit might not have been so mad if I had told her myself. After all, 419er or no, was I not still Kingsley? Was I not the man who had come to my family's rescue after my father had failed? Was I not the man setting aside my own dreams for the sake of my mother and my siblings? Was I not the man still making efforts to reach out to my mother, even when she had been so judgmental and unreasonable?

I flung the phone on the table and hissed. I felt like screaming, grabbing the crockery from the table, and flinging each item against the wall. Instead, I placed my head in my hands and leaned my elbows on the dining table.

What a rotten world. Other poor people found women to marry them, other 419ers were besieged with desperate Misses. Maybe I was the one who suffered from bad luck – surrounded by ingrates and utopians. But no matter what, my siblings would have the best education I could afford. And I would never go back to a life of poverty and lack. Not for anyone dead or alive.

Perhaps Merit would understand. By morning, her anger would have subsided and I would explain everything to her. I was not a criminal. I had gone into 419 so that my mother could live in comfort and my siblings have a good education. Yes, I should have told her but I was not sure how to broach the topic, and I was very sorry for deceiving her. Besides, things were on the verge of changing. I would soon start work at the Ministry of Works and Transport. I would soon have a respectable job. I would soon have business investments.

Godfrey and his friends brought their noise back downstairs.

'Charity, is Kingsley still in the dining room?' I heard Godfrey ask from the staircase.

I raised my head quickly and turned back to my meal. My appetite had definitely fled, but I dipped my hands into the soup and pretended to be deep in chow.

His friends sat in the living room with my other siblings while Godfrey strutted over to me, pulled a dining chair noisily, and sat. The fragrance of his freshly sprayed Eternity wiped out every trace of the *egusi* aroma from the air.

'Kings, there's something I've been wanting to discuss with you,' he began without any ceremony.

I looked at his two friends sitting within earshot of us and looked back at him. He did not seem to mind their presence, so why should I?

'Kingsley, I've been thinking about it for some time. I've decided that I want to quit school. I've been thinking about it for a long time and I've decided that there's no point. I really don't want to go on. I'm thinking of going into business.'

'You want to go into business?'

'Yes. I'm tired of school. There's no reason for me to keep wasting my time in school when there's so much money to be made out there. The sooner I start making my own money, the better.'

Without a doubt, this boy was crazy. From the depths of my vexation, I borrowed from Cash Daddy's patented lingo.

'Godfrey, is your head correct? Have you been drinking? Are you on drugs?'

He appeared surprised at my reaction. Then he toughened up his face and seemed to be bracing himself for a stronger argument.

'Kings, let me ex—'

'Shut up!' I barked. Like Azuka, he sounded so idiotically confident. 'Just forget about it. End of discussion. Forget it. There's nothing to talk about. It's not my business what else you do with your life, but you must remain in school and you must graduate. Don't ever raise the matter again.'

Godfrey watched me while I washed my hands, put my phone into my pocket, grabbed my glass of water, and stood. When I started walking away, he also stood.

'Kings, you're the last person I'd expect to be making such a fuss. Look at you. After all your education, you're not even doing anything with your degree. What was the point? Do you think I don't want to make my own money for myself? You're just being hypocritical.'

The glass cup dropped from my hand and colonised a large portion of the marble floor. I stopped in my tracks and mutated into another being. My brother had the guts to spew this breed of rubbish after everything I had been through for them? Was I being hypocritical when I put their welfare and comfort ahead of mine? I turned round and gave him a wholehearted slap on the face.

'Do you think this is the sort of life I wanted to live?! Do you think I had much choice?!'

I slapped him again, grabbed his shirtfront, and pushed him against the wall.

'Don't you realise that I made the sacrifice for you people?!'

I tightened my grip on his shirt, pulled him towards me, and screamed into his face.

'I am the *opara*! I did it for you people! Do you understand me?!'

Right from childhood, Godfrey had had the formation of a gangster. He did not squeal, he did not try to escape, he did not beg for me to stop. And because of the age difference that granted me automatic authority to discipline him, he dared not fight back. He just stood there looking at me through squinted eyes and using his arms to shield himself from my blows.

By this time, Eugene, Charity, Godfrey's two friends, my cook, my washer man, my gardener, my mother's niece's daughter had gathered. They all pleaded and begged and blocked. They were wasting their time.

'Kings, pleeeeease! Please leave him! Please leave him!' Charity wept and screamed.

I dragged my brother by his shirt collar and yanked him towards the staircase. I turned round to the sympathetic crowd.

'Nobody should follow me upstairs!' I warned.

My cook, whose communication with me never exceeded 'Yes, sir!' 'No, sir!', shouted, '*Oga*, abeg no kill am, abeg no kill am!' and ventured up the first stair. I pulled off the right foot of my natural viper snakeskin slippers and flung it at his head. The slipper missed, but he learnt his lesson.

I hauled Godfrey into his bedroom and deposited him in a heap on the floor. I shut the bedroom door and looked round. The first thing that caught my eyes was the sound system that stood by his dresser. I punched it. It fell with a huge crash.

In one sweep of my hand, everything on his dressing table tumbled to the floor. The air filled with the aroma of a mixture of designer fragrances. I yanked open the wardrobe and grabbed an empty bag. I dragged his clothes from the hangers and stuffed as many of them as I could fit into the bag. There was no time for me to pause and tear them into shreds like I really wanted to do. I heaved the bag across my shoulder and caught Godfrey by his shirt collar again. On my way out, I reached out my free hand and knocked the compact disc rack. The stack of disks rattled to the floor in a pile. I brought down my left foot on them. They crackled with each fresh stomp.

Outside, the sympathetic crowd had regrouped by the bedroom door. With more pressing tasks to tackle, I ignored their disobedience and descended the stairs with my two pieces of load. I went straight to my Lexus and tossed Godfrey and the travelling bag inside.

'Open the gate!' I shouted.

The terrified gateman rushed to obey.

My foot did not leave the accelerator until we arrived in Umuahia. Godfrey sat in stunned silence as I sped straight to the flat on Ojike Street and deposited him and his luggage outside the door.

'I never ever want to see you in my house again,' I warned.

My mother was on her way out of the house when I jumped back into my car and vroomed off.

Forty-four

Of all the emotions that kept me wide awake that night, the one that stayed with me until the following morning was anger. I was angry with my mother, angry with my father, angry with myself for allowing my family to exercise so much control over my existence. Cash Daddy was right. Relatives were the cause of hip disease. And schizophrenia and dementia and hypertension and spontaneous combustion. Someday, even Charity might look me in the face and call me a hypocrite, and tell me that I had no right to tell her whom not to marry.

I was tired of trying to please everyone, of making sacrifices that no one seemed to appreciate. Many mothers would give an arm and a leg to have an *opara* like me. Yet my own mother was still bound by the mental shackles of a husband who had lived from beginning to end in a cloud. Perhaps, I should just be like Cash Daddy and do and say as I pleased. With time, people would learn to accept me for who I was. And so what if Merit did not want me? There were many Thelmas and Sandras out there who would gladly jump at the opportunity to wear my ring on their finger. After all, if Cash Daddy had paid attention to people like my father and my mother, he might never have made it this far.

Someone knocked on my door. I ignored it. The person knocked again. I still ignored it.

'Kings,' Charity said in a grasshopper voice, 'Mummy and Aunty Dimma are here.'

Last night, my sister had almost slid into the wall when I passed her on the staircase, as if she were afraid that I would sting if her body made contact with mine.

'I'm coming,' I replied.

I rolled out of bed and pulled a T-shirt over my boxer shorts.

Aunty and Mummy were seated in the living room when I

entered. My mother had actually persuaded Aunty Dimma to forgo her Sunday morning service to accompany her here today? The gravity of their mission was evident on their faces.

Charity was nowhere in sight. I greeted them and sat. For a while, we sat looking at each other. Finally, Aunty Dimma glanced at my mother and whispered.

'Ozoemena.'

My mother then took in a deep breath, exhaled noisily, and opened up her case.

'Kings, what happened between you and Godfrey yesterday?'

I kept quiet.

'Why did you almost kill your brother?' she added.

I continued keeping quiet.

'Kings, am I not talking to you?'

'Mummy, why didn't you ask him what he did? Why did you have to come all the way to Aba to ask me that question?'

The women exchanged glances. Aunty Dimma's glance seemed to be saying, I told you so.

'Kings, what is coming over you?' my mother asked. 'You don't even seem to realise that what you've done is very evil. Whatever your brother did, is that the way for you to behave? Couldn't you find another way to resolve the issue without . . . without trying to kill him?'

'There's nothing to resolve,' I replied coolly. 'I can sponsor Godfrey and give him whatever he needs. But if you want your son to remain alive, he'd better stay in Umuahia with you. Maybe that will help tighten some of the screws that have gone loose in his head.'

'Jesus is Lord!' Aunty Dimma exclaimed.

Ha.

'Jesus is Lord. Education is gold. God will provide. You people should continue living in your dream world.'

Aunty Dimma glanced at my mother again. My mother stood up and leaned forward with one hand on her waist and the other pointing at me.

'Look at how you're talking. See who's talking about loose screws in the head. What about you?'

I still had some left over of yesterday's oomph. I jumped up from my chair, slammed my fists in the air and stared her in the face.

'I'm tired of all this rubbish! I'm tired! Whether you people appreciate it or not, I've been making all these sacrifices for the family. It's because of you. And all I get is insults and derogatory remarks.'

Charity had reappeared. She was watching from the bottom of the stairs.

'It's not for us you're doing it,' my mother spat through clenched teeth. 'I told you long time ago that I don't want any of your dirty money. If your father were alive, none of this would have happened. Your father is there turning in his grave and wondering how his son, his own flesh and blood, can be living this sort of despicable life. This is not the way we brought you up. As far as I'm concerned, you're a disgrace to your father's memory.'

'Let him keep turning in his grave,' I said. 'That's why he died a poor man. If he had done what other people were doing instead of sitting there and idealising, he would still be alive today.'

Aunty Dimma covered her mouth with her hand and allowed her eyes to do the exclaiming instead. My mother became a column of ice and focused her frozen eyeballs on my face. Gradually, she thawed. Then, rushed over and landed two slaps on my right cheek.

'Kingsley,' she said, with tears rising in her eyes, 'your father and I did not raise you to be a conman. You hear me? Enough is enough. You have to stop this 419. If not, I will never mention your name again as my son. As far as I'm concerned, you no longer exist.'

She sniffed. The tears had now overflowed the banks and were creeping far out to shore.

'Since this your fast money has given you the guts to talk about your father in this manner, then you might as well just forget about me. Until you stop this 419, I will never, ever set foot in your house again. And I don't want you to come and visit me. If you ever see me here in your house again, that is the day I will drop dead. You had better not think for one second that I'm joking. I mean every single word I'm saying.'

She grabbed her handbag and stormed out. Even the sound of Charity's sobbing was drowned out by her footsteps.

'Kingsley,' Aunty Dimma said. 'Don't allow the devil to use you to wreak havoc in this family! Don't allow—'

'You people should learn to be realistic,' I cut in gruffly, recalling Cash Daddy's long-time-ago imitation of how rich people behaved and spoke. 'This has nothing to do with the devil.'

'That's what you think! Even the devil was not always the devil, God made Lucifer then Lucifer turned himself into the devil. You might not know it, but money is turning you into a devil. You'd better stop yourself before—'

'I don't want to hear any more of this rubbish. Aunty Dimma, I've tolerated your tongue enough. All this talk . . . Does it put food on the table? Does it pay school fees? Me, I don't believe in film tricks, I believe in real, live action.'

Whatever else she wanted to say got stuck inside her throat. She looked on in disbelief while I stormed past her and headed for the stairs.

For the first time in the history of womankind, Aunty Dimma's tongue appeared tied.

I sat on my bed and swept the room with my eyes. My Rolexes and Movados on the dresser, my five bunches of car keys on the bedside stool, my Persian rug, my six pillows, my rows of shoes by the split-unit air conditioner – a mere fraction of what I had in my closet. None of this was worth losing my mother for. And, truth be told, I would have loved to have Merit in my life.

Nevertheless, I could not face poverty again. Never again. My best bet was Cash Daddy's suggestion. Once I took up his job offer at the Ministry of Works and Transport, my mother – and Merit – would definitely be appeased. So what if it was just a façade?

I noticed that my cellular screen was flashing. I grabbed it from the edge of my pillow and saw the five missed calls. All were from Cash Daddy's number. I rang back immediately.

'Kings, they got him, they got him,' Protocol Officer said over and over again.

'Got whom?'

'Kings, Cash Daddy is dead.'

Then he started sobbing, making the sort of noises you should hope never to hear from a grown man.

Forty-five

At first, nobody was sure how it happened. Early on Sunday morning, the Indian girls had suddenly started screaming and scampered out of the room. Nobody had understood what they were saying. The security personnel had rushed in. Cash Daddy was lying stark naked on his belly with white foam gathering at the corners of his mouth and blood dripping from his rectum.

Protocol Officer was summoned. Cash Daddy was rushed to a private hospital. Shortly after, the next democratically elected executive governor of Abia State was pronounced dead. Death by poisonous substance.

For starters, the Indian girls were arrested and carted off to the police station. But after hours of questioning, the officers of the Criminal Investigative Division were unable to get any sensible information out of them. One of the smarter policemen then came up with an idea. Mr Patel, the CEO of Aba Calcutta Plastics Industry, was invited to interpret.

The girls said that everything had gone very well till Saturday evening. But after his nightly snack of fried meat and wine, curiously, Cash Daddy had declined all their offers of amusement, stumbled into bed, and fallen asleep. In the morning, they prepared themselves for his body rub – one of his favourite daybreak pleasures. They tickled him. Cash Daddy did not stir. They shook him. He still did no stir. Then, one of them climbed onto his back. She noticed the foam at the corner of his lips and screamed. The other two also saw it and joined in.

The police thanked Mr Patel for his services but still held onto the girls.

Next, all the staff of the hotel restaurant – both waiters and chefs – were rounded up and also taken to the police station. Each of them proclaimed undying love for their dead master; they all swore that their hands were clean. The police tried different methods to get a confession, all without success.

Eventually, Protocol Officer suggested investigating all the staff's bank accounts. An unexplainable two hundred thousand naira was sitting snugly in the Diamond Bank account of one chef. The Indian prostitutes were released, the other staff were released, the chef kept swearing that he had received the money from a 419 deal. But when a quarter of his back had turned raw and red, the man finally confessed that someone had paid him to poison Cash Daddy's 404 meat. He insisted it was two men whom he had met only once. He could not give any further information about them, not even when the rest of his back was raw and red.

If Cash Daddy had lived to see the drama in the days following his death, he would have been very proud of himself.

The Association of Pepper and Tomato Sellers, Aba Branch, took to the streets in angry protest. Not wanting to be left out, the street touts joined in. Their placard carrying, 'Death to the murderers!' chanting, and wanton looting lasted for three whole days, grinding all commercial activity in Aba to a halt. The mayhem made it into the nine o'clock news headlines. The entire nation of Nigeria was forced to take note.

Newspaper and soft-sell headlines screamed in anger. Politicians of timbre and calibre – Uwajimogwu included – granted press briefings to publicly condemn the senseless killing of yet another one of Nigeria's great politicians. The president of the Federal Republic of Nigeria was not left out of the tirade.

'Enough is enough!' he declared. 'It is time for God to punish whoever these assassins are! They shall never cease to entertain sorrow in their homes, they shall never know peace, their grief shall be passed on from generation to generation of their families.'

The inspector general of police went on national television and made a golden pledge to the nation.

'Whoever is behind this dastardly act will soon be unmasked!' he promised.

As proof that he meant it – this time – he had invited the British Metropolitan Police into the investigation.

'Not because our police officers are not capable of handling it,' he explained, 'but right now, we lack the required forensic facilities for the successful investigation of these assassination cases.'

Journalists and opinion-editorials immediately went berserk.

'Why not invite the whole British government to come run the rest of Nigeria?' some asked. 'Then maybe we would have electricity, running water, good hospitals, and our highways would cease to be death traps.'

'The rampant assassinations are the fault of the electorate,' some others said. 'They are the ones who reward the assassins by victory in the polls.'

Yet others cautioned the public about automatically assuming that all assassinations were political; some could actually have been in-house engineered.

Protocol Officer did not buy that talk. When he turned up suddenly at my house a few days after the murder, he told me exactly what was on his mind.

'I'm sure it's Uwajimogwu,' he insisted. 'Everybody else loved Cash Daddy. There's no one else it can be.'

That opinion was shared by the majority of people in Abia State. The rioters had even razed Uwajimogu's campaign office headquarters in Aba. With Cash Daddy's relocation to the other world, he was the new flag bearer of the NAP gubernatorial ticket, certain to become the next democratically elected governor of Abia State.

Mrs Boniface Mbamalu had come all the way from Lagos to take her position as widow in Cash Daddy's living room. Each morning, she appeared wearing a different black designer dress and a different pair of designer shades. With his fresh complexion, his gentlemanly clothes and English manners, her *opara* sat by her side. So far, eleven condolence registers had been filled. Still, the dignitaries continued pouring in.

'I can't believe Cash Daddy has gone like that,' Protocol Officer continued. 'Just like that. Every morning I wake up and expect him to ring my phone. I spend the whole day waiting for him to ring.'

I also was still finding it hard to believe. Cash Daddy was one of those people who seemed as if they were born never to die. Even after Protocol Officer's phone call, I had to see for myself. I jumped into my car and accelerated all the way to the mortuary and saw him lying with his name – complete with nickname – tagged to his big toe. His face was contorted and pallid. I clutched my head, stumbled out of the cold room, and collapsed in the hall.

To think that I had heard the last Igbo proverb and that I would never again have to shield my ears from his thunderous 'Speak to me!' How could Cash Daddy be dead? The man who had taken me under his wing. The man who had given me a new life. The man who had given me an opportunity to prove myself when everybody else kept turning me down. I had not just lost an uncle and a boss, I had lost a father.

And Cash Daddy would have been good for Abia State. After all was said and done, my uncle loved his people. He might have pocketed a billion or two in the process, but in the long run, our lot would have been better. We would have had better roads. We would have had running water. We would have had a public officer who could not bear to watch his brothers and sisters in distress. Abia had just lost the best governor we could ever have had. I wailed even louder.

Eventually, an elderly man who could have been a morgue attendant or a fellow-mourner or a ghost, tapped my shoulders firmly.

'Be a man,' he said sternly. 'It's enough. Be a man and dry your tears.'

He waited beside me until I wiped my eyes and got up. I realised that I was barefooted, in boxer shorts and T-shirt.

I did not feel like going home. I drove to the office and was startled. There were two giant black padlocks on the main gates and on the front door.

Could it be the Economic and Financial Crimes Commission who had barricaded our office? Could it be the FBI? Had our friends in the police abandoned us so quickly after Cash Daddy's death? With panic, I rang Protocol Officer.

'I'm the one that locked it,' he said, in a teary but firm tone. 'I don't want anybody to tamper with any of Cash Daddy's things. Nobody should go inside.'

Amazing that he could function so effectively even at a time like this. He must have dashed out to lock the office immediately after learning of his master's death. But then, no one could blame me for having been paranoid. First Azuka, then Cash Daddy. Who knew where the lightning was planning to strike next?

Perhaps, we were being punished for all the mugus. I pushed away the thought. The only offences I had committed were against the people I loved. I replayed my misbehaviour towards Godfrey and my mother. I was consumed with shame. Truly, I was becoming a devil.

Nay, I was a devil.

Back at home, I rang Merit.

'Merit is busy,' her brother said calmly.

She was still busy the fifth time I rang.

I got dressed, drove to her house and waited outside, hoping to see someone whom I could send inside to call her. To my relief, after about two hours, the gates opened and her skinny brother appeared. He was dressed casually in singlet, jeans and bathroom slippers, as if he was just taking a stroll.

'Hello,' I called out to him.

He froze when he saw me, then scurried back inside like a mouse caught in full view on the kitchen floor when the lights were turned on suddenly in the middle of the night. I waited for another hour without anybody going in or coming out. Finally, I left.

I changed my mind about driving to Umuahia to see my mother. What would I even say to her? I locked myself in my bedroom and stared at the ceiling till dark. With the assistance of two tiny tablets, I had been managing about three hours of sleep per night ever since Cash Daddy's death.

But my deep sorrow could certainly be nothing compared to whatever Protocol Officer was feeling. I had always thought of him as the real McCoy Graveyard, but today, he talked and talked and talked. In between, he sobbed. At some point, I reached out and placed my hand on his shoulder. My own eyes had no more tears left to shed.

He talked about how some wicked people were spreading the rumour that Cash Daddy had expired in the throes of orgasm. He talked about how the people that really mattered were being left out of the planning for Cash Daddy's funeral. The National

Advancement Party, in collaboration with the Abia State government, had announced plans to honour 'our great man of peace, who has left a great example of politics without bitterness' with a befitting state burial. He talked about how poorly the crime scene had been managed. Cash Daddy's hotel room had not been cordoned off for several hours after his body was discovered, and the British police had gathered more than 5,000 fingerprints. He talked about how Cash Daddy had been a peace-loving man; if not, he would have got his opponents before they got him.

Finally he stopped. I removed my hand from his shoulder. We were quiet, then I chortled. Protocol Officer looked at me askance.

'Knowing Cash Daddy,' I smiled, 'I won't be surprised if he rises up from the coffin while all of us are gathered round during the funeral.'

He thought about it briefly. To my relief, he giggled.

'Cash Daddy, Cash Daddy,' he said. 'There are no two like him in this world.'

We went back to quiet again. Suddenly, he dipped his hand inside the inner pocket of his jacket, brought out a sheaf of papers and placed them on my lap.

'What is this?' I asked.

At the same time, I looked at them and gasped. Sheet after sheet of foreign bank account details. Cash Daddy's holiest of holies.

'What is this?' I asked again. This time, my question meant something different.

'Kings, Cash Daddy thought very highly of you. You're the only one who can take over the work.'

He also brought out two large, shiny keys from his socks and stretched them towards me.

'The keys to the Unity Road office,' he said. 'You can reopen it whenever you want.'

I stared at the keys and at the documents.

'Why did you bring them to me?'

'Kings, if Cash Daddy knew that anything was going to happen to him, he would have handed them over to you.' He paused. 'I'm sure.'

I continued staring at the keys. A wave of emotions flooded my heart. Unlike my natural father, who had left me nothing but grand ideals and textbooks, Cash Daddy had left me a flourishing business. I was touched. And proud.

I reached out for the keys in Protocol Officer's outstretched hand.

I remembered my mother. I remembered Merit.

My mind changed gear.

Perhaps this was my opportunity to gather my takings and leave the CIA. Going cold turkey would certainly not be easy, but with the millions I had stashed away in the bank, I could gradually start my life afresh. My father had steered me to engineering, my uncle had persuaded me to 419. For a change, I would decide what I wanted to do with my own life. I retrieved my hand without touching the keys.

'No,' I said to Protocol Officer. I gathered up the sheets and transferred them to his lap. 'No, I don't want them.'

'Kings?' Protocol Officer gaped.

I continued shaking my head. He continued staring with mouth agape. For the very first time in my life, I felt in control. I was the master of my destiny.

Epilogue

Good mothers know all about patience. They know about lugging the promise of a baby around for nine whole months, about the effort of pushing and puffing until a head pops; they know about being pinned to a spot, wincing as gums make contact with sore nipples; they know about keeping vigil over a cot all night, praying that the doctor's medicine will work; they know that even when patience seems to be at an end, more is required. Always more. That is why Augustina could hardly believe that the day had finally come.

The forty-five minute journey from Umuahia to Aba felt more like three hours. Throughout, Augustina hummed the first two stanzas of 'How Great Thou Art'. All the plants seemed to have an unusual splendour, despite having leaves caked in Harmattan dust. A wrinkled man in the owner's corner of an oncoming V-Boot winked, mistaking her smile as being directed at him. Augustina looked away and sighed. If only Paulinus had lived to make the trip with her. Quickly, she pushed away the greedy thought. Today was what she had and she was grateful. She could be happy enough for both of them..

The car veered off the expressway and onto a dirt road. An *okada* zoomed past carrying a woman with two toddlers straddled between her and the driver, and a baby strapped to her back with an ankara cloth. Augustina was saying a silent prayer for the baby's safety when her own head bumped against the Mercedes S-Class roof. But the second and the third and the fourth potholes did not catch her unawares. Her arms were already wrapped firmly around the headrest of the front passenger seat. All this excitement about democracy. Yet so much was left undone.

At last, they came onto a tarred road. The driver pulled up at a grand storied building and waited for her to dismount before going off to park the car. The building was painted pure white, broad, and tall. Augustina did not need anyone to give her directions. The signboard on the ground floor was enough. More than enough. To Augustina, it was everything.

KINGS VENTURES INTERNATIONAL

The large hall was as crowded as an anthill. Rows and rows of computers, and there was barely sitting space left. People clicked away at keyboards, clusters giggled around screens, queues on benches awaited their turns. Friendly notices, against using Kings Cafe computers to download pornography or to participate in terrorism, hung beside stern warnings from the Nigerian Economic and Financial Crimes Commission – official admonitions proclaiming that customers caught engaging in internet fraud would be handed over to the police. These EFCC notices were a symptom of the many changes sweeping across Nigeria.

Recently, a proliferation of internet service and cable TV providers had brought the rest of the globe a little bit closer to the man in the street. GSM technology meant that more people could afford mobile phones, never mind the murderous per minute cost of calls. The other day, Augustina had actually seen a pepper seller in Nkwoegwu market laughing loudly into a mobile phone. There were even rumours of cash machines and shopping malls coming soon.

Kings Cafes were the largest and most popular business centres in Aba, Umuahia, and Owerri. In addition to facilities for browsing the Internet, there was also a section for private phone booths and another where registered customers could read national dailies free of charge. All sections were fully air-conditioned. This main branch in Aba also served as head office for Kings Ventures International, which was comprised of importing and exporting of computer equipment and GSM phone supplies.

Most of the Kings Cafe customers came to send requests to relatives abroad or to chat with lovers in distant lands. But today, customers who should have been busy making good use of their hard-earned cyber time had turned away from their screens, their faces hopeful of a full-blown fight.

The cafe manager was on the brink of exchanging blows with a young man in plaited hair whose eyes were flashing murder, and their voices were raised to a frenzied pitch.

Augustina froze in her steps. If only young people of these days could learn that violence was not the way forward. Back in her days, young people worked off their excess energy by climbing trees or digging ridges in the farm, and any issue that needed resolving was tabled before an elder. As the only real adult around, Augustina considered intervening. But then, she did not want to tempt trouble on a beautiful day like this. Any man who went around with plaited hair must surely be a hooligan; he could easily despise her grey hairs and knock her to the ground. Kingsley might be better off leaving this arena to his hot-blooded customers and relocating his private office to another building.

Out of nowhere, a magisterial voice boomed.

'Odinkemmelu, what's all the hullabaloo about?'

In the wave of silence that came next, you could almost hear the swishing of angel's garments. All eyes in the hall sought out the sound of the voice. The manager and the man in plaited hair stopped being barbarian and turned.

Standing an authoritative few paces behind the squabbling men was Kingsley.

Augustina's heart pumped with pride. In his cream linen suit, oxblood shoes, and budding potbelly, her son was as elegant as a lord. His back was straight, his hands stayed deep inside his pockets, and his gaze was clear and unflinching. Without a doubt, Augustina knew that her *opara* was the man in charge.

'What's the problem?' Kingsley repeated.

'Chairman, I have try explain for him,' Odinkemmelu responded quickly. 'His ticket have expire.'

'I don't care what he says,' the young man howled through gritted teeth. 'I want my money back!'

'Chairman, he is buy the ticket from last week—'

'It's a one-hour ticket. I only used five minutes out of it.'

338

'I am told him that our ticket is expire after five days. It didn't matter if he use it or don't.'

'Look, if you don't want trouble—'

Kingsley stared casually as the duet continued, his face giving nothing away. Augustina remembered her husband and the way he never exchanged words with house helps. Really, there was something about being educated that made a man stand out from the crowd.

Eventually, Kingsley raised the open palm of his right hand. The two men shut up.

'Young man, what exactly is the problem?' Kingsley asked calmly.

The man in plaited hair proceeded to explain. It was exactly as Odinkemmelu had said, except in more conventional grammar.

'It's all right, it's all right,' Kingsley said while the man was still expressing himself. 'This time, we'll let it pass. But, young man, next time, please be aware that our tickets expire after five days. Odinkemmelu, give him another ticket.'

'Thank you, sir,' the young man exhaled.

Gradually, the spectators turned back to their computer screens. This must have been an anticlimax to what had started out as a great show.

Without moving, Kingsley watched while Odinkemmelu issued the fresh ticket. Augustina made her way eagerly towards her son. She reached him as the man in plaited hair strutted away victoriously with the slice of paper that had his new log-on code.

'Mummy!' Kingsley exclaimed with excitement.

'Ma Kingsley, welcome, Ma,' Odinkemmelu mumbled with downcast gaze.

Augustina embraced her son. From the corners of her eyes, she was pleased to note that many customers were glued to this less brutish show.

'Kings, I hope I'm not disturbing your work,' she said, smiling brightly.

'Of course not! Come, let me show you round.'

He took her by the hand. Abruptly, he paused in his stride and turned, resuming his CEO composure.

'I don't want to see this again,' Kingsley reprimanded Odinkemmelu quietly, wagging his finger at him. This kind of scene must be avoided.'

'Chairman, I am told him before about our ticket. It's not a lie. I am told him.'

Odinkemmelu was still a rough diamond. A short while ago, he had decided that he had exceeded the acceptable age of being a dependent relative. He wanted to earn an income and help his parents and siblings in the village. His dream was to open a provision store, and he had found a kiosk to let on the same street as Augustina's tailoring shop. Odinkemmelu approached Kingsley for the capital at about the same time that Kingsley was facing a challenge of his own.

The graduate of economics he had employed as manager of the Kings Cafe's main branch, Aba, had been caught doctoring the books. Over a period of weeks, the man had silently siphoned off several thousands of naira. He vanished into a puff of smoke the moment his crookedness was discovered. Kingsley was outraged. Augustina then advised her son.

'That's why it's better to employ relatives,' she had said. 'If they steal or misbehave, you can always trace them to their homes. No matter how efficient strangers are, they can do whatever they want to do without fear of being traced.'

Her son had paid heed to her advice. Odinkemmelu was offered the job. He moved from Umuahia to Kingsley's house in Aba and took up his white collar job with zeal. Now, in his yellow shirt, red trousers, and green tie, Odinkemmelu trembled, apparently fearful that he had bungled so soon.

'I'm not saying you did anything wrong,' Kingsley said. 'But one does not scratch open his skin simply because of how badly he feels an itch. Learn not to overreact. The cost of one ticket is not worth all the disturbance that man was causing. I could hear him all the way from my office.'

'Chairman, am very sorry, sir,' Odinkemmelu said.

Kingsley took Augustina on a tour of all four floors. He showed her the different kinds of equipment for sale and explained their functions. She shuddered at the heavy price tags. Her main enjoyment derived from the staff gazing upon her in awe. The CEO's mother.

Kingsley then led her into his private office. Tears sprang to Augustina's eyes. If only Paulinus had lived to see the fruits of his labour in their *opara*.

The office was large and uncluttered, with a refrigerator in a corner and a wide, mahogany cabinet displaying several exotic vases and several awards extolling her son's financial contributions to different organisations, and a smiling portrait of Thelma in a gold frame. Not for the first time, Augustina wondered how her son's sweetheart could bear the burden of those enormous breasts on such a petite figure.

But Augustina soon lost interest in the awards and the photograph. Her eyes and heart had settled on the large mahogany shelf filled with books. And not just any books. Augustina recognised many of her husband's priceless textbooks and smiled. Really, there was no better legacy a father could bestow on his son than knowledge as vast as eternity.

'Your office is lovely,' she said, a broad grin on her face. 'Anyway, you've always had good taste. Just like your father.'

Augustina noticed that her son's expression did not acknowledge the compliment. It was probably his way of showing humility at being compared to such a great man. Kingsley offered her a seat and sat in the grand leather chair behind the executive desk.

'How about the MBA?' she asked. 'Have you started applying?'

'I just downloaded the forms for the Manchester Business School today,' he said, swivelling to the right. 'I'll send them off by tomorrow.'

'Oh, good! Have you confirmed the fees?'

He swivelled to the left and told her the amount.

'Really!' she exclaimed. 'That means Imperial Business School is even cheaper.'

'Yes, but Manchester is one of the top three in Europe.'

'Oh.' She was quiet. Then, 'your father would be very happy if you went to his alma mater.'

Kingsley laughed a brief, staccato laugh.

'Mummy, the same medicine that is good for the eyes may not be good for the ears. Daddy studied Engineering, mine is an MBA.'

Augustina went quiet. She remained quiet.

'OK,' Kingsley said at last. 'If that's what you really want, I'll fill out the application forms to Imperial as well.'

'Kings, that would be lovely,' she said, smiling brightly. 'That would be really lovely. Imperial is still a very good school, no matter what you're studying.'

The important thing was for people to see that her son, the CEO of Kings Ventures International, had an MBA from a foreign university. In Nigeria, foreign degrees carried huge respect, whether they were from Manchester or Imperial or Peckham. And now that it seemed as if democracy had indeed come to stay, hordes from the diaspora were shaking off their phobias and coming back home, and people with local degrees were becoming more and more invisible. In the next few years, Augustina was confident that her son would do well enough to become one of the most respected entrepreneurs from this part of the world. An MBA from a reputable foreign school would definitely go a long way in making him stand out farther from the crowd. And in an economy that was so shaky and unpredictable, it would also be a good insurance policy to fall back on, in case business went awry.

A harsh tune pierced the air. Kingsley brought his phone out of his pocket and looked at the screen. He excused himself, rose quickly, and strode towards the window at the far end of the room.

'Hello Mr Winterbottom,' he said with quiet authority.

Augustina lost control of her mouth and giggled.

'I was just about to ring you now, but my mother dropped by and I got busy attending to her.'

That was something Augustina loved about her son: family always came first.

'I've confirmed that the funds have definitely been sent to your bank,' he said, 'but the delay is from the brokerage firm. They said they can't conclude the transfer without first receiving their commission. That's their policy.'

He turned from the window and glanced quickly at her.

Augustina smiled and waved her hand for him to continue with his conversation. She did not mind; she was not in any hurry.

'One per cent. That's the standard fee on all transactions.' He paused. 'Yes, one per cent of the 420 million.'

He nodded. He nodded again and again.

'Just let me know as soon as you've made the payment to them, so that I can follow up and make sure there are no further delays.'

Kingsley returned to his desk, his face aglow with a gigantic grin.

'One of my foreign investors,' he explained.

Augustina nodded.

Exactly as she had guessed.

Paulinus had always said that their *opara's* brains would some-day make him great beyond Nigeria's shores. This was only the beginning.

Acknowledgements

Special thanks to:

~ Kirsty Dunseath, my editor, for giving me a wonderful home.

~ Daniel Lazar a.k.a. Master, my literary agent of inestimable value. Charming, long-suffering, conscientious, filled with remarkable wisdom.

~ Bibi Bakare-Yusuf, my trailblazing Nigerian publisher, for believing in me from the very beginning.

~ Brenda Copeland, my US editor, for the endless tutoring and enthusiasm.

~ My friends, both old and new. I'm convinced that no one in the universe has a circle more amazing. I started mentioning your names but it went on for two whole pages, and yet, I was not finished!

~ Uluobi Andrea, for making sure that my bank account never ran dry.

~ Uncle Sunmi Smart-Cole, for those beautiful *'awoof'* photographs.

~ Dr. Chioma Ejikeme, for constantly telling me that I was making the whole family proud.

~ Fred Ukachi Onuobia, for the unflinchingly high expectations.

~ Aunty Mary Ibe, for taking care of me.

~ Professor Adigun Agbaje, for all the intellectual advice.

~ Eyo Ekpo, my veritable 'Encyclopaedia Africana'.

~ Gilda O'Neil, for that dramatic boost.

~ L. M. Stephenson Jr, for the great suggestion which I initially found amusing.

~ My 419 sources and acquaintances, for kindly or inadvertently allowing me a peep into your surreal world.

~ Magnus, Uwasinachi Dave and Ekwueme, for being part of us.

~ My life coach and my mentors, for teaching me that, truly, anything is possible.

~ The One who put the talent in my hands and blessed me with the *mimshach*.

I Do Not Come to You by Chance

Reading Group Notes

In Brief

The village experts said that women did not need to know too much 'book'. It was therefore a waste of time sending Augustina to secondary school. Reverend Sister Xavier felt so strongly about this that she came all the way to sit opposite Augustina's father and tell him he was wrong. She told him that all across the world women were achieving great things, and that Augustina should be given the chance to join them. He was so unused to women telling him what to do, Augustina's father agreed.

Changing the world was not to be Augustina's destiny, however, and after she completed school she was apprenticed to her father's sister, who was a tailor. Her exemplary marks at school made no difference, there was to be no further education for Augustina. All this was swept from Augustina's mind when she first saw Engineer. He was on leave from his government job, and Augustina loved him from the moment he stepped from his Peugeot 403. He had studied in the United Kingdom, and he behaved like a white man.

He was also handsome, and when he began to take an interest in Augustina she couldn't have been happier.

Engineer encouraged Augustina to continue her studies and even helped with her fees, promising to marry her when she graduated. Engineer was sure that their children would be everything he dreamed: doctors, scientists, lawyers . . .

The soup should have been thick, rich and delicious. But it was thin, weak and depressing. It was a good indication of how bad times were. Kingsley knew things had not always been like this. After his parents had married they had gone to England and gained Masters degrees. His father had returned to a good job in the Ministry of Works and Transport, and his mother had taken on a good size tailoring shop. But the years of rising inflation had eaten up his father's stagnant salary, and when his ill health proved to be diabetes, the cost of the treatment had caused their descent to this present precarious position.

Kingsley's life had been tailored to one goal. He would study to the exclusion of all else, and he would get a good job in a big company as a chemical engineer. This was not open to discussion. The plan had gone well so far, but Kingsley was struggling at the last hurdle. He could get interviews, but no one was offering him a position. It was getting rather worrying.

After receiving the latest rejection letter Kingsley had gone in search of his one shining light in this murky darkness: his beloved Ola. Even she had seemed less pleased to see him than usual, and there had been something different about her room. It had taken Kingsley a while to work out what it was, but alarm bells certainly rang when he realised that the pictures of him had gone from her bedside. Things were going from bad to worse.

Kingsley's life would change when his father became seriously ill. They needed money quickly so a hospital would treat him, and there was only one place to go. So Kingsley set out to ask the favour of his uncle, Boniface. Cash Daddy, as his uncle Boniface was known, was just the sort of person Kingsley's father would not want Kingsley to grow into. Making his enormous fortune from email scamming, Cash Daddy had money to burn, and would surely help. As Kingsley approached the guarded offices, he was uncertain what he would find.

What he found changed his life. Kingsley just wasn't sure if it was for the better. . .

About the Author

Adaobi Tricia Nwaubani grew up in the eastern part of Nigeria, among the Igbo-speaking people, whom many believe to be the major culprits of 419 scams. She won her first writing competition aged 13. She now lives in Abuja, Nigeria. *I Do Not Come to You by Chance* is her first novel.

For Discussion

◆ Is the benefit of education the ability 'to change the world to suit', as Engineer thinks?

◆ How is the changing culture of Nigeria reflected in the novel?

◆ 'The past is constraining but the future has no limits.' Is this true?

◆ 'Perhaps it was natural to find all sorts of silly things funny when you had a pocketful of cash.' Is it?

◆ 'My father had no quarrel with the white man.' What is Kingsley's relationship with the white man? Does it differ from Cash Daddy's?

◆ 'In his own special way, my uncle was an honest man.' Is Kingsley right? Is there an honesty about Cash Daddy?

◆ How does the author feel about 419ers?

◆ What does the novel say about education?

◆ 'Kissing may be the language of love, but it's money that does the talking.' Is this true, do you think? What does this tell us about Cash Daddy?

◆ 'Besides, the petty enmities that exist between one man and another suddenly disintegrate when they are linked with the bond of affliction.' How far is the novel about financial insecurity?

◆ 'Every human being deserved at least one person to laugh at his jokes, no matter how dry.' What does Kingsley want?

◆ 'After all, 419er or no, was I not still Kingsley?' What do we learn of Kingsley from this thought?

Suggested Further Reading

The Thing Around Your Neck
by Chimamanda Ngozi Adichie

Things Fall Apart
by Chinua Achebe

This House Has Fallen: Nigeria in Crisis
by Karl Maier

The White Tiger
by Aravind Adiga

Nervous Conditions
by Tsitsi Dandarembga

Graceland
by Christopher Abani